MAUREEN CHILD

is a California native who loves to travel. Every chance they get, she and her husband are taking off on another research trip. The author of more than sixty books, Maureen loves a happy ending and still swears that she has the best job in the world. She lives in Southern California with her husband, two children and a golden retriever with delusions of grandeur. Visit her Web site at www.maureenchild.com.

PEGGY WEBB

and her two chocolate Labs live in a hundred-year-old house not far from the farm where she grew up. "A farm is a wonderful place for dreaming," she says. "I used to sit in the hayloft and dream of being a writer." Now, with two grown children and more than forty-five romance novels to her credit, the former English teacher confesses she's still a hopeless romantic and loves to create the happy endings her readers love so well.

When she isn't writing, she can be found at her piano playing blues and jazz or in one of her gardens planting flowers. A believer in the idea that a person should never stand still, Peggy recently taught herself carpentry.

MAUREEN
CHILD
PEGGY
WEBB

Summer Surrender

Silhouette Books

Published by Silhouette Books
America's Publisher of Contemporary Romance

SILHOUETTE BOOKS

ISBN 0-373-23024-9

by Request

SUMMER SURRENDER

Copyright © 2004 by Harlequin Books S.A.

The publisher acknowledges the copyright holders
of the individual works as follows:

THE NON-COMMISSIONED BABY
Copyright © 1998 by Maureen Child

INVITATION TO A WEDDING
Copyright © 2001 by Peggy Webb

This edition published by arrangement with Harlequin Books S.A.

® and TM are trademarks of Harlequin Books S.A., used under
license. Trademarks indicated with ® are registered in the United States
Patent and Trademark Office, the Canadian Trade Marks Office and in
other countries.

Visit Silhouette Books at www.eHarlequin.com

Printed in U.S.A.

CONTENTS

Dear Reader,

Seeing one of your books reissued is always exciting for a writer. Seeing *this* book reissued is especially so. *The Non-Commissioned Baby* was one of my first BACHELOR BATTALION books and one I had a lot of fun writing.

The idea of a man with absolutely *no* experience with children suddenly becoming responsible for a baby seemed filled with humorous—and touching—possibilities. And Captain Jeff Ryan didn't let me down.

Not only did the baby, Miranda, turn Jeff's tidy world upside down, but her temporary nanny, Laura Morgan, shook the foundations of his life.

I hope you enjoy reading about a Marine Corps captain as he discovers that *nothing* is quite as formidable as a baby—except of course, falling in love.

Love,

Maureen Child

THE
NON-COMMMISSIONED BABY
Maureen Child

For Jaime and Kirk Brogdon
with love to celebrate Hayden.
A baby is a wonderful gift.
Enjoy every minute of your little miracle.

One

"**D**amn cats." Jeff Ryan muttered and swung both legs off the edge of the mattress. Stumbling across his bedroom in the heavily draped darkness, he slammed his big toe into the leg of a chair.

He jerked his foot up, cursed viciously, grabbed the throbbing toe and hopped to the closed door. Yanking it open, he let go of his foot and hobbled across the living room, wincing at the jagged slices of sunlight slanting through the half-opened blinds.

What was wrong with people? he thought. Why couldn't they keep their blasted cats at home instead of letting them sit outside his door howling like lost souls on the way to Hell?

Well, he'd had enough. This time, he'd catch the little beast and carry it straight to the manager's apartment—or the pound.

In a foul mood that was getting worse by the second,

Jeff slid back the dead bolt, threw open the door and made a lunge for the cat.

One small problem.

That was no cat screaming from its roost in the basket just outside his door.

"A *baby?*"

At least, he told himself as he stared down in horror at the red-faced, screaming mass of humanity, he *thought* it was a baby. At the moment, it more resembled something out of *Aliens*.

What was going on around here? He looked up and down the length of the short hallway as if he expected to find the culprit who'd abandoned a baby like something out of a 1930s movie. But no one was there.

He looked down at the baby again, still stunned to find it on his doorstep.

Fat little arms and legs swung wildly in the air, while chubby hands grabbed for something that wasn't there. And the baby's howl was designed to puncture eardrums.

"Hey, kid," he said, bending down to jiggle the basket awkwardly. "Stick a sock in it, will you?"

The infant snorted, sniffed, looked at him, took a deep breath and screamed again.

And people wondered why he had never wanted kids.

Scowling in disgust, Jeff looked up and down the third floor's long hallway again. Not a sign of anybody. Wouldn't you know it? Where were his nosy neighbors when he really needed them? Sure, at eleven o'clock in the morning, no one was around. But let him come home at 2:00 a.m. with his date for the evening, and at the very least, old Mrs. Butler would have her head poked out her open door.

Glancing back at the Scream Machine, he noticed an envelope jutting up from the side of the basket, half-covered by a brightly colored knitted blanket.

Despite the thread of worry that had suddenly erupted in his bloodstream, Jeff reached down and plucked the envelope free. Slowly, dreading what he would find, he turned it over.

He cursed again, louder this time, as his gaze locked on his own name scrawled across the front of the envelope.

Captain Jeffrey Ryan, United States Marine Corps.

A baby on the doorstep? Things like that didn't really happen, did they? His fingers suddenly clumsy, he tore at the sealed flap and pulled out the folded papers. Smoothing them out, he read the note first.

Captain Ryan—Sorry to just leave the baby like this, but you weren't answering your door and I've got 45 minutes to catch a transport to Guam.

He paused. A fellow *Marine* had done this to him?

I volunteered to bring you the baby. The Sarge's will is enclosed, too, just so's everything's legal. A shame about the Sarge, but we all know you'll do right by his kid. Signed, Corporal Stanley Hubrick.

The Sarge? Jeff wondered. Sergeant who? And what did Corporal Hubrick mean, he knew Jeff would do right by the kid?

Head pounding from the baby's continued screeching, he skimmed the will once, then again, hitting only a few, significant words. Horrified, he lowered the papers and stared accusingly at the infant.

"No offense, kid, but I am *nobody's* guardian."

Ten minutes later, Jeff was on the phone, the receiver tucked between his ear and his shoulder as he rocked the incredibly unhappy baby in his arms.

At least it had stopped screeching. For the moment.

"I can't believe this," his sister repeated for the fifth time.

"You already said that."

"You're the baby's guardian?"

"According to this will, yes."

"Amazing."

"Peggy," he tried to reason with his sister, "you don't understand. I can't do this. What do I know about kids?"

"I don't know nothin' 'bout birthin' no babies, Miss Scarlett!" she said.

He inhaled sharply and gritted his teeth as she laughed.

"Very funny," he snarled a moment later, the humor in the situation completely escaping him. "Now, are you going to come down here and help me or not?"

"Not," Peggy said, amusement still touching the tone of her voice.

"Peg—" He stared, horrified as the baby started chewing on the sleeve of his T-shirt. Drool ran down the baby's checks and chin, pooling in the white fabric. "That's disgusting," he muttered.

"What?"

Snapping back to the bigger problem, he said, "Never mind. Peg, you've got to come."

"I always said you'd make a great father."

Yes, she had, but she had been the *only* one to think so.

"Cut it out." Silently, he shouted at his long-dead parents for gifting his sister with such a warped sense of humor. "This is serious. I've got to see about correcting this mess. Fast."

"What's to correct?" she said, and in the background, he heard one of his nephews apparently trying to behead his niece.

Jeff winced. Maybe he'd called the wrong person for advice on kids.

Her hand obviously half over the phone, Peggy calmly said, "Teddy, don't twist your sister's arm, you'll break it."

Unbelievable. Teddy. A nine-year-old enforcer.

"Honestly, Jeff," Peggy spoke to him again. "You're just going to have to deal with this. Whose baby is it, anyway?"

The name would be forever etched into his memory. "Sergeant Hank Powell. We served together in the Gulf. According to the note, Hank and his wife were killed in a car accident."

"Oh," soft-hearted Peggy sighed. "How terrible."

"Yeah," Jeff muttered, with a glance at the infant staring at him through wide blue eyes. Heck, he hadn't seen Hank in years. What had Jeff ever done to make the man hate him enough to saddle him with his kid?

"Oops," his sister said abruptly. "Gotta run. Thomas's violin lesson is in fifteen minutes. Then Tina has ballet and Teddy has—"

"Karate?"

She laughed. "No, what am I, nuts? Drums."

Good Lord. Then, realizing she was hanging up on him, he panicked. "Peg, I need help. At least until I can figure out how to get out of this."

His sister sighed dramatically. After a moment, though, she perked right up. "Of course!" she said. "I'll call Laura."

"Laura?" he repeated. "Laura who?"

"I don't know why I didn't think of her right away," Peg went on, mostly to herself. "I'm sure she'd be willing."

"Willing to what?"

"Really, Jeff," Peggy said abruptly. "I've got to rush. Call you later to tell you when to expect Laura."

"Laura who?" he demanded again.

A dial tone hummed in his ear.

Abandoned, Jeff replaced the receiver and looked down at the finally quiet baby cradled against his side. Actually, when it was silent, holding it wasn't an entirely unpleasant sensation. A peaceful expression crossed the infant's face, and Jeff breathed a sigh of relief. Maybe the worst was over.

A moment later, he frowned at the sudden, damp warmth spreading down his hip and thigh. Realization dawned. He held the baby out at arm's length and stared down at his military green boxers.

Soaked.

In a much more disgusting manner than his T-shirt sleeve.

Slowly, he swiveled his appalled gaze to the baby.

It laughed at him.

Judging from the screams coming from the other side of the door, Peggy's brother had his hands full. Laura Morgan winced slightly as the baby's wail hit a particularly high note.

She forced herself not to reach for that doorknob. Every instinct she possessed told her to go inside, pick up that baby and comfort it. But she had to be sure before she did any such thing.

Laura laughed at herself. A little late for rethinking. If she hadn't been sure, would she have taken a commuter flight from Santa Barbara to San Diego almost immediately after talking to Peggy? Would she even now be standing outside Captain Jeff Ryan's apartment, her life neatly packed into three battered suitcases?

Okay, fine. So she wanted the job. So it had seemed like a gift from the gods the minute Peggy had mentioned it. Laura loved babies. Had always planned on having several of her own by now. She frowned slightly. The best-laid plans, et cetera.

Now here she was, thirty years old, single and hoping that her best friend's brother would hire her for the summer. Because the only way she could ease the baby fever still holding her in its grip was with other people's children. There were no husband and kids in her future. All of those dreams had died with Bill eight years ago.

Well, that's a good start on the summer, she told herself. Drown yourself in a tidal wave of self-pity. Always a great party favor. Designed to win friends and influence people.

"Psst!"

Laura frowned and looked to her right, but she didn't see anyone.

"Psst!" The voice was a little louder this time.

Studying the hall carefully, Laura finally spotted one of the apartment doors opened no more than half an inch. Staring at her through that narrow gap was one bright blue eye.

"Are you talking to me?" Laura asked hesitantly.

The door opened a hairbreadth wider, displaying a bit of the face that eye belonged to. A woman. Small, birdlike features, lined and etched by time, topped by wispy, snow white hair. "Are you going in there?" the woman asked.

"Yes," Laura answered with what she hoped was a friendly smile. Maybe the woman was too afraid to step into the hallway. But heck, the nightly news was enough to terrify Laura, for that matter. "I'm here to look after the baby."

"You look after yourself, missy," the woman said softly. "That one in there, he's a ladies' man."

"Is he really?" Laura turned a speculative eye on the door from behind which she could still hear the baby's cries.

"You don't look his usual type," the woman continued. "But I thought you should be told. Forewarned is fore-armed, you know."

With that intriguing statement, she closed her door. In quick succession, Laura heard four locks slam home.

Interesting start to a new job, she thought. Yet she couldn't help wondering what Captain Ryan's type *was*.

Then she dismissed the old woman's warnings, steeled herself and lifted her right hand to knock. She stopped short when she heard a man shouting to be heard over the baby.

"Yeah?" he asked. "If Laura Morgan's so great, why isn't she here yet? I had to take the baby to the grocery store! And it wasn't pretty!"

Laura drew her head back and stared at the closed door as if she could see through the heavy wood to the angry man inside.

"Peggy," he shouted, "this isn't *funny*."

Laura had to smile. Peggy Cummings's sense of humor was one of the things she liked best about her.

"I need help," he said. "Where the hell is this friend of yours, anyway?"

That cue was just too good to pass up. Quickly, she rapped her knuckles against the door.

It opened immediately.

The harried-looking man clutching a cordless phone to his ear stared at her. Well, he didn't match the description given to her by his sister. Peg had described her brother as "gorgeous, meticulously neat and with enough self-confidence for three healthy people."

The man in front of Laura now, though, looked wild. Short hair standing almost on end, he wore a white T-shirt stained with several different types of baby food, and a wet patch on his sharply creased trousers, which clung to his thigh. Bare feet only added to the image of a man on the edge.

None of that did a thing to take away from his good looks, though. His sharply defined features, strong jaw, straight nose and slightly full lips worked together to form a man too handsome for his own good. Peggy hadn't lied. He *was* gorgeous. Yet it wasn't only his face that was attractive. There was a strength about him that seemed to call to her. A knot of warmth uncurled in her stomach, sending ribbons of awareness spiraling through her limbs.

She breathed deeply, shifting her gaze to his eyes. A pale, icy blue, they seemed to look straight into her soul, poking and prodding to discover her secrets.

Laura shook her head slightly and looked away from his even stare deliberately. One thing she certainly *didn't* need was to start getting fanciful.

"I think she's here," he said into the phone. "Call me later."

He punched the disconnect button and set the phone down on a small table near the door.

"Are *you* Laura?" he asked, his blue-eyed gaze sweeping up and down her body in a flat second.

Instinctively, she stiffened, forgetting all about that instant, momentary bolt of attraction. Straightening her shoulders, she lifted her chin slightly. She had to do that anyway, to look him in the eye, but she hoped that the action looked defiant to him. Laura knew exactly what he was seeing when he stared at her.

A thirty-year-old woman, no makeup, wide brown eyes, dust brown hair pulled back into a ponytail. She wore comfortable penny loafers, baggy jeans and an oversize sweatshirt that proclaimed Ain't Life Grand? across the front.

Not very impressive, maybe. And as his neighbor had pointed out, probably not his type at all. But at least *she* could take care of a baby without looking as though she'd waded bare-handed through a war zone.

"Yes," she answered stiffly, giving him the same slow once-over that he had given her. "Jeff Ryan?"

He nodded abruptly, stepped past her into the hall and grabbed up her suitcases. Dropping them next to the wall, he closed the front door, then faced her.

"Where the heck have you been?" he demanded. "I expected you a half an hour ago."

She winced against the blare of the TV combining with the baby's cries. Pitching her voice a bit louder than normal, she snapped, "The plane was delayed."

Before he could comment on that, Laura sailed past Jeff Ryan into the unbelievably messy apartment. She paused long enough to turn off the TV, then followed the baby's screams to a basket set on the floor. Inside that straw-colored wicker bed, the infant lay on a handmade quilt, its chubby arms and legs pumping madly against the air.

Laura's heart melted.

Forgetting all about the man coming up behind her, she bent down, scooped up the baby and cradled it close to her chest. "It's all right, sweetie," she murmured as she rocked slowly back and forth, her right hand smoothing up and down the baby's back. "You're all right now. Laura's got you."

The screaming stopped.

The baby relaxed against her, its tiny body trembling as it sniffed and hiccuped.

"That's amazing," Jeff said softly, clearly afraid to break whatever spell Laura had woven around the child.

"Not really," she said, sparing him a quick sidelong look. "A little comfort goes a long way."

He pushed one hand through the little bit of hair allowed by military regulations and shook his head as he looked over the wreckage of his living room.

"I could use a little comfort myself," he admitted. "She hasn't been that quiet all day."

A girl.

"What's her name?"

"According to the papers, it's Miranda. Miranda Powell."

"Well, hello, Miranda Powell," Laura whispered. She kissed the little head that was nestled just beneath her chin.

The baby's fingers tugged at the material of her sweatshirt, but Laura felt the small pulls all the way to her heart.

Jeff collapsed onto the cluttered sofa, then winced, lifted one hip and reached beneath him to pull a half-empty baby bottle out of his way. Tossing it onto the floor with a fatalistic shrug, he turned his gaze back to Laura. "You're not what I expected," he said.

She was rarely what anyone expected and had long ago ceased to care. But she was already in love with this baby. Laura wanted the job enough to remain pleasant as she asked, "Really, why?"

He shrugged, his gaze running over her carelessly. "Peg said you're a teacher, but you look like a kid yourself."

Translation, she thought, *short.* It was hardly her fault that there were no tall genes in her family. "I'm thirty years old and a kindergarten teacher," she told him. "I have references if you'd like proof."

He held up one hand and shook his head. "Peggy's word is good enough for me. Besides—" he waved one hand to encompass the destruction around him "—as you can see, I'm in no position to quibble. I need help with her until I can figure out what to do about her."

One light brown eyebrow lifted. Laura felt it go up and tried to stop it, but she couldn't. What was there to figure out? she wanted to ask. There was only one thing to do with a baby.

Love it.

He must have read her expression because one corner of his mouth lifted slightly. She didn't want to notice what exceptional things even a hint of a smile did to his already handsome features. But she did.

"So," he asked, "you still want the job?"

She shouldn't. That sizzle of awareness she had experienced the second she laid eyes on him was not a good sign. But Laura couldn't have said no even if she wanted to. Not with Miranda's warm little body cuddled so closely.

"Yes."

"You understand that it may be for the entire summer?" he asked. "I mean, if I can handle everything right, the baby shouldn't be here more than a month or so. But you never know."

Any interest Laura might have had in him dissolved at his obvious haste to rid himself of the baby. Which was just as well anyway. She had already had her shot at love—and she'd lost. Besides, she could never be attracted to a man who so obviously didn't like children. Still, she wondered, what kind of man could turn his back on something so tiny? So defenseless?

"I understand perfectly," she said, and watched him give a satisfied nod.

"Good." He pushed himself up from the couch. "We can talk about salary tonight, if that's all right with you. My rules are simple. *You* take care of the baby. Agreed?"

"Agreed," she said.

He gave her a quick nod and started past her toward one of the closed doors on the other side of the room. He stopped dead in his tracks, though, when she said, "Hold on a minute, Captain. Now it's time for *you* to hear *my* rules."

Two

Jeff turned around slowly to face her.

All he really wanted was a shower, a nap and a change of clothes. Marine Corps boot camp hadn't been as rough on him as that one small baby girl had been. And yet, he thought as he looked into a pair of suddenly remote brown eyes, he had a feeling that his troubles were just beginning.

"Your rules?" he asked, determined to keep the upper hand in whatever argument was beginning to erupt. "Since when do employees make the rules?"

"Since now," she declared firmly.

Jeff rubbed the back of his neck. He should have known it wouldn't be easy. Any friend of his sister's was bound to be stubborn and independent as hell. He stared into those soft brown eyes of hers again and felt a stirring deep within him. Despite the fact that she was dressed like a refugee from the Goodwill, Jeff found himself wondering what her legs looked like when they weren't being hidden by seemingly *miles* of denim fabric.

Why would she dress like such a frump? What was she hiding from?

And why did he care?

He didn't, Jeff told himself. He couldn't afford to feel the sense of awareness already creeping through him. Laura Morgan was going to be living in his house, taking care of that baby. He wasn't about to mess that up by allowing his hormones to do his thinking for him.

Still, he told himself, he must be lonelier than he had thought, to be intrigued by a tiny woman dressed in clothes two sizes too big for her.

The look in her eyes as he continued to stare at her only grew frostier. So much for her sweatshirt, he smirked inwardly. He'd be willing to bet that she hadn't found anything "grand" about life in years.

But, since the baby was cooing contentedly, he was willing to put up with the poor man's Mary Poppins. As for his hormones—apparently, he needed to spend some time with one or two lady friends. That should take care of any bizarre interest in Laura Morgan.

"Okay," he said at last, folding his arms across his chest and completely ignoring the sticky substances on his T-shirt. "What are these *rules?*"

She nodded. "I'll stay here and take care of the baby for the summer, but…"

"Yeah?"

She inhaled sharply and tried to draw herself up to a formidable height. He could have told her it was a futile attempt. She couldn't be more than five foot one. And that was no one's idea of intimidating.

"You're not hiring me to be your housekeeper." She paused for a look around at the mess his apartment had become. *"Or,"* she added, "your cook and laundress."

Insulted, Jeff tried to defend himself. "Look, until this morning, everything was under control—"

"Also," she said, cutting him off neatly, "there will be no walking around naked, no women strolling in and out of the apartment—"

"What are you—?"

"One of your neighbors thought it prudent to warn me about the fact that you're what she calls a 'ladies' man.'"

He shook his head and gave a resigned sigh. "Let me guess. White hair, big blue eyes?"

She nodded, but he thought he saw the ghost of a smile twitching at her lips.

"Agnes Butler," he said, the elderly woman's features forming in his mind. "For lack of anything better to do, she spies on me."

Twin brown eyebrows arched high on her forehead. "Spying? Sounds a little paranoid."

Briefly, he recalled all the times he had strolled down that short hallway and spotted his neighbor, her eye glued to a partially opened door. Yeah, *spying* was the right word.

"You're not paranoid," he told her, "if they really *are* after you."

A moment or two of silence passed. At last, she nodded and said, "Yes, well, the rest of the rules are pretty simple."

"There's more?" he asked.

She smiled. "No foul language—"

"Now, just a minute—" he said, trying to interrupt, but she was on a roll.

"No talking before coffee in the morning, and no loud TV or radio after eleven at night."

Jeff stared at her. Was she finished? Or just pausing for breath? A few seconds ticked by, and he told himself that apparently, she'd reached the end of her demands. Well, fine. Now it was *his* turn.

He would tell her just what she could do with her rules. This was *his* house after all. Where did she get off telling him when he could or couldn't watch *his* TV? And what about women? So he didn't exactly have a parade of females trooping in and out of his apartment every day and night. If he *wanted* to, he wasn't going to be stopped by her.

"Listen up, lady," he started, "I don't know who the hell you think you are…"

She froze, stiffening for a fight.

Miranda sniffled, shifting against a suddenly tense body.

Recognizing the signs of baby distress already, Jeff lowered his voice and spoke in a quiet, reasonable tone. "You can't order me around. *I'm* the employer here, you know."

"I can tell you what I expect," Laura countered, her voice matching his. "And if you don't like it, you can find someone else."

He didn't believe the threat. Even as she said it, her arms were tightening around the baby as if afraid that he would try to take Miranda from her forcibly.

No worries there.

But with the position he was in, he couldn't afford to take the risk. If she left, he'd be right back where he started that morning. In deep trouble, begging Peggy for help.

All right, he could swallow a little bit of pride for the sake of his sanity. And he could even learn to deal with her ridiculous rules. *Anything* to keep her here and the baby quiet. After all, it wasn't forever. Just for the summer. By the end of three months, he would either have found a suitable replacement guardian for the baby or, God help him, a permanent nanny to help him raise Hank Powell's kid.

Abruptly, he said, "Fine. Agreed."

"Thank you." She accepted his defeat gracefully. "But as long as we're discussing this situation, I should like to add one more rule to my list."

He snorted disbelievingly. "What's left?"

"I'd like to state clearly right from the first," she said, "that I am *not* interested in you romantically, so I would appreciate it very much if you would keep your distance."

Jeff laughed, the first good laugh he'd had all morning. Pointedly running his gaze over her slowly, he shook his head and said, "No problem."

Once Jeff was out of the shower—and Laura had even resorted to turning on the TV so she wouldn't have to listen to the spray of water and imagine it pummeling his naked, no doubt gorgeous body—they set things to rights.

The living room was a disaster.

With a fed and changed Miranda watching happily from her wicker basket, Laura and Jeff worked together to rebuild the place. So much for her rule about not being a housekeeper. As most of the clutter was cleared away, she noticed that the apartment wasn't exactly homey. In fact, it was surprisingly impersonal.

A sprinkling of framed photos and commendations hung on the beige walls, but there were no paintings. Tweed fabric covered the couch and two chairs that sat on the tan wall-to-wall carpeting. There was an impressive stereo system and a large-screen TV on one wall, and a fireplace that looked as though it had never been used stood on the opposite wall. A two-person table sat at the end of the kitchen, and there were two bedrooms, one on either side of the single bathroom.

She tried not to think about having to share that bathroom with Jeff Ryan for the next three months. Luckily for her, she no longer noticed things like just how good-looking Jeff Ryan was. If she had been the slightest bit interested in finding a man, these next few months could have been torture.

Of course, she had thought she was past noticing the fresh, clean scent of a man's aftershave, too.

"So," he said, and snapped her attention to him. He folded up yet another brown paper grocery bag as he asked, "How come a kindergarten teacher didn't already have a summer job nailed down?"

She stacked the last can of formula in what had been an empty cabinet, then closed the door and straightened up. "I did," she admitted. "This one sounded like more fun."

He snorted a laugh. "More fun than what?"

"Transferring card catalogs to computer in the local library."

He whistled low and long. "You're right, not fun." He glanced at the baby a few feet away. "But this is?"

"Sure."

"Lady, you've got a strange sense of fun."

Peggy had told Laura that Jeff not only had no experience taking care of children, but also that he didn't even like them.

She frowned at him. "Your sister has three kids. Don't you remember how cute they were when they were little?"

He shrugged and bent down to neatly place the folded bags in the appropriate rack just inside the pantry door. "I remember they cried. A lot," he said as he stood up again and closed the door. "They smelled bad and they couldn't even talk to tell you *why* they cried all the time."

"No wonder you never visit Peggy and her family."

He looked at her. "Is that what she said?"

Was he offended? How could he be? "It's true, isn't it? You see them about once a year?"

"Yeah, it's true." He folded his arms across his chest and leaned one hip against the blond wood countertop. "She tell you why?"

"She said you're uncomfortable around kids." Laura didn't tell him the rest. Did he really need to know that his own sister, though she loved him, thought he was too self-involved to be concerned about family?

"That's part of it," he admitted, letting his gaze slide from Laura to the baby, now chewing contentedly on her own fist. "But mostly it's because I can't even talk to Peggy and her husband anymore."

"Why not?" Laura asked. Peggy and Jim Cummings were two of the nicest people she'd ever known. Was the woman's own brother too dense to see that?

He shook his head and smiled without humor. "Before they had those kids, Peggy and Jim and I had some good times. Skiing, sailing, took a few trips together."

"And?" she prodded, interested now.

"And, the minute the first kid was born, it was all over." He pushed away from the counter, walked across the utilitarian kitchen and stood, staring down at the baby in the basket. "They became *parents* in the worst possible sense. All they talked about was Thomas. His teeth. His upset stomach. His first steps. The first time he used a spoon by himself, you would have thought he was Einstein reincarnated."

Laura smiled to herself as she stared at Jeff's broad back. His sister was *still* like that. Just a few weeks ago, Peggy had called to crow over Tina winning the second-grade spelling bee.

Like any other good parent would.

"But that's perfectly natural," Laura said, and walked to stand beside him. Looking down at Miranda, she smiled. "They're proud of their children."

"They're boring," he countered, swiveling his head to stare at her. "They used to have plans. Ambitions. Now those ambitions are all for the kids."

An emotion she couldn't quite identify flickered in his pale blue eyes briefly, then disappeared. "All parents want good things for their kids," she said quietly.

"Sure," he countered. "But do they have to stop being people themselves to be good parents?"

"Peggy and Jim are *terrific* people," she argued, defending her friends.

He shook his head as he looked at her. Once again, Laura felt a flutter of awareness dance through her bloodstream. Deliberately, she squashed it.

"Is it so wrong to have ambitions and dreams for your kids?" she asked, determined to keep this conversation going, if only to keep her mind too busy to daydream.

He thought about her question for a long minute, then shrugged. "Not for Peggy and Jim," he said, shifting his gaze back to the baby, now intently staring up at the two adults. "But that's not me," he continued. "I have plans for my career. Plans I've worked toward long and hard."

"Everybody makes plans," she said.

It was as if he hadn't heard her.

"I'm going to be the youngest general in the corps," he stated. Then he glanced at the wicker basket. "And I'm not going to let *anything* stop me."

Three

A nightmare.

In less than twelve hours, his life had become a waking nightmare.

Jeff stumbled across the living room, stepped on a fallen pacifier and grunted as the dull yet stabbing pain lanced from his arch straight up his leg.

"Are you all right?" Laura asked, her voice high enough to carry over the baby's wailing.

"Dandy," he muttered, then flopped down beside her on the couch. Instantly, he lifted one hip and pulled a leaking baby bottle from under his butt. "How can one kid need so much *stuff?*" he grumbled to no one in particular as he slammed the plastic bottle down onto the coffee table.

Laura had only one lamp on, and in the dim light, he surveyed what had, only that morning, been his sanctuary.

Blankets, clean diapers, bottles, pacifiers, lotion, powder—there was enough junk in the already small room to satisfy a battalion of babies. So why wasn't the only baby present happy?

"Why is she screaming like that?" he demanded.

"I think she's teething," Laura said, and hitched Miranda higher on her shoulder.

"Perfect," he said. "How long does *that* last?"

In the soft light, Laura smirked at him. "According to my watch, she should be finished in another three and a half minutes."

His eyebrows lifted. He knew sarcasm when he heard it, and if he wasn't so damn tired, he might have taken a shot himself. As it was, his heart just wasn't in it.

Laura whispered to the baby while stroking the infant's back in long, gentle motions. Jeff watched her, at first for lack of anything else to do, but after a moment, because he couldn't seem to look away.

And he also couldn't figure out why. That nightgown of hers certainly wasn't alluring. An oversized T-shirt emblazoned Life Is A Trip, Don't Miss It hung to midthigh. Although, he thought, the surprisingly shapely legs revealed by that shirt were not bad at all. As he watched, she shifted slightly, tugging the hem down fruitlessly.

Her thick brown hair lay loose on her shoulders, and he had to admit that the casual style complemented her features far better than the scraped-back ponytail she'd worn earlier. Her high cheekbones were more sharply defined in the soft light. Light brown eyebrows arched high over eyes that looked as deep and mysterious as a moonless night. Her generous mouth was curved in a half smile even as the baby in her arms flailed tiny fists against her face. Laura merely caught one of those fists, opened it and kissed the small, chubby palm.

His jaw tightened, and something inside him twisted. A curl of desire trickled through him, and he deliberately squashed it. Shifting position on the sofa, he wished he had taken the time to grab his robe before leaving his room. Wearing only a pair of boxer shorts, Jeff felt suddenly, decidedly uncomfortable.

He was staring.

In the shadowy light, Laura saw his pale blue eyes darken as he watched her. Her gaze slid away, unfortunately dropping to his bare, muscular chest. Her heart beat faster, and her palms were damp. Breath after breath straggled into her lungs even as she told herself that she was probably just too warm in the overheated apartment.

All she needed was to turn the heater down.

This had nothing to do with how attractive he was. After all, she didn't even notice things like that anymore.

Laura's gaze flicked to his again, then quickly away. Her stomach fluttered and twitched. Why was he looking at her so strangely? She wasn't exactly a supermodel, so what did he find so fascinating that he couldn't stop watching her?

Miranda sucked in a gulp of air, coughed, choked, then cried again, pumping her little legs against Laura's chest. Immediately Laura dismissed Jeff Ryan and the strange things he did to her stomach and concentrated on the baby.

"It's all right, sweetheart," she soothed in a low, humming tone.

"No, it's not," Jeff said, his voice grumpy. "Is she ever going to shut up so I can get some sleep tonight?"

Laura frowned at him, furious at his impatience. Carefully, she shifted the baby to her lap and began to rock slowly. "Well, now that you've told her that she's disturbing you, I'm sure she'll settle right down," Laura snapped. "After all, how can the throbbing pain of new, sharp teeth slicing through her gums compare with your being tired?"

He scowled at her and sat forward, leaning his forearms on his thighs. "You know—" he started to say.

"Yes, I do," she cut him off neatly. "I know that you don't give a—" she broke off, searched for a word, then continued ''—*hoot* about this baby. All you care about is yourself.''

"Up until eleven this morning," he reminded her, "that's all I *had* to worry about."

"Well, things've changed."

"Tell me about it." He waved one hand at her and the baby. "In less than twenty-four hours, I've inherited a baby and a snotty nanny."

"Snotty?"

"Snotty," he repeated.

Bouncing the baby a little faster on her knee, Laura's rocking motion became a bit jerky. "You are the one who needed my help," she told him stiffly, still smarting from the "snotty" remark.

"Help," he clarified. "Not harassment."

"Now I'm harassing you?"

"What do you call it?" he asked hotly.

"I call it looking out for this baby when no one else seems willing."

Miranda sniffled and rubbed her eyes with both fists. Then, reaching down, she snatched at the hem of Laura's nightgown and lifted it. Jamming the fabric into her mouth, she chewed furiously.

"I didn't say I wasn't willing," he said.

"Of course you did," Laura countered, paying no attention to the suddenly quiet baby in her arms. "Not five minutes after I got here, you were talking about finding a way out of this situation."

A long silent moment passed, neither of them aware that Miranda had stopped screaming. Finally, Jeff stood up, and ran one hand across the top of his head. Something Laura had already noticed he did quite often when he was upset.

"Look," he said, gazing down at her in the half-light, "maybe we got off on the wrong foot."

"How's that?" She looked up at him, determined to

keep her gaze locked on his face. Thankfully, she was immune to the distraction of a well-muscled chest, but there was no point in taking chances.

"I'm not some kind of monster," he told her, and his voice sounded distant, quiet. "I don't even *hate* kids."

Wow. A testimonial. Her hold on Miranda tightened protectively.

"It's just that I'm not..." He shook his head and looked off into the shadowy corner of the room. "Hell, I'm nobody's idea of father material."

Was that a wistful tone in his voice? "You could be," she said hesitantly. "If you tried."

He snorted a choked laugh. "You're a lot more sure than I am, Mary Poppins," he commented.

Laura stood up, hitching the baby higher in her arms. Forcing herself to look into Jeff's eyes, she said, "I thought Marines weren't afraid of a challenge."

One corner of his mouth lifted in a sardonic half smile. She told herself that it was lucky for her she was beyond noticing things like the dimple he had in his right cheek.

"Challenges, no," he told her. "Slaughters, yes. And I have a feeling that kid's already got me outnumbered." Pausing, he listened for a minute, then said, "Hey, she's not crying anymore."

True, Laura thought. Miranda had finally settled down, and neither one of them had realized it.

Jeff looked at the baby in her arms, then pulled in a deep breath as his gaze slipped lower.

Laura saw his jaw tighten. Glancing down, she looked for whatever it was that had caused such a reaction in him. Her eyes widened immediately. The hem of her nightshirt was drawn up to just beneath her left breast. Exposed to Jeff's view was not only a wide expanse of flesh, but the electric blue lace bikini underwear she wore. Laura's one concession to femininity in her wardrobe had always been her secret weakness for beautiful lingerie.

Well, it wasn't a secret anymore.

"Oh, my goodness," she blurted as she tugged at the fabric even while turning her back on Jeff.

"Wow," he murmured.

Laura silently thanked heaven that it was so dark in the living room. She felt the heated flush of embarrassment rush to her cheeks and was relieved he wouldn't see it.

"Who would have thought you'd be hiding lace under all that camouflage you were wearing earlier?"

It would have been too much to hope for that he would ignore what he'd just seen. But did he *really* have to talk about it, too?

"I think it would be better if we just pretend this never happened," Laura said as she tugged at the fabric, hoping to restore her dignity. But the baby, happily chewing on the soft cotton, was blissfully unaware of Laura's predicament. Little fingers curled into the material and hung on with a surprisingly strong grip.

"Nothing *did* happen," Jeff stated.

Laura shot him a quick, furtive look over her shoulder. An odd gleam shone in his eyes, but she dismissed it as a trick of the low lighting. For whatever reason, he wasn't going to talk about her underwear anymore. That was enough.

"Good," she said quickly. "Now, if you'll excuse me," she grunted as she stepped around him, keeping her back to him at all times. "I think I'll put Miranda down. She seems contented enough now."

He chuckled.

She heard him, but since she still wasn't decently covered, she didn't turn around. "What's so funny?" she demanded, stopping just outside her open bedroom door.

"Nothing," he said, his voice low and intimate. "It's

just that I was thinking how alike Miranda and I are after all.''

"What does that mean?'' she asked, knowing even as she did so that it was a mistake.

"It means that pulling a woman's nightgown up always makes me pretty content, too.''

She inhaled sharply. Straightening her shoulders, she ignored the deep chuckles coming from behind her and walked into her room. When the door was safely closed, Laura leaned back against it.

Miranda laughed, let go of the nightgown and patted Laura's cheeks.

"Oh, sure,'' she said to the smiling baby. "*Now* you cooperate.''

Jeff cupped his head in his hands and inhaled the scent of the strong black coffee in front of him. His eyes felt like two marbles in a bucket of sand.

Between the baby's restless first night in his apartment and the heart-stopping peep show Laura had unwittingly given him, he had lain awake most of the night. Visions of blue lace and smooth, lightly tanned flesh had haunted him.

Even now, he could see her, flustered and embarrassed as she turned away from him. If the light in the room had been better, Jeff was willing to bet that he could have seen a blush steal across her cheeks.

How long had it been since he'd known a woman to blush?

He inhaled sharply, blew the air out of his lungs in a frustrated sigh and told himself that he would be in real bad shape if he was attracted to women like Laura Morgan.

Thankfully, he wasn't.

Give him a well-dressed, sophisticated career woman every time. The motherly type had never done a thing for him. Although, you really couldn't classify those blue lace bikini panties as *motherly*.

He groaned quietly.

Should have taken another sick day, he thought. A man just couldn't function on two hours' sleep. Unless of course, he thought as he leaned back in his chair, he was on a battlefield. Live ammunition whizzing past your head had a way of waking you right up.

"Captain?"

Jeff blinked groggily, almost surprised to find himself in his office. He looked at the younger man poking his head in the doorway. "What is it, Corporal Warren?"

"A Private Higgins is here, sir. Says he has those files you wanted."

"Send him in," Jeff ordered sharply. He'd been waiting all morning for these records to arrive.

A young, eager-looking redheaded kid in the standard camouflage utility uniform strode into his office. File folders tucked neatly beneath his left arm, the kid came to an abrupt stop in front of Jeff's desk and flashed a picture-perfect salute.

Nodding absentmindedly, Jeff reached for the files.

"This is all I could find, sir," the private said as he handed the manila folders over. "If you'd like, I could make a few calls, see if there's anything else available."

Jeff opened the files and glanced quickly over the pages inside. Then he looked up again. "That won't be necessary, Private. Thank you."

"Aye, sir." Another salute, an abrupt about-face and the kid was gone.

"Corporal Warren," Jeff called. His clerk appeared instantly.

"Sir?"

"Close my door, Corporal. No interruptions."

"Aye, sir."

In seconds, the door was closed and Jeff was alone. Picking up his coffee, he started reading all about the man who had given him Miranda. Not that he didn't remember him. But it had been more than five years since he'd seen the sergeant. And in the military, an officer served with so many men—sometimes names and faces blurred without a good prodding of the memory.

Twenty minutes later, Jeff sat back in his chair, flipping the file closed with the tips of his fingers. Setting his elbows on the arms of his chair, he steepled his fingers and stared at the windows opposite his desk.

Memories raced through his mind. Desert sun, mind-boggling heat and the constant adrenaline rush of impending battle. Days and nights spent in the company of men willing to die at a moment's notice.

Abruptly, he reached for his phone and the Rolodex on the corner of his desk. He flipped quickly through the cards until he'd found the one he wanted.

Punching in a phone number, he held the receiver to his ear, sat back again and waited.

Laura woke up instantly and lay perfectly still.

Even before her mind had assured her that everything was all right, she heard his voice, a hushed whisper in the darkness.

Turning her head on the pillow until she was facing the newly purchased crib against the far wall in her room, Laura saw Jeff, leaning his forearms on the top rail, staring down at the sleeping baby.

"I remember your father now, kiddo," he was saying, his voice oddly tight. "I called up his service records today."

The baby whimpered in her sleep, and Jeff reached down to awkwardly pat her. Laura smiled in the darkness.

"He was a good man, your dad," Jeff said. "Got a Bronze Star for bravery."

Miranda kicked her blankets off, and Jeff carefully replaced them.

A trickle of warmth moved through Laura. Maybe she had misjudged him. Maybe he cared more for the baby than even *he* knew.

Moonlight, peering through a part in the curtains, washed her otherwise dark room with a pale ivory cast. In the indistinct light, Jeff was no more than a shadow, yet she could read tension in every line of his body.

"We fought together, you know." He sighed heavily and shook his head, as if lost in the memories. "Hank kept me from making a damn fool of myself during my first battle. And I saved his sergeant's stripes for him when he came up against a major with more brass than brains."

Laura held her breath, wanting to say something to him, to let him know that she wasn't asleep. But at the same time, she wanted him to go on. She wanted to know more about him.

She told herself that it was only because she was working for him and would be living in his house for the next three months.

But it was more than that, and she knew it.

Somehow, in the past twenty-four hours, he had forced some of the ice around her heart to melt. Why and how, she wasn't sure.

Maybe it was the helpless expression on his face when he looked at Miranda. And maybe it was what he did for a pair of boxer shorts.

She scowled to herself, disgusted at this turn of events. Laura didn't want to care about another man. She'd already found and lost the love of her life. What was the point of settling for second best?

"You had a good dad, Miranda," Jeff said quietly,

bringing Laura's attention back to him. "I'll do my best to see to it you get a good one again." He reached into the crib and smoothed his palm gently across the top of the baby's head. "Good night, kiddo."

So much for her giving him the benefit of the doubt. All of her warm, fuzzy feelings for nothing. Apparently, he still had every intention of finding a way to squeak out of being Miranda's guardian.

Laura bit down hard on her bottom lip to keep from speaking. *How* could she possibly be attracted to a man who could so casually walk away from a baby entrusted to his care?

Her gaze followed him to the door and the slice of light spearing in from the living room. Laura ground her teeth together in frustration. She couldn't say anything. If she did, he would know that she had deliberately lain there eavesdropping.

"And good night to you, too, Laura," he added softly, just before leaving and closing the door behind him.

She sat straight up in bed.

Blast him. He had known the whole time that she was awake! He must be laughing himself sick right now, guessing what it had cost her to keep her mouth shut.

Well, he wouldn't laugh long. Whether he knew it or not, he had just given her permission to make a few comments on what he'd been telling Miranda.

Casting a quick look at the baby, Laura climbed out of bed and headed for the door. She paused briefly to snatch up her bathrobe and throw it on.

If they were going to talk, she'd make sure his mind was on what she was saying. *Not* on her underwear.

Four

In the kitchen, Jeff smiled to himself as Laura's bedroom door opened, then closed again softly. He'd known she wouldn't stay in her room. In fact, he'd been counting on it. For reasons he didn't want to explore at the moment, he wanted, no, *needed* to see her.

Picking up the chilled bottle of wine, he poured each of them a glass and was turning around to hand it to her when she walked in.

Surprised, she blinked and stopped dead.

Instantly, the taunting memory of blue lace bikinis withered and died along with his fantasies. Looking her over quickly, he wondered just how old that bathrobe was.

Faded pink terry cloth hung on her small frame with all the grace and dignity of a drunk clutching a light pole. The nubby fabric, rubbed smooth in places, was a patchwork of stains and tears. Long, loose threads waved lazily every time she moved, and the single front pocket looked stuffed with tissues and God knew what else.

"Nice robe," he commented wryly.

She tightened the threadbare sash around her waist and tossed her hair back behind her shoulders. One light eyebrow arched high on her forehead as she looked him up and down quickly. "Nice camouflage," she snapped. "Were you out hiding in the forest?"

He grinned. Ratty robe or not, he was glad to see her.

"You knew I was awake the whole time, didn't you?"

Her cheeks were flushed, and her hair looked soft and tousled, as if a man had spent hours running his fingers through it.

Jeff inhaled sharply. Better if he didn't let his mind wander too far down *that* road. Deliberately, he took another look at her worn robe before meeting her deep brown eyes. Those shadowy depths sparkled with impatience and suspicion as she watched him.

"Not the whole time," he said with a shrug, and held out one of the crystal wineglasses toward her. "Wine?"

She ignored the offer. "Why didn't you say something?"

"I was talking to Miranda," he said, wondering now why it was that he'd wanted to see her. "Do you want the wine or not?"

"Oh." She looked at the glass, then back to him. "I don't think so."

Still holding it toward her, he said, "It's only half a glass, Laura."

She thought about it for a moment longer, then reached out and took it from him. "All right. Thanks."

Inclining his head slightly, he said, "You're welcome." Taking his wine, he walked past her into the living room. A single lamp had been left on. The room lay mostly in darkness, with deeper shadows gathering in the corners.

Tossing his hat onto the coffee table, Jeff sat down on the couch, leaned his head against the high back and sighed heavily. Damn, it felt good to relax. He propped one foot on the edge of the table, and as proof of his tiredness, didn't move a muscle when Laura stepped over his extended leg to take a seat beside him on the sofa.

Turning his head slightly, he looked at her. She was watching him again, with that solemn stare he was already getting used to.

"Bad day?" she asked.

"Long day," he corrected.

Moments of sweet silence stretched out between them. After being surrounded by people and the noise and hustle at the base all day, Jeff had always craved the peace and quiet of a few minutes alone. Solitude helped him think. Gave him time to consider his past, his future.

He'd been alone for so many years, this small ritual was second nature to him. But tonight it was different. Tonight there was someone else's breathing whispering into the darkness. Instead of absolute, undisturbed silence, he heard the hush of skin brushing against skin as she crossed her legs beneath her, Indian style. When she took a sip of her wine, the tiny clink of her front teeth hitting the crystal sounded out.

Surprising himself, Jeff found that he was actually enjoying sharing this moment of quiet with someone who valued peace enough to know not to talk.

It was…comforting in a way he hadn't expected.

"Was it true?" she asked softly.

Jeff smiled to himself. Apparently, Laura *could* be quiet. She simply preferred not to. "What?" he asked.

"Everything you said about Miranda's father?"

"Yeah." He nodded, took a drink of wine and sat higher on the couch, half turning to look at her.

"But you said yesterday that you didn't even remember him."

"I know." He reached up and rubbed one hand across his face. Jeff had read through Hank Powell's files three times. Each time, he had asked himself how he could have mentally misfiled the man.

The only answer he had come up with was one he was sure Laura wouldn't understand.

"I just don't get it," she said. Scooping one hand through her hair, she propped her elbow on the sofa back. "How can you forget a friend?"

Jeff shook his head. "I didn't say he was a friend."

"You said he saved you from making a fool of yourself."

He winced tightly. There was a memory he didn't particularly want to relive.

"He did," Jeff admitted, hoping she'd let it go at that. He should have known better.

"Then—"

"He wasn't my friend," Jeff interrupted. "He was my sergeant."

In the dim light, he saw her shake her head in confusion. Suddenly unable to sit still, he got up, walked to the nearest window and yanked on a nylon cord. The window blinds flew up with a loud clatter. When they were secured, Jeff set his wineglass down on the windowsill, leaned both palms on either side of it and stared through the glass at the town outside.

Bright splashes of neon decorated the night. Shimmers of primary colors reflected off the night sky. Convenience stores, gas stations, even the theater down the street added to the blazing clutter.

He stared at civilization's landmarks until they faded into a kaleidoscopic blur of light and color. Slowly, his mind replaced the familiar view with one he'd spent years trying to forget.

A sun-washed desert rose up in his memory. Men and machinery moving across endless miles of sand and heat under a sky so wide and empty it glittered in the noonday sun like a stainless steel skillet.

Hank Powell, a grizzled, tough, no-nonsense first sergeant, had had the guts to look a fresh, young, know-it-all lieutenant in the face and tell him he was wrong.

Jeff smiled slightly at the memory of what had been an embarrassing and infuriating moment. It had been hard enough admitting to himself that he didn't know what he was doing. But to have First Sergeant Powell call him on it was especially humbling. He'd made every effort since then to forget it.

"What happened?" Laura asked from behind him.

The desert slid back into the past where it belonged. Jeff half turned to look at her. "It was my first tour. I was young and stupid." He shook his head slowly. "But thankfully, not too stupid to learn. I made a mistake that could have gotten me and my men killed."

"What?" she asked, and he could see the curiosity stamped on her features.

"Doesn't matter now. All that matters is that Hank Powell stopped me in time." Picking up his wineglass, Jeff eased down onto the windowsill, perching on the edge as he faced her. Memories swelled around him. "Hank was the kind of Marine that would make John Wayne look like a sissy."

She gave him a tentative smile. "Sounds scary."

"You bet."

"You liked him."

He thought about that for a long minute. *Like* the first sergeant? "I admired the hell out of him," he finally said, and even then that wasn't really enough to explain the relationship. Jeff drained the rest of his wine, then twirled the empty glass between his fingers. "He taught me a lot."

"Yet you didn't remember him."

"I never actually said I didn't remember him. I knew

the name." He shot her a sidelong glance. "I hadn't seen him in at least five years."

"Still…"

Jeff's grip on the fragile crystal tightened noticeably. He looked down at whitened knuckles and deliberately forced himself to relax his hold on the slender stem. Taking a deep, calming breath, he said, "I remember people fine, Laura." His voice sounded rough and thick, even to himself. "Every time I close my eyes, I see their faces clearly."

"Who?"

"The dead."

Laura sucked in a gulp of air. Even from across the room, she saw the shadows in his eyes. Instantly, her mind furnished images of what he must see. What he must recall about battles she had only read about from a safe, insulating distance.

She took a sip of wine, forcing the cool, smooth liquid past the sudden knot in her throat. Then she leaned forward and set the unfinished drink carefully down on the coffee table.

What could she say? She watched him for a long, quiet moment and knew he wasn't in the room with her anymore. His features shifted, tightened. Clearly, the memories, once unleashed, raced through his brain. Memories she had prodded him to relive.

Suddenly, she wanted to go to him, slip her arms around his shoulders and comfort him like she would a lost child.

But he was no boy.

And the feelings he stirred in her weren't entirely altruistic. *Or* motherly. In the soft glow of the single lamp, she saw the sharp, strong planes of his face as if in a dream. Her gaze drifted over him and locked on his hands. His long fingers toyed with the empty crystal glass, turning it this way and that, slowly, hypnotically.

She watched his fingers stroke the foggy glass, tracing

the intricate pattern etched into the crystal. She wondered what it would feel like to be touched by hands as gentle as those. To be explored with the same finesse and care.

To be the woman he turned to when his dreams refused him sleep.

Her stomach fluttered uneasily, and her heartbeat quickened. One minute she was sympathizing with him, wanting to ease a years-old pain, and the next, she was caught up in sensual imagery that left her body throbbing with an ache she hadn't known possible.

Yet more disturbing than those sensations was the emotional ache he caused in her. She felt herself wanting to give. To soothe. To love.

Quickly, she took a mental step backward.

Closing her tired eyes, she hoped to rid herself of the fantasies building within her. It didn't work. As if in a dream, Jeff leaned over her, whispering her name. She arched toward him, lifting her arms in a welcoming embrace.

He held her close to his chest, and she listened to the steady, reassuring beat of his heart. In her drowsy, half-asleep state, she snuggled into him. "Where are we going?" she murmured.

"*You're* going," he said quietly. "To bed."

She tightened her arms around his neck and leaned her head back to look up at him. "You're dangerous, Captain."

He glanced down at her as he stopped outside her bedroom door. His arms tightened slightly around her. "Me? I'm a Marine," he said. "One of the good guys."

She shook her head slowly, unsure if he was purposely misunderstanding her or not. Lifting one hand, she stroked her fingers along the line of his cheek and felt his jaw muscle tighten in response. Oh, yeah. He knew exactly what she was talking about.

"It wouldn't be a good idea," she told him.

"Probably not," he agreed, and turned his face into her touch.

"I'm not interested in a relationship, you know."

"Me, either," he said, his teeth nipping at the pads of her fingers.

Electrical charges skittered through her bloodstream.

"We'd regret it, Jeff."

"Maybe, Laura," he whispered. "But we'd never forget it."

Oh, good heavens, she thought. What had she gotten herself into?

Without another word, he opened the door, carried her into the darkness and crossed the room to her bed. As if she were the most delicate flower in the world, he laid her down on the mattress. Bracing his hands on either side of her head, he leaned in close and brushed a kiss across her lips.

Her heart stumbled, stopped, then started beating again, much quicker than before. Staring up at him, Laura, for the first time in years, couldn't think of a single thing to say.

Jeff straightened up slowly, whispered, "Sleep well," then left the room as if the hounds of hell were on his heels.

Laura lay wide-awake in the darkness, listening to Miranda's baby noises and the wild, frantic beating of her own heart.

Hours later, muted sunshine drifted in through her bedroom curtains. Morning. Laura sat up, groaned and rubbed her eyes. No doubt about it—a person really did need more than one or two hours' sleep a night.

Helplessly, she shook her head. She was in deep trouble here. She'd only known Jeff Ryan a couple of days, and already he had begun to sneak past the barriers she had erected around her heart.

Suddenly, the three long months of summer stretched out

ahead of her like an eternity. How would she ever survive living in such close quarters with the man?

That night over pizza, Jeff looked at the woman sitting across from him at the table. Hair scraped back into a high ponytail, no makeup and a lime green sweatshirt that read, Don't Sweat The Small Stuff, she was not the kind of woman dreams were built around.

So why, he wondered silently, did *his* dreams furnish her with a starring role? All night, he'd been haunted by the memory of her slight form cuddled in close to him. By the taste of her lips. By the soft sigh of her breath.

Good God—he was digging himself a trench here.

"Have you been looking into Miranda's guardianship papers?" she asked suddenly.

Grateful to end his disturbing train of thought, he nodded. She hadn't said one word about their little tryst in the darkness, and he was profoundly grateful for *that,* too.

"I talked to my lawyer yesterday," he admitted, remembering the call he'd made after reading Sergeant Powell's record.

"I've never known anyone who had their own lawyer," she said.

He shrugged. "He's actually the brother of one of the captains on base. We all go to him with legal questions."

"And what was your question?"

Jeff picked up a slice of pepperoni-and-mushroom pizza, then set it back down again. Almost guiltily, he glanced at Miranda, her little face covered with a layer of strained green beans. "I told him about how I found her and explained the note and the will that was with her."

"And?"

He leaned back in his chair, his appetite suddenly gone. "And, though he says the means of delivering Miranda to

me were fairly unusual, the guardianship can be legalized—
if I consent.''

Laura nodded, her attention squarely on him. She was
practically quivering in her chair. He knew damn well that
she wanted to prod him for more information. But she
wouldn't, so he took pity on her.

"And no, I haven't called child welfare."

She released a pent-up breath.

"But that's not saying I won't."

Her lips tightened.

Why should she be able to make him feel guilty? He
hardly knew her. Of course, she made him feel lots of *other*
things, too. Don't go there, he told himself silently. "Laura,
it's too early for me to decide anything."

"I understand," she said tightly.

"That's nice," he returned. "I'm not sure I do."

"What do you mean?"

He glanced at the baby. She was smearing her green
beans across the tray of the high chair. Her soft, fine hair
was dotted with leftover mashed potatoes, and a stream of
drool was running down her chin.

Just looking at the small disaster area should have made
up his mind for him. Why it didn't was beyond him.

Jeff shook his head wearily. "I don't understand why I
can't decide what to do."

Over the next few days, the three of them settled into an
uneasy routine. While Jeff was at the base, Laura concentrated on Miranda, trying to keep the captain out of her
mind entirely. Sometimes, she would even go hours without
once thinking about him.

But eventually, thoughts of him drifted across her brain,
and she snatched at them like a child grabbing for the string
of an escaped balloon.

Laura groaned, closed her mind to thoughts of Jeff and

concentrated instead on bathing the baby. A task that seemed to be never ending.

Jeff took the stairs to the third floor of the old building and stopped as he entered the hall leading to his apartment. Mrs. Butler, just a step or two ahead of him, was staggering under the weight of an overstuffed grocery bag.

Instantly, he hurried to her side and lifted the bag from her painfully thin arms. "Didn't you tell me a couple of weeks ago you were going to start having the groceries delivered?"

She glared up at him out of the blue eyes that marked his every movement. "They charge extra for that, y'know," she told him, then scuttled to her apartment door, Jeff right behind her.

"Wouldn't it be worth it?" he asked. The older woman was as stubborn as she was nosy. Once, he'd even offered to get the old bat one of those rolling carts to carry her groceries in. She had informed him that only *old*, old people used those things and she wasn't that bad off yet.

When she had the last of her locks opened, she pushed the door open, then turned to him, reaching for the bag. "I'm keeping a close watch on you and that baby, mister," she said, her voice as creaky as an old iron gate.

"I never doubted it for a minute, Mrs. Butler."

"Humph!" She sniffed pointedly. "That woman you got staying with you seems nice enough."

A compliment? Stop the presses.

The woman's features softened considerably for a moment. "Saw the two of them today," she said. "Out for a walk, they were. That Miranda is a doll."

Jeff smiled to himself. Who would have guessed that his nemesis had a soft spot for babies?

She spotted that smile.

Her features stiffened. Snatching the bag of groceries, she stepped into her apartment and slammed the door shut.

Grinning now, Jeff listened for the four locks to be set in place before calling out, "You're welcome."

Leaning over the edge of the bathtub, Laura smiled down at the chubby little face turned up at her. Miranda's two small hands clutched a bright yellow rubber duck that squeaked if the little girl managed to squeeze it hard enough.

The baby, chattering happily in a language all her own, suddenly smashed the duck down into the water, splashing Laura's face and chest.

"Well, thank you," she said, swiping one hand across her eyes, then pushing wet hair off her forehead.

Miranda laughed, tipping her little head back and closing her eyes tightly with delight. Then, smacking her open palms against the surface of the water, she watched the duck rock in the resulting waves.

"Having fun?" A deep voice from right behind her startled Laura, and she gasped aloud.

"You scared me," she snapped, glaring at him over one shoulder.

"Sorry." He leaned against the doorjamb and looked down at the two of them. "Thought you heard me come in."

"Not likely," Laura told him, jerking her head toward the baby.

One corner of his mouth lifted. "She is a little loud, isn't she?" Then his gaze settled on the dampness on Laura's shirt and the slicked-back hair on top of her head. "Thought you were supposed to be bathing *her,* not the other way around."

God, he looked great, Laura thought before her good sense could prevent it. If the big-name clothing designers could just see him, they'd hustle out a spring line of camouflage wear. She inhaled slowly, deeply, and reminded herself that she no longer noticed how good-looking a man was. That was something she put behind her years ago.

Sure. So why was her pulse racing as though she'd just completed a marathon? Oh, she needed some distance between herself and the captain.

"As long as you're home early," she said, coming up on her knees, "you can finish bathing the baby while I fix something for dinner."

He straightened up and stiffened like he'd been shot. Against the dark greens and browns of his uniform, his face paled. His gaze shot from her to the baby and back again.

"No way," he declared, holding one hand up, palm out. "Uh-uh. The deal was *you* take care of the baby."

If she wasn't in such a hurry to get away from him, this whole thing might have been laughable. "I also said I wouldn't be the cook around here, either," she reminded him. "But *who* has been doing the lion's share of that lately?"

He frowned at her. "I didn't ask you to cook for me."

"That's not the point," she said, and spared a glance for Miranda. The little girl was still happily busy with her duck. "The point *is,* now that you're here, we can share some of the chores."

"Fine," he said, and half turned to leave. "I'll cook."

"Lord, no!" she snapped, remembering the salmon steak he had broiled two nights before. If the poor fish had been as tough when it was alive, it would have been able to pull the fisherman who caught it into the ocean and beat the heck out of him with its fins.

"Come on, *Marine.*" She said it slowly, sarcastically, making sure he heard her mentally throwing down the gauntlet. "You can handle a *baby* for a few minutes, can't you?"

Hell, Jeff thought. He could hardly handle being in the same room with Laura! Her cheeks were flushed with the warm, moist air in the bathroom, tendrils of brown hair curled softly around her face and her eyes looked dewy, despite the spark of challenge she was shooting at him.

His insides twisted with an unexpected pang. Obviously, he thought in disgust, his attraction for her hadn't weakened any, despite his hopes.

Jeez, only a week ago, he was a perfectly content man. His life and career were running smoothly. Now, everything around him was in turmoil.

All because of one small person.

Jeff let his gaze slide from Laura's flushed cheeks to the little girl sitting in the tub. Bubbles drifted past the sturdy, chubby body, and as they did, Miranda tried to catch them with quick, clumsy movements. Something inside him shifted as he watched the child.

He'd done his best to keep a safe distance between him and the tiny interloper. But no matter where he went in his apartment, evidence of her presence was already there. Her bottles, blankets and toys were strewn across the once painfully neat place.

He no longer walked barefoot through his house anymore, since the night his arch slammed down on the straight edge of a pacifier. He didn't sleep late on his days off, and even staying up late was out of the question because he couldn't play his stereo at the deafening levels he preferred.

One small scrap of humanity had completely altered his life.

Hell, Mrs. Butler had smiled at him!

At that moment, Miranda looked up at him and gave him a wide, sloppy grin. Twin dimples deepened her fat cheeks. Blue eyes sparkled with life and laughter. An infectious, rolling giggle shot from her throat, and he found himself reluctantly returning that silly smile.

Something warm and soft and completely alien to him settled in his chest. He didn't want to like it. He tried to ignore it. Tried to pretend he didn't feel a thing when he looked at that baby.

But the bottom line was, she was reaching him as no other female ever had.

And that scared the hell out of him.

"Well?" Laura asked, drawing him back from his terrifying thoughts. "Are you going to take over or not?"

He could do this, he told himself. He was a captain in the United States Marine Corps. He could damn well bathe a six-month-old infant. In his career, he had survived enemy gunfire, eager new recruits and overbearing officers.

One little girl was *not* going to defeat him.

"Okay," he said, stepping into the small room. "I'll do it."

"Kneel down here," Laura told him, scooting over a bit.

He didn't particularly want to be that close to Laura at the moment, either. If Miranda tugged at his heartstrings, Laura touched him on a much deeper, more basic level. Yet she managed to scare him every bit as badly as the baby did.

"Wouldn't this be easier if you moved out of the way first?" he asked shortly.

She shot him a look usually reserved for a dog who'd made a mess on the carpet. "*Never* leave a baby alone in a bathtub."

"She's not alone," he protested even as he surrendered and kneeled down beside Laura. "I'm right here."

"Anything can happen," she told him, her features serious, her gaze lancing into his. "In a matter of seconds, an untended baby can drown in just a couple of inches of water."

"For God's sake," he said harshly, "I'm not going to toss her into a lake and tell her to swim for it."

Laura laid one hand on his. A wild electrical current seemed to spring into life between them. He felt a sharp, jagged blast of heat rocket up his arm and burst in his chest like a mortar shell.

He knew being close to her was a bad idea.

She must have felt it, too, because she pulled back instantly. When she spoke again, her voice shook a bit.

He didn't blame her. He felt a little shaky himself.

"I mean it, Jeff. Don't take your eyes off of her for an instant."

This is what he got for hesitating when she asked him to take over. Now Laura probably figured that he was too incompetent to wash a child.

"I think I can handle the responsibility," he assured her, the words dripping with a sarcasm she apparently didn't notice.

"I'll check on you in a minute."

"That's not necessary," he said as she stood up and moved around him.

"It's no trouble," she told him. "I'll just go throw the steaks on the broiler. If you need help—"

"When people need help," he interrupted, reaching down into the tub for the rubber duck, "they usually *send* for the Marines."

Unimpressed, she retorted, "Yeah? Well, then who do you guys call for help?"

Slanting her a long look over his shoulder, he said proudly, "There's only one force stronger than us."

She paused in the doorway, obviously curious. "Who's that?"

"There's the U.S. Marines…and then there's God."

Five

Halfway through the bath, Jeff was silently calling on that higher power in desperation.

"C'mon, Miranda," he said, and winced at the pleading note in his voice. "If you don't sit still, we can't get the job done."

She laughed at him and slithered out of his grasp like a greased piglet.

Jeff reached for her and tried his Marine voice. Stiff, stern, demanding attention. "All right, recruit. Straighten up."

She flipped onto her tummy and started crawling across the floor of the tub. Exasperated, Jeff lunged for her. After he had her, though, he turned her around to face him, and she slapped both of his cheeks with bubble-covered hands. He blew the soapy water off his lips and managed to close his eyes in time to avoid the tidal wave of water she kicked at him.

Bubbles cascaded down his face as the wet soaked into the front of his cammies. His knees slid on the bathroom rug, and his chest slammed into the edge of the tub. His grip on the baby didn't loosen, though. Grumbling under his breath, he plopped her down again and grabbed a neatly folded washcloth.

"You and I have to come to an understanding, kiddo," he said as he ran the soaped cloth over first one arm, then the other.

She kicked her legs in the water, splashing him again.

He sighed, resigned now to the cold, clinging material of his uniform. Reaching for one foot, he rubbed the cloth over her pink skin. "You've pretty much been calling the shots around here, you know?"

She giggled deep in her throat.

He reached for the other foot. "But if you're going to be staying here—" he heard that statement come out of his mouth and quickly amended it "—for *a while,* you've got to understand that *you're* the private and *I'm* the captain."

She giggled again and tried to pull her foot free. He held on.

"We do things *my* way in this outfit," he went on, rubbing the cloth over her arch again just so he could hear that giggle.

She didn't disappoint him. Then she leaned over, her little fingers tugging and pulling at his hands.

"Ticklish, huh?" he asked with a smile.

The baby scooted around on her bottom, flashing him another grin.

He dropped the washcloth into the soapy water and lifted her, his hands beneath her fat little arms.

She clapped her hands and kicked her feet, but he had taken the precaution of lifting her high enough that she couldn't soak him again.

"We did it," he said. "Got through the bath with no

problems. See? All you have to do is remember who's in charge around here and we'll get along fine.''

As if in answer, he heard the distinct sound of water trickling into water.

Looking at Miranda through wary eyes, he saw her self-satisfied smile and knew instantly what she'd done.

''Oh, man…'' he said on a defeated sigh.

The town park was crowded on Saturdays.

Sunshine poured from a sky so blue it almost hurt to look at it. A few puffs of white clouds danced in the breeze that lifted kites high over the treetops.

Keeping a close eye on Miranda, Laura sat on the quilt Jeff had spread out on the grass beneath an ancient oak tree and watched the parade of people whirl by.

Bicyclists in helmets, pads and skintight suits raced along the path winding through the park, darting around slower-paced strollers pushed by proud fathers and tired-looking mothers. A few in-line skaters roared past her, their wheels grinding on the pavement with a soft whirr. Off to one side, two boys were playing catch with their father, and in the sand-filled playground to the left of her, smaller children were gathered. Toddlers laughed as they scrambled over concrete statues of dinosaurs and bounced on fiberglass ponies mounted on stiff springs.

Laura sighed and smiled. It had been a lovely afternoon, she thought lazily. She'd been surprised but touched when Jeff had suggested a picnic. Maybe he was getting used to the idea of having a baby in his life. She glanced at the little girl scooting across the blanket with determined, crab-like movements.

Laura leaned forward, scooped her up and sat her down again, this time safely trapping the baby between her legs.

Over the past few days, Jeff hadn't again mentioned finding a replacement guardian for Miranda, and Laura was sure that was a good sign. Given enough time, the sweet baby would be able to worm her way into even an ogre's heart.

And Jeff Ryan was no ogre.

Despite what he seemed to think.

Miranda watched the children playing. Her little hands clapping, she made another stab at an escape, but was easily bought off with a teething biscuit.

Tired, Laura looked off toward the parking lot, where she could just see Jeff closing up the car again and starting back toward them, Miranda's sweater in his hand.

Honestly, she thought. The man looked good enough to be illegal. Even from a distance, she could see how well his faded, threadbare Levi's fit his long legs. And the red polo shirt he wore made his blond hair seem lighter, while at the same time giving his tan a deeper, warmer tone.

And here she sat, huddled under a tree, because the slightest amount of sunshine made her look like a boiled lobster.

Her heartbeat stuttered into high gear. Silently groaning, Laura tried to ignore what had become an all too familiar sensation lately. Two weeks, she thought. Two weeks with Jeff and Miranda and she was a goner. Oh, she'd been prepared to fall in love with the baby. She never had been able to resist one. But Jeff was another matter entirely.

She'd sworn off love a long time ago. And in all the years since, she had never once been tempted to fall off the wagon.

Until now.

As he came closer, Laura studied him, trying to ignore her quickened heartbeat and the rush of adrenaline. What was it about him that created such a wild tangle of emotions?

He smiled, and lifted one hand in greeting just as a boy on a skateboard sped past him. Laura laughed shortly as

Jeff did a fancy two-step to avoid falling. The expression on his face was priceless.

Shaking his head, he stepped off the path onto the grass and headed straight for her.

It was as if a steel band had tightened around her chest. Lord help her. If she hadn't already given up on love, Jeff Ryan would definitely be a man to watch out for.

Jeff studied her as he approached. In a park full of women wearing shorts and clingy T-shirts, why was he so completely taken with a woman dressed in baggy jeans and a T-shirt that would have been big on him? Her hair was pulled back into a ponytail at the base of her neck, and a few wisps of shorter hair flew about her cheeks.

Their gazes locked, and as she tucked a strand of hair behind her ear, he noticed that she suddenly looked kind of sick. He sat down beside her in the shade, tossed Miranda's sweater to one side and asked, "You all right?"

"Yeah," she replied a little too quickly. "Why wouldn't I be?"

"You just looked a little…"

"What?" she asked.

"Nothing," he said, backing down. He wasn't in the mood for a fight now, and it sounded like she was. Whenever Laura's voice got that tight, controlled sound to it, he knew there was an argument headed his way. And it was just too nice a day for it. Who would have thought that he could enjoy a simple picnic so much? "Boy," he commented absently, "this place gets nuts on the weekend."

"It's the first nice day all week," she said.

He shot her a quick look, then turned away again, frowning. Were they really going to talk about the weather? There was so much he wanted to know about her. Like why a kindergarten teacher? Why wasn't she married? And if she loved kids so much, why didn't she have one or two of her own?

But mostly, did she want him as much as he wanted her?

He didn't ask any of his questions, though. For some reason, he couldn't think of a way to start. Hell, he'd never had a hard time holding a conversation with a woman before. What was it about her that unsettled him so?

Miranda pulled herself across Laura's legs and crawled to him. Grateful for the distraction, Jeff lowered his gaze to the determined baby. Holding on to his shirtsleeve, she slowly drew herself up to wobble unsteadily on her bare feet. Her tiny toes curled into the blanket as if she were trying to get a grip on the world.

"Hey," he said, afraid to move lest he spoil her balance. "Look at you!" An unreasonable swell of pride filled his chest. She looked so pleased with herself, he suddenly wished he had a camera. Good Lord, what was happening to him? Then Miranda gurgled at him, and something around his heart tightened a notch.

"What a big girl you are!" he said.

Miranda laughed up at him and swayed as she patted his chest with one hand.

Chuckling, Jeff scooped her up in one arm and held her in front of him. The now familiar weight of her in his arms was comforting. She smelled of baby powder and giggles. It was a scent he would always remember.

With his thumb, he wiped away a streak of drool from her chin, realizing ruefully that only two weeks ago, he would have grabbed a paper towel to handle the small task. "You're something, kiddo," he said with a smile. "Don't you know you're too young to walk?" He glanced at Laura, suddenly unsure. Heck, he didn't have a clue what babies should be doing at any given age. "She *is,* isn't she?"

"Yes," she confirmed, with a slight shake of her head. "But not too young to be trying."

"Ooo-rah, Miranda," he said, looking back into blue

eyes surprisingly like his own. "Always reach high, kiddo."

"Look out!" someone called a moment before a bright-blue-and-yellow ball bounced into the middle of the quilt.

Laura grabbed it just as a harried-looking mother ran up to them, apologies spilling from her lips. She looked like a magazine ad for the typical southern California mom. Short blond hair, healthy tan and a well-toned body displayed by white shorts and a pale yellow tank top.

"Sorry about that," she said, and took the ball Laura offered her. "My five-year-old's got quite a kick. His father is already planning his career in the NFL." She took a deep breath, tucked the ball beneath her right arm and bent down to take a good look at Miranda. Reaching out one hand, she chucked the baby's chin and sighed, "What a cute little girl."

"Yeah, she is," Jeff said shortly, not sure how to react to the woman. He shot Laura a quick glance and noted her proud smile as the stranger admired Miranda.

"She has your eyes," the woman commented, looking at him.

He frowned slightly, the sense of pride he'd experienced only moments before suddenly at war with a different emotion blossoming in his chest. An emotion that caused him to blurt out, "She's not mine."

The woman blinked.

Miranda bounced in his arms.

A brief, strained silence reigned before the woman then looked to Laura. "Sorry, my mistake. Your daughter's a beauty, though. Always wanted a girl myself." She shrugged and kept talking, as if to smooth over the tension in the air. "Instead, I got four boys." Turning a wistful look on Miranda, she muttered, "If somebody could guarantee me one like that, I'd be willing to go again."

"Hey, Mom!" a boy's voice hollered.

"Coming," the woman called back, and stood up. "Better get going," she said. "Sorry again." Then she turned and ran back toward her family.

Jeff watched her go with pleasure. If she hadn't interrupted a perfectly nice afternoon, he wouldn't now be feeling so…what? Guilty?

"Why'd you tell her Miranda wasn't yours?" Laura asked when they were alone again.

"Because she's not." Even to him, his voice sounded strangled, harsh.

"Maybe not biologically," she corrected. "But legally…"

Jeff's features tightened, and Laura couldn't help wondering what he was thinking. How could he hold that baby, play with her and take such obvious pride in the little things she did and still not want to claim her?

"You know," he said through clenched teeth, "it's real easy for you to say, 'She's yours—keep her.' But I don't see *you* with any kids. Why is that if you're so nuts about children?"

Laura paled. She felt the blood drain from her cheeks and was helpless to stop it. "I'm not married," she hedged.

"Neither am I, in case you haven't noticed."

"This isn't about me," Laura countered, knowing it was a weak argument.

"Why not?" Jeff turned the baby around, plopped her down onto his lap and looked at Laura steadily. "Why don't we make this about you for a change?"

"I'd rather not talk about it."

"You don't have any trouble telling me what I should do with *my* life."

"Jeff…" Horrified, Laura felt the sting of tears fill her eyes. She dipped her head and hurriedly blinked them back.

"Come on, Laura," he prodded, "tell me. Why is someone who is so crazy about kids still single?"

When she thought she could trust herself not to cry, she lifted her head and looked at him. Apparently, her eyes were still awash with tears, though. The expression on his face was too stricken to mean anything else. Before he could speak, she sucked in a deep breath and said simply, "I was engaged once. He died."

"Oh, man…" Jeff sighed heavily, reached across the blanket and took one of her hands in his. Giving her a gentle squeeze, he said softly, "I'm sorry. I shouldn't have said anything."

"No," she told him. "You were right. It *is* easy for me to tell you to raise a child you hadn't counted on having." Her gaze dropped to Miranda, now happily gumming Jeff's thumb. "But I just don't understand how you could *not* want her."

"Wanting something…or *someone,* is one thing. Figuring out if it's the best thing for everyone is something else."

Seconds rolled into minutes, and the silence between them stretched on and on. Finally, Jeff asked quietly, "Do you still love him?"

She inhaled sharply. A few weeks ago, her answer would have been a quick, decisive yes. Now, if she was to be honest with herself, it was a different story. Lord, what was happening to her? "He'll always have a place in my heart," she said at last.

Jeff nodded slowly. "That doesn't answer the question."

She met his gaze. "It's the only answer I have."

The muscle in his jaw ticked spasmodically as he gave her a short, sharp nod.

"Here," he said abruptly, handing the baby over. "You take her while I go pack up the car."

"We're leaving?" she asked, cuddling the squirming baby close. "Already?"

"Yeah," he told her, gathering up the picnic basket and

a couple of stray napkins. "I've got some things I should be doing back at the base."

"What things?" She had the distinct impression he was trying to run away. From her? To where? "I thought you had the day off."

"Just things, all right?" he snapped, and stood up quickly. He looked at her for a long minute, then said, "Get the baby ready—I'll be back."

He marched down the path, like a soldier going off to war. Eyes straight ahead, he looked neither right nor left, ignoring everyone and everything around him.

What had just happened here? she wondered. Did it bother him that much to know she would always care for Bill?

"And why is he fighting you so hard?" Laura asked the baby. "Why can't he just admit that he loves you? Is it really so hard for him?"

The baby blew a spit-bubble raspberry.

One eyebrow arched high on Laura's forehead. "My sentiments exactly."

That night, Jeff turned the stereo on, needing the soothing sounds of his favorite music. In deference to the baby, he kept the volume at a level just below earsplitting.

He had hardly plopped down onto the couch before Laura came out of her bedroom. That stupid nightshirt of hers looked ridiculously sexy, which told Jeff that he'd been without a woman way too long. After glaring at him for a minute, she strode to the stereo and pushed the Power button.

Silence dropped over the room like a heavy blanket.

"What are you doing?" she demanded, pushing her hair back behind her ears.

"Listening to music," he said, getting up from the couch. "Like I used to, every damn night."

He walked to the stereo and hit the Power switch with a stab of his index finger. Instantly, guitars roared into life.

Laura punched the same button a breath later. She stood, arms crossed, chin lifted, foot tapping solidly against the floor.

In the charged silence, Jeff stared down at her, anger and frustration pulsing through him. He'd spent the entire night in his office on base, trying to keep busy enough that he didn't think about this frumpy, short woman who had invaded his life so thoroughly.

It hadn't worked.

Even now, when he wanted to scream and shout and rage at her, one question kept sliding through his mind. What color underwear was she wearing tonight?

Groaning, he reached up and shoved both hands along the sides of his head, as if he could quiet the fantasies that had nagged him all night.

Damn it, if she and the baby weren't there, everything would be fine. He wouldn't be dreaming about ugly nightgowns and gorgeous lingerie. He wouldn't be taking cold showers every morning and tiptoeing through the house at night.

Mrs. Butler wouldn't be smiling at him every time he passed her in the hall.

He could have his life back. The simple, uncomplicated life that he had never truly appreciated as much as he did now that he'd lost it.

But that wasn't going to happen, and he knew it. Even if Laura and Miranda were to disappear tonight, nothing would be the same as it had been before they'd come. Because no matter what, there were memories of the two of them. Vivid mental images that would always be with him.

He would never have true solitude again.

Gritting his teeth at the thought, he turned the music back

on and grabbed Laura's hand before she could hit the button.

"Leave it on," he growled, his fingers tight around her small wrist.

"It'll wake the baby."

"She'll go back to sleep."

"When I first came here, I told you my rules," she said, jerking her hand from his grasp, then rubbing at the skin on her wrist.

"Your rules," he repeated with a short bark of laughter.

"That's right," she said. "And you agreed to them."

"I was desperate," he argued, unwillingly remembering that first, hideous day when he'd begged his sister for help, not knowing that he was asking for even more trouble than he already had.

"You still agreed."

"I would have agreed to a human sacrifice that day, and you damn well know it." He looked away from her, his throat aching with the effort of forcing angry words past a tight knot of anxiety.

"Why are you so upset?"

His gaze swung back to her instantly.

She reached for the stereo again, but instead of turning it off, she only lowered the volume.

The familiar beat of an old rock song thrummed in the darkness like a heartbeat. Seconds ticked by. At last, Jeff crossed the room to the wide window and opened the blinds.

"What is it?" she asked, pitching her voice just loud enough to be heard over a rattle of drums.

He felt more than heard her walk up behind him. It was as if he could sense her position in the room. Tiny electrical currents seemed to stretch from her to him, digging at him, prodding at him.

"Jeff?" she asked, closer now.

He inhaled sharply and shook his head, staring out at the neon patchwork quilt beyond the glass. "This isn't going to work," he finally said.

She stopped beside him. Heat from her body reached out to him, sinking into his bones. His soul. He sensed her gaze on his face and deliberately kept from looking at her.

"What's not going to work?" she asked, obviously not going to be put off.

A snort of laughter shot from his chest, and a hard knot of pain settled in its place.

"None of it's working, Laura. Not the baby..." He paused and glanced briefly at her. "Not you."

"You don't know it won't work. It's only been a couple of weeks."

God, just barely two weeks, and the world as he had known it was completely gone.

"Exactly," he said. He heard the snarl in his voice but was helpless to stop it.

"That's no time at all," she argued, tugging at his upper arm, trying to turn him toward her. "You haven't tried—"

With a low growl of frustration, Jeff turned on her. Grabbing her shoulders, he gave her a shake. There was no way out. He had to admit to the one shameful truth that he had realized only that night.

"Don't you get it?" he demanded, his voice slicing the music-filled air. "Maybe I don't *want* to try."

She yanked herself free. Anger flashed in her eyes, and he was almost relieved. It was easier to deal with anger than disgust.

"So *this* is how you meet responsibility? You run from it? Find someone—*anyone* else to raise Miranda?"

"I'm not talking about letting her be raised by wolves, for Christ's sake."

"Why *not* wolves? As long as it's not you, what do you care who does it?"

"I want what's best for her," he said. "She deserves a family. People who know how to take care of kids. What to do for them." He shook his head. "You know as well as I do that's not me."

She planted her palms on his chest and shoved him with all of her strength.

He didn't budge.

Reaching up, Jeff rubbed the back of his neck viciously. "I'm thirty-five years old, Laura. I'm too old to learn this stuff." He inhaled sharply and blew it out on a heavy sigh. "I'm too old to become an overnight father."

Once the words were out, he felt as though he'd finally managed to shove a gigantic boulder off his chest. Maybe she would understand now, he told himself.

He should've known better.

"That's just an excuse," she snapped. "You're looking for an easy way out."

"Shouldn't I be?" he asked, leveling a long look on her. A wave of guilt and shame swamped him as he reached back to the moment earlier that afternoon that had slapped him with a harsh, undeniable reality.

One that even now he was having a hard time facing.

"Sergeant Powell trusted you," she said hotly. "He left you his *child*. That has to mean something to you."

"Why?" he growled. "Because it would to you?"

Laura's head snapped back as if he had slapped her.

Damn it. None of this was her fault. She didn't deserve to be yelled at just because she was handy. He tilted his head back on his neck and stared briefly at the shadowy ceiling. He concentrated on pulling what was left of his self-control together. But it wasn't easy.

Man, this was one of those times when he really wished he were a drinking man. But that was stupid. Even if he did go off and get roaring drunk, the situation he faced wouldn't have changed by the time he sobered up.

Jeff felt her staring at him and sensed the hurt in her. He was really batting a thousand. He couldn't seem to make the call to child welfare that would get him out of this mess. And hurting the woman who was there to help him.

Shifting to look at Laura again, he tried to explain what he meant.

"Look," he said tightly, "I never *wanted* kids. It's not that I don't like 'em," he added. "I like my sister's kids fine."

"It's a wonder you don't go and visit more than once a year, then," she countered stiffly.

Thanks, Peggy, he thought. He sucked in a gulp of air, trying to ease the knot of helpless anger practically choking him. "Damn it, Laura, I decided a long time ago that I wasn't going to *have* a family. I wanted a career and I figured rather than do two things halfway, I'd do one thing well."

Her brown eyes shone with a film of tears that he hoped to God she wouldn't let spill over.

In a quieter tone, he added, "Not everybody in the world *wants* kids, you know."

Her head bobbed in an abbreviated nod.

"I have my own plans. Plans that don't include kids." He looked away from her, out at the night. His hands curling around the windowsill, he continued, "I didn't know Hank had named me as guardian to Miranda." Quietly, he added, "If I had, I would have told him not to."

"Everybody makes plans, Jeff," she said, her voice as soft as his had been.

"You, too?" He asked, then remembered the late fiancé.

"Of course, me too."

"You *planned* to be a temporary nanny?" He didn't want to talk about the man she had once loved—maybe still *did* love.

She chuckled and he felt a bit better.

"No," she answered.

"What happened?" he asked, half turning to look at her. Damn. He didn't want to know and yet he did. *Nothing* made sense anymore.

"The same thing that happened to you." She shrugged eloquently. "Life. And when life shakes up your plans, you have to adapt. To accept."

He stared at her thoughtfully. She may have accepted, but she hadn't adapted.

"It's not easy," she said, her voice dropping a bit. "But you do it anyway."

"I don't know," he answered, his grip on the windowsill relaxing a bit. "All I *do* know is, in the park, when that woman said Miranda looked like me—" he shook his head and forced himself to say it all "—my first instinct was to deny all claim to her. I knew that if I claimed her in that moment, then it was decided forever. There'd be no going back. I wasn't ready to make that decision." He pulled in another deep breath and exhaled on a rush. "What kind of father is that?"

The remainder of Laura's anger drained away instantly. She heard pain and confusion in his tone. She knew he was ashamed of his reaction to that woman's innocent statement and that he was trying to deal with it.

"It was completely natural," she said softly.

He laughed shortly and shot her a sidelong look. "Natural to say, 'No, no, that's not *my* baby.'"

"You're not used to her yet."

When he spoke, his words came so softly, Laura had to lean in close to hear him.

"What if I *never* get used to her?"

Six

Laura took a long, deep breath and laid her hand on his forearm. An instantaneous burst of heat rocketed up her own arm, settling in her chest. She tried to dismiss the sensation and concentrate.

The muscles beneath her hand flinched at her touch.

"Is it fair to Miranda," he asked through gritted teeth, "to be raised by a man who might *never* be the kind of father she deserves?"

Laura felt a rush of warmth that had nothing to do with the chemistry between them well up inside her. She had thought he didn't care. That he didn't want to be bothered by the responsibility of Miranda.

She'd been wrong.

"I'm sorry," she said suddenly, and he swiveled her a look.

"About what?"

This wasn't easy, she thought, but it had to be said.

"I thought you didn't care about the baby, but I should

have known better.'' She shook her head slightly. "I've watched you with her. You *do* feel something for her.''

"She's not easy to ignore,'' he said, a rueful smile on his face.

"True.'' Laura steeled herself. "But mostly, I'm sorry for what I was thinking about you.''

Two blond eyebrows lifted. "An intriguing statement.''

Now it was her turn to give him a reluctant smile. "You were right. I did expect you to want the baby because *I* would have in your shoes.'' Shaking her head slightly, she said, "It's just that I always wanted kids of my own. I guess I was judging you by my feelings. Arrogant, I know.'' Throwing both hands up in a helpless shrug, she continued. "You have every right to *not* want kids. Not everyone does. Besides, I know what a huge responsibility she would be for a man like you.''

"Like me?''

"Single, career oriented.''

"Ah…''

She wasn't quite sure how to interpret that last comment, so she left it alone. "All I'm saying is that I'm sorry. I, better than anyone, should have remembered what it's like to have your life's plan splintered in one quick blow.''

She hadn't meant to give him that much information. It would have been too much to hope for that he would ignore it.

"What happened to your neatly arranged world, Laura?'' he asked, his voice dropping to mingle with the deep, fluid notes of the music swelling around them. "What little bombshell did Fate drop on you?''

"It doesn't matter,'' she said. Laura didn't want to explain about Bill. For some reason, she felt as though this moment, this night, belonged only to her and Jeff. Not even memories were welcome. "This is about you, not me.''

His features tight, worry lines deepened at the corners of his eyes and between his eyebrows. His mouth a grim slash, she knew he wanted to ask her more questions. But Laura was through talking about herself. Determinedly, she went back to their original subject, hoping he would leave her past where it belonged.

"You would be a good father," she said firmly.

He frowned, clearly not happy with the shift in the conversation. But he went along with it. "Yeah? What makes you so sure?"

"Because you're already worried about doing the job right. A bad father wouldn't care either way."

He seemed to think about that for a long minute. Then slowly, the muscle in his arm relaxed. Reluctantly, she let her hand drop to her side.

"Maybe," he finally said, his gaze caressing her face. "I don't know."

"You'll see." She wanted him to believe her.

He lifted one hand and smoothed her hair back from her face. The pad of his thumb stroked her cheekbone, sending a trembling response through her body.

"Don't misunderstand me," he told her, his voice as soft as his touch. "I'm not saying anything's changed. I'm still not convinced that Miranda being with me is the right thing for her. Or me."

Laura stared at him, confused. Hadn't they just been discussing that very thing? "But I thought—"

"I know," he said, and let his fingertips trail along the length of her throat. "And I appreciate what you said. But this is a big decision, Laura. One I'm not going to make overnight."

It wasn't fair of him to touch her while talking to her about something this serious. She couldn't concentrate. All she could do was feel. It had been so long, she thought, her eyes sliding shut. So long since anyone had touched her like this. So long since she had *wanted* a man's touch.

But it wasn't just any man she wanted, she admitted silently.

It was *this* man.

She moaned softly at the realization.

For eight long years, she had kept her heart, her emotions carefully locked away. After Bill's death, she had buried her wants and desires. She'd thrown herself into her work, satisfied with teaching and loving other people's children.

Now, suddenly, it wasn't enough.

Maybe it never had been.

Jeff stepped in closer to her, as if sensing her surrender.

His hands moved to her shoulders, and she felt the warmth of his touch right down to her soul. The dark corners of her heart were filled with a searing light that banished shadows and illuminated desires.

Moonlight poured through the window, bathing them both in a pale ivory glow. A new song drifted from the stereo. The rock guitars had given way to a slow jazz piano and a soulful saxophone. The plaintive notes of the horn sounded like stereo sex.

Hot, slow and mesmerizing.

She swallowed heavily.

His right hand dropped to her waist. "Dance with me," he whispered.

Laura knew she should say no. As vulnerable as she felt at the moment, the safest place for her to be was somewhere far away from him. But she couldn't refuse. Already, her body was surrendering to the seductive music.

Sliding her left hand up onto his shoulder, she stepped into his embrace. Her right hand caught by his left, she felt the surprisingly erotic sensation of their palms brushing together.

He began moving in a slow, tight circle. He swayed slightly with the rhythm of the music, and she moved with him. His arm around her waist tightened, pulling her closer to him. Her breasts flattened against his chest, she felt his heartbeat thundering in time with her own.

Her knees weak, Laura's breath caught when his denim-clad thighs rubbed her bare legs. His right hand slipped to cup her bottom, pressing her tight enough to him that she was aware of his own need and knew it was as powerful as the sexual flames licking at her center.

The sensuous music rose up and around them, drawing the two of them together, into a net built of the breathless desire shimmering between them. Shadows and moonlight shifted around her as she stared up into his eyes. Her breathing shallow, her heartbeat quickened even further until her pulse became nothing more than a thundering roar in her ears.

She knew the moment he decided to kiss her. She read it on his face and realized that this was her last chance to escape. In the same instant, she admitted silently that she didn't want to run. For the first time in eight long years, she wanted to feel.

If only for one night.

Then he bent his head to hers, and all thought stopped. His mouth dusted across her lips gently, tentatively. Drawing his head back, he looked down at her, his features tight with an emotion she didn't want to explore too closely.

One dance ended and another began.

He stopped, and moved his hands to cup her face. Then he kissed her again, and from behind closed eyes, Laura saw the bright flash of exploding stars.

He parted her lips with his tongue, his breath invading her mouth even as his kiss conquered her soul. Laura groaned quietly and leaned into him. A film of tears burned her eyes as a sweet ache began to grow within her.

He grabbed her and pulled her hard against him. Laura's arms wound around his neck, and she pressed herself as tightly to him as she could. Her hardened nipples throbbed for his touch. Her knees weak, she sagged into him as his tongue continued to plunder the defenses she had maintained for too long.

Jeff broke the kiss and bent his head lower, dragging his

mouth along the line of her throat, tasting her pulse beat beneath his teeth. When she sighed and tipped her head to one side, allowing him access, he muffled a groan against her neck. His body aching, he inhaled her scent and knew he would carry it with him always.

The magic in her kiss was like nothing he had ever known.

Her skin was as soft as he had imagined it would be. Her fingers tugged and pulled at his shoulders, holding him tightly, silently urging him on.

Lifting the hem of her nightshirt, his right hand dropped to explore the curve of the bottom he had dreamed about so often. When his palm encountered only smooth, warm flesh, his breath was trapped in his lungs.

Straightening slightly, he looked down at her, an amazed half smile on his lips. "Here I've been trying to imagine what kind of lacy delight you were wearing under this hideous shirt—" he shook his head, stunned "—and you're not wearing any underwear at all."

She looked insulted. "Of course I'm wearing underwear."

"But..." He ran one hand over the bare flesh of her behind. It was only then that he noticed the tiny thread of fabric lining the cleft of her bottom. His fingertips smoothed across it, following it down. Shaken, he whispered, "A thong?"

She shivered as his fingers explored her, but finally, she nodded.

"Good God," he murmured huskily, his mind providing the image it was too dark to see. His groin hardened until he thought he might explode. "What color?"

She rose up on tiptoe to whisper in his ear. "Red."

"You're killing me, Laura." He groaned then and reclaimed her mouth, his tongue dipping in and out of her warmth in a hunger that built with each passing moment.

Scooping her up into his arms, he carried her to the sofa

and sat down with her on his lap. Kissing, tasting, nibbling at her bottom lip with his teeth, Jeff reveled in her, exploring her body as thoroughly as he had dreamed of doing for days.

Sliding his hand up under the hem of her nightshirt, his fingertips encountered the scrap of red lace that was his undoing. He didn't need to see her. All he needed at the moment was to touch her.

She arched into his arms, her legs parting slightly for him. Devouring her mouth with his, he slid his right hand beneath that bit of lace and down to the damp heat that was at her core. Laura trembled in his arms as his hand cupped her.

Stirred by her response, Jeff drew his head back to look at her. He stared down into her face while slipping his fingertips farther, deeper into the secrets she guarded with lace barriers.

"Jeff," she whispered brokenly, and licked her lips with the tip of her tongue.

Something inside him shifted, but he swallowed back the groan of hunger roaring through him.

She lifted her hips when he dipped first one finger and then two deep within her. His breathing short and shallow, he indulged himself in her. In counterpoint to the raging desire coursing through his bloodstream, he explored her slowly, lazily. Her heat burned him; her passion fed his own. He bit back another groan as he watched pleasure steal across her features.

Again and again, his fingers moved within her, forcing her higher, faster as she strained to reach the completion awaiting her. Dipping his head, he kissed her, needing to taste her mouth and feel the intimate connection of their tongues mating.

Her response was instantaneous. Her tongue twisted and brushed around his in a silent erotic dance. She gave and took, submitted and conquered.

Gently but firmly, his thumb stroked across the small, sensitive nub of flesh. Her body jerked in his arms. She broke the kiss, moaning his name in a tearing whisper.

Her fingers clutched at his shoulders. Her body writhed in his arms, and when the first violent tremors shook her, Jeff felt the force of them himself. Tears leaked from the corners of her eyes as her hips rocked frantically against his hand. He claimed her mouth again in desperation, swallowing the last of her cries and using them to muffle his own.

Laura lay across his lap, feeling practically boneless. Relief shimmered through her even as inside her body, tiny, rippling convulsions still trembled on. She'd never experienced anything like that before. Had her climax been so overwhelming simply because it had been so long since her last one?

No, she decided, not without a pang of guilt. It was more than that. As much as she had loved Bill, he had never taken her so high…made her feel so much.

Instantly, that small sliver of guilt blossomed and grew. What was she thinking? How could she possibly compare what she had had with her fiancé to what she had just experienced? She had *loved* Bill. Hadn't she?

Of course she had. If he hadn't died, they would have been married eight years now. She would no doubt be the mother she had always longed to be. And she would be having regular, loving sex with her husband.

No doubt, with practice, she assured herself, their lovemaking would have become every bit as stimulating as— she bit down hard on her bottom lip—as stimulating as this first time with Jeff had been.

Oh, goodness, she thought, a sinking sensation developing in the pit of her stomach. If his hands alone could drive her above and beyond anything she had ever reached before, what might his actual lovemaking do to her?

Slowly, she tried to straighten up on Jeff's lap. Tugging

at the hem of her nightshirt, she scooted her hips back and instantly gasped as a new rush of sensation poured through her. His hand was still cupping her, his fingers still deeply rooted within her passage.

"Laura," he whispered, his breath brushing against her cheek. "That was—"

"Please don't say anything," she interrupted him.

"I have to," he continued, and dropped a quick, firm kiss on the corner of her mouth.

Deep inside her, Laura felt the strength of his fingers, pressing against the walls of her body. Unbelievably, her muscles contracted around his hand, drawing him in, welcoming his touch. It was as if she had no defenses against him.

"Jeff," she managed to say, and grabbed his hand, hoping to stop him. "This was a mistake," she said, and knew it for the understatement of the century.

He lifted his head and smiled gently at her. "The only mistake we made was waiting so long to try it."

"No," she said even as his thumb brushed across that one incredibly sensitive spot again. "Oh!" Her breath caught as her body exploded into need again. No, it couldn't be. Not so soon. Not after what she had already experienced.

"Laura," he said, claiming short, damp kisses to punctuate each word, "this is special. This is right."

"No." She had to argue. This couldn't be right. If it was right, then what had she felt for Bill all those years ago?

"Yes," he insisted, moving within her, touching, stroking.

Her hips ground against his hand. Beneath her bottom, she felt the solid, thick ridge of his need pressing into her. He had given her release. He had taken her to heights she hadn't known existed, all the while ignoring his own clamoring desire.

The night pressed down on them. Music, low and full,

surrounded them. Laura, knowing that she would regret this later, reached for the button at his waistband.

He sat perfectly still, his gaze locked with hers. "You don't have to, Laura."

But she did. Tomorrow would be soon enough to deal with *should have*s and *would have*s. Tonight, she wanted to feel everything she had denied herself for eight long, lonely years.

Leaning into him, she covered his mouth with her own, teasing him with long strokes of her tongue even as her fingers quickly undid the button fly of his jeans.

He sighed into her mouth as she took him in her hand. Her fingers caressed the hard length of him and gently rubbed the tip of his erection. His body tensed beneath her. His fingers dipped in and out of the liquid heat at her center.

When he finally groaned, pulled his hand free of her and in one quick move, yanked her red thong off and threw it onto the floor, she was beyond ready. His hands at her waist, he turned her on his lap until she was straddling him, their faces only a breath apart.

Kneeling on the sofa, her hands on his shoulders, Laura slowly lowered her body onto his. Inch by slow inch, she took him inside. His hands at her waist tightened, his fingers digging into her flesh. She sighed and moved on him again, rocking her hips slightly until she had welcomed him fully into her depths.

Laura's head tipped back. Her eyes closed, she concentrated on the incredible feel of him locked deeply within her. She twisted her hips in a slow, torturous pattern, moaning softly at the overwhelming sensations sputtering through her.

Jeff whispered her name and slid his hands up under her nightshirt, then pulled it off over her head. He tossed it to one side and captured her breasts with his palms. His thumbs rubbed at her hardened nipples until her breathing staggered.

As he tugged and pulled gently at the rigid peaks, Laura moved on him. Her hips lifted and lowered as expectation built low in her belly. She knew it was coming. Knew how overpowering it would be. And she raced toward it, eager to feel it again. To ride the crashing waves of satisfaction as they thundered through her.

Jeff watched her. Moonlight dusted across her flesh, dazzling her in a pale glow that made her seem like part of a dream. But if this was a dream, he never wanted to wake up.

Reluctantly, he dropped his hands from her magnificent, full breasts. Grabbing her hips, he guided her into a quicker rhythm. Each time she took him inside, it felt like the first time. Each time she lifted herself from him, he died a little.

She raised her head and looked at him. He saw the swirl of passion dancing in her eyes. Her features tightened. Her back arched. Her lips parted, and she cried his name aloud as a shuddering climax claimed her.

Her interior muscles contracted around his body. He groaned and held her down on him tightly as he exploded into her warmth.

When it was over, Laura sagged against his chest. She felt his arms go around her and was numbly grateful for the support.

Every muscle in her body was almost liquid. Yet at the same time, she felt more *alive* than ever before. Her head on his shoulder, Laura listened to the ragged gasps of his breathing and knew that she wasn't the only one so completely affected by their lovemaking.

Lovemaking.

No, she couldn't think of it like that. This was sex. Pure, simple, glorious sex. Lovemaking had been what she had done with Bill, the man who would have been her husband.

The passion she shared with the man beneath her had nothing to do with love. It was something much more basic, more elemental than that. Lust, she supposed, was an old-fashioned word. But it certainly seemed to fit the situation.

Suddenly uncomfortable, Laura eased herself off of Jeff and groped in the darkness for her discarded nightshirt. When she found it, she immediately pulled it on.

"Laura," Jeff said softly. "I think we should talk about this."

She was profoundly thankful for the shadows filling the room. At the moment, she didn't want to be able to see his face too clearly. Shoving her hair back from her face, Laura glanced at him, then averted her gaze again, instead looking in the grayness for the thong panties she'd been wearing.

"I don't think that's necessary," she said. Spotting the tiny triangle of lace and elastic draped over the arm of a chair, Laura got up from the sofa to retrieve it.

Her knees were weak, and her body ached in places that hadn't been used in years. She stumbled a bit, caught herself and went on. Snatching up the red lace, she crumpled the pair of panties in one fist.

Her underwear, tossed across the room by a man caught up in the throes of passion. Good Lord, what had they been thinking? What had *she* been thinking?

He stood up and came around the coffee table to stand in front of her. He had already adjusted his clothing. To look at him, no one would guess what had just happened between them.

She envied him that control.

"I didn't mean for this to happen," he said, reaching for her.

Laura took a quick sidestep away from him. "Neither of us did, Jeff," she told him, and hoped her voice sounded steadier to him than it did to her. "But we're both adults. I'm sure we can put this behind us."

"Behind us?" he asked.

The lacy garment in her hand scratched against her palm. Laura knew she would never again be able to wear the panties without remembering this night and the stolen passion that had ignited something inside her. Something she hadn't even known existed.

Swallowing heavily, she said, "Jeff, I know you're trying to be…nice about all of this, but I really would rather not talk about it now." Or ever, she added silently.

He lifted one hand toward her, but let it fall to his side before touching her.

"Laura…" he started to say.

Thankfully, Miranda chose just that moment to cry. More of a whimper than a wail, at the moment it sounded like the sweetest music in the world to Laura. The baby crying provided just the excuse she needed to make a graceful escape.

She made it as far as the bedroom door before his voice stopped her. Closing her eyes and holding her breath, she prayed that he would let her go.

"Not tonight," he said, a promise ringing in his tone. "But we will talk about what happened, Laura. I'm too old to play games about something like this." He paused a moment. "And so are you."

She didn't answer. She couldn't have spoken if her life had depended on it. Turning the knob, she opened the door, slipped into the dark room and closed the door firmly behind her.

Briefly, she leaned back against that door, thinking about the man on the other side. How had this all become so confusing? she asked herself.

And how would she ever survive the entire summer here?

Seven

Jeff stretched out on his bed and turned his head on the pillow to stare at the doorway of his room. He heard her moving around in her room and the soft sound of her voice as she soothed Miranda back into sleep.

He groaned and punched a closed fist against the mattress. What kind of a twisted man was he that listening to a woman crooning to an infant could make him hard and eager for her?

It took every ounce of willpower he possessed to lie where he was and not go to Laura. He wanted an explanation. He wanted to know why there had been such incredible heat between them. And he wanted to feel it all again.

Basically, he thought grimly, he wanted her.

Again and again.

Inhaling sharply, he jammed his pillows behind his head, laid one arm across his chest and shifted his gaze to the ceiling.

Damn it. He didn't need this complication. Especially now. He hadn't expected to be drawn to such a frumpy little thing. Jeff snorted at the thought. Frumpy? He remembered his first sight of that red lace thong, the thin bands of elastic stretched across her small curves.

Beneath the hideous clothes she insisted on wearing was a body that could drive a man insane.

No, she wasn't frumpy. But she was warm and kind and gentle. All the things he'd tried to steer clear of in a woman for years.

Damn it, he should be feeling better. He'd made love to her. He'd experienced what his dreams had been tormenting him with for weeks. He should be relaxed, satisfied. Instead, his body was tight with need. Rather than easing his hunger for her, making love had only whetted his appetite.

Images raced through his mind. Shadows, deep, reverberating music, her body bathed in moonlight, their frenzied, almost mindless coupling in the darkness.

Mindless.

Realization shot through his brain.

He sat bolt upright in bed. How could he have been so careless? Swinging his legs off the mattress, he rushed across the room, out the door and into the living room.

Heading straight to her room, he lifted his right hand and gave three short, quiet raps on the wood.

She opened it immediately, one finger against kiss-bruised lips. Pushing him back, she eased out of her room and closed the door behind her. "Be quiet, you'll wake her again."

"Laura, I just thought of something," he said, and cursed himself again for being so damn stupid.

"Jeff," she said, "I'm tired and I'd really rather not talk right now—"

No time now for niceties.

"Are you by any chance taking the Pill?" he asked bluntly.

She frowned up at him, then slowly that frown changed to a look of appalled disbelief.

"I take it that means no," he said. He ran one hand across the back of his neck. *More* complications. As if there hadn't already been enough.

"Of course I'm not," she said, wrapping her arms around her waist. Her soft, dewy eyes looked haunted. "It's not as though I had a big use for it up until tonight."

"Damn it," he whispered.

"This doesn't necessarily mean anything," she told him, but it sounded as though she was really reassuring herself. "My chances of actually conceiving have to be slim. It was only the one time."

How many couples, he wondered, had soothed themselves with that particular line over the centuries?

"I should have taken care of it," he said. He *always* took care of it. He'd never believed in trusting one means of birth control alone.

But tonight, for the first time ever, he hadn't taken the time to think. Instead, they'd acted like a couple of kids in the back seat of a car. Now they could have a major problem on their hands.

"This is my fault," he said, even knowing that it was pointless to assign blame. "I'm sorry, Laura."

"Stop it," she said softly but firmly. "I'm a big girl. I should have been looking out for myself."

Then why did he feel so lousy?

"This is getting us nowhere," he told her. "We can't do anything about it now, anyway. When will we know?"

"Hmm?" She shook her head, clearly distracted by the possibilities. "Oh. In another couple of weeks."

He nodded stiffly. Two weeks. Right now, that sounded like an eternity. But look at what had already happened to him in a couple of short weeks. He had been a reasonably carefree bachelor. Now he had a baby, a nanny and possibly *another* baby on the way.

Good Lord.

Looking at the two of them now, no one would guess that less than half an hour ago, they'd been locked in each other's arms. Even though he was standing right in front of her, Jeff felt the distance between them growing with every passing second.

Hoping to bridge the gap before it widened to an impassable chasm, he lifted one hand toward her.

She stepped back, neatly avoiding his touch. Reaching behind her back, she twisted the knob and opened her bedroom door. Pausing briefly, she said, "Good night, Jeff," then she slipped into her room, shutting him out.

He placed his hands on either side of the door frame and leaned forward, scowling into the darkness. What a mess. Jeff sighed and remembered the look on her face just before she closed the door.

If he was any judge, there wouldn't be a repeat of tonight's performance.

Thoroughly disgusted with himself, Jeff gave the closed door one last look, then went back to his empty bed.

The next morning, Laura managed to stay in her room until after Jeff had left for work. Miranda was a bit fretful, but even she cooperated by waiting a little longer than usual for her morning bottle.

As soon as the coast was clear, she hustled to the kitchen, sat the baby down in her high chair and hurriedly prepared Miranda's breakfast.

She was so tired she could hardly keep her eyes open. Of course, that was hardly surprising. She hadn't gotten a wink of sleep all night, what with the images of Jeff darting through her mind…along with the worry that she just might be pregnant.

Laura groaned quietly and reached up to rub her temples. How could she have done something so completely out of character? Not only had she made love with a man she hardly knew, but also she hadn't even *considered* the possibility of a pregnancy.

Only fools and children made that kind of mistake.

And she was no child.

A child. She stopped cold and leaned her forehead on a cabinet door. Please, she prayed silently. She couldn't be pregnant. How could she face her colleagues at school next September? A pregnant, unmarried kindergarten teacher? No, she was sure *that* wouldn't go over well with her principal.

Her eyes squeezed shut on a wave of misery. It wasn't fair. How many times had she dreamed about having children? Ever since she was a girl, she'd longed for a family of her own. When Bill died, she'd put all of those hopes and dreams aside, resigning herself to the fact that she would always be alone.

Now, she very well *might* be pregnant and found herself having to pray frantically that she wasn't.

It could all have been so different, she thought tiredly. If only Bill had lived. Laura kept her eyes firmly closed and tried to draw up a mental image of her former fiancé.

But the once familiar, comforting features blurred and shifted. The harder she tried to focus, the more the images fought her. Faded by the years, her memories of Bill had become distant recollections of warmth.

On the other hand, a vivid portrait of Jeff Ryan leaped into her mind instantly. His eyes, his hands, his mouth as he leaned in to claim a kiss.

Tears filled her eyes as she pushed those mental pictures aside.

Blast you, Bill, she thought angrily. Why did you die? Everything was so much simpler then. So clear. With him, she had known who she was and what she wanted.

With Jeff, everything was different. *She* was different. In ways she would never have expected, she felt herself reacting to him and to the new world she found herself in.

Making love on a couch? With no protection?

That was definitely *not* the old Laura Morgan.

A single tear rolled from the corner of her eye. She caught it with a swipe of her hand and told herself to leave the past in the past. Though she felt safe living with her memories, they offered her no solutions to her current problems. Right now, the present demanded her full attention.

Straightening away from the cabinet, she glanced at the baby, saw that she was happily chewing on the end of the safety strap and smiled softly.

The phone rang while she was stirring baby oatmeal. She grabbed up the receiver, tucked it between her chin and her shoulder and said, "Hello?"

"Hi, Laura," a familiar voice answered. "It's Peggy."

"Peggy," Laura said, glad for the distraction of a friendly voice. "How are you?"

"I'm fine, I wanted to know how *you* were doing."

"I'm sorry," she said, spooning a bit of the cereal into Miranda's open, birdlike mouth. "I should have called you."

"Hey, it's no biggie," her friend countered. "You've been busy."

Busier than she knew, Laura thought with a grimace.

"So what's my new niece like?"

Laura smiled. She couldn't help it. "Right now, she's smearing oatmeal over her face."

Miranda laughed, as if she knew she was being discussed. Smacking both palms down on her high-chair tray, she opened her mouth wide for another mouthful.

"Tell that brother of mine to bring her up for a visit, okay?" Peggy's voice sounded wistful.

"I will," Laura said automatically, then bit her lip before saying, "you know, he still hasn't decided if he's going to keep her or not."

"He'll keep her," Peggy assured her.

"How do you know?"

"I know my brother," Peggy answered, then added to one of her kids, "I said *one* cookie." Speaking to Laura again, she asked, "So, what do you think of Jeff?"

Now, *there* was a loaded question.

"He's…" What? Gorgeous? A wonderful lover? Terrifying? Perhaps the father of her unborn child? She shuddered and settled for "Nice."

"Nice?" Peggy sounded appalled. "That's it? Nice?"

"What did you expect?" Laura said, spooning the last of the oatmeal into Miranda's messy little mouth.

"*Expect* isn't the right word," Peggy told her on a sigh. "*Hoped* would have been more accurate."

Laura picked up a towel, wiped the baby's face, then handed her a bottle. Two chubby fists closed around it and tipped it up.

"Peggy," Laura said, leaning back in the chair.

"You can't blame a girl for trying," Peggy interrupted. "I've thought for the longest time that you and Jeff would be perfect together."

Laura flushed and thanked heaven that her friend couldn't see her face. They had been perfect. More than perfect. But sex wasn't everything.

"Forget it, Peg," Laura said, more for her own benefit than her friend's. She wouldn't fool herself into thinking she and Jeff were madly in love. If she was more attracted to him than was comfortable to admit, no one but *she* had to know that. "I already had my chance at love."

"Please," Peggy groaned. "Don't start telling me about Saint Bill again."

"He was a wonderful man," Laura said hotly, determined now, more than ever, to defend his memory. It was one thing for her to realize that what she and Bill had shared wasn't even close to the chemistry between her and Jeff. It was quite another to let someone else talk about the man she would have married if things had been different.

"I'm sorry. I'm sure he was." There was a long minute of silence before Peggy went on. "But he's gone, honey. And you're still alive. Is it right for you to pack yourself up in mothballs?"

She hadn't been in mothballs. She'd had a life the past eight years. She just hadn't had a man. There was a difference.

"Look," Peggy said, apparently sensing the need for a change of topic. "Tell me about Jeff and the baby. Is he nuts about her?"

Thankful for safe, neutral ground, Laura smiled. "He's so good with her. But he doesn't seem to think so. It's as if he hasn't even noticed how much time he spends with her. And how much he enjoys it."

"Then maybe you should show him."

"What do you mean?"

"I mean," Peggy said, and Laura could hear the grin in her voice, "keep the baby away from him. Have her asleep by the time he gets home. Make him do without her so that he'll see how much he already loves her. And how much he'd miss her if she was gone."

Not a bad idea, Laura thought. "Okay," she agreed, reaching out to smooth the baby's flyaway hair. "I'll do it. But only because I know what a terrific parent he would be."

"Of course he's good at parenting," Peggy exclaimed. "He's *my* brother, isn't he?" Then in a louder, sterner voice, she ordered, "Teddy, put those scissors down this minute. Don't you *dare* cut your sister's braid off!"

Laura chuckled and wasn't surprised when Peggy said, "Gotta go," and hung up.

Standing up, she pulled Miranda from her high chair and cuddled the messy little person close. "Remember, Miranda," she said, "when you go to visit your cousins, stay clear of Teddy."

Miranda grinned around the nipple in her mouth, and a river of formula ran down her chin.

Jeff opened the door to the apartment, not really sure what kind of a reception he would get. All day, he'd had to balance his duties at work with thoughts of Laura. It hadn't been easy, concentrating on the piles of paperwork he was expected to handle while his brain kept conjuring up images of the night before. Laura in his arms. Laura sighing. Laura crying his name.

Not to mention the image of Laura pregnant.

He'd never been so affected by a woman. He'd never allowed whatever female he was seeing to invade other aspects of his life. He had always been able to keep his career and his private life separate.

Until now.

Whatever it was between him and Laura, he couldn't allow it to affect his work. They were going to have a talk, whether she wanted to or not. He gritted his teeth and closed the door quietly, telling himself to get a grip. His gaze scanned the inside of the apartment, looking for her. But there was no sign of either Laura or the baby. Irrationally, a hollow emptiness opened in his chest. What if she'd left? What if she had taken the baby and gone?

He knew it was stupid. Laura wouldn't sneak off and she sure as hell wouldn't take the baby if she did.

Still, he was amazed at the sweeping relief he felt when

her bedroom door opened and Laura stepped into the living room. She turned, saw him and stopped abruptly. Her gaze met his for an instant before sliding away.

She wore an oversize white T-shirt again and a pair of pale blue shorts, exposing her shapely, lightly tanned legs. He couldn't help wondering what she had on *under* those baggy clothes. That thought brought up the memory of a red lace thong, and his mouth went dry.

For an uncomfortably long minute, he simply looked at her, not sure what to say or where to start.

Ridiculous to feel suddenly tongue-tied.

Jeff tossed his camouflage uniform hat onto the nearby table, then shifted his gaze back to her, willing her to look at him. It didn't work. Finally, he asked, "Where's the baby?"

"Asleep," Laura said, and started for the kitchen.

Asleep? At six o'clock? He checked his watch just to make sure of the time. Normally, Miranda didn't even have her bath until seven-thirty. "Why so early?" he asked, crossing the room to join her.

Laura shrugged. "She seemed tired. Maybe she just didn't get enough sleep last night." Her voice sort of trailed off on the last part of that sentence.

"I know how she feels, then," he said, glad she'd given him an opening.

She ignored him, bent down and pulled a saucepan from the bottom cupboard. "Is soup all right with you?" she asked. "I'm really not very hungry."

"I thought you said you weren't going to cook for me." He deliberately brought back the memory of their first day together, hoping she would smile. She didn't.

"I'm cooking for me," she explained. "There's simply enough for you, too."

"Fine," he said.

"Soup, then." She walked to another cabinet, opened it and stared up at the rows of cans. "Chicken noodle okay?"

"I don't care," he answered impatiently.

She grabbed one can and opened a drawer, rummaging for a can opener.

"Laura," he said.

She didn't even turn around. Just started in on that can of soup as though it were the most important thing in the world.

"Laura, we should talk about last night," he said, still waiting for a response.

"Would you hand me that pan?" she asked.

Grumbling under his breath, he stalked across the small kitchen, grabbed the pan and handed it to her across the table.

"Thanks."

"You're welcome," he said. "About last night..."

"I think it's better if we just pretend last night didn't happen," she said, dumping the condensed soup into the pan. Stepping over to the sink, she filled the can with water, and went back to the stove. As she stirred the mess together, she continued, "It was an accident. Something I'm sure we both regret. Let's go past it, shall we?"

"Go past it." He stared at the back of her head, wishing he could see her expression. Look into her eyes.

"I think that would be best."

"Oh, well..." He nodded sharply, though she couldn't see him, either. He'd wanted to have a reasonable discussion. He'd wanted to have a chance to explain to her that just because the sex had been incredible, it didn't necessarily follow that there would be a relationship between them.

Damn it, *he* had wanted to be the calm, reasonable one.

Briefly, he wondered why he was so upset. Wasn't this just what he'd wanted? Hadn't everything worked out fine?

All day, he'd wondered and worried about a conversation that she had just initiated and ended in about five sentences.

A flicker of anger sparked into life inside him. Who the hell did she think she was, deciding something this important for both of them? The fact that he had been going to do the same thing was irrelevant.

"And what if you're pregnant?" he forced himself to ask. "Do we just go past that, too?"

She went completely still. "We'll worry about that if we have to."

"You can't avoid looking at me forever," he snapped.

Slowly, she turned around to face him. Color stained her cheeks. Her eyes glittered with an emotion he couldn't identify, and her spine was so stiff, she looked as though she might snap in two.

"Happy now?" she asked.

"Delirious." He wasn't sure how to reach her. She seemed more remote now than she had the day she arrived. "Damn it, where is the woman I was with yesterday?" he demanded.

If anything, the splotch of color on her cheeks deepened. "She's gone," Laura said. "Let her go."

"Not yet," he countered grimly. Why was he fighting this? Why was he poking and prodding for a response even though it would be easier for him if she maintained this unbreachable wall around her?

He didn't know. All he knew was that he wanted to see the other Laura again. The Laura who had demanded his passion and given her own.

Coming around the table in a couple of quick steps, he grabbed her upper arms and pulled her close. She tipped her head back to stare up at him. Jeff tried to read the emotions swirling around in her chocolate brown eyes, but they shifted and changed too quickly to be identified.

"I've been thinking about you all day," he admitted, his

gaze moving over her features like a dying man looking for signs of heaven. "I couldn't even work. I kept seeing your face, hearing your voice."

"I'm sorry," she said tightly, letting her gaze slide to one side.

He shook her gently. "I don't want an apology," he told her. "I want…"

"What?" she snapped, suddenly breaking free of his grip and taking a step away from him. "What *do* you want?" she repeated. Her voice sounded hollow. Empty.

He looked down at his hands, then let them fall to his sides. Lifting his gaze back to her, he shook his head. "I don't know," he admitted. "But I know I don't want you pretending last night didn't happen. It did, damn it." He reached up and pushed both hands along the sides of his head. "Ignoring it or brushing it under the rug doesn't change anything."

She blinked, opened her mouth, then closed it again.

His reaction didn't even make sense to him. But they had shared something incredible the night before. Something that had touched him more deeply than anything ever had, and he would be damned if he'd let her pretend otherwise.

"Laura," he said, more softly this time, "I know neither one of us *wanted* it to happen…"

She shook her head and bit down on her bottom lip.

"But it did," he went on, determined to reach her. "And I think you felt the same magic I did."

"Magic?" she asked.

"Yeah," he said, taking a cautious step toward her.

"It wasn't magic, Jeff," she corrected, backing away again. "It was lust, pure and simple."

"Lust?" It had been a while since he'd had that word applied to him. The last time, he thought, was when he was sixteen and the father of his prom date had "escorted" him to his car.

"Don't misunderstand," she added while he was still testing the sound of that word in his mind. "I enjoyed it."

He already *knew* she'd enjoyed it.

"But it can't happen again."

He'd been telling himself the same thing all day. Strange that hearing her say it sounded so much more final.

"Laura—"

"I'm not hungry after all," she said thickly. "You can have the soup." Then she turned and scuttled off to her bedroom.

Alone, he didn't move from that spot until he heard the chicken-noodle soup boiling over on the stove.

Eight

Three days later, Laura was hurrying down the short, carpeted hallway toward the apartment. Nearly five o'clock, she thought with a hasty glance at her wristwatch.

Her grip on the stroller handle tightened. She shouldn't have stayed so late at the park. But Miranda had been having so much fun on the baby swings, Laura hadn't had the heart to drag her away from them.

Now, she ran the risk of running into Jeff.

For the past few days, Peggy's idea of keeping the baby away from him had been working fine. By the time he came home from work, Miranda had eaten her dinner and was tucked into bed. In the mornings, the baby had her bath *after* he had left for the base.

The beauty of Peggy's plan was that now, on the few occasions Laura had spoken with Jeff, he didn't want to talk about their night of lovemaking. Instead, he was peppering her with questions about Miranda. Was she still teething? Did she eat the vegetables she hated so much?

He'd even come home early the night before, trying to catch Miranda still awake. He hadn't succeeded, but Laura was expecting him even earlier tonight.

Halfway down the hall. She hurried her steps a bit, determined to get the baby fed and down for the night before Jeff arrived.

A door on the left opened, and Agnes Butler stepped out of her apartment. Not now, Laura thought. She just didn't have time to listen to another tirade on the dangers of living with Jeff Ryan. Besides being in a hurry, there was that old adage...locking the barn door after the horse was already out and frolicking in the corral.

The older woman, one hand behind her back, scowled at Laura briefly, then bent down to look at the baby. For the past week, Mrs. Butler had managed to catch Miranda and Laura every time they left the apartment. Maybe there was something to Jeff's notion about being spied on.

"Hello, sweet pea," the older woman crooned, and Miranda kicked her feet excitedly against the stroller. "Look what Agnes has for you." Pulling her hand from behind her back, she offered the baby a pastel pink, crocheted, stuffed bunny rabbit.

Miranda babbled incoherently, then grabbed at the toy, immediately stuffing one of the long ears into her mouth.

Stunned by the gesture, Laura stared at the happy baby for a long moment before turning to study the suddenly surprising woman beside her.

The heavily lined features were softened as she watched the baby, and there was definitely a glint of some undisguised, warm emotion shining in her eyes.

"Agnes Butler," she said thoughtfully, "you're a fraud."

The old woman shot her a sly glance from the corner of her eye. "Don't know what you're talking about," she said.

Laura smiled and shook her head. "Yes, you do," she

countered, a chuckle in her voice. "You've got Jeff fooled, you know."

Twin snow-white eyebrows lowered over those sharp blue eyes.

"Me too, until now." Impulsively, she reached out and squeezed the other woman's hand gently, noticing the fragile, papery feel of her skin. "You snap and snarl at everybody, then spend *days* making something like this for a baby you hardly know." She shook her head again. "You know what you are, Agnes?" she asked. *"Kind."*

"Kind." Agnes waved one hand, dismissing the notion entirely. "Nothing kind about it. Feels good to have somebody to do it for. Selfish, really."

"If that's what you call selfish, I can't wait to see your definition of generous."

Agnes sniffed, snatched her hand away and rubbed at the tip of her nose. "You're a nice girl," she said, looking Laura up and down. "And I got to say you're quite the improvement over the sort of females he *used* to bring around here."

Unwillingly, Laura felt a twinge stab at her heart. Which didn't make the least bit of sense. When you're in lust with a person, you don't feel jealousy and envy. For heaven's sake, lust isn't *love*.

"What kind of women?" she asked before she could stop herself.

"Oh, the high-strung type," Agnes said, tipping her nose up with the tip of a finger. "Raw-boned skinny, tight smiles, silk dresses."

Suddenly depressed, Laura glanced down at her own stunning ensemble and grimaced helplessly. A damp, sand-splattered white T-shirt, baggy gray sweat shorts and tennis shoes. And no one would ever call her skinny.

"But haven't seen one of 'em for months," Agnes was saying.

"Months?" Why did that news feel like a bright ray of hope?

"Yeah. Here lately, at least till you came along, keeping my eye on him was about as interestin' as watchin' grass grow."

"I'll try to do better from now on." A deep voice sounded out from right behind Laura.

Blast it, she'd *known* he would be home early today. Instead of turning around to face him, Laura watched Agnes Butler's relaxed, almost friendly features tighten up into a familiar, disapproving mask.

"Anybody ever tell you it's rude to listen in on conversations?" the older woman snapped.

"Not a soul, ma'am," he responded.

"I thought not," she countered.

Laura swiveled her head to look at him as he stepped up beside her. His lips twitched with the beginnings of a smile as he bantered with Agnes.

"You could teach me manners," Jeff offered.

"I should live as long as that would take," the older woman retorted, then snorted, already turning into her apartment.

"You'll live forever," he assured her.

Agnes stopped. Cocking her head, she glared at him suspiciously over her shoulder. "How do you know?"

He grinned. "Only the good die young."

Agnes sputtered, but Laura noted the spark of humor in her eyes.

"Rude, I tell you. Just plain rude." With that, the old woman closed her door and systematically turned all four locks.

Still surprised by the exchange, Laura stared at the closed door for a long moment of silence before turning to look at Jeff. "She likes you, doesn't she?"

"*Like* is pretty strong," he said, hunkering down to smile at the baby. "*Doesn't hate* is probably closer to the truth."

After ruffling Miranda's hair, Jeff stood up and looked at the woman who continued to haunt his dreams.

"You're home early," she said.

"I have to be these days," he told her. "If I want to catch a glimpse of you or Miranda." Her gaze shifted away from his, but not before he saw a gleam of guilt flash across her brown eyes. "I don't know what you're up to lately, but do you realize that I haven't even *seen* Miranda in days?"

Laura pushed the stroller toward the apartment. "Isn't that the way you wanted it?"

"Wanted what?" he asked as he followed her.

"You didn't want to be bothered by the baby." She dug in her pocket for her set of keys. "I'm seeing to it that you're not."

"Who put you in charge of making Miranda invisible?" Jeff nudged her to one side, unlocked the front door, then opened it, stepping back so she and the stroller could precede him inside.

"You did," she said softly.

"Bull," he countered. "I never said I wanted her hidden away in an attic."

"You don't *have* an attic." Laura shot him a quick look. "But you *did* say that you never wanted kids. That if you had known Hank was going to make you guardian, you would have stopped him."

"That's different. That's how I felt before."

"What's changed?"

He didn't answer. Hell, he wasn't sure *how* to answer.

Shooting a quick glance at the baby, he felt something inside him turn over. She looked as though she'd grown in the past few days. Stupid, he thought. Of course she hadn't grown in a couple of days.

But seeing her felt good. Better than he had thought it would.

It had been a hard thing for him to admit to himself—that he actually missed Miranda. And he didn't think he was up to the challenge of admitting that fact to Laura. Not yet.

Quietly, he closed the front door behind him, automatically turning the door lock.

"What about you?" he asked, watching her.

"What about me?" She bent down to scoop up the baby.

"You've been keeping out of sight, too."

"I've been with the baby," she replied.

A quick answer. Too quick.

"It's more than that," he said. "You've been avoiding me. Deliberately."

She glanced at him covertly, then concentrated on smoothing Miranda's flyaway wisps of hair. "Shouldn't I be?"

"I never said I didn't want a nanny in my life," he stated quietly.

She stilled. A tenuous thread of awareness leaped up between them, practically vibrating in its growing intensity.

"I'm not in your life," she told him, moving for her bedroom with quick, determined strides.

Every step she took hammered at him. It was as if she were walking out of his apartment, distancing herself from him. Jeff couldn't stand the thought of it.

He caught up with her before she could open the door and disappear again. She held Miranda close to her chest, one hand beneath her little bottom, the other splayed protectively across her back.

"You're here, Laura," he said, curling his hands into fists to keep from touching her. "In my home. In my life." The words *In my heart* hovered on his tongue, but he closed his mouth on them.

"Temporarily."

"Now," he corrected.

"Don't do this," Laura pleaded, her voice breaking slightly.

"Do what?" he asked. "Tell you I've missed you? That I dream of you every night and think of you all day?"

She gasped, held the breath trapped in her lungs for a long minute, then released it on a sigh.

"I can't keep my mind on the job," he told her, realizing even as he said it that that was a gross understatement. Hell, the way he'd been feeling lately, the base could have been invaded and he would hardly have noticed.

"Instead," he continued, "all I see is a pair of soft brown eyes—" he reached up and slowly touched the pad of his thumb to her lips "—a completely kissable mouth—" he let his gaze drop to her sand-covered shorts "—and lace-covered skin."

She shivered and he wanted to shout. He knew that she wanted him as badly as he wanted her. He felt it in her. He sensed the heat already building between them.

"Jeff," she said, taking a hasty half step backward, clutching the baby tightly to her. "I..." Clearly, she was reaching for something to say. Something to put him at bay and keep him there. He had no intention of helping her.

She sucked in a deep gulp of air, making a deliberate attempt to steady herself. "You'll have to excuse me," she said stiffly, "I have to bathe the baby and feed her and..."

"I'll do it tonight," he said, already reaching for the baby, who leaned toward him eagerly.

Odd that he should be so willing to take on a task that he had resented in the beginning of his forced fatherhood.

The past few days, he had almost been able to believe that he was again alone in his apartment. He'd had time to himself. Quiet. Uninterrupted peace.

That should have made him happy. Lord knew in the

first few days after Miranda's arrival, all he'd done was silently complain about his lost privacy and the burden of responsibility he'd been handed. Now, though, after just a taste of what his life had been like before the baby, he realized that he didn't like it one damn bit.

In fact, he wouldn't have believed this possible a month ago, but he actually missed being a part of something more than just his own life. He missed seeing Miranda and had caught himself wondering about her at odd times of the day. He'd become accustomed to the baby's presence in his life, and her absence had left a void he had never expected to feel.

Miranda's smile made him feel as though he could conquer the world, and her tears broke his heart.

Strangely enough, in a few short weeks, he seemed to have become somebody's daddy.

Miranda's sturdy little body felt right in his arms. The baby laughed up at him and patted his cheek with her grubby fingers. He smiled at her.

Jeff lifted his gaze from the baby to Laura. A fist tightened around his chest, squeezing until he thought drawing a deep breath would be impossible.

Yes, he had missed Miranda.

But he longed for Laura.

Every night, he lay in his bed and listened for the sounds of her moving about her room. He fantasized at work about her oversize sweatshirts and the perfect breasts they hid. His dreams were filled with visions of her, in the silk-and-lace underwear he knew she loved. He remembered every moment of their one night together, and those memories kept his body tight and his temper with co-workers short.

Something had to be done.

"I've missed her," he said softly.

Laura nodded, a film of water glimmering in her eyes.

"I've missed you, too."

Her gaze snapped up to his. "This isn't helping."

"What *would* help, Laura?" he asked, stepping in close to her.

"I don't know that anything can," she said quietly.

"Damn it, why are you making this so hard?" Jeff reached out with one hand, caught her chin with his fingertips and tilted her head up until he could look into the brown eyes that seemed to be deeper and more velvety every time he saw them. "It doesn't have to be."

"Of course it does," she said with a slow shake of her head. "Neither of us planned on this happening."

Plans. She surely was big on plans. But then, he admitted silently, he used to be, too. Until about fifteen pounds of female trouble had landed in his lap and shattered any sense of planning that he'd ever done.

Suddenly, something Laura'd said to him the night they had made love came back to him, and in the next instant, he heard himself tossing her words back at her.

"Didn't you tell me that plans don't always work out? That life has a way of just happening?" Her gaze shifted from his. He went on. "You said you had to adapt. To adjust."

"This is different," she protested, her voice husky as it scraped past her throat.

"How?"

She shook her head, apparently unable to come up with a valid reason. Hurriedly, Jeff pushed on.

"I've wanted you, Laura," he said, willing her to hear the hunger in his voice. "I dream about holding you again. Burying myself inside you. Feeling your heartbeat thundering against my chest."

She dragged in a long, shaky breath and slowly lifted her gaze to meet his.

She was weakening; he could feel it. Desire roared through him.

"Tonight, Laura," he demanded, and congratulated himself on making his voice work despite the knot of need lodged in his throat. "Give me tonight, and we'll let tomorrow take care of itself."

Her breathing quickened and shallowed out. Her teeth pulled nervously at her bottom lip.

A long moment passed, and Jeff wondered desperately if he'd pushed too hard, or not enough. He was only certain of one thing. He couldn't spend another long, lonely night with her so close and yet so far away.

He needed her, damn it.

"It's a mistake," she whispered.

"It's inevitable," he countered.

"We shouldn't," she said.

"But we will?"

"Yes," she agreed helplessly. "We will."

By the time Miranda was bathed, fed and put down to sleep, Laura's nerves were as tightly strung as piano wire. Her stomach pitched and rolled constantly, and a low, burning ache had settled at her center, reminding her of what was coming.

She flipped the faucets on and turned the handles until the stream of water rushing from the showerhead was just the right temperature.

The small bathroom filled with steam slowly. It crept from behind the edge of the white shower curtain and swirled over the tiled floor like warm fog. Then it lifted in a slow, writhing dance, twisting around her calves and thighs as it reached for the ceiling.

Laura stared into the mirror as she pinned her hair up on top of her head. Her gaze slipped over her reflection idly, and she couldn't help wondering what Jeff found so appealing about her figure. Her breasts were too small to be voluptuous, her hips too rounded to be fashionable, and she would never have a small waist. Her legs were her best feature, and they were far too short.

Self-consciously, she wrapped her arms around her middle and wasn't surprised to find that her hands were cold, despite the rising, damp heat in the bathroom.

She shouldn't have agreed to this, she told herself sternly. She should have been strong. She should have told him that adding to their first mistake would only compound the problem.

Instantly, visions of their time on the couch raced through her mind, and her nipples tightened in anticipation. She groaned quietly and admitted that it was pointless to fight it. Whatever attraction lay between her and Jeff, it was too strong to ignore.

Sighing, she turned, stepped into the tub and drew the curtain closed behind her. She moved beneath the spray of water, letting it pour onto her face and chest. The hot, stinging, needlelike drops pelted her skin and teased her already raw nerve endings.

Snatching the bar of soap, she rubbed it between her palms, working up a good lather before applying the suds to her shoulders and neck.

"Can I do your back?" a deep, rumbling voice penetrated the steamy wall surrounding her, and Laura jumped, startled.

"Go away," she ordered, instinctively keeping her back to him as he drew the curtain aside and stepped over the rim to join her beneath the rush of hot water.

One of his hands touched her shoulder and slowly, lazily drifted along her spine to her behind.

Laura shivered.

"We both want to take a shower," he said, the rumble of his voice echoing in the small room. "Why not save water while we're at it?"

Laura groaned inwardly. It was one thing to make love

to a man in the dark shadows of a bedroom—or a living room—she qualified silently. It was quite another to stand in the bright fluorescent light of a bathroom and have him share a shower in a tub that seemed to be shrinking by the second.

"Laura?" he said softly.

She shot him a quick, backward glance and knew immediately that she was sunk.

Clouds of steam wound around his head. Pale blue eyes shimmering with the heat of desire watched her. Droplets of water clung to the faint brush of dark blond hair that dusted his broad chest. Her gaze dropped farther, landing on the hard, thick proof of the need he felt for her.

"Hand me the soap," he coaxed.

Wordlessly, she did as he asked. She watched as he worked up a lather, then held her breath as he reached for her.

His strong hands fell on her shoulders. His fingers rubbed at either side of her neck, and she felt her muscles liquefy as he gently eased away the tight knots of tension.

Laura leaned forward, resting her forehead on the cool, wet, tiled wall and concentrated on the feel of his hands. Soapy lather made his skin glide along hers, down the length of her spinal column to the curve of her bottom.

His palms cupped her behind, caressing and kneading the tender flesh until she moaned with pleasure and leaned more heavily against the wall. Her right hand gripped the porcelain soap dish bolted to the tiles and her knuckles whitened with the effort to hold herself erect as he continued exploring her body.

"Lovely," he murmured in a husky voice pitched just above the rush of the water. "So lovely."

Her knees wobbled, and she stiffened, locking them into position. She absolutely refused to dissolve into a mass of sensation at his feet.

Then one of his soap-covered hands dipped between her legs, urging them to part for him. The soft, slick feel of his fingers on her thighs brought another gasp and a low, throaty moan from her. Laura pressed herself fully against the blue-and-white tiles, turned her face to one side and closed her eyes.

"Let me touch you, Laura," he whispered.

Instantly, she opened her thighs, widening her already precarious stance on the slippery tub floor. Her breath quickened. Her stomach tightened, and her mouth went dry. Holding on to the soap dish for dear life, she waited for the intimate caress she knew was coming.

Then he kissed the back of her neck.

Laura jolted as electricity sizzled along her nerve endings. His lips and tongue teased her nape before moving down, along her spine. Gooseflesh leaped up on her skin and raced across her body in his wake.

"Jeff," she murmured, and tasted the sweetness of his name on her lips.

She felt him kneel behind her and wanted to protest, but the words wouldn't come. His long, soapy, slick fingers rubbed and smoothed skin that had become so sensitive, she trembled at each touch.

One of his hands slipped between her thighs from behind, and she tensed, everything within her coiled tightly in anticipation. He dipped two fingers into her liquid heat, stroking and pressing against her internal muscles until her entire body was a quivering mass of sensation.

She groaned brokenly and spread her legs farther in a greedy attempt to feel more of him. The still rising steam held her in its foggy grasp, surrounding her with damp heat and blinding her to all but the mist and Jeff's touch.

Then he kissed her bottom, raking his teeth across the tender flesh gently but firmly. Slowly, he stood up, rubbing the length of his body along hers. His thickened groin prodded at her, reminding her that there was more to come.

Laura's breath caught in her chest. Her heart slammed against her ribs in a wild, unsteady beat. Her knees trembled. Her grip on the soap dish tightened even further.

When he had his front firmly pressed to her back, he pulled his hand free of her body, despite the slight whimpering noise that escaped her at his desertion.

But he didn't move away. Instead, he slid his right hand around to the front of her, down over her abdomen and past the triangle of curls at the apex of her thighs.

Grateful and eager, Laura whispered, ''Yes, Jeff. Oh, please, now.''

He bent his head to kiss her cheek, the corner of her mouth. She couldn't move. Dared not inch away from the tiled wall that had become her only support now that her limbs were useless to her.

As his hand smoothed along her wet flesh to cup her hot, throbbing center, she shivered violently. His thumb brushed across a hardened nub of desire. He whispered to her, his words lost in the rush of water and the pounding of her heart. Her hips moved frantically as he pushed her relentlessly along a path she had thought never to wander again.

Her body bucking against his hands, she twisted this way and that, desperately seeking a release that seemed to hover just out of reach. Jeff moved even closer to her, aligning his body to hers.

Breathing labored, she gasped for air in the tiny, steam-filled enclosure. Helpless to do anything but ride the incredible wave of pleasure just peaking within her, Laura shouted his name as the first explosion took her over the edge.

Nine

His hands shaking, Jeff shut off the water, and stepped out of the tub. He turned and pulled Laura into his arms. She sagged against him, her body still trembling as she sighed his name. He didn't bother to grab towels. He wanted her now. Wet and flushed from the steam. Silently, he headed for his bedroom.

He'd wanted to make love to her in the shower. Watching her as a climax tore through her had shaken him to his soul and pushed his control to its limits.

But he wouldn't make another mistake with her. This time, he would show her the care he should have used their first time together.

Entering the dark bedroom, he walked directly to the bed and laid her down atop the fresh white sheets. She stretched languidly, opened her eyes and smiled up at him. Wet tendrils of her hair snaked out in a star-burst around her head. Her eyes were clouded with the fresh memories of her passion.

She whispered his name and lifted her arms toward him.

He gritted his teeth, yanked the bedside table drawer open and fumbled in its contents blindly. After a long moment, he found what he needed, picked up the foil packet, then slammed the drawer shut again.

His fingers, suddenly clumsy, tore at the wrapper.

"Jeff," she said softly, and came up on one elbow, her free hand held out toward him. "Let me."

He sucked in a gulp of air, incredibly aroused at just the thought of her hands on him. Deliberately, he steadied himself and handed her the packet.

Laura sat up and scooted closer to the edge of the bed. Jeff's breath came in short, shallow puffs. He watched her pull the cream-colored latex free of its wrapping, then held his breath as she reached for him.

Her fingers closed around him tightly. Her thumb stroked the underside of his shaft, and he surged forward, into her grasp, just managing to muffle a groan aching in his throat.

"Laura," he said tightly. "I'm walking a real fine edge here."

She smiled, a knowing, completely feminine curving of her lips. Leaning into him, she kissed his belly, and jagged spears of heat sliced through him. He muttered a curse as more of his control fell away.

"Jump off that edge, Jeff," she urged him softly.

He looked down at her and felt his heart stop. Her mouth just a breath away from his rigid arousal, she leaned in even closer. His teeth ground together. His hands curled into fists as if searching for something—anything—to grab hold of. The only possible way for him to maintain his too ragged sense of self-control would be for him to close his eyes.

Yet he couldn't look away.

He watched her lips touch him. Felt the soft hush of her breath caress his hardened flesh.

A low rumble of need escaped him. Her damp hair

against his thighs served as a dramatic contrast to the fire she had started elsewhere. A moment. Two. He luxuriated in her intimate touch and at the same time craved to be inside her. To be buried so deeply within her that they would never be truly apart again.

Suddenly, Jeff couldn't stand it anymore. Reaching for her, he set his hands at either side of her head and tipped her face up to his. When their eyes met, he was humbled and rocked to his core by the raw emotion he read in her gaze.

Through tightly gritted teeth, he said, "Put the condom on me, Laura. I need to be inside you and I can't wait much longer."

"I need that, too, Jeff," she told him, though her voice was thin and wavering. "More than I thought possible."

"Hurry, Laura," he urged. "Hurry."

Her fingers stretched the latex and slowly, carefully, rolled the shield down over his length. Its tightness bit into his flesh, but any discomfort was wiped away by the knowledge that this was his only means of protecting her. Cherishing her.

She scooted back on the mattress, stretched out and parted her thighs. Then she reached for him, arms wide in welcome. He couldn't wait another moment. The sweet torment had already gone on too long. A wild need burned in him now with an energy that wouldn't be denied.

He knelt between her thighs, slid his hands beneath her bottom and lifted her hips slightly for his entry. As he pushed himself into her warmth, he paused, reveling in the feel of her closing around him. Even shielded from her, he experienced the same overpowering sensation he had the first time.

It was like coming home.

With his next breath, he thrust deeply inside her, satisfaction rippling through his bloodstream. In seconds, an ancient rhythm claimed him and drove him on relentlessly.

Laura's hands clutched at his shoulders and forearms. He felt her short fingernails digging into his flesh. He leaned over her, bending his head to claim first one rigid nipple and then the other. His tongue rolled across the tender flesh, drawing it deeply into his mouth. He suckled her, working her flesh with his lips and tongue until she writhed and twisted beneath him.

Her hands moved to his chest. He felt her fingertips brush across his flat nipples, and a bolt of lightning shot through him. He redoubled his efforts at her breasts, lavishing his attentions on them, each in turn.

"Please, Jeff," she whispered. "It feels too good." She shook her head against the sheets, her hair spread out and around her shoulders. "I can't do this again. It's too soon."

"Again," he muttered thickly. And again, he thought, lost in the sensations she brought him. Caught in the web of her scent, her taste.

Despite her protests, her hips rose and fell in tandem with his. He felt the change in her as another tearing climax approached. Her breathing sped up and she drew one ragged breath after another. She raked her fingernails down his chest, around his waist and then up his back.

He lifted his head and drove himself into her, pushing them both higher, faster than they had gone before.

Jeff looked down into her face and watched her features tighten as she strained to reach the goal that came closer with each of his powerful thrusts.

Her legs came up and wrapped around his hips. She pulled him deeper, closer. Her back arched, she tipped her head back into the mattress and cried out brokenly. He set his hands at either side of her head and bent over her, claiming her mouth as the pleasure took her, rocked her.

As her trembling eased, his own release rushed through

him. He parted her lips with his tongue and took her breath for his as he shuddered in her arms.

He rolled to one side, keeping one arm around her and drawing her close. She snuggled into his warmth, using the last of her strength to lay one arm across his chest so she could feel the steady, thunderous beat of his heart.

Laura's own heartbeat slowed, and the wild sizzle in her veins gradually dimmed to a low hum of satisfaction. She drew a deep breath and let it shudder out of her lungs. If she had had to run for her life at the moment, she would be in big trouble. Every muscle in her body was limp. Even her bones felt as if they had turned to mush.

Jeff's fingertips dusted across her back. Laura smiled sadly, regretfully. His gentle touch twisted a silken cord of tenderness around her heart. She didn't want to acknowledge it. Couldn't bring herself to admit to any feelings beyond contentment. To do that would be to invite disaster.

Her chest tightened with an overwhelming emotion she refused to name, even to herself.

A film of tears blurred her vision suddenly, and she closed her eyes against a pain she knew would eventually assert itself. Nestling her head into the hollow of his shoulder, Laura closed her mind, shutting off the thoughts that threatened to ruin this one beautiful moment.

For now, she only wanted to rest in his arms and listen to the heartbeat of the man who had become too important to her.

A soft sound of distress woke him from a sound sleep. Jeff stared at the ceiling for a long moment, trying to figure out just what he'd heard.

Laura sighed and moved in closer to him. Her head on his chest, her warm breath brushed across his skin like a whisper. He smiled into the darkness and pressed the memory of this moment deeply into his brain. The silky texture of her skin. The warmth of her body curved into his. The sensual drape of her unbound hair spilling across his arm.

He committed all of those senses to memory. Fifty years from now, he wanted to be holding her just like this and be able to reach back in time and relive their beginning.

He stopped, stunned at the thought. His smile faded as he tried to shy away from it, but it was too late. It was as if his subconscious had already accepted the fact that he and Laura would be together forever.

Before he could wrestle with his own feelings, the sound that had awakened him came again. A thin, mewling cry that tugged at his heart.

Miranda.

He looked down at the sleeping woman in his arms and smiled to himself. He wouldn't wake her. No reason for both of them to have their dreams interrupted. Carefully, Jeff slipped from under Laura's outflung arm and eased off the mattress. Pausing long enough to grab his robe from a nearby chair and tug it on, he started for the open doorway.

Darkness didn't slow his steps. He could find his way safely through the apartment even if blindfolded. At the door of his room, though, he paused for a brief glance at Laura.

Even the deep shadows couldn't keep him from seeing her. Her form neatly outlined against the plain white sheets, she slid her arm across the mattress as if searching for him in her sleep.

How perfect she looked in his bed.

How good she felt in his life.

Vaguely, he wondered how he had lived as long as he had without her. And how he would ever survive when she left him at the end of the summer.

Jeff brushed one hand across the top of his head, then scowling, tugged the belt of his robe tighter around his waist. A moment later, he turned his back on Laura and headed off to the other bedroom.

Slivers of moonlight pierced the darkness, pointing the way to the crib, where Miranda lay fretting, her blankets twisted around her legs. Jeff stared down at her for a long minute. She rubbed her eyes with two little fists and squirmed uncomfortably, her tiny mouth forming a pout in her sleep.

Jeff reached across the crib rail and gently released her from her cocoon. Immediately, Miranda flipped onto her side, dragged the stuffed bunny close and drifted back into her dreams.

In the hush of darkness, the baby's deep, even breathing measured the passing seconds. Leaning his forearms on the rail, he stared down at the child who had changed his life in so many ways.

Shaking his head softly, he realized just how small, innocent...defenseless she really was.

Something tightened in his chest, threatening to strangle his heart. There were so many things in the world for her to explore, discover. Joy. Pain. Love.

He reached into the crib again and gently ran his fingers along her cheek. Her mouth worked frantically, as if she were sucking on a bottle filled with her favorite drink.

That silly pink bunny stared up at him through wide, green-yarn eyes. Another change wrought by Miranda. Who would have guessed that Agnes Butler had such a soft spot for babies?

He shook his head slowly. "Why should that surprise me, though?" he asked in a whisper. "Look what you managed to do to me."

Miranda slept on, unaware of the man talking to her.

"I never wanted kids, you know," he confessed. "But you probably guessed that early on." He pulled her blanket a bit higher up on her shoulders. "Didn't seem to stop you any, though. You kept right on, looking cute and smiling at me. Expecting me to fall into line." He chuckled gently. "Just like a woman. Sneak under a man's defenses. Change his life until he can't remember what the world was like without you and then reel him in."

His smile slowly disappeared as he sunk down to kneel on one knee beside her crib. At eye level with her, he stared at Miranda, captivated by the sweep of eyelashes across her cheeks and by the tiny mouth, still working in her sleep.

Love blossomed in his chest, swelling and growing to painful proportions. He was good and caught, he thought. He couldn't give her up. This tiny baby had become an integral part of his life. He couldn't imagine not being around to see her take her first steps. Hear her first word.

The realization that had been building within him for weeks reared up and demanded to be acknowledged.

There would be no neat adoption.

He wouldn't be calling child welfare, looking for a way out. Where Miranda was concerned, he thought with a smile, there was no way out.

He swallowed hard and began whispering again, forcing the words past a tight throat.

"I'm no prize, Miranda," Jeff said. "I don't know much about being a father. I'll probably make lots of mistakes, too." She should be warned about just what she was letting herself in for, he told himself. "But I promise you, I'll try." He reached through the bars of her crib and curved the palm of his hand gently around the back of her head.

Inhaling sharply, he blew it out in a rush and added, "I love you, Miranda." He smiled, feeling the relief at finally admitting to the emotion that had been plaguing him constantly. "Believe me, I'm just as surprised as you are. I didn't count on this happening. Heck, I would have bet money on it never happening to me."

He shrugged and chuckled quietly. "But if I've learned

anything since you first came to me, it's that life *does* change when you least expect it. You and Laura both taught me that," he said. "I can't even imagine my life without you two in it," he admitted, his voice tinged with the wonder he felt at that one simple fact.

The baby shifted, cooed something unintelligible and turned her face into his touch.

Jeff's breath caught. He felt the responsibility of her care settle on his shoulders, and amazement flooded him as he realized that it didn't feel at all like a burden. More like a blessing.

His vision blurred suddenly and he blinked to clear it. "I promise you, Miranda," he said softly, "I will do everything in my power to keep you and to make sure you're happy. I may not be much of a daddy yet, but you can work on me." He paused thoughtfully. "Daddy. Sounds kind of nice, doesn't it?"

One corner of his mouth lifted and a protective pride rose in his chest. "But there is one thing you should know right off, for when you get older," he said sternly. "There'll be no boys hanging around the house. Since no one will ever be good enough for you anyway, I don't want a bunch of teenage Don Juan's coming after my baby."

She sniffed, rubbed her tiny nose and made a grab for her bunny again.

Slowly, Jeff stood up and stared down at her. "My baby," he repeated, liking the sound of it. "My little girl."

Laura swiped at the tears coursing down her cheeks.

Standing in the shadowed darkness of the living room, wearing only one of Jeff's camouflage uniform shirts, she kept to the side of the doorway where she could hear him and not risk being seen. Quickly, she glanced into the room and saw him leaning over the crib as he made heartfelt promises to a baby he had grown to love.

Laura straightened up again and struggled to control the rising tide of tenderness washing over her. His words had reached into her heart and opened up all the dark corners she had lived with for too long.

She ached to go to him, lay her head on his chest and feel his arms close around her. At that moment, there was nothing she wanted more than to experience the warm safety she found in the circle of his embrace.

But Laura didn't move. Not only because she didn't want him to know she had again eavesdropped on him as he spoke to Miranda. But also because of something he had said about her.

He couldn't imagine his life without her.

Did that mean he loved her, too?

A sense of panic shot through her bloodstream, obliterating the tender feelings and the overpowering longing she felt for him.

She ran her palms up and down her arms, feeling the rough fabric of his shirt scrape against her skin. His scent clung to the material, teasing her with every breath she took.

A sudden chill crept along her flesh.

This couldn't work. Her own fears would defeat her. Whatever it was that lay between them was destined to fail. She'd known that all along. Ever since the first time she'd kissed him.

Another tear trickled from the corner of her eye, and she quickly brushed it away.

She couldn't stay much longer, she told herself. She couldn't be around him as he made plans for his and Miranda's future. A future Laura could have no part in.

Briefly, her mind drew up an image of the long, lonely years stretching out ahead of her. She pictured the faceless woman who would replace her in Miranda's life. Would that same stranger take her place with Jeff, as well?

Would he and Miranda forget all about her once she was gone?

A sharp stab of regret pierced her heart at the thought.

But there was nothing she could do about it. Nothing at all, beyond enjoying whatever time she had left with the two people she'd come to care for so deeply.

Pulling in a series of deep, ragged breaths, she scuttled back to his bedroom and crawled onto the mattress. Laura reluctantly took off his shirt, tossed it to the floor and lay down, drawing the sheet up over her.

If she was very lucky, by the time he came back to bed, she would be asleep.

Ten

Born under a lucky star she wasn't.

Laura could have feigned sleep, but the truth was, she didn't want to. What she wanted was to feel Jeff's arms slide around her, listen to his heartbeat and content herself with the moment.

He settled himself against the pillows, and when she moved up close to him, he wrapped one arm around her and held her tightly to his side.

"Everything all right?" she whispered, despite knowing that all was well.

"Yeah," he said, his tone as hushed as hers. "She's asleep again."

"Good."

"I'm going to keep her, Laura. Raise her as my own."

Despite the situation, she smiled and kissed his chest. "I knew you would."

He chuckled, and she felt the rumbling sound beneath her cheek.

"Then you knew more than I did," he said.

"You should always bear that in mind," Laura countered, striving desperately for a light, teasing note.

"Laura—" he tightened his hold on her as if expecting her to dart away from him "—there's something else. Something I want to talk to you about."

Panic opened up inside her. The darkness seemed to creep closer, threatening to swallow her. She couldn't let him talk. The serious tone of his voice warned her that whatever it was he wanted to say…she couldn't allow herself to hear it.

She lifted her head and looked up at him. His gaze, soft and warm, was locked on her. "Not tonight," she whispered, and she heard the plea in her voice. "No more talking tonight."

"But…" He lifted one hand and smoothed her hair back from her face.

"Please," she whispered, turning into his touch and dropping a quick kiss in the center of his palm. Sliding up over him, Laura bent her head to kiss him, giving him everything she could.

Everything she dared risk.

Jeff rolled over, flipping her onto her back. His hands glided over her skin as he traced her curves with questing fingers. The magic that lay between them burst into glorious life, splintering the darkness with brilliant shards of color and light.

Staring down into her liquid brown eyes, he at last realized the depth of the love he felt for her. It both terrified and amazed him.

He wasn't sure when it had happened, not that it made a difference. All that mattered was that he had actually been granted something that he had long since decided would never be his.

Passion, desire, love, swept through his bloodstream, carrying him to a place just short of madness. He wanted to say the words out loud and savor the taste of them. And he wanted to make her admit to loving him, too. He knew she did. He felt it every time she touched him. He heard it in her voice and sensed it in her caresses.

But as he continued to look into those incredible eyes of hers, he reluctantly accepted the fact that she clearly wasn't ready. Hadn't she hidden from him for days after the first time they'd made love? For what reason if not to hide from the depth of her emotions?

He would have to wait. Wait until she was as sure of this new love as he was.

Disappointment was relieved by the knowledge that he had until the end of summer to convince her.

He wouldn't lose her.

Not now. Not after finally realizing what he had found with her.

Laura lifted one hand and pulled his head down to hers. Thoughts and plans for the future dissolved as he gave himself over to the present and the joy of loving her.

In an effort to keep her sanity and quiet her mind, the next morning, Laura went shopping. She had Miranda dressed, in her stroller and out the front door early enough to be on the spot when the stores opened.

It wasn't that she needed or even *wanted* anything in particular. But she knew she couldn't sit in that apartment all day with nothing but an infant and her own thoughts for company.

She needed open spaces. She needed to feel the wind in her face. She needed to walk off some of the nervous energy that had been pumping through her body since the night before.

Since she had overheard Jeff's plans for the future and realized that she couldn't be a part of them.

Instantly, she recalled the determined look on his face when he had come back to bed. Every instinct she possessed had screamed at her that he was about to make a proposal. A proposal she would have had to reject. She couldn't risk love again. The pain of loss cut too deep. Thankfully, she had managed to keep him from saying the words that would have ended their time together. For now.

Her fingers curled around the stroller handle, squeezing it tightly. Laura wasn't sure just how much longer she could bear to stay, pretending to be a member of this little family. She would never be able to last out the summer though; that much she was sure of.

The sleepy coastal town was small, with more touristy stores than general merchandise, but Laura hardly noticed. She and Miranda browsed through craft stores, card shops and in a baby boutique, Laura purchased a sweet romper and sun bonnet for Miranda. Afterward, they stopped at a coffee house for a well-deserved break of formula and lattes.

Finally, window shopping on their way back to the apartment, Laura stopped dead in front of a small ladies' clothing store.

Sunshine sparkled on the clean glass and danced across the scrolled letters spelling out Francine's Finery. But Laura wasn't admiring the well-clothed mannequin in the window or trying to see past the glare into the shop.

Instead, her attention was caught by her own reflection. She tightened her grip on the stroller handle reflexively as she studied the woman she had become.

Somehow, she'd never actually paid much attention before now. The woman in the glass looked at least ten years older than thirty. Hair in an untidy ponytail, figure hidden beneath a baggy yellow tunic top and a calf-length full skirt that ballooned around her in the breeze. Even her shoes looked matronly. Sensible loafers, no stockings.

Lifting her gaze back up to meet her reflected eyes, she stared at a woman who suddenly seemed like a stranger.

"What have you done to yourself?" she whispered, and lifted one hand to smooth back a wild strand of hair, plucked free by the wind.

She used to be cute.

Okay, maybe not cute. But *interesting* looking, certainly. What had happened? Even as her mind posed the question though, she knew the answer.

Bill's death had happened.

Laura lifted one hand from the stroller and plucked at her too large shirt. Teeth worrying her bottom lip, she admitted that right after Bill's accident, she had gone into hiding. Oh, she hadn't locked herself away in a tower somewhere. It might have been healthier if she had. At least then she would have been forced to go out once in a while, if only for food.

But no. She'd built a tower around herself. She'd hidden away behind baggy clothes and messy hair. Hiding from the pain of loving and then losing someone, she had also been hiding from the world. She had thought that by dressing like a ragpicker and avoiding makeup and a decent hairstyle, she would be able to keep any man from becoming interested. She hadn't wanted to risk feeling again. Loving again.

"The joke's on you," she told the woman in the glass. "It didn't work."

Jeff had seen through the frumpy exterior she offered the world, to the woman she really was. Somehow, he had touched her soul despite the safeguards she had erected so carefully.

Now the sad clothing she wore didn't represent anything but bad taste.

Although she couldn't allow herself to be in love again,

there was no longer any reason to hide behind ill-fitting clothes.

"Well," she said thoughtfully, with a glance at the baby in the stroller, "since frumpery didn't help anyway, why don't we go inside and see if we can find something that suits me better?"

Miranda kicked her feet and squirmed excitedly.

"You're right," Laura said, determinedly steering the stroller toward the front door. "I believe it's time for the real me to rejoin the world. A little bit at a time."

He stepped into the apartment and paused to take a deep, appreciative whiff of the delicious aromas drifting out of the kitchen.

Man, how things changed. Only a few weeks ago, he would have been coming home to an empty apartment, a microwavable dinner and maybe a rented movie.

Domestic bliss. Who knew it would feel so good?

From the kitchen came Miranda's garbled attempts at talking and the distinct sound of Laura, singing.

Grinning, he tossed his hat onto the table and started across the room. In the entryway, he stopped dead.

"Hi," Laura said. "I didn't hear you come in."

Stunned, Jeff's gaze swept over her from head to toe and back again. The transformation started with her hair. She'd had it trimmed, and now it lay neatly just above her shoulders in a soft wave that tempted him even from across the room to run his fingers through it. But she hadn't stopped with her hairdo.

She wore a pale peach tank top, its thin, delicate fabric caressing and outlining the swell of her breasts. The hem of that shirt came to an abrupt end just above her waist, giving him a tantalizing glimpse of skin. Pastel yellow shorts clung to her hips and thighs, with the determined grip of a lover's hands, displaying every curve with detailed precision.

Shaking his head, Jeff rubbed his suddenly dry mouth and muttered a fervent "Wow."

Laura's smile warmed him. "Thanks," she said.

"What's the occasion for the shopping trip?" he asked, wondering why all of a sudden she had come out from under wraps, so to speak.

"No occasion," she told him, and tore the lettuce into salad-size bites. "I just decided it was time."

"I approve," he said, in a gross understatement.

"Good," she told him. "Now, you're just in time to set the table."

Smiling, he bent down, kissed the top of Miranda's head, then walked to the cabinet where the plates were kept.

He hadn't been able to take his eyes off of her all through dinner. Hell, Jeff thought, if someone asked him what he had just eaten, he couldn't have said. For all he'd tasted of it, it might as well have been sawdust.

From the moment he'd seen her in those new clothes, he'd felt hope shimmering through him. There had to be a reason for her abrupt shift from frump to fashion plate. He couldn't help thinking that maybe it wasn't just a new wardrobe she was in the market for. But a new life, as well.

A life with him.

"Do you smell something?" Laura asked suddenly, wrinkling her nose.

"What?" It took him a moment to come back from his daydreams. He sniffed the air and frowned. Definitely something burning. Glancing behind her, he asked, "Did you leave a burner on accidentally?"

"No," she said, but dutifully got up, walked to the stove and checked anyway. She shook her head as she looked at him.

He pushed up from his chair and walked quickly around the apartment. Odd. The smell seemed to get stronger the closer he moved to the front door. That couldn't be right.

Then he heard it.

A shriek of sound, muffled but distinct. Almost like a— Realization dawned with the impact of a bullet.

Reacting instantly, he shouted, ''Smoke alarm downstairs. There's a fire.'' He reached the kitchen in a few short strides and snatched Miranda from her high chair. The baby yelped at such abrupt treatment, but he couldn't take the time to reassure her.

Old but not forgotten feelings surged in his bloodstream. A strange mixture of terror and calm, panic and logic asserted itself in his brain. As if he were on a battlefield again, he took charge, already planning the best way for his troops—now his family—to survive.

His gaze shot to Laura. He saw her cheeks pale and watched her brown eyes widen in alarm. Immediately, he snapped, ''Don't panic.'' He waited for her gaze to clear as she looked at him. Only then did he continue. ''We probably have lots of time. Let's just get outside. *Now*.''

She jerked him a stiff nod, then turned, not for the front door, but for her bedroom.

''Where the hell are you going?'' he demanded.

''To get Miranda's jacket.''

''Forget the damn jacket,'' he told her, taking the few steps that separated her from him. Grabbing hold of her arm, he started dragging her toward the only exit. ''Get out of the building—that's all that's important.''

Clutching Miranda to his chest, despite her struggles to get free, Jeff stopped at the door and took the time to touch his palm to the wooden panel. Cool. He breathed an inward sigh of relief. At least he knew there wasn't a wall of fire in the hallway, waiting to engulf them.

He twisted the knob, poked his head out the opening to

check the situation, then stepped into the hall. "Come on," he said to Laura.

She moved out to stand beside him and reached for the baby.

"I'll carry her," he said, his tone brooking no arguments. "You stay behind me. Take hold of my belt and don't let go." No matter what else happened, he didn't want to take the chance of losing her. If she was holding on to him, he would know where she was at all times.

They passed Agnes Butler's door, and he stopped long enough to pound on it. "Agnes!" he shouted, then paused to listen for an answer. When none came, he told himself she was already outside. He couldn't wait. His instincts told him to get his Laura and Miranda to safety quickly.

The door of the only other apartment on the top floor stood open. Apparently, that tenant hadn't even bothered to close his door on the way out.

Jeff kept going along the carpeted runner. Strange, he didn't remember the hall being this long before. It seemed to be taking forever to reach the stairs.

His gaze narrowed sharply. At the end of the hall, just past the elevator, a tentacle of smoke reached the head of the stairs.

His chest tightened. His mouth went dry.

The ribbon of gray mist curled and twisted on the ceiling before sidling farther down the hall, toward them. The shrill bleat of the smoke alarm was louder now and sounded like the screams of the damned.

Ignoring the whisper of fear rattling around in his head, Jeff hurried his steps, forcing himself to lead his family into the smoke. There was no other way. They couldn't take the elevator. They had to use the stairs.

"Jeff," Laura said tightly, "the baby. She'll choke."

The smoke was at eye level now and falling with every

passing second. Soon none of them would be able to draw a breath without gasping.

"She'll be all right," he answered, then he shifted Miranda so that her small face was turned into his chest. He cupped the back of her head, holding her in place. She'd still be able to breathe, but hopefully she wouldn't take in much smoke. "Stay down," he said. "Keep low." They hunched their shoulders, trying to keep their faces below the dropping gray curtain. "Okay," he told her. "Let's go."

They plunged down the stairs, their bodies slicing through the wisps of smoke, tearing it into strips that writhed around them like ghostly ropes, trying to hold them back. Keep them inside.

The front door stood open, and Jeff made right for it.

On the lawn, people from all over the street were gathered. A surfer and a middle-aged businessman type had garden hoses in their hands, the streams of water aimed through the windows of one of the three apartments on the ground floor.

Down the four short steps to the grass, and still he didn't stop. Not until he had Laura and Miranda a safe distance from the fire that had threatened everything he held dear.

Under the heavy limbs of a gnarled maple tree, he released Miranda from his stranglehold and laughed when she made a face and howled her displeasure. She sounded wonderful. In the next instant, he half turned, pulling Laura into the circle of his arms, while still juggling an infuriated infant.

"All right?" he asked, dipping his head to plant a kiss on Laura's forehead.

"Yeah," she answered, tipping her face up to his, showing him a small, frightened smile.

She was breathing heavily, and her eyes still looked a little glassy, but otherwise, she was fine. Jeff sent a quick, heartfelt prayer of gratitude heavenward, then shifted his gaze to look over the group of people.

Absently, he noted the sound of sirens as emergency vehicles raced their way.

Jeff frowned and swept the faces of the crowd again, looking for and not finding one particular person.

"Agnes," he muttered. A sinking sensation flared up in the pit of his stomach and slowly unfurled fingers of dread.

"What? What about her?" Laura asked, turning her head to stare at the building behind them.

"She's not here," he said, his voice scraping against his throat. He handed the baby to Laura and started walking toward the apartment house. "She didn't get out."

"Are you sure?" Laura asked, following in his footsteps.

"No," he turned his head this way and that, checking out the faces surrounding him. No, he wasn't sure. She might have gone to a neighbor's, but the neighbors were all here, watching the commotion. "I don't see her anywhere."

Laura's hands gripped the baby tightly. "Oh God, Jeff..."

He had to check. He had to make sure the older woman had made it to safety. Just the thought of Agnes Butler trying to maneuver her way through a burning building alone was enough to get him moving.

"Stay here," he ordered in a tone that had been known to make privates and corporals leap for cover. He paused long enough to stroke her cheek, then he was running. Running toward the open doorway where smoke billowed out into the evening.

Laura watched him disappear into the thick gray fog and kept her gaze locked on the last spot she'd seen him. She couldn't look away. She couldn't draw a breath.

Lord. Standing beside her one minute, he'd been gone

in the next. Maybe forever. What if he was overcome by the smoke? What if the fire spread despite the neighbors' efforts? What if the fire department got here too late?

So many risks. So many dangers.

Her heart pounding, she told herself that he was a trained soldier. He would be all right. Her blood chilled. A career Marine. A man schooled in war and battle. A man who could be sent off to fight in some far-off place at any time.

Danger and risk were a part of his life. Death was never too far from a man whose job it was to fight his country's enemies.

Tremors rocked her. How had she allowed herself to become even remotely involved with Jeff? Why hadn't she ever once stopped to think about his being a Marine? A warrior?

Oh God, oh God, oh God… The phrase kept repeating in her brain, over and over like some ancient chant designed to ward off evil spirits. But she knew that frantic prayers and hastily offered deals to the Almighty didn't work. Nothing worked. Nothing could keep him safe if some odd twist of Fate decided that tonight was his night to die.

Oh, *please,* she thought, terrified. Not Jeff. Not now. Not yet. Not yet? her brain screeched. When, then? After they'd lived together and loved together and had more children? Would *then* be the time to lose him? Would the pain be less or more?

Tears stung her eyes. She told herself they were caused by the smoke, but she knew that one for a lie even as she thought it. Fear was the enemy here. Her fears. Her weaknesses. Her body trembled, and her grip on Miranda tightened in response.

She couldn't do this. Couldn't risk it.

Not again. Not ever again.

She didn't realize just how tightly she was holding on to Miranda until the baby squirmed against her uncomfortably. Immediately, Laura loosened her grasp a bit, trying at the same time to fight down her fears. The infant's cries continued to blast into the lavender twilight and seemed to intensify when the emergency trucks pulled up behind them.

In seconds, firemen were streaming across the lawn. Pushing the crowd back to safety, they unreeled their water hoses and took over the task of quelling the fire.

A man, a paramedic she thought, came up to her, wanting to check her and the baby over, but Laura only shook her head. They were fine, she knew. Maybe later, she would let the man examine Miranda, but not now. For now, she had to concentrate her focus and her prayers on that front door.

Jeff, she thought frantically, what's taking him so long? Why wasn't he out yet? Why wasn't he there, beside her?

Old fears rose up and threatened to choke her. Her throat closed up tight, and she had to struggle to breathe. Not again, she prayed. Please don't let the man she loved die. Not again.

She groaned, an aching rumble of fear and pain that came from deep in her soul. She wasn't merely *involved* with the man. It was far worse than that. Dear God, she loved him. Despite her efforts. Despite everything, she loved him. More deeply, more completely than she had ever loved before.

Tears pooled in her eyes as she acknowledged that her feelings for Bill couldn't compare to the depth of the emotions she felt for Jeff.

She doubted anything could.

Swiping one hand across her eyes, she jiggled Miranda on one hip and squinted into the smoky haze filling the entryway of the apartment building. As if she could *will* him to safety, she concentrated on the image of his face and tried to silence the terror building inside her. But it wouldn't be denied its chance to torment her.

Where was he?

Why hadn't he come out yet?

Fear rippled along her spine. Dread echoed in her brain as one word repeated itself over and over. Gone, gone, gone.

Laura choked back a sob. No. She couldn't go through this again, she told herself.

She would never survive the pain.

Laura dragged a deep gulp of air into her lungs and reminded herself that this was why she had hidden for so long. This was why she had decided not to love again. *This* was the agony she'd thought and hoped and prayed to avoid.

To no avail.

Desperate tears stung her eyes as endless seconds ticked by.

Then he was there.

Agnes Butler clutched firmly to his chest. Jeff, his face sooty, stepped through the now thinning haze.

His gaze found hers instantly.

And Laura lived again.

Eleven

It wasn't much of a fire really, more smoke than flame. Someone had allowed the water in a pan to boil away and by the time they'd caught it, their kitchen was filled with smoke, driving them outside.

The quick-thinking neighbors with their garden hoses had pretty much saved the day. A few hours later, the fire department allowed the tenants back into the building.

Adrenaline still pumping through his blood, Jeff stood at the window in the living room while Laura put the baby to bed. He stared out at the neon and what stars he could make out in spite of the reflected lights of the town and tried to calm himself.

Everyone was fine. Nothing tragic had happened. Although, he thought with a brief smile, Agnes Butler might never be the same. She'd been wearing earphones to listen to her stereo and hadn't heard the smoke alarms go off. Jeff still wasn't sure how she had finally heard him pounding on her door, but he'd never forget the look on her face when he'd told her there was a fire in the building.

She'd even submitted to being carried out because, though it had hurt her pride to admit it, she was too slow to make good time.

Idly, he reached up and touched the cheek she had deigned to kiss once he'd carried her to safety. Of course, he realized that her newfound fondness for him probably wouldn't last long.

Inhaling sharply, he set his hands on either side of the window frame and leaned in, resting his forehead on the cool glass pane.

He shouldn't be as churned up inside as he was. Why wasn't he calming down now that the threat to his family was over? Abruptly, he shoved away from the window and started pacing. His footsteps echoed through the room like a thundering heartbeat.

Was the threat gone, though? he wondered. Pushing both hands across the sides of his head, he shot a quick glance at Laura's closed bedroom door. Inside that room were the two most important people in the world to him. And he could have lost them both tonight.

Hell, what was driving him insane was that he could *still* lose Laura. He'd seen the look on her face and recognized it. Shell shock. The same expression he'd seen carved into the features of people who had watched their homes and lives destroyed by war.

People who had given up on life.

The bedroom door opened quietly, and he snapped his head around. She stood framed in the doorway. Dim light from the corner lamp fell on her, dusting her in a pale ivory glow. His chest tightened as his gaze locked on her shadow-filled brown eyes.

He had the distinct feeling that she was drawing away from him even as they stood there, staring at each other.

Laura had heard him before she'd opened the door. His footsteps quick, almost angry, he'd been pacing the apartment floor like a caged tiger.

If there had been a way to avoid him, she would have. Cowardly or not.

She let her gaze slide from his. Her emotions were still too close to the surface. She didn't want him to be able to see the conflict raging inside her.

"Miranda all right?" he asked, his voice a low growl.

"Yes. She's asleep." Keep the sentences short, she told herself. Don't invite a conversation.

"Good," he said. "Because we have to talk."

"Not now," Laura told him, and rubbed her hands up and down her arms, hoping for some warmth to dispel the chill that seemed to have settled in her bones.

"You can't put this off," he said, starting toward her.

Laura quickly sidestepped, moving for the kitchen. Keep busy, she thought. Make coffee. Do the dishes. *Anything.* "Hasn't there been enough activity for one night?" she asked quietly from over her shoulder.

"No," he said, then paused. "Damn it, Laura," he continued, following her into the tiny kitchen. "Stand still and listen to me."

She shook her head, refusing to turn around and face him. Looking into his eyes would only make this so much harder.

He wouldn't be put off, though. He stepped up behind her, grabbed her arms and turned her around. Her back pressed to the edge of the counter, she met his blue eyes and saw a flash of emotion that shot a tremor of warning down her spine.

"Laura," he spoke more softly now, his gaze moving over her features like a caress. "What happened tonight scared the hell out of me."   -

Her heart breaking, she said, "It scared all of us." She

would never forget the image of Jeff racing into danger. She *couldn't* forget the mind-numbing minutes she'd spent waiting to see if he'd survived.

"I know you were scared, too." His hands gentled on her arms, and his thumbs moved over the fabric of her nightshirt. "But the fear made me think, too."

"Jeff, don't," she pleaded, even knowing that it was too late. Love shone in his eyes. Determination etched into his features, and she realized there was no way to escape hearing the declaration she knew was coming.

Logically, Laura knew she was being foolish. She should be happy that such a man loved her. But happiness was an ephemeral emotion. And despair stretched on forever.

"I have to say this," he told her. "Tonight made me realize that what we have together is too fragile to be taken for granted." Abruptly, he let her go, took a half step away from her, then stopped and ran one hand across the back of his neck. His voice dropped as if he were speaking to himself, not her, as he continued. "I figured I'd have all summer to convince you."

No, he wouldn't have, she thought sadly, forcing herself to keep from reaching for him. She never could have stayed the whole summer. But he didn't know that.

"Now I know that I can't take the chance of waiting." He shrugged helplessly. "For all I know, I could step into the street tomorrow and get run down by a truck."

Her breath caught. Memories of a long-ago car accident that had shattered her world rose up, and she relentlessly battled them down again.

He came back to her, cupping her face in his hands, his fingers spearing into her hair at her temples. "I don't want to wait another day to tell you that I love you."

Her eyes filled with tears, and she blinked them back. What she wouldn't have given in that moment to be able to tell him that she loved him, too. Three small words. How could they both warm her and terrify her?

"I know you don't want to hear this," he said in a rush, apparently sensing her turmoil. "But, Laura, life's too fragile to not say the things that are important to us."

Panic burned in the pit of her stomach. She knew very well just how fragile life was. Fragile enough that to care about anyone as much as she did him was to leave yourself open to disaster and unbearable pain. She couldn't do that. She couldn't risk everything only to have Fate snatch it away from her again.

"I want you to marry me," he blurted, then stopped and smiled at her. "Man, there's something I never figured to say."

Her eyes widened. Suddenly frightened, she worried that just by his speaking the words out loud, he'd thrown a challenge at the feet of the gods of happiness.

"Don't say anything more," she whispered, and reached up to lay her fingertips across his mouth to silence him, though it was already too late.

He kissed her fingers, then spoke anyway, refusing to be hushed. Her hand dropped to her side.

"I'm going to say it, and you have to listen. I realized tonight that I couldn't take the chance of losing you, Laura." His voice dropped, husky with emotion. "You're to important to me. I can't even imagine living without you." He sucked in a gulp of air. "I thought I could wait. Give you time. But I can't. I need a commitment between us, Laura. I need to be married to you."

She gathered up her remaining strength and said, "Being married isn't a guarantee, Jeff."

He gave her a half smile. "I didn't say I needed guarantees. I just need you."

She needed guarantees. She needed someone to tell her that this time it would be all right. This time, the man she loved would live forever. But since she couldn't have that promise, she wouldn't risk loss again.

She started to speak, but he cut her off.

"Don't answer yet," he said quickly, his gaze boring into hers. "Think about it. Think about us. Miranda." He slid one hand down to cover her flat belly. "You may be pregnant, Laura. Think about that, too."

His eyes closed and he leaned toward her, pressing his brow to hers. "I *love* you, Laura," he whispered. "And I know you love me and Miranda. Neither of us planned for this to happen. But didn't you tell me once about life shattering your plans and how you had to adapt? Accept?"

She nodded stiffly and remembered the eight long, lonely years she'd hidden her heart and soul from the world.

His arms closed around her, pulling her flush against him. "We could be happy together, Laura, the three of us." He kissed the top of her head. "Hell, maybe the *four* of us. But I think you already know that."

Yes, they could be happy. If only the risk weren't so great. As for the chance of her being pregnant, she wouldn't worry about that yet. She still had another week before they would know. Time enough then.

Although, she thought, the idea of Jeff's baby growing inside her was somehow a comforting one.

"Love me, Laura," he said, bending his head to give her a kiss. "And let me love you."

She leaned into him. The instantaneous flash of heat between them warmed her to her soul. Tonight, she thought, giving herself over to the incredible sensations he created in her. They could have this one last night together. They deserved at least that much, didn't they?

She reached up, wrapped her arms around his neck, and when he lifted her into his arms, she sighed into his mouth. Quickly, he carried her to his bedroom, and in seconds, their clothes were scattered across the rug and they lay entwined in each other's embrace.

His hands seemed to be everywhere at once. Stroking, caressing, his palms moved over her familiarly, rediscovering her body as if for the first time.

Laura arched into him as his mouth closed over her breast. She felt every flick of his tongue as an arrow piercing the coldness wrapped around her heart. He suckled her, and she felt him draw the last of the loneliness from her. Her hands cupped around the back of his head, she held him in place, silently demanding more of him.

He gave. Lavishly, he adored her breasts, one after the other, while his hands moved expertly over her flesh, stoking the kindling in her blood to a raging blaze.

When he moved to slide along the length of her body, Laura moaned softly. His lips and tongue forged a trail across her skin. New patches of desire rippled to the surface as he slowly, deliberately drove her.

Each kiss was a promise. Each caress a blessing.

At last, he moved to take a position between her thighs.

Hungering for the feel of him inside her, Laura lifted her arms to hold him, but he made no move to lie atop her. Instead, he slid his hands under her bottom and lifted her hips from the bed.

"Jeff," she whispered, "what are you doing?"

His eyes glazed with passion, he met her gaze squarely. "Loving you," he answered, and lowered his head.

She gasped aloud when his mouth came down on her center. Her fingers curled into the sheet beneath her, searching for purchase in a suddenly spiraling world.

His tongue swirled over and around a tiny piece of sensitized flesh. She jerked in his grasp and couldn't quite contain the groan of pleasure that ripped from her throat.

He lifted his head and smiled at her. Moving his hands

from her behind, he shifted first one of her legs, then the other, to his shoulders.

She looked at him, caught by the gleam in his eyes. Mesmerized, she continued to stare at him as he slowly, teasingly, covered her with his mouth again. Laura's eyes closed briefly, then flew open again.

Helplessly suspended in air, Laura could do nothing but feel. She watched him take her. Erotic sensations sizzled through her body as he gave her most intimate flesh long, luxurious strokes with his tongue.

Her hips lifted, her heels digging into his back. She swayed unsteadily as his mouth took her to heights she had never dreamed of before.

Then he slipped one finger inside her, and the last of Laura's composure splintered. Too many sensations at once clamored through her brain, demanding to be recognized. Her breath came in short, ragged gasps as her hips lifted into his touch again and again.

The world around her rocked as the first tremors rippled through her. His lips and tongue worked faster now, urging her on. Her eyes slid closed as a final, overpowering surge of pleasure rocketed around inside her.

Jeff set her down gently on the mattress, reached into the nightstand drawer and pulled out the condom he needed so desperately. When he was ready, he pushed himself into her, relishing her soft moan of pleasure.

Fed by an almost frantic desire, he raced toward the completion waiting for him and, with one final thrust, joined her on the other side of passion.

Some time later, Laura stirred from her dreams and turned into Jeff's embrace. He muttered something in his sleep and tightened his grip on her.

Caught halfway between being asleep and being awake,

Laura sneaked a peek at the bedside clock—2:00 a.m. The night was almost gone, and they were wasting it in sleep.

She pressed a kiss onto his chest, then shifted her head until she could run her tongue across his flat nipple. He sighed heavily.

A sheen of tears blurred her vision, but she blinked them back determinedly. She wouldn't allow herself to cry. Not now, anyway. There would be plenty of time for tears later. In the months and years she faced without him.

Lifting her head, she looked down at him, memorizing each of his features, etching them into her heart. If things were different, she thought. If she were braver, if he had a less dangerous job, if there were guarantees...

No. No more *ifs*. She'd made her decision. It wasn't an easy one, and God knew she already had regrets. But there was really no other choice. She couldn't face a lifetime of worry. Fear.

She bent her head and kissed the corner of his mouth. His eyes opened to slits. He looked up at her and gave her a grin that would haunt her forever.

This had to be enough, Laura told herself. She would have tonight with Jeff.

Tomorrow, she would leave.

By midmorning the following day, the sky was overcast and dreary. Heavy gray clouds threatened rain but did nothing about it. The weather matched her mood perfectly.

The phone rang just as she was zipping her last suitcase.

Laura straightened up and stared at it. If it was Jeff calling, she didn't want to talk to him. She was afraid he would be able to tell by the tone of her voice that something was wrong. It would be better...easier if he didn't find out about her leaving until the deed was done.

On the other hand, if he decided to come home to find out why she wasn't answering the phone...

Instantly, Laura hurried to the table and snatched the receiver off the hook. "Hello?"

"Hi," Jeff said, his voice low and intimate. "What took you so long?"

"Uh—" she shot a glance at the baby in her stroller "—I was changing Miranda."

"Give her a kiss for me."

"I will," she said, her heart breaking.

"Give one to yourself, too."

Laura's grip on the phone tightened until she was afraid she'd snap the instrument right in half.

"Is everything all right?" he asked.

"Yeah," she answered after clearing her throat. "Everything's fine. Uh, I'm taking Miranda out for a couple of hours." She flinched at the lie. "So if you call, I won't be here."

"No problem," he said. But she heard an undertone of concern in his voice. "Have fun."

"We will," she said, eager now to hang up.

"Laura…"

She bit back a sigh. "Yes?"

"About last night…"

She didn't want to think about last night. She couldn't. Not when she was leaving him.

"Jeff," she told him brusquely, "I've got to go before Miranda starts getting cranky."

"Sure," he agreed quietly. "Go ahead. We can talk later."

"Later." She nodded to herself. Later she would be gone.

"I love you, Laura."

She winced, squeezing her eyes shut. On a sigh, she whispered, "I know."

Laura set the receiver back in its cradle and caressed it absently before turning away. She picked up her purse and the suitcase from the couch and paused to glance at the sealed envelope she'd left on the coffee table for Jeff. Then she pushed Miranda's stroller into the hall, where the rest of her bags were already waiting.

Agnes's door was open, the older woman standing on the threshold, watching her.

"I appreciate you taking care of the baby this afternoon, Agnes," Laura said.

She nodded her gray head and peered at Laura through those sharp blue eyes of hers. "I'll enjoy it," she replied. "Though I think you're makin' a big mistake."

"I can't stay," Laura answered, and closed Jeff's door firmly. Just she was closing the door on any future she might have had with him. "The new nanny will be here tomorrow." Her bottom lip trembled slightly at the thought of someone else caring for *her* baby, but she had no choice. "I spoke to the head of a very reputable agency a couple of hours ago. She assured me that their nannies are extremely well qualified and that Miranda would be in good hands."

"You're bein' a damn fool," Agnes said quietly.

Laura's gaze snapped to the other woman's.

"Oh, Jeff Ryan's no prize, but he's a good man." She wagged one gnarled finger at Laura. "You should be snappin' him up, not runnin' for cover."

"Agnes, it's just not that simple."

"Love is always simple," the other woman asserted with a slow shake of her head. "It's people who make it hard."

"Life makes it hard," Laura whispered.

"Runnin' doesn't make it any easier," Agnes said, a trace of compassion in her voice. "You'll find that you can't run far enough or fast enough to leave what you feel behind."

The older woman's words echoed in the hollow blackness that had become Laura's heart.

Agnes stepped up closer to her and gave her an awkward pat on the arm. "Why not stick around a bit longer?" she suggested. "Give it another day or so."

Every day she stayed only made it harder to leave. It was now or never.

"I have to go," Laura said. "My plane…"

"Hope you know what you're doin', girl."

"I do," she whispered. The only thing she *could* do.

"One of these days, y'know," Agnes added, "you're going to regret this. A lot."

Laura gave her a watery smile. "That's where you're wrong, Agnes," she said. "I already regret it."

Twelve

Jeff held the huge bouquet of flowers behind his back as he opened the front door. Foolish perhaps, but he wanted to catch the look of pleased surprise on Laura's features when he presented them to her.

"She's not there."

Frowning, he turned around to face Agnes Butler, standing in her open doorway. Sympathy shone in her eyes, and he tried to ignore it. "What? Where'd she go?"

"She's gone."

Amazing the effect that two simple words could have on a man's nervous system. His mouth dry, he managed to croak out a question. "Where?"

"Home, she said."

Home. Apparently *he* had been the only one to consider this place her home, as well as his.

"The baby?" he asked.

"Inside." She nodded toward her own apartment. "Sleeping."

He nodded stiffly. His fingers tightened around the cellophane-wrapped bouquet he still held. The rustling sound seemed to echo around him. Drawing the flowers from behind his back, he smirked down at them. *Surprise.*

"She said she left you a note," Agnes continued.

"A note." He nodded again, congratulating himself on the movement. After the night they'd shared. After his proposal of marriage. She'd left him a note and disappeared.

A hollow emptiness opened up inside him.

Damn it, he'd had a feeling something was wrong. When he'd talked to her earlier on the phone, he'd heard a tremor in her voice that had worried him. But he'd convinced himself that all was well. That they would talk everything out when he got home.

He'd never guessed that she would simply run away.

"Jeff? You all right?"

He glanced at the older woman. Strange that his old nemesis should now feel like his only friend. "I'll be right over to get the baby."

"No hurry," she said. "Take your time."

Jeff stepped into the apartment and closed the door behind him.

Nothingness greeted him. Not one interesting smell from the kitchen. No Miranda gurgling happily in her high chair. No Laura singing softly to herself.

The emptiness in his soul began to slowly fill with anger. How could she just leave, without a word?

Then he remembered. A note.

Grinding his teeth together, he let his gaze shoot around the room. He spotted it almost instantly. A plain white envelope, his name scrawled across it, lay on the coffee table.

A muscle in his jaw ticked. He tossed the bouquet down onto the sofa and grabbed the envelope. Quickly, he tore it open, pulled out the single sheet of paper inside and read it.

Dear Jeff,
The baby is with Agnes, and I've arranged for a new
nanny to start working for you tomorrow. I didn't want
it to be this way, Jeff, but I can't marry you. Please
understand and don't follow me. I'll always remember
you and Miranda.

Love, Laura.

"'Love, Laura'?" he asked aloud. "How the hell could
she sign a goodbye note 'Love, Laura'?"

And "Please understand"? Understand what? That she
had no guts?

Glancing down at the note in his hand, Jeff slowly, thoroughly crumpled it into a ball. "It's not that easy, Laura,"
he said, fury rising up like bile to choke him. "If you're
going to leave me, you're going to have to say it to my
face."

Still grumbling, he headed for the phone. Quickly, he
dialed Peggy's number. His sister would know where he
could find Laura.

On the fifth ring, she answered, clearly out of breath.

"Peggy, it's me," he said shortly.

"Thought I'd be hearing from you," she countered.

"Why?" he asked. "Have you talked to Laura?"

"Yeah. A couple of hours ago."

"She left me, Peg." Lord, those words hit him hard.

Peggy sighed heavily. "I know. I told her I thought it
was a mistake."

Jeff pushed one hand across the top of his head and
glanced at the crushed roses and daisies lying on his couch.
"Why is she doing this?"

"I guess she has her reasons," Peggy evaded nicely.

"Like what?" he demanded, anger pulsing in him.
"What could possibly be a good enough reason for her to
run away like some damn teenager?"

"Here's a thought," she snapped. "Why don't the two of you talk to each other and stop using me as an interpreter?"

He inhaled sharply. She was right. Any answers he got, he wanted directly from Laura. Damn it, he deserved that much.

"That's why I called you. I need her address."

"Good," Peggy said quickly. "I thought maybe you were going to let her go."

"Not a chance," he whispered, more as a promise to himself than to his sister.

"Got a pencil?" she asked.

He rummaged around for one, then said, "Shoot." After writing down the address, he tore the sheet of paper off the pad and stuffed it into his pocket. "Do you think you could watch Miranda for me while I talk to her?"

"I'd love it," she said, then louder, "Teddy! Put Whiskers down! Cats aren't supposed to fly!"

"I'll call before I come," he said, and then warned, "And while she's there, keep that kid away from my baby."

"Yeah, yeah. Gotta go," Peggy said, and hung up.

Jeff replaced the receiver and stared blankly into space. It would take him a few days to wrap up some outstanding projects on the base and then to arrange for leave. But by the end of the week, he'd be looking Laura square in the eye, daring her to deny she loved him.

Laura let herself into her apartment and was greeted by voices from the radio she'd left playing while she went to the grocery store. An old song from the sixties streamed into the painfully neat room. She'd unpacked and put all her suitcases away four days ago. Her weary gaze slid around the place she'd called home for eight years. Overstuffed furniture, rag rugs on highly polished wood floors and white lacy curtains fluttering in the breeze drifting under the partially opened windows.

The place used to give her such pleasure. She'd thought it cozy. Homey. Now it just seemed empty. And lonesome. What she wouldn't have given to spy a pacifier lying on the floor. Or that silly pink bunny.

Tears filmed her eyes, and she wiped them away with the back of her hand. She had already cried oceans of tears and found no release from the pain that hammered at her day and night.

She missed him. She missed him so badly it was a constant ache that throbbed in time with her broken heart. Her only consolation was that *this* pain was nothing compared to what she *might* have suffered if she had dared to stay and then lost him.

Slowly, she walked across the room to the kitchen. As she unpacked her grocery bag, she gulped back tears again. No formula. No diapers. Single-serving meals.

And tampons.

Laura's hand dropped to her belly. There was no child nestled there. The proof had arrived only that morning. She should have been relieved, she knew. But strangely enough, she wasn't. Now, not only was she going to have to live without Jeff, but she had also lost her only chance at a family. Children.

She was alone.

Jeff checked the paper in his hand, then marched down the long hallway to the door at the end. He stopped outside her apartment and stared at the closed door in front of him.

Four days without her, and it felt like a damn eternity. What made her think she could just pick up and walk away without a backward glance?

Anger pulsed through him. Damn it, she *loved* him. He knew it. He lifted one hand to knock, then paused, anxiety suddenly wiping away the fury he'd lived with for the past four days.

What would he do if she refused to come back with him?

Jeff's jaw tightened. He bit down on his teeth hard enough to crack them. And with worry still battling hurt and anger, he pounded on her door.

"Who is it?" she called.

He closed his eyes at the sound of her voice. Pain and hunger rose up inside him. It felt like centuries since he'd last seen her. Heard her. Held her.

Breathing deeply, he opened his eyes again and tried to mentally prepare for the fight of his life.

"Laura?" he said in his loudest, made-to-be-heard Marine Corps voice. "It's Jeff. Open this door."

There was a long pause, then she said, "Go away."

"I'm not going anywhere until I say what I came to say," he yelled. Absently, he heard a couple of doors down the hall open up. He glanced to one side quickly and noticed two or three people peeking out of their apartments. He ignored them. "Do you want me to shout it out for everyone to hear? Or are you going to open up?"

He waited what felt like forever, then he saw the doorknob turn. She opened the door and stepped onto the threshold as if her slight body could keep him out.

She looked miserable, and he felt a quick zap of hope blast through him. Purple half circles smudged the flesh beneath her eyes, and her face was pale, giving stark contrast to those shadows. The meadow green, sleeveless summer dress she wore made her skin look even creamier than he remembered.

Jeff's heart staggered painfully. His arms had ached to hold her, and now, suddenly, there she was. Instinctively, he grabbed her, pulled her tightly to him and took her mouth with his. The kiss was long, and hard and deep.

Vaguely, he heard her groan and thought he felt her hands slide up his arms before she let them fall to her sides again.

He tasted her tears and inhaled the soft, sweet scent of her, dragging it into his lungs like a drowning man coming up for air for the last time.

Finally, he broke the kiss and released her. She stumbled backward, lifting one hand to cover her kiss-bruised lips.

"You scared the hell out of me," he told her grimly. "Don't *ever* disappear like that again."

"I left you a note," she countered, but her voice sounded high and tight.

"Damn your note," he snapped. "And damn you for making me love you and then leaving."

She blanched, her skin going another shade paler. Nervously, she bent forward, saw the interested faces of their audience and straightened up again. Stepping back into the apartment, she said, "Come inside. Where it's private."

His blood boiling, Jeff marched past her and strode across the room like he was crossing a parade ground. When he reached the opposite wall, he turned around.

As she closed the door and faced him, she asked, "Where's the baby?"

"Do you care?" he nearly shouted.

"Of course I care," she said, and rubbed her eyes with the backs of her hands.

He took a deep breath and exhaled loudly. "She's with Peggy. I didn't want any interruptions to our 'talk.'"

She nodded stiffly and wrapped her arms around her waist as if for support.

"I would have been here sooner," he told her, "but I have responsibilities. I *can't* just take off anytime I feel like it."

She blinked, but had no defense.

He waited. One minute. Two. When it became obvious

that she wasn't going to start the ball rolling, Jeff growled out one word. "Why?"

She swallowed heavily and avoided his gaze.

"You owe me that much at least," he snarled. "Why the hell did you leave? I asked you to marry me, damn it."

"I know," she shouted, and squeezed her middle more tightly. "That's why I left."

He snorted a choked laugh and shook his head. "A simple no would have been enough."

"Would it?" she snapped, taking two hasty steps toward him before stopping short. "Would you really have accepted my refusal?"

He didn't even have to think about that one. "Probably not," he conceded. "But we could have talked about it."

"Talking won't change anything."

"Neither did running away," he said, and had the satisfaction of seeing her flinch from the direct hit.

"Tell me why you're doing this, Laura." Desperately trying to control the wild swirl of emotions churning through him, he struggled to keep his voice even. "Tell me why you're willing to throw us away."

She looked at him then. Her eyes were so pain filled, it hurt him to look at them. He steeled himself against the pang of sympathy he felt for her. Sympathy wouldn't win the day. Only honesty could bridge the gap that had leaped up between them.

A long silent moment ticked past. Finally, though, she shouted, "Because I can't go through this again."

"What?" he demanded.

As if she'd reached her breaking point, the words burst from her lips in a torrent. She told him more about Bill, about his death two weeks before their wedding. About the pain she'd lived with and finally conquered. And about her fear.

"Don't you understand?" she cried, "I love you more

than I have ever loved *anyone* in my life! If I lost you like I did Bill, this time the pain would kill me.''

"You want guarantees?" he asked.

"Yes, damn it. Promise me. No, swear to me here and now that you won't die. That if we get married we'll live forever!"

"I can't do that."

"Then I can't marry you."

"You're punishing me because Bill died?" Unbelievable.

"I'm not punishing you."

"What is this, then?"

"Self-protection."

"Bull."

"What?" She looked at him like he was speaking some weird foreign language.

"I said that's a load of garbage." Damn it, he wouldn't lose her to a fear that he had no way of easing. "You're just hiding, Laura. Trying to dig a big enough hole to disappear into."

"You don't know what I went through—" she started to explain.

He cut her off, jumping with both feet into the most important battle of his life. "Another lie." Throwing his hands wide, he shouted right back at her. "I know all about death. I've seen it. Up close and personal. And I know that the most important thing death can teach us is to *live*. Live every moment like it's your last. Squeeze every last damn drop you can out of life. Enjoy every minute for the gift it is."

"You don't understand."

"Yes, I do," he countered. "You're so busy trying not to die, you've forgotten how to live."

She reacted as though he'd slapped her. Drawing her head back, she stared at him through watery eyes.

"I'm not afraid to die," she whispered, her hands at her throat as if choking the words out. "I just don't want to watch *you* die."

"You'd rather watch me walk out of your life?"

"*Yes!* Do it now. *Please.*"

Laura moved back a pace, keeping the distance between them. It was safer that way.

"Trying to hide didn't help, did it?" he demanded. "You didn't want to love me. Or Miranda. But you do."

She looked into those blue eyes of his and couldn't deny the truth. "All right, yes. I do love you. Both of you. But I can't let that love make my choices for me. I *won't* set myself up for that kind of pain again."

"You're crying now," he countered.

Laura lifted one hand to brush across her cheeks.

"What pain have you managed to avoid by leaving me?"

She sniffed and tried to focus on him through the film of water flooding her eyes. "This grief will pass," she told him brokenly. Laura prayed she was right. "But if we become a family and something should happen to you and Miranda..." She shook her head sorrowfully. "That kind of agony would kill me."

Jeff groaned, a tortured sound that erupted from his chest. Closing the space between them, he grabbed her upper arms and gave her a shake. Glaring down into her eyes, he said harshly, "I can't believe you're willing to toss aside something I never thought I'd have."

Her head fell back on her neck. She felt the tension rolling off of him in waves.

"Damn it, Laura, I *love* you. Don't you see what a miracle that is?" He sucked in a gulp of air, held it a moment, then blew it out again, clearly struggling for calm. "Yeah, love is risky. It makes life messy and frightening. Hell, I don't know what will happen tomorrow." His gaze bored into hers, and Laura wept harder at the desperate love she read in his eyes. "I can't give you a guarantee, Laura. I can only tell you that living without love makes for a cold, lonely existence. I know," he said, more softly now.

His hands moved to cup her face. His thumbs brushed her fresh tears away, and she felt the heat of his tenderness reach into the dark corners of her soul and warm them.

"I know what life is without you," he said, "and I don't want to go back to that. I want to love you. I want to make babies with you."

Her hand lifted to cover her abdomen.

"Laura?" he asked suddenly. "Are you...?"

"No," she admitted, and felt the emptiness inside threaten to swallow her whole.

He actually looked disappointed, she thought, and when he spoke, he confirmed it.

"I'm sorry. I had been hoping." He shook his head again. "Laura, come with me. Build a family with me."

Jeff. A family.

It was what she had always wanted. Everything inside her screamed at her to throw her fears aside and say yes.

"If only," she whispered, "if only I *knew* everything would be all right this time..."

Jeff bent down and dusted a kiss on her forehead. Love for her filled him so completely that he thought he might burst with it. "Ah, sweetheart," he said tenderly, "I can't promise you that. No one can. The only guarantee I can give you is that I will love you forever." He smoothed her hair back from her face, keeping his gaze locked with hers. "That's all I can say. Our lives are in your hands, Laura."

More scared than he'd ever been on the battlefield, Jeff held his breath and watched her as she looked around her small, quiet apartment.

Laura forced a calming breath into her lungs. Jeff's hands on her face sent ribbons of warmth trailing through her body. Silently, she acknowledged that this was the first time she hadn't been deathly cold since she ran away from him and Miranda. Since she had turned her back on the gift of love. These days without Jeff had been empty. As empty as her life would be if she continued to live scared.

The fear of losing him would probably never disappear completely, she knew. And the prospect of pain was a terrifying one. But, she realized as she turned her gaze back to the face of the man she loved, the reality of living without Jeff Ryan in her life was much more terrifying.

Slowly, she reached up and covered his hands with hers. When she spoke, her voice was hushed. "Eight years ago, I thought my life was over."

He took a breath and held it. Worry lines deepened at the corners of his eyes.

"But it wasn't, Jeff," she said, turning her face into his palm to kiss it. "It's just beginning." She paused and looked into his eyes before saying tenderly, "You are the love of my life. Will you marry me?"

"Yes." A slow, relieved smile curved his lips as he exhaled on a sigh. "I don't mind saying, you had me scared for a while."

"Me, too," she admitted, and moved into his embrace. His arms closed around her, and it felt like a homecoming.

They held on to each other for several minutes, just savoring the joy of being together again.

"Remember," he asked suddenly, "when I told you that I wanted to be the youngest general in the corps?"

She nodded against his chest. His arms tightened protectively around her.

"I've decided to go after a better promotion."

Laura tilted her head back to look at him. "What?"

"To be the best damn husband and father you ever saw."

"You've got my vote, Marine," she said, and went up on her toes to meet his kiss.

* * * * *

Dear Reader,

When I created Ben Standing Bear as brother to the hero in *Standing Bear's Surrender,* I knew he had to have his own book...and a very special woman. I pulled out all the stops with Josie Bell Pickens. She's feisty, independent and full of fun, laughter and music. She embraces lost causes, ridiculous relatives and a stubborn chocolate Lab named Bruiser.

My best friends say Josie Bell is me. In a way, that's true. There's a little part of me in every novel I create. It's impossible for me to write without putting my heart and soul on every page.

It's also impossible for me to write without infusing the stories with bits and pieces of my beloved Deep South. *Invitation to a Wedding* is set in a small Mississippi town very much like the one where I grew up. I claim firsthand knowledge of the town, but I categorically deny that any of the characters are my relatives!

I'm thrilled you loved Ben and Josie enough to want another madcap romp with them. I write because I love the beauty of words and the art of storytelling. But I also write because of *you,* dear reader. For twenty years you have remained loyal fans, and many of you have become good friends. I am deeply grateful to you, for a book without a reader is a book forever lost.

With gratitude,

Peggy Webb

INVITATION TO
A WEDDING
Peggy Webb

Prologue

Ben Standing Bear, Family Medicine. His shingle had been hanging for only one week when the invitation came in the mail. Otherwise, except for a Wal-Mart flyer, his box was empty.

Who would be sending him an invitation? He hadn't been in Pontotoc long enough to know anyone. He'd have thought it was a mistake except that it had his name on it, and how many doctors in Mississippi were named Standing Bear?

None, would be his guess.

Ben slit the envelope and pulled out the card: *Mrs. Betty Anne Pickens requests the honor of your presence at a pre-nuptial party for her daughter, Josie Belle Pickens and Jerry Bob Crawford.*

Josie Belle. Ben hadn't seen her in years but her name conjured up her image as if it had been only yesterday— wide smile, the bluest eyes this side of heaven and red hair as wild as she was. They'd been pals in college, *study buddies* Josie Belle called them, and he guessed it had been true. He'd studied the books and she'd studied ways to get into trouble.

He smiled thinking about her. She'd been an impulsive scamp, a rebel, a modern-day Carrie Nation who loved nothing better than being the ringleader in a sit-in or a picket line for whatever cause struck her fancy. And many of them did. She'd picketed for a ban on net-fishing in known dolphin waters. She'd marched for protection of the snail darter on the Tennessee-Tombigbee Waterway. She decried the slaughter of the mountain gorilla, air pollution, chemical dumping into rivers and streams.

If you had a worthy cause, Josie Belle Pickens was the girl you wanted on your side.

Of course, she was a woman now, a woman about to get married.

Funny. He'd never imagined her settling down for anybody. Besides, who would be brave enough to hitch his wagon to hers for that wild ride she called life?

You could bet your britches Ben Standing Bear was going to find out. In fact, he could hardly wait.

Chapter One

"I do hope you're not wearing that red dress to the party tonight, Josie Belle."

Actually, she'd been planning to wear the blue, but now that Aunt Tess had thrown down the gauntlet, Josie was bound and determined to pick it up. Her mother's older sister thought she knew everything there was to know about *everything,* and besides that she acted as if she was on a mission from Moses to save the entire Pickens family from rack and ruin.

Josie would wear the red dress tonight or die.

"I most certainly am, Aunt Tess. I like to wear red."

"It clashes with your hair."

"It makes me feel powerful."

"What I'd think you'd want to feel in front of Jerry Bob's mother is meekness. You know how Clytee Crawford thinks she's the most important woman in town. If I were you I'd want to stay on her good side. At least until after the wedding."

"She doesn't have a good side."

"Josie Belle!" Her mother, who had been anxiously watching the exchange between a daughter she openly called willful and a sister she privately called meddling, felt compelled to offer a mild rebuke. "Behave yourself."

"I'm glad you finally put your two cents' worth in, Betty Anne. Talk to your daughter. I can't do a thing with her."

Tess got up from the kitchen table where they'd all been enjoying a cup of coffee until the discussion of the red dress surfaced, and picked up everyone's cup, even though her sister had barely started drinking her coffee.

"You two will have to sort this out without me, Betty Anne. If I'm going to put on a pretty face for tonight's party, I'd better go and get started."

Tess Clemson disappeared through the doorway, and Betty Anne shot her daughter a warning look.

"Don't say it, Josie Belle."

Josie gave her a wicked grin, and suddenly Betty Anne dissolved into laughter. She laughed so hard tears rolled down her cheeks.

"All right. I'll say it for you. Tess couldn't put on a pretty face even if she tried." Never one to be prepared for emergencies or otherwise, Betty Anne wiped her face with the corner of the tablecloth. Then she waved a hand at her daughter. "Go on. Get out of here. Wear the red dress. Jerry Bob's is the only other opinion that matters, and he's crazy about you no matter what you do."

"God help him," Josie said.

And she meant it. Jerry Bob Crawford of Crawford's Tractors had to be a saint to put up with her. How he'd ever got up the courage to give her a ring was beyond Josie's comprehension. Even more puzzling was how she'd said yes.

As she pulled the red dress over her head, Josie waxed philosophic. She seemed to be doing that a lot since she'd left the glitz and glamor of Chicago and moved back to Pontotoc to be close to her mother after her father had died. If she wasn't over-the-moon happy about her impending marriage, she was practical.

"If you can't have the man you want, then marry the man you can have," she told her dog, and the big chocolate lab with soulful eyes thumped his tail on the hardwood floor in complete agreement.

That was the best thing about Bruiser. He agreed with everything she said.

Against her will a certain Sioux with dancing black eyes and a devilish smile whispered through Josie's mind. If she were the kind of woman who pondered over what might have been, she'd have worked herself into a fit of the blues. But she wasn't.

Instead, she fluffed up her hair that was doing just fine on its own, then went downstairs to meet her fiancé.

He whistled when he saw her, then looked worried.

"Hon, don't you think you ought to get a wrap?"

"Why? It's ninety-five degrees."

"Mama's going to be there."

She started to say, "I'll bet she's seen these before," then she caught herself. In one week she was going to marry this man, this good, long-suffering man.

Standing on tiptoe she kissed him softly on the mouth.

"You worry too much, Jerry Bob," she said, then she linked her arm through his. "Let's go to the party and have fun."

Fun with Jerry Bob consisted of weekend football games at Mississippi State, visits with friends and an occasional sedate game of bridge, which was a far cry from what she used to do for kicks. But in time she hoped to get used to it. Perhaps she would even learn to enjoy the settled life.

By the time they arrived at the country club she'd mentally geared herself for a toned-down evening. But heck, it was *her* party and she planned to enjoy every minute of it no matter how dull it got.

Jerry Bob parked his Dodge pickup beside an ancient black Cadillac that had been made back in the days when tail fins and titanic proportions were in style.

"Mama's already here," he said.

He got that anxious look that always made Josie want to pat him on the head as if he were a little boy and say, "Everything's going to be all right." Her feelings for him bordered on the maternal, and that scared her a little.

She'd always dreamed she'd sweep to the altar on a tidal wave of passion. Instead she seemed to be floating along on a small current of coziness.

"Lordy," he added, casting a skeptical glance at Josie's red dress.

Josie felt like bopping him over the head with her purse. And his mother, too. Instead, she decided to be magnanimous. She figured it would be good practice for the future.

"Let's go in and say hello to her."

"That's all you're going to do, isn't it, Josie? Say hello?"

He was referring to the last time she'd spent an evening in his mother's company, the command performance at one of Mrs. Crawford's ritual Sunday dinners. Josie'd bitten her tongue through Clytee Crawford's narrow religious views, but the minute she'd attacked dogs in general and Bruiser in particular, Josie went into battle.

Her daddy used to say, "Josie, you're a quick draw with that invisible sword you carry around."

"It's my sword of justice," she'd say, and they'd both laugh.

Clytee Crawford didn't understand about the sword when she'd said, "I think anybody who keeps dogs in the house ought to have their heads examined." Then smiling sweetly, to show she could bloody your head without malice, she turned to her future daughter-in-law.

"I do hope you're planning to get rid of that mutt before you and Jerry Bob marry. I shudder to think what it would do to a nice house."

"Bruiser will bring a loving heart and good manners to my house, which is more than I can say for some people."

Later Jerry Bob told her, "It took Mama three days to recover from that remark."

Josie didn't plan on making any outrageous remarks tonight. The week before a wedding should be one of the most joyful times in a person's life. She didn't want to spoil it for Jerry Bob.

What about you, Josie?

As the party guests swarmed around congratulating them, the question burned through Josie's mind. She suddenly felt cold all over.

I can't go through with this, she thought as Jerry Bob was borne away from her on a tide of a well-wishers.

"Cold feet," her mother had told her two months earlier when Josie told Betty Anne she was thinking of returning Jerry Bob's ring because she didn't love him the way a man deserved to be loved. "Every bride-to-be gets them. Don't worry, darling. Everything's going to be all right."

Josie sincerely hoped so.

"Hello, Josie."

A voice from the past. Her cheeks burning and her heart racing, she turned around and fell into the deep black eyes of Ben Standing Bear.

"I got your invitation," he said. Then he smiled, that heart-stopping, breath-stealing smile that had haunted her for years.

She'd had no idea he was coming, or even that he was in town. Her mother had sent the invitations while Josie had been up to her ears with the usual round of teachers' seminars that preceded the opening of school.

"Ben." Reason deserted her. She longed to be brilliant and witty for him. She yearned to impress him with her charm, her gaiety. But all she could think of was her wedding. It loomed before her like doomsday.

The man of her dreams had come too late.

Ordinarily she'd have thrown herself into his arms for a huge hug. After all, he'd once been the best friend she had. But that was a long time ago, and she was no longer free to launch herself at him, even in friendship.

"I'm so glad you could come," she said, offering her hand.

"I wouldn't have missed it for the world."

His hand closed over hers, and she wanted to sit down and cry. How could she have been so foolish? How could she have been so mistaken? If you couldn't have the man you loved, it *wasn't* all right to love the man you could have, for on doing so you were no better than a liar and a thief.

Holding Ben's hand was joy indescribable. She'd robbed herself of that pleasure. In saying yes to the wrong man she'd consigned herself to years of traveling the dull interstates when she might have been on a rocket ship to the moon.

"You look *great,* Josie." Ben was still holding her hand, and she wasn't about to be the first to let go. "What are you doing with yourself these days? Besides getting married?"

She wished he hadn't added that last part. At the moment she wished she'd never heard the word *marriage.*

"I teach drama at the local high school."

"If anyone is suited to drama, it's you."

"I take that as a compliment."

"That's exactly the way I meant it, Josie Belle."

Josie wished she were the swooning type. The way he said her name made her want to fall into a heap of crushed red taffeta and melted bones.

"And you, of course, are a doctor now. Where's your practice, Ben?"

"Right here in Pontotoc. I assumed you knew."

Oh, God. Not here. Anywhere but here.

Josie wanted to die. She wanted a big hole to open up and swallow her. She wanted to race to the highest hill in northwest Mississippi and scream until her throat was raw.

How was she ever going to spend the rest of her days with Jerry Bob Crawford while the man she wanted was living in the same town? Pontotoc was not that big. In fact, it had only two major streets. She was bound to run into Ben at the grocery store, the drugstore, on the town square, at the courthouse. For Pete's sake, she'd see him practically every day of her life. See him and yearn.

"No, I didn't know. I've been too busy to even pick up the newspaper."

"Weddings must take a lot of planning."

He looked deeply into her eyes, and she felt the impact all the way to her toes. They gazed silently at one another, still holding hands. People were beginning to turn and look their way, but Josie didn't care. She was going to hold on to his good solid warmth as long as she could.

All of a sudden Ben let go, as if he'd just recalled why he was there.

"When am I going to get to meet this fiancé of yours?"

For a heady moment she'd forgotten Jerry Bob existed. Scanning the room she saw him standing beside the punch bowl with his mother, both of them scowling in her direction.

There was no way she could take Ben to them for an introduction. First she'd have to smooth the waters.

"Don't move a muscle. I'll go fetch him."

The dazzling smile she gave Ben was the best job of acting she'd done since the night she received her engagement ring.

"I'll wait for you, Josie," Ben said, and she left him to face the music.

Jerry Bob met her halfway across the room, and his mother was not far behind.

"What on earth are you thinking of, Josie? You've been over there holding hands with that man for hours."

"He's an old college friend, Jerry Bob, and we haven't *been* here for hours. We've only been here twenty minutes."

Josie hated being put on the defensive. Even more, she hated resorting to excuses. She'd opened her mouth to tell Jerry Bob a few things about trust when his mother arrived, her mouth working like a fish.

"I'm absolutely mortified," she said. "Who on earth invited that Indian?"

Josie was so outraged she didn't dare speak. She shot a pleading glance at Jerry Bob. He could set his mother straight in a diplomatic way, whereas Josie would definitely burn bridges.

A frown creased his forehead and sweat beaded his upper lip.

"Mother's right, Josie. People are beginning to talk." Her feathers fell, as Aunt Tess was fond of saying. But it was Jerry Bob's next remark that drove a stake through her heart. "It would be bad enough if he was someone we know, but an *Indian,* Josie!"

He waited expectantly for her to apologize and make the peace. Instead, she was going to burn bridges. Oh, she was *definitely* going to burn bridges, for in the last few moments she'd discovered that there was no way in heaven or earth she could marry Jerry Bob Crawford.

The simple thing would be to hand him his ring and walk

away, but Josie had never in her life done the simple thing. Besides, she had a better plan; she was going to let Jerry Bob *ask* for the ring back. That way he'd save face; she'd gain her freedom.

And along the way, extract a little revenge for her best friend, Ben Standing Bear.

"Well, Josie." Clytee Crawford pursed her lips and lifted her eyebrows into her starched hairdo. "What do you have to say for yourself?"

"That *Indian,* as you call him, happens to be a very fine Sioux doctor named Ben Standing Bear, and when you get sick and in need I hope he takes your scalp."

Clytee's mouth fell open and Jerry Bob made a strangling sound.

"Furthermore, *I* invited him. He's my friend, and one hell of a dancer."

Josie put an extra wiggle in her hips as she marched off. She detoured by the bandstand with her request, then sashayed in Ben's direction.

"They're playing our song," she said, reaching for his hands.

The great thing about Ben was that he never questioned her. Their connection was so deep it didn't need words.

He swept her into his arms and onto the empty dance floor. They'd won a prize once when Josie had talked Ben into entering a local dance competition. Their winning number had been the tango.

On fire with the hot Latin beat and the nearness of the man that time couldn't erase from her heat, she molded herself against Ben. But not merely to feel his rhythm. She was feeling his soul.

Flames leaped into his eyes as he caught her close, then dipped her so low her hair brushed against the floor.

"This is the only acceptable way of making love in public," he said.

"Yes. I know."

Chapter Two

Just like old times, Ben thought as he and Josie danced. Though he hadn't danced in years, he'd forgotten neither the steps nor the rhythm. What he had forgotten was the feel of Josie in his arms.

Suddenly he knew it wasn't like old times at all. If holding Josie had felt this good in college, he'd have remembered, wouldn't he?

"I'd forgotten what a great dancer you are, Josie."

"I haven't forgotten a single thing about you, Ben. Not one, including how you always get that bemused look in your eyes when you dip me. I've always wondered what it meant."

Josie had always been the most honest woman he'd ever known. That was one of the things he liked about her.

"You must not have wondered very much, Josie. All I got from you after college was a couple of Christmas cards."

"That's more than I got from you, Ben Standing Bear. One lousy birthday card."

"You didn't like it?"

"I like roses." She swiveled closer to him, if that were possible, and whispered, "Can you make this dance look a little sexier?"

"Your wish is my command, Josie."

It always had been. That's why he hadn't questioned her when she'd asked him to dance. He hadn't had to ask: her face said it all. He'd witnessed the exchange between her and Jerry Bob Crawford. He'd seen the set expressions on the faces of her future husband and the woman he assumed would be Josie's mother-in-law, heaven help both of them.

Josie's eyes had been shooting fire when she'd left them gawking in her direction with their mouths hanging open. She frequently left people in that condition.

That was another thing he liked about her: she never gave half measure on anything. With Josie it was whole hog or nothing. She was as passionate about her opinions as she was about her causes.

And speaking of passionate, what she was doing to him right now ought to be against the law. Everything about her was provocative, from the way she moved her hips to the way she gazed deep into his eyes. He was finding out the hard way that his feelings for another man's intended were anything but appropriate.

As the Latin beat pulsed through him, he pulled her so close you couldn't get a straw between their bodies, then executed a move that censors would have given an X-rating. Ben was too introspective to pretend, even to himself, that he was merely following Josie's instructions. Quite the contrary. What he was doing on the dance floor with Josie Belle Pickens was not what he had done with his best friend in college. What he was doing was what any sane man would do with a girl he used to know who had turned into the most exciting woman he'd ever seen. He was performing a mating ritual as old as time: The man postures and preens and shows all his colors hoping to attract the attention of the most desirable of the female species.

And that would be Josie Belle Pickens. Formerly his best friend. Most recently, a tantalizing woman completely out of his reach.

If she's so out of your reach, why isn't she dancing this way with her fiancé? Ben decided to break his long-standing code with Josie: no questions asked.

Her full skirt spread over the floor like the petals of an exotic red flower as he dipped her low, then bent close to her face, so close he could see the golden starburst in the center of her incredible blue eyes.

"Just what is this game you're playing, Josie?"

"Don't you like it?"

"I didn't say I didn't like it." He swept her up so close her lips were almost touching his. Suddenly it was hard for him to think. "I asked a question that deserves an answer. Right now your soon-to-be husband is looking at me as if he's planning a hanging party and I'm the featured guest."

"Good. He deserves to stew in his own oils."

"I don't plan to stew along with him. Out with it, Josie. What's the story?"

"You made me miss a step."

"You might as well stop trying to avoid the question. You know I don't give up, Josie."

"Lord knows, do I ever. Who could forget that ball you knocked clear out of the park after everybody had written you off?"

He'd been playing college baseball, the team was having a winning season, and his own stats were breaking records. Then he'd been sidelined with a broken wrist, written off for the rest of the year by the coach, the players, the sportswriters and all the fans. "Even if you play again this season," the doctors warned him, "don't expect to hit home runs. The wrist will be weaker, you'll have less mobility. It's going to take a long time to come back a hundred percent, if you ever do."

So he'd sat on the sidelines and watched his team fall behind in the conference ratings, then slowly and painfully begin to lose the game that would decide whether they advanced to the championship.

"Put me up at bat," he'd told the coach. When Ben wouldn't give up, Pat Slader had finally agreed. With bases loaded, two out and two strikes against him, Ben had smashed the ball out of the stadium. They still hadn't won the game, but it was a play everybody had said was impossible for Ben. It was the play nobody would ever forget.

Bear on the Warpath Again, the headlines had shouted. But he hadn't been. Not really. He'd been approached by the majors, but his injury made Ben understand once and for all how fleeting fame can be, and how quickly it can be taken away.

And so he'd chosen the long, arduous path toward a medical degree, and in the process had lost touch with the one person he'd thought would always be around—Josie Belle.

Ben didn't believe in coincidence. Fate had set her in his path once more, but for what purpose? He supposed he'd find out in time…if he lived long enough.

The song had ended, Josie was still clinging to him like a honeysuckle vine and Jerry Bob was headed their way.

"Hang on to your hat, Josie. Here comes trouble."

"Good. Let 'er rip."

She wiggled closer to Ben. What could he do but be a gentleman and protect her the way he always had? Ben kept his arm around Josie and watched her fiancé coming. A big man with a little too much girth, he moved like a freight train under full steam.

He didn't even bother to acknowledge Ben, but turned the full force of his wrath toward Josie.

"Josie Belle, I've had about enough of your shenanigans."

"Good." She gave him an impudent grin.

"I'm not kidding. You're embarrassing Mama. Come on here and stop acting like this."

"Make me."

Something more was going on here than a lovers' quarrel, and from the dark looks Jerry Bob cast his way, it didn't take Ben long to solve the mystery. He was not only a foreigner in the heart of a small Southern town, but he was breaking their codes of behavior. He'd been around long enough to know the protocol: be polite, smile a lot, tell a white lie when the truth ruffles feathers and, above all, don't act as if you're a part of the crowd until you're invited. Especially don't dance the tango with the bride-to-be.

"Gosh danged, Josie Belle. Now stop that."

Jerry Bob loosened his collar with his finger. If he weren't being such a jerk, Ben would feel sorry for him.

"This is not what you think," Ben said. He was a peacemaker by nature. Besides, getting off on the wrong foot was not a good way to set up a practice in a small town. Most of the people in this room would at one time or another end up in his office with sniffly noses and hacking coughs and one of the viruses running rampant. "Allow me to introduce myself. I'm Josie's old friend from college, Ben Standing Bear."

Keeping one hand planted firmly around Josie's waist just in case, he held out his other hand. Jerry Bob ignored it.

"I know who you are. What I don't know is how come you're trying to steal my wife."

"Now wait a minute…" Ben said.

"I am not your *wife,* Jerry Bob. Not yet."

"Saturday you will be."

"Saturdays can be a *long* time coming." Suddenly Josie spun away from both of them, then waving two fingers she said, "Ta-ta. You two have fun."

"Josie, you'd better not be up to any more tricks." Ignoring her fiancé, Josie kept on walking. Ben noticed she put more swing than necessary in her hips. Not that he was complaining. Not by a long shot. "What are you up to now, Josie?" her fiancé called after her.

She glanced over her shoulder and winked. "Watch me and find out, Jerry Bob."

She sashayed up to the bandstand, but instead of making another song request, as Jerry Bob obviously had assumed she would, Josie mounted the steps and took the microphone.

Thunderstruck, Jerry Bob waved his arms at her, a frantic signal for her to come down.

"This song is for a very special friend, somebody I haven't seen in a long, long time." She leaned over to consult with the bandleader.

What was she going to do? Jerry Bob looked ready to have a stroke, but Ben was intrigued. That was the thing about Josie. She'd always intrigued him. He'd never known what to expect from her, and only now with the perspective of years did he realize how exciting that could be.

The guests began to be aware that there was high drama taking place in their midst, and started gathering around the bandstand. By the time Josie returned to the microphone, she had quite an attentive audience. There was a collective gasp when she started singing. The song she'd chosen was "Amazed," a top seller by the group called Lonestar and one of the most romantic tunes to come down the pike in a long time.

Josie had a great bluesy voice and she knew how to wrap it around a song. Furthermore, she knew how to deliver. And there was not a single doubt in anybody's mind who she was delivering the song to. It was the stranger in their midst.

Ben was by turns pleased, amused and shocked. The song was a love ballad, the words such a straightforward declaration that they left no doubt whatsoever as to their meaning.

This was a song Josie should be singing to her fiancé. With every gesture, every move, every nuance, she made it clear that she was not. She was singing to one man, and one man only, Ben Standing Bear.

For one shining moment he believed what Josie was singing to be true—they were two people in love. For one heart-aching interlude the crowd vanished and he was alone in the room with a woman he'd viewed all these years as merely a friend. Loss settled like a stone in the pit of his stomach. He'd been too busy to see what was right before his eyes: a woman worthy of a man's full attention, a woman who would be so easy to love, a woman who went through life with her arms and her heart wide open, a woman you could hurt if you weren't very careful. A woman who now belonged to another man.

And that man had no idea of the treasure he possessed. He wanted to take a magic fairy and turn her into a toad. He wanted to clip her wings, silence her voice, tame her spirit.

Jerry Bob Crawford wasn't worthy to tie Josie's shoes.

Ben's heart hurt for her. He hurt for all the dirty looks and frantic directives her husband would send her way. He wanted to tuck her under his arm and run so that she would never suffer the humiliation of being considered an embar rassment to the Crawford family when she should be considered the brightest jewel in the family's crown.

By the time Josie finished the song, the crowd had a new drama to witness: Jerry Bob's much-deferred-to mama went into a swoon and required three people to carry her to one of the sofas near the bar. A woman who possessed more good intentions than good sense raced to the bar and returned with a glass brimming with whiskey. Mama came out of her swoon long enough to send the glass flying, then screech, "You know I don't touch that stuff. I leave it to the likes of Josie Belle Pickens up yonder on that stage acting like a strumpet."

Rage robbed Ben of his senses. There was no telling what he would have done if the woman hadn't faked another swoon. Flattened against the faded cabbage roses she began to moan and carry on as if she were about to give birth. Every now and then she'd lift her head and let out a pitiful wail to her son.

"Jer-ry Bo-o-o-b, I need you."

Jerry Bob didn't rush right to his mama's side because he had other fish to fry. His jaw tight, he started stalking toward the stage. Ben blocked his path.

"If you harm one hair on her head I'll take your scalp."

"Move out of my way."

"Not until you calm down. I think there's been enough sensation for one evening, don't you?"

"You should have thought of that before you and Josie showed off out on the dance floor."

"It's called the tango."

"I don't care what it's called. It looked vulgar to me. Now get out of my way."

Jerry Bob tried to skirt around him, but Ben moved quickly, depriving him of his target once more. And once more Ben found himself in the role of peacemaker.

"Josie is a high-spirited woman," he said. "That's all.

Apparently you did or said something to make her mad, and she's getting even with you.''

"She didn't act like this till you came along."

"Josie's not acting. She's being her usual delightful self."

"I don't think I like the way you refer to the woman I was planning to marry."

"Why don't you and I go outside and walk around till you calm down?"

"And leave Josie up there to mortify Mama again?"

It was taking three hefty men, all in waiters' jackets, to mop up the mess Mama had made.

"It looks like she can take care of herself. Josie's the one I'm worried about. She's so full of bravado she makes you think she could whip the world with one hand tied behind her back. But underneath is a soft, vulnerable woman who needs understanding and lots of hugging."

"Well, she's not fixing to get it from me. Not after tonight."

"What are you talking about?"

"If you'll get out of my way, I'll show you."

"I'm not moving until I know your intentions."

Over on the sofa Mama let out another moan, and Jerry Bob began to twitch like a man possessed.

"Lordy." Jerry Bob mopped his brow with a handkerchief. "All I want to do is get my ring back and get Mama home."

Ben's relief was all out of proportion to the situation. After all, Josie was merely an old friend he was still protecting out of habit, wasn't she?

"That's all you intend to do?"

"What do you take me for? A heathen?"

"No. I knew the minute I spotted you that you were a gentleman." Ben stepped out of Jerry Bob's way, then fell into step beside him.

"What do you think you're doing?" Jerry Bob asked.

"I'm going with you just to make sure your gentlemanly conduct doesn't fail you."

Ben was glad that Jerry Bob didn't argue. He'd come to the party anticipating a lively time because that's what happened everywhere Josie went. She wore excitement the way some women wear a favorite perfume. What he hadn't expected was being at the center of it all. He didn't want that kind of notoriety in the town where he was just getting started. He didn't want that kind of distraction. His life was carefully mapped out.

We don't always get what we want. He'd have to write that down in his journal when he back to the apartment he called home. If he ever got home.

Josie saw both of them coming, Ben looking ready to take on a passel of wildcats, and Jerry Bob looking like a man who had been poleaxed in the gut. Remorse slashed her, but it was fleeting. After all, he had said cruel things about Ben, and he deserved everything he'd got.

If looks were any indication, her plan had worked: Jerry Bob was coming to break off the engagement. Josie climbed off the stage. Her desire had been a public revenge, not a public humiliation.

What was sure to come was best done without an audience. Except one, of course. From the looks of him, Ben had no intention of leaving Jerry Bob's side.

She smiled as she slipped through the crowd and out the side door. It felt wonderful to have her old friend and protector back on the job.

A few stars sprinkled the sky and a moon as big as a galleon rode the topmost branches of an ancient magnolia tree. Josie made her way to the tree and climbed up until she was perched on a thick branch with a natural curve just right for sitting. She kicked off her shoes and started swinging her legs. She never could sit still when she was nervous.

While she watched the door, she hummed a snatch of "Amazed." She wondered if Ben had known the song came from her heart. She hoped not.

She'd learned a powerful lesson with this Jerry Bob business: hearts left wide open got hurt. And even though she'd wanted the breakup, even though she'd initiated it, still a small place in her heart hurt.

She felt not that love had failed her, but that she had failed love. Love was a precious thing, to be cherished and revered, but above all to be *recognized*. She should have known from the very beginning that what she'd felt for Jerry Bob was not love. She should have guarded her heart—and his—more carefully.

No, she didn't want Ben Standing Bear to know how she felt about him. Not yet. Not until she could figure it out for herself. Sure, he'd been her best friend all those years ago. Sure, he'd been her protector, her guardian angel, her shoulder to cry on. And there was no denying he was one of the most appealing-looking men she'd ever known. Nor could she deny the way her heart's rhythm picked up every time she looked at him. Nor that unexpected rush of joy she felt merely hearing his voice, standing at his side.

And the dancing...well, she couldn't even bear to think about that. Her feelings were too new, too raw, too powerful to make a swift judgment. She needed to let them simmer, to peek inside herself at random moments over the next few days, the next few weeks, and see what was cooking.

Maybe it was love. Maybe not. Josie wasn't even sure she knew what love was.

Jerry Bob's voice cut through her musings. "Josie Belle. Where are you? I know you're out here."

"Here I am, Jerry Bob. Up a tree."

Ben chuckled. It was one of the sweetest, most reassuring sounds she could imagine. And exactly what she needed.

"I want to talk to you."

"You'll have to come over here then, because I'm not coming down."

Jerry Bob kicked a fallen limb out of his way, then stood under her tree craning his neck upward.

"I'm not even going to ask how come you did what you did in there, Josie Belle." That was a relief to her. She didn't want to get into any long discussions with him. She merely wanted him to set them both free. "I just want you to know that the wedding's off."

She could have wept for joy. And truth to tell, a tear did squeeze out of the corner of her eye. She was glad it was dark so that nobody could see.

"I'm sorry, Jerry Bob," she said, and she really meant it. "But I do think you're doing the right thing. I would never fit in with the Crawford family. I'm afraid I would have made you a terrible wife." She twisted the ring off her finger. "You'll be wanting this back."

"I most certainly will. It's a family heirloom." He reached up a long arm, and she dropped the diamond into his palm. Josie felt as if she'd shed a two-ton weight.

Jerry Bob closed his fist over the ring, then stood with his face still turned up to hers as if he didn't know what to do next. The maternal feelings she'd always had for him surfaced.

"Then you should guard it carefully, Jerry Bob. Don't go giving it to the next pretty girl who turns your head. You need somebody sedate and steady, somebody whose interests don't range much beyond the kitchen and the nursery."

"Are you saying I'm dumb, Josie Belle?"

"Not at all, Jerry Bob. I'm saying that you need a soft dependent woman you can protect."

"Who asked your opinion? When I want your advice I'll be asking for it."

"Another thing, Jerry Bob, when you choose a woman for a wife you should leave your mother's side and move over to hers. No woman wants to play second fiddle. Every woman wants to be the whole orchestra, the first prize, the grand trophy."

If he kept standing under her tree with his neck craned, he was going to have a crick in the morning.

"I never meant it to turn out this way," she added. "I never meant to hurt you." The silence went on for so long you could drive a Mack truck through it.

"Thanks for nothing, Josie Belle." Hands crammed deep into his pockets, head ducked, Jerry Bob hurried back toward his mama.

Ben took his place under the tree, but instead of craning his neck up, he caught Josie's feet and held them still.

"I'm here now, Josie. Everything's going to be all right."

She tipped her face toward the moon and squeezed her eyes tight against the tears. Ben Standing Bear had never lied to her in his life. He *was* here, and in spite of the way her heart hurt and her spirit felt battered and her pride felt bruised, she had to believe that what he said was true. She had to cling to that hope.

"Thanks, pal," she said, and Ben could hear the tears in her voice. Josie was hurting, and that made him hurt. Funny how that could still happen after all these years. "I can always count on you," she added, and suddenly her voice was small, like a little girl's.

"That's what friends are for."

He felt her legs twitch as she tried to start swinging her feet again. Except for growing more lush, more beautiful, Josie hadn't really changed in all the years they'd been apart. She was still a little girl in a grown-up's body, begging for the attention of a father who never showed her he loved her.

Thomas Jefferson Pickens. Ben remembered him well. Their freshman year in college, the year they'd met, Josie had invited him home to Pontotoc with her for Thanksgiving. His brother had been off somewhere performing with the Blue Angels, and his parents had been dead since he was two years old and he had nowhere to go except perhaps back to the orphanage to pay his respects to the only mother he'd ever had, and so he'd accepted her invitation.

It hadn't taken long to get the lay of the family territory. Josie's mother was one of those natural beauties who had probably been told all her life that a woman who looked like her could have the moon and the stars without ever lifting a finger. And that was the role she played to the hilt.

All she had to do was widen her eyes and her husband raced to her side to see what she wanted. Clearly he was besotted with her. And clearly she loved him beyond all reason. Their love would have been beautiful to see if Ben hadn't also seen how completely it shut Josie Belle out of the picture.

She was strong and self-sufficient, her parents' attitude seemed to say. She didn't need anybody to look after her, whereas Betty Anne was the kind of woman who would melt into a pool of helpless tears at the least provocation.

It was suddenly clear to Ben why Josie embraced every cause, took center stage at every party, put herself in the middle of every controversy. Sure, she was high-spirited as well as a natural leader. But she was also deeply vulnerable, a woman crying for the attention of a father who would never look beyond his lovely needy wife and a mother who was so wrapped up in her husband she hardly knew her daughter existed. Josie Belle had always been left to fend for herself.

As far as he could tell that was still true. Her father must be dead for only her mother's name had appeared on the party invitation. Surely Betty Anne Pickens had been at the party. But during the entire series of outrageous events she had been conspicuously absent. Not once had she appeared at her daughter's side to offer guidance, support or a motherly shoulder to cry on.

Ben would bet his last dollar that Josie now shouldered the burden her father had carried, being caretaker for a woman who had never learned that she had the inner resources to help herself.

"Are you all right up there? Do you want me to join you on that limb?"

"Why don't you just get an ax and chop it off? That's what everybody else in this town will be wanting to do right now. I've just succeeded in living down to Clytee Crawford's opinion of me."

"Since when have the opinions of others mattered to you, Josie? You've always marched to the beat of your own drum."

"That scares the hell out of most people. Why aren't you running, Ben?"

"You don't scare me, Josie."

"Oh, yeah?" He was glad to hear her laughing again. He didn't like the idea of Josie sitting out on a limb all by herself, crying. "After I started singing that song, I thought for a minute there that you were going to bolt out the door."

"A Sioux run from battle? Never!"

"You knew a battle was coming, didn't you?"

"It was bound to, Josie. Trouble seems to follow you around. What I don't know is why you brought this one on."

She was quiet for so long he tipped his head back so he could see her face, but it was too dark. All he could make out was a pale clear orb surrounded by a bright nimbus of hair.

Her red dress shimmered in the moonlight, and she looked like some kind of glorious red bird perched high in her tree, exotic and unattainable. Ben started stroking her feet, whether from habit or need, he couldn't say.

"I did what I thought was best at the time," she said, breaking her silence.

"Best for whom?"

"Jerry Bob."

"What about you, Josie? Did you do what was best for you?"

"Maybe. I don't know. I guess only time will tell."

"I think you did, Josie. I can't imagine you married to Jerry Bob Crawford. That family would smother you."

"I'm glad you agree with my motives...if not my tactics."

"Who said I didn't agree with your tactics? I've always enjoyed watching you in action, Josie."

"You have?"

"Yes. You're an exciting woman."

The sudden tension in her body came all the way down to her toes. They curled under, and her whole foot stiffened.

"You think I'm exciting?"

"Yes. I always have."

"You never told me."

"You never asked." It seemed a safe enough answer. The truth was, Ben hadn't really known until tonight how Josie thrilled him. "Are you ready to come down now?"

"It seems a longer way to the ground than it did to the top."

"Jump. I'll catch you."

"What if I fall?"

"Don't I always catch you if you fall?"

She stretched her toes and flexed her feet, loosening up.

Ben smiled into the darkness. He could tell what Josie was thinking by holding her feet. It was fun, too. And strangely intimate. It made him wonder if the rest of her body reflected her feelings, and how she would feel as she ran the gamut from anxiety to acceptance.

"All right, then," she said. "Here goes. Ready?"

"Yes."

"Say ready, set, go."

"Just let go, Josie. I'm here for you."

"Promise?"

"Always."

Her skirt billowed around her as she turned loose from the limb and plummeted toward him. He made a quick shift to the left in order to be directly in her path. She landed with a soft *whump* in his outstretched arms, then beamed at him, her face only inches away.

"You *did* it, Ben."

"Just like catching a fly ball."

"I'm considerably bigger than a fly ball. Heavier, too, I dare say."

A lovely flush stained her cheeks, and a light sheen of moisture dampened her skin. It was a soft Southern night, exactly right for holding a lush woman in your arms.

Ben tightened his hold, and her arms stole around his neck. He was going to kiss her, and she was going to kiss him back. He could feel it in his bones, see it in her eyes.

"Josie." Was he warning her, asking her permission, or merely stating a truth as old as time? Sometimes the whole world can be wrapped up in a name.

Suddenly his lips were on hers, and she was everything he'd thought she would be, sweet and yielding and so responsive he wasn't sure he'd ever be able to stop. It was a heady experience and one he was totally unprepared for.

He'd come to the party to celebrate her engagement to another man, and here he was kissing the woman who, bu for the grace of God and some lively shenanigans of her own, had almost been a bride. And he wasn't about to stop. That much he knew. He was going to hold on to her and see where the kiss would take them.

"Yoo-hoo!" It was a female voice, hailing them out of the darkness. "Josie Belle? Are you out here?"

Josie pulled away and looked at him, stricken, then closed her eyes and leaned her forehead against his.

"Ashley," she whispered. "She's a friend of mine."

"I suppose I'll have to let you go."

Josie sighed. "I suppose." He released her, and she smoothed down her dress before stepping out of cover of the tree. "Here I am, Ashley." She reached back and squeezed Ben's hand, then walked swiftly toward the slender blonde who was tripping through the grass on stiletto heels. Ben considered it a miracle Ashley didn't fall down and break her neck.

While Josie joined her friend, he leaned against the tree and learned how to breathe all over again. Amazing, the impact of one small kiss.

Voices floated to him on the still summer air.

"You'd better come back inside, Josie. Everybody's looking for you. Especially your aunt Tess."

"Oh, lordy, what now?"

"Jerry Bob and Clytee left the party in a huff, then your aunt got up to the microphone and told everybody to start dancing, that it was just a lovers' tiff that would blow over and she'd see them all at the wedding on Saturday."

"Oh, no."

"So, Josie, what happened? Is there going to be a wedding on Saturday?"

Ben couldn't hear Josie's answer. They were out of range.

He closed his eyes, keenly aware of the taste of Josie's lips and the beating of his own heart. If there was a wedding on Saturday, if Josie married Jerry Bob Crawford, a part of Ben would die. It was that simple.

Chapter Three

"If you think you're going to get by with this, young lady, you're sadly mistaken."

Nobody could lay down the law quite like Aunt Tess. She made her point by jabbing her index finger in the air and waving her arm as if she were directing a full-fledged circus parade complete with dancing bears and performing elephants. Josie figured that's where she got her own flair for drama.

She leaned her hip against the kitchen cabinet and watched, partially amused, partially outraged, as her aunt paced the kitchen floor and lectured her audience of two. Josie's mother sat with her mouth pinched and her shoulders hunched as if blows were being rained down on her.

There would be no help from that quarter. Josie was in this alone, as she'd been so many times before.

"Just what did you think you were trying to pull, embarrassing poor Clytee and mortifying us all?"

"She deserved everything she got after the nasty things she said about my friend Ben."

"That dark, good-looking young doctor who's hung his shingle across town?"

"That's the one."

"Well, no wonder. If I were twenty years younger he'd light my fires, too, but there's a quite a big difference between getting your fires lit and letting everybody in town know it."

Josie didn't bother to correct her aunt, for to tell the truth, Ben really had lit a few of her fires. She'd spent the better part of last night and a good chunk of the morning remembering their kiss under the magnolia tree. The unexpectedness of it. The beauty. The passion. The way Ben Standing Bear kissed ought to be declared illegal.

She wondered what would have happened if he'd ever kissed her that way while they were in college. Would she still be sitting in her mother's kitchen listening to Aunt Tess rant about a wedding that wasn't going to take place?

"When are you going to learn to be discreet, Josie?"

"Never. Games are for wimps and cowards. I always let my feelings show."

"May I remind you this is Pontotoc, Mississippi, and not Chicago, Illinois?" Aunt Tess pronounced it *El-ee-noise,* in three distinct syllable with emphasis on the last.

"I know where I am, Aunt Tess. And I know where I'm going. I'm going to the high school to start cataloging the stage props for this fall."

"You most certainly are not, young lady. You're going to get on that telephone and apologize to Jerry Bob and his mother."

"Hell will freeze over first. It's over, Aunt Tess. Jerry Bob asked for his ring back, and there's not going to be a wedding."

Josie looked toward her mother for some support, but

Betty Anne was clinging to her chair as if she might be putting down roots.

"What about that wedding dress hanging in the closet, not to mention the cheese balls taking up all the room in the refrigerator and the three hundred miniature quiches in the freezer that Betty Anne and I slaved over for days?"

"I'll take the dress back, and we'll give the food to the Salvation Army kitchen."

"We will do no such thing. A hundred and fifty people are going to show up next Saturday for a wedding, and you're going to give it to them if I have to hog-tie you and drag you there."

Josie cast another beseeching look toward her mother, but Betty Anne was now twisting the edge of the tablecloth into knots.

"Good grief, Aunt Tess. This is the twenty-first century. Nobody raises an eyebrow about a cancelled wedding."

"You'd better speak to your daughter, Betty Anne." Aunt Tess crossed her arms and tapped her foot in an angry rhythm on the linoleum.

"What can I say?" When Betty Anne cried she didn't just shed a few tears; she let loose a river that had to be mopped up with a whole box of tissues.

"Now see what you've done, Josie? Your poor father would be mortified. In fact, you've mortified us all. Over the years I've tried to keep my mouth shut, but now that you've embarrassed the entire Pickens family in front of the whole town, I can no longer hold my peace."

Aunt Tess had worked herself into such a tantrum that her face was red and her dress had big wet patches under the arms where she'd sweated in spite of the fact that the air conditioner was going ninety to nothing.

"I'm not fixing to stand by and let you disgrace us, to boot," she added. "You'd better get your ducks in a row and make up with Jerry Bob."

Betty Anne flung the top half of herself across the kitchen table, sobbing as if the world was about to come to an end.

Something inside Josie snapped. "All right, then. I'll give you a wedding."

She marched out of the kitchen with her head high and all her war flags flying. In the hall she whistled for Bruiser, who loped down the stairs with his tongue hanging out and a goofy grin on his big hairy face. Josie grabbed the leash and hooked him up.

"Let's go for a walk, boy."

He thumped his big tail on the floor, and the minute he was out the door he took off like a rocket, dragging Josie along behind. For once she was glad he'd refused to learn to heel. She didn't want a sedate walk. She needed to go flying down the sidewalk and whizzing by trees and dodging hydrangea bushes. She needed to have to concentrate on not getting dragged into traffic and killed. She needed anything except to think about what had taken place in her mother's kitchen.

The small town passed by at dizzying speed. Bruiser didn't let up until they had reached the town square. Then he suddenly sat on his haunches and looked up at her, panting, his tongue lolling sideways and dripping on her shoes.

She plopped into the grass beside him and looped her arm around his thick neck.

"Now what am I going to do, Bruiser?" He tilted his head to one side and gave her his goofy grin. "You wouldn't know what it's like to have Aunt Tess trying to run your life while your mother hides behind her tears, would you?"

Now that she was out of the pressure cooker, Josie sorely regretted her impulsive statement. How could she possibly give Aunt Tess and her mother a wedding? She wouldn't marry Jerry Bob Crawford and his mother if they were the last people on earth.

She wished that just once she could hold her tongue. She wished she didn't have to rise to every challenge, snap at every bait, leap before she looked.

"Maybe I can just show up at the church on Saturday and tell everybody there's not going to be a wedding, but they can come to the reception and eat the cheese balls and the quiches. And the wedding cake. Oh, Lord, I forgot about the wedding cake."

She'd ordered it from Nancy Cunningham down at Cakes Galore, and there was a two-week cancellation policy. The only thing she could be thankful about was that Aunt Tess hadn't thrown that in her face, too.

Nor the wedding presents. *Good grief.* There were all those wedding presents taking up space in the dining room that would have to be packed up and returned.

"Why can't life be simple, Bruiser? Answer me that."

He bathed both her hands and her face with his big pink tongue. As long as he had food and shelter and plenty of pats on the head, he was happy.

"It's a dog's life, huh, boy?"

Think of something, she told herself. She'd always been able to think her way out of a dilemma.

Suddenly she thought of Ben Standing Bear. *If you ever need me, all you have to do is call.* That's what he had told her last night right before he left the party.

She'd gone inside with Ashley to face the music, and much to her relief she'd found most of her guests dancing and drinking, concentrating more on having a good time than on what had gone on between her and Jerry Bob, who, she saw thankfully, had already departed with Clytee.

"Did he announce that the wedding was off?" Josie had asked her friend.

"No, he just told everybody his mother wasn't feeling

good, and he was going to take her home. I felt kinda sorry for him, he looked sort of lost.''

''You've got a marshmallow heart, Ashley. Better watch that. It'll get you into trouble.''

''Not nearly as much trouble as your impulsive ways, Josie.''

Lord, wasn't that the truth? Josie thought now as she sat on the town square. Her latest impulse had landed her into the midst of a pot of boiling water, and she could think of only one way out.

She stood up, dusted off her shorts, and tugged on Bruiser's leash.

''Come on, boy. Rest time's up.'' He didn't budge. Instead he gave her a look that said, can't you carry me? Or how about calling a taxi? She tugged again. ''I mean it, Bruiser. I'm not kidding around this time. This is important.''

Something in her voice must have communicated her sense of urgency, for he lumbered onto all fours, thumped his tail once, licked her hand, then trotted along beside her as if he'd learned leash training as a puppy, and it was his favorite thing in the world to do.

''Good boy,'' she said. ''Did you know you're the smartest dog in the world?''

His lopsided grin said he knew that, too, but that a dog couldn't hear enough praise.

Ben saw her coming. Standing on a ladder outside his soon-to-open office, he spotted the flaming red hair a block down the street. Smiling, he shaded his eyes to watch her. She made a fetching picture, a beautiful woman walking her dog.

Did she just happen to be in the neighborhood, or was she coming to see him? He'd dreamed of her last night,

An Important Message from the Editors

Dear Reader,

Because you've chosen to read one of our fine romance novels, we'd like to say "thank you!" And, as a **special** way to thank you, we've selected <u>two more</u> of the books you love so well **plus** an exciting Mystery Gift to send you— absolutely <u>FREE</u>!

Please enjoy them with our compliments...

Pam Powers

Lift here

Peel off seal and place inside...

How to validate your Editor's
"Thank You"
FREE GIFT

1. Peel off gift seal from front cover. Place it in space provided at right. This automatically entitles you to receive 2 FREE BOOKS and a fabulous mystery gift.

2. Send back this card and you'll get 2 brand-new *Romance* novels. These books have a cover price of $5.99 or more each in the U.S. and $6.99 or more each in Canada, but they are yours to keep absolutely free.

3. There's no catch. You're under no obligation to buy anything. We charge nothing—ZERO—for your first shipment. And you don't have to make any minimum number of purchases— not even one!

4. The fact is, thousands of readers enjoy receiving their books by mail from The Reader Service. They enjoy the convenience of home delivery...they like getting the best new novels at discount prices BEFORE they're available in stores... and they love their Heart to Heart subscriber newsletter featuring author news, horoscopes, recipes, book reviews and much more!

5. We hope that after receiving your free books you'll want to remain a subscriber. But the choice is yours— to continue or cancel, any time at all! So why not take us up on our invitation, with no risk of any kind. You'll be glad you did!

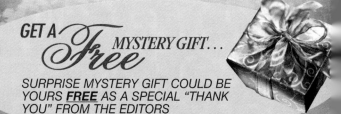

GET A *Free* MYSTERY GIFT...

SURPRISE MYSTERY GIFT COULD BE YOURS **FREE** AS A SPECIAL "THANK YOU" FROM THE EDITORS

The Editor's "Thank You" Free Gifts Include:

- *Two BRAND-NEW Romance novels!*
- *An exciting mystery gift!*

Yes! I have placed my

Editor's "Thank You" seal in the space provided above. Please send me 2 free books and a fabulous mystery gift. I understand I am under no obligation to purchase any books, as explained on the back and on the opposite page.

**PLACE
FREE GIFT
SEAL
HERE**

▼ DETACH AND MAIL CARD TODAY! ▼

393 MDL DVFG   193 MDL DVFF

FIRST NAME

LAST NAME

ADDRESS

APT.#

CITY

STATE/PROV.

ZIP/POSTAL CODE

(PR-R-04)

Thank You!

The Reader Service — Here's How It Works:

Accepting your 2 free books and gift places you under no obligation to buy anything. You may keep the books and gift and return the shipping statement marked "cancel." If you do not cancel, about a month later we'll send you 3 additional books and bill you just $4.74 each in the U.S., or $5.24 each in Canada, plus 25¢ shipping & handling per book and applicable taxes if any.* That's the complete price and — compared to cover prices starting from $5.99 each in the U.S. and $6.99 each in Canada — it's quite a bargain! You may cancel at any time, but if you choose to continue, every month we'll send you 3 more books, which you may either purchase at the discount price or return to us and cancel your subscription.

*Terms and prices subject to change without notice. Sales tax applicable in N.Y. Canadian residents will be charged applicable provincial taxes and GST.

If offer card is missing write to: The Reader Service, 3010 Walden Ave., P.O. Box 1867, Buffalo, NY 14240-1867

BUSINESS REPLY MAIL

FIRST-CLASS MAIL   PERMIT NO. 717-003   BUFFALO, NY

POSTAGE WILL BE PAID BY ADDRESSEE

THE READER SERVICE
3010 WALDEN AVE
PO BOX 1341
BUFFALO NY 14240-8571

NO POSTAGE
NECESSARY
IF MAILED
IN THE
UNITED STATES

and she was the first thing he'd thought about when he woke up. That bewildered Ben.

He led a carefully planned, tightly focused life. Always had, always would. Currently his focus was on carving out a place in the community and building a good practice. Romance was not part of his plan now or in the foreseeable future.

Friendship was another thing, though. And after all, Josie was merely a friend, wasn't she?

She was close enough now to see him, and she waved.

"I hope you don't mind drop-in company," she called, even before she turned up his walkway, even before he could get his heart to behave.

"Not at all. Especially when the company is you."

She tilted her head to one side and studied him solemnly. "Just when did you get to be such a charmer, Ben Standing Bear?"

"If I did, which I sincerely doubt, it was while you weren't looking."

"Hmm, I'm going to have to keep my eye on you. There's no telling what you'll do next."

"That's a great idea, Josie." He climbed off the ladder and took her hand. "A woman has to stand pretty close to keep an eye on a man."

He loved the way she blushed. He loved the way her eyes crinkled at the corners when she laughed. He loved the way the tip of her tongue appeared briefly, as if she were tasting her own smile.

Ben wanted to kiss her. Right there on the sidewalk.

Stop, he warned himself. *Stay focused.*

Besides, she'd only recently broken her engagement. Who knew what was happening to her heart?

"You want to see my office, Josie? There's still a lot of work to be done, but I think you can get the general idea."

"Can Bruiser come in, too?"

"Certainly." He smiled. "A lab named Bruiser?"

"Shh, he doesn't know he's a lab. I gave him that name so he'd think he's a fierce watchdog."

"I see." He took her elbow and led her through the door of his clinic. Sunlight poured through the windows and pickéd up dust motes rising from the unfinished hardwood floor. "Like I said, it's not much right now."

"It's charming. I can picture you here." Josie walked from room to room with Bruiser right at her heels, making certain he was between Ben and Josie.

They ended up in his office, the only room in the clinic that was fully furnished. "It's wonderful!" she said, and seeing it through Josie's eyes, Ben was glad he'd brought in his books, hung his diploma, put the Oriental rug under his desk.

"Sit down, Josie. I'll get us a couple of colas, and a dish of water for your dog."

"That'll be great. I don't usually walk Bruiser in the middle of the day when it's so hot, but something came up, and I just... Cola sounds great, Ben."

Josie was actually nervous. That wasn't like her. As he poured their drinks over ice and drew a pan of water for the dog he wondered what else had happened since the party. Had Jerry Bob come back and tried to make amends? He hadn't seen the ring on her finger, but then he hadn't been looking at her hands. He'd been mesmerized by her face and her hair and her long, tanned legs.

"Here you are," he said, handing her the drink, and the first thing he noticed was that she wasn't wearing Jerry Bob's ring.

"Thanks. I needed this."

They drank in silence, eyeing each other over the tops of their glasses. Josie finally set hers aside.

"I guess you're wondering why I'm here."

"You don't have to have a reason to visit me, Josie. I thought you knew that."

"I wish I didn't," she said. "Have a reason, I mean."

"Why the long face? Is that any way for a woman who worked so hard to become disengaged to look? I thought you'd be celebrating."

"So did I. But Aunt Tess had other ideas."

"The one I met at Thanksgiving so many years ago? The barracuda in the beehive?"

That had been Josie's term for her aunt, not his. They'd both laughed about it as they drove back to the campus after the Thanksgiving holidays were over.

"That's the one. She says I'll disgrace the entire family if I don't go through with the wedding. She wants me to make up with Jerry Bob."

"Do you want my advice, Josie?"

"Yes."

"I don't think you should do that. It was obvious to me that he's wrong for you. I don't think you could ever be happy in the Crawford family, and I'd hate to see my old study buddy with her light hid under a bushel."

"Thanks, pal."

"Any time. I'm glad I could help. I told you last night, and I meant it...if you need me, all you have to do is let me know."

Josie had a habit of biting her lip when she was trying to make up her mind about something. She was doing it now, and studying Ben as if she were trying to see his soul.

"I need you."

That's all she said. Three little words that felt as if they might change his life forever.

Ben didn't know what to say, and so he waited, watching Josie. She was no longer uncertain. He could tell by the way she looked directly into his eyes.

"I'm in trouble, Ben." *Oh, God, not that. Not pregnant.*

"Aunt Tess backed me into a corner, and, as usual, I acted on impulse. I told her there would be a wedding on Saturday."

He felt as if he were on a seesaw, going from relief to doldrums in seconds.

"So you're going to marry Jerry Bob, after all?"

"No."

"No?"

"I was hoping to marry you."

The seesaw swung upward and stayed there. Ben had the sensation that if he looked down there would be nothing under his feet except sky.

"I'm afraid I don't understand."

"I'm proposing to you, Ben."

"You're serious, aren't you?"

"About the wedding, yes. Unless you're involved with somebody else, of course. I wouldn't want to be the cause of a breakup if you have a girlfriend."

"There is no one else." He started to add, *romance is not in my plans,* but thought better of it.

"Good." She laughed, nervous. "I didn't mean that the way it sounded. It would be nice for you if you had a girlfriend, if she was wonderful, of course. You deserve somebody wonderful, Ben."

"So do you."

She bent down to pet her dog, and he couldn't see her face. He knew Josie. She was hiding something. But what?

"Where does that leave us, Ben?"

"You said something about a wedding Saturday."

"Well, yes…see, if you would just walk down the aisle and say *I do,* then we could go our separate ways and in a reasonable length of time, say five or six months, we could get an annulment and everybody would be happy."

Ben was too stunned to speak. What she was proposing went beyond unconventional. It was outrageous, unthinkable…and yet, all the other times he'd rescued Josie he'd never had regrets.

"We have enough time for the blood tests and license and all," Josie said. "That is, if you'll agree. And I want you to know that it's okay if you don't. We'll still be friends, and I'll go home and face up to Aunt Tess." Suddenly her face clouded over, and she stood up so fast she startled Bruiser, who barked, then hid behind her legs.

"I never should have come here. I should have stood up to Aunt Tess, and that's what I'm fixing to do. Go home and face the music, damn the torpedos, full speed ahead, it's not as if I'm pregnant or anything, it's just that I get so tired of fighting alone, sometimes I…"

Ben stopped her flood of words the only way he knew how. He kissed her until he could feel her relax. A shudder ran through her, and when he let her go she leaned into him, boneless, her head against his chest, her hand resting over his heart.

"Better?" he asked.

She nodded. "Better."

"I want to marry you, Josie."

"You don't have to…"

"Did you hear what I said? I didn't say I'll be happy to help you out. I said I *want* to marry you."

She tipped her head back and studied him. "Why?"

How like her to ask the hard questions. Josie had never been one to beat around the bush.

"Because you're my good pal, and the best times I've ever had were with you. I can't wait to see what happens next."

It was the truth, but only part of the truth. Josie needed support right now, not an airing of his own confused feelings. She didn't need to hear that he'd never been so moved by a woman. She didn't need to know that the bargain she proposed appealed to his sense of the romantic. She didn't need to hear that rescuing her made him feel noble.

What she needed was his full support and a chance to get over Jerry Bob.

A temporary marriage need not sidetrack his own plans nor change his focus. He'd look upon this as another great adventure with Josie, and when it was all over they'd laugh about it.

She could forget going their separate ways, though. Even if this was a temporary arrangement, he would do it properly, the way he did everything else in his life.

But he'd deal with that later. Right now, he had other things on his mind, namely cheering up his best friend.

Dropping to one knee, he caught Josie's hand. "Josie Belle Pickens, will you do me the honor of becoming my wife?"

She laughed. "You're crazy."

"Is that a yes?"

"It's a resounding hallelujah-thank-you yes."

"Good, then let's celebrate. The usual way?"

"You remember?"

"Of course, I remember. How can I forget sitting cross-legged on the floor with you surrounded by Hershey Bar wrappers and mountains of buttered popcorn?"

"Ben, how is it that you always know exactly what I need?"

"Because I'm this romantic, wonderful guy, see? And I'm planning to marry an exciting, wonderful woman."

Laughing, she squeezed him around the waist. It was a spontaneous gesture she'd made many times. Strange how this time, Ben wanted to hold her close and not let go.

"When?" she asked.

"Tonight? My place? I'll pick you up."

"No. We can't tip off the enemy before Saturday. I'll come to you."

He watched her leave with her dog, watched until she disappeared from view. Then he went back inside to call his brother. There was no way he was going to stand up in a church Saturday without his brother as best man for the wedding, even if the wedding wasn't real.

Jim and Ben had been a team since their parents had died in a freak accident at the state fair: the roller coaster they'd been riding jumped its tracks and plunged to the ground while Jim and Ben watched from a nearby carousel. Ben still remembered how his older brother had watched over him in the orphanage, a fierce protector, a staunch friend. At the age of twelve Jim had become mother and father to his two-year-old brother. They had formed a bond that could never be broken.

Ben dialed his brother's number, and Jim picked up on the first ring.

"Ben! How's Pontotoc treating you?"

"I'm already a sensation." *Literally.* Jim laughed as Ben recounted last night's tango and its aftermath.

"The Sioux always did know how to take a place by storm. Wait till I tell Sarah."

Sarah would get a kick out of the story, too. Anything involving her husband's family delighted her.

Ben loved his sister-in-law and wanted her at the wedding, too. As well as his niece and nephew.

Family was important to Ben, perhaps because he'd never had anyone except his brother, but mainly because he was a man who loved deeply and truly. No one-night stands for him. No casual sex.

Ben had known from the minute he met Sarah Sloan that she was the perfect woman for his brother. When the time was right, he hoped the same thing would happen for him.

"There's something else you can tell Sarah. I'm getting married Saturday, and I want you to be my best man."

Jim whistled. "I've always known that you move fast, Ben, but don't you think that's a little hasty?"

"It is a bit rushed."

Jim went into his older-brother-caretaker mode. "Is she pregnant?"

"No. You know me better than that."

"I thought I did. Where have you been keeping this woman?"

Ben had always been totally honest, but for the second time that day he found himself telling only partial truths. If he spilled the beans about why he was marrying Josie he would be disloyal to her, and besides that, Jim, the practical big brother, would try to talk him out of it.

If Ben thought too much about it, he might talk himself out of the wedding. The trick was not to cogitate. Josie used to tell him, "Ben, you think too much. Don't you know, if you analyze magic it vanishes?"

"You know her, Jim. It's Josie."

"*Josie?*" Jim chuckled. "That explains it. She never did a conventional thing in her life." He laughed again. "By the way, Ben, I approve."

It was what Ben had been waiting for, his brother's blessing. Call him superstitious, but he considered it a good omen.

"Good. Then I can count on you and Sarah and the children being here Saturday?"

"You can always count on me, Ben. For anything. And don't you forget it."

Ben was in such a chipper mood after he hung up that he walked downtown and bought flowers for Josie. After all, didn't a woman about to be married deserve some pampering?

Chapter Four

Jerry Bob was waiting for Josie. When she saw his pickup truck parked in her driveway she started to turn around and go back to the park. Or back to Ben.

Why did it feel so good to run to Ben? Why was it that the minute he'd come to town Josie had turned into the kind of woman who longed to be held in the protective embrace of a kind and gentle man?

She'd always prided herself on her independence. She'd always fended for herself. She didn't need somebody else to do that job. Being dependent relinquished power, made her weak, didn't it?

Bruiser whined. He was hot and ready to flop down on the cool hardwood floor.

"Might as well face the music, Bruiser. Don't tell what we've been up to. And you might take a bite of Jerry Bob's leg. Just a little nip. Enough to send him on his way."

Josie took a deep breath and went inside. It helped that

Jerry Bob looked silly. Most of him was perched atop her mother's ridiculously small Victorian chair, and the rest of him hung over, then sort of draped over the carved roses.

No one else was in sight. Her mother was probably up in her bedroom, overcome with the vapors, but she'd bet her bottom dollar that Aunt Tess was lurking somewhere, fixing to listen to every word.

What would she do if Josie said, "Sic 'im, Bruiser"? She'd probably come barreling out from behind the tacky silk potted palm Josie had always hated.

She smiled at the thought. As it turned out Bruiser sniffed at Jerry Bob's pant leg, then lifted his nose in disdain and flopped down in front of the sofa.

"I don't see what you have to be so happy about, Josie Belle. I've been waiting for you."

How like Jerry Bob to put her on the defensive. Josie had opened her mouth to defend herself when she realized that she didn't ever have to answer to this man again.

"You no longer have any reason to do that, Jerry Bob. I gave you back your ring. Remember?"

"How could I ever forget, Josie Belle? Nobody in town will. They'll be talking about the spectacle you made of yourself for years. It just about killed Mama. She's had a headache ever since."

"Maybe she should see a doctor. I know a good one."

"Now you cut that out. I came here to make the peace and you've got me all mad again."

This was a complication Josie hadn't counted on. If she expected to pull off a wedding without Jerry Bob on Saturday, she had her work cut out for her.

"Go home and put an ice pack on your mama's head, Jerry Bob. I'm not going to marry you. Not Saturday. No ever."

"Is that your final word?"

"You can paint it in big red letters and paste it to the front of your mama's Cadillac."

Jerry Bob stood up so fast his chair toppled over. It was like dominoes. The chair fell against the brass umbrella stand which fell against the Oriental screen which toppled onto Aunt Tess, who let out a bellow.

"Lordy, Miss Tess..." Jerry Bob plucked Tess boldly from the mess and set her down in the middle of the living room where she stood with one arm raised like an outraged Statue of Liberty. Pins spewed from her beehive, and no matter how hard she tried, she couldn't keep up with the damage.

"I didn't mean to knock you over." If Jerry Bob had had a tail, it would be tucked between his legs. Josie felt sorry for him. Almost.

"Just go on home, Jerry Bob," Aunt Tess said. "I told you it wouldn't be easy. We'll deal with all this tomorrow after Josie's had time to calm down."

"I am calm, Aunt Tess," Josie told her after Jerry Bob left.

"Well, then, what do you have to say for yourself, young lady?"

"Number one, I'm not young, and as you well know, I'm hardly a lady, so you can stop calling me that, starting here and now. And number two, I promised you a wedding and you're going to get it, so you can just go on about your business and let me handle things."

Aunt Tess stood with her mouth working like a fish, then she walked stiffly out of the room without saying word.

"Why does it have to be like this?" Josie whispered after her aunt left the room.

Why did her mother's sister have to turn everything into a pitched battle? And why did Josie always take up her sword?

As Josie headed toward the front door, Bruiser trotted along behind her. She bent down and patted his head.

"Not this time, boy. I have lots of things to take care of, and you'd just slow me down."

Bruiser went to the window, and she could see him watching her all the way down the sidewalk. She didn't feel a bit silly as she turned and waved to her dog, then she headed in the direction of Ashley's house. If she planned to pull off Saturday's wedding, she'd need a co-conspirator.

Ben kept watching out the window for Josie like a teenager on his first date. Laughing at himself, he left the window and checked the refrigerator to see if the wine was cool. It was a good chardonnay, a vintner's reserve.

He didn't even know if Josie liked wine. Though they'd been best friends years ago, there were still lots of thing he didn't know about her.

"Well, pal, looks like you're going to get a chance to find out," he said. Talking to himself. A sure sign of nervousness.

Now that it was all over, now that he'd given his word and invited his brother, it suddenly occurred to him that there was no turning back. He was, indeed, getting married Saturday, and he didn't know whether to laugh or cry.

Fortunately he didn't have time to think about it. Josie knocked smartly, then realized there was a buzzer, and gave it a short punch. He could picture her standing outside his door, feeling a bit embarrassed that she hadn't noticed the buzzer first.

"Saved by the bell," he said, then opened the door, and there she stood with the setting sun shining in her hair, and he forgot everything except happiness.

"It's great to see you, Josie."

She laughed. "You just saw me earlier this afternoon."

"Every time I see you, it's great."

"Didn't anybody ever tell you? Remarks like that can go to a girl's head."

"Good. I'll try to think up some more."

They stood in the doorway smiling at each other. Ben got lost in the blue depths of her eyes. It was like drowning. Sinking softly into oblivion. And loving every minute of it.

"Somebody might see us," she said finally.

"Come in." He took her hands and pulled her into the room, and then he didn't want to let go.

And why should he? Saturday, he was going to marry this woman. Seized by impulse, he bent down and kissed her.

"Oh," she murmured, then her arms stole around his neck and she was kissing him back.

The music he'd put on earlier was playing somewhere softly in the background, and a part of him recognized the song—"Amazed." It was the song Josie had sung to him. Forever after he would think of it as *their* song.

His brother had always accused him of being a romantic, and Ben guessed it was so. Else why had he turned the lights down low and lit candles before Josie came? Why had he bought flowers? And a wedding gift?

Why was his heart racing as if he'd run around the block? And why couldn't he seem to stop kissing Josie?

Ben's kiss shook her all the way to her toes. She was going to have to put a stop to this. It felt too good. She could get used to it. Worse, she could become dependent on it.

Josie gently disentangled herself, trying to think of something witty to say. All the clever remarks she'd think of tomorrow took flight, and all she could do was smile at him.

"What, Josie?"

"You're spoiling me," she said, then hurried across the room and stood looking out the window as if she'd never seen Pontotoc before. She felt lost without his arms around her, so she wrapped her own around herself.

She could feel Ben watching her. What must he be thinking? She couldn't worry about that. She had enough things on her mind without taking on Ben, too. He could take care of himself. He was the strong type, the kind of man who always knew exactly what to do in every situation.

"Josie." He had come up behind her and was standing only inches away. She could feel his body heat, sense the size and shape of him. "Turn around and look at me."

She turned slowly, and Ben smiled at her. "I have something for you."

Whatever he had was hidden behind his back. When he pulled out the flowers Josie almost cried. They were gardenias, exquisitely beautiful and so fragrant they perfumed the entire room. She buried her face in the waxy white blossoms and inhaled.

"I *love* them. But you didn't have to do this, Ben."

"I didn't *have* to, Josie. I wanted to." Suddenly he seemed almost shy. "Now, how about that candy and popcorn? Is microwave all right with you? I'll melt extra butter."

She patted her hips. "I'll appreciate it, and so will my saddle bags."

"If you're fishing for compliments, you've come to the right place." Ben circled her slowly, taking in the view with one eyebrow raised and a satisfied smile on his face. Josie had never found a man's perusal so unnerving. For a minute she thought of sucking in her breath, then she knew he would know, and she flushed all the way to the roots of her hair.

"Nice," he murmured. "Very nice."

Everything he said sounded intimate to her. Maybe it was

her state of mind. Maybe it was her overactive imagination. Whatever the cause, she had to make some changes, and fast.

"We'd better get cooking, or I'm liable to be here all night."

"I could handle that."

That, too, sounded suggestive, though Josie knew full well that Ben Standing Bear was merely being his usual take-it-all-in-stride self.

He put a bag of popcorn into the microwave, then got a small sauté pan and began to melt a big chunk of butter.

"I'll get a bowl. Where do you keep them?"

"Left of the sink. Bottom shelf."

"If you'd asked me that question I wouldn't have been able to tell you. How do you always know these small details, Ben?"

"Habit. For instance, I know that you used to eat all the plain chocolate in the Hershey Bar first and save the parts with the almonds for last. Do you still do that?"

Josie laughed. "I do. Do you still hide your potato chips so nobody will know you don't always eat healthy?"

"Who, me? Keep heart-attack-in-a-bag?" He opened a cabinet and shoved aside two rolls of paper towels to reveal a bag of vinegar-and-salt potato chips. "We know each other better than most couples getting married, Josie."

He made it all sound so normal, so real, that Josie was having a hard time remembering that Saturday's wedding would be a farce.

"I've been thinking about that, Ben."

"Don't worry, Josie. Most brides get cold feet."

"How do you know? You're the wrong gender."

"I read it somewhere."

"You shouldn't believe everything you read, Ben. But I wasn't thinking about changing my mind, I was thinking about how I could make sure Jerry Bob doesn't come near the church.''

"Popcorn's ready. Let's think over food.'' Ben spread a quilt on his floor in the living room. "Dig in, Josie. I'll be right back.'' When he returned he was carrying a bottle of wine and two glasses. "I hope you like chardonnay.''

"Love it.'' First flowers, and now this. "I'm going to get a big head, Ben.''

"It's not every day a man gets married. I thought we'd celebrate in real style.''

He said it as if he sincerely meant it. Or was he merely being kind? He was the kindest man she'd ever known, and someday some woman was going to be very, very lucky.

All of a sudden Josie felt as if she was standing on the sidelines watching while everybody passed her by, two by two, couples with hands joined, laughing, while the music played on. She imagined Ben on the carousel with another woman, the lucky somebody he would meet someday, while Josie stood nearby with nothing but a faded wedding bouquet and a yellowed marriage certificate.

What had she done? In asking Ben to be a stand-in for Jerry Bob at a wedding that wasn't real, she had effectively destroyed any possibility of getting to know him as anything except a friend. Instead of calling him to come over for dinner and letting things take their natural course, she had cast him once more in the role of rescuer for the scamp Josie.

Now Ben could never view her in any way except as the woman he was *obligated* to protect.

"What's wrong, Josie? Did I say something to upset you?''

"No.'' Her smile, like everything else about their current relationship, was false, and how Josie hated that. "I went woolgathering for a minute, that's all.'' She held out her glass. "Pour, please.''

When their glasses were full, Josie clinked hers against his. "To us," she said, "in remembrance of the good times."

He smiled. "To us, in anticipation of all the good times ahead."

He was so sweet, so positive, she almost wept. In order to take her mind off serious matters, she dug into the popcorn. Sitting with his long legs stretched out and his back against the sofa, Ben watched her. His intent perusal sent shivers over her.

She ate in silence for a while, then, when she could stand it no longer, she swung around and found herself looking straight into his eyes. The question she'd meant to ask died on her lips.

"You have butter...right there." He leaned over and wiped her chin with the tips of his fingers. "And there," he said, tracing her lips.

Josie couldn't move. She couldn't do anything except stare into his almost-black eyes and wish he would kiss her. Instead he leaned back and sipped his wine.

Josie grabbed her glass and took a big gulp. She could feel it going down, flowing through her body like fire. Or was that Ben? She took another big swallow.

Ben refilled her glass. "You always did have a lusty appetite, Josie."

She supposed ladies would mince at their food and sip their wine. *Real* ones, the kind Ben was bound to be attracted to.

"I like that," he added.

It was funny how the simplest remark could take on significance if the right person said it. And Ben was definitely the *right* person.

The right person for what, she didn't know. She took another drink of her wine. The buzz took away some of her confusion. She wondered if she was the kind of person who could become an alcoholic.

She'd have to ask Ben. He was a doctor. He'd know those things.

She opened her mouth to ask him, then closed it again. It was getting far too easy to depend on Ben. She'd just have to figure it all out for herself.

"You haven't touched the candy, Josie."

Chocolate. Now there was safe subject.

"I'm fixing to remedy that." She ripped into a Hershey Bar. "Prepare to watch me do major damage." She took an enormous bite, then closed her eyes as the confection melted in her mouth. "Hmm. Delicious. No wonder they say chocolate is the next best thing to sex."

Oh, dear. Now she'd done it. She couldn't bring herself to look at Ben. Was he amused? Horrified? Worried? He probably thought she leading up to something.

To consummate or not to consummate. That is the question.

Oh no, now she was thinking in Shakespeare.

"I'm waiting, Josie."

"Waiting for what?"

"For you to open your eyes."

"Why?"

"So I can figure out what's going on in that pretty head of yours."

Ben was the kind of man who believed that the eyes were windows to the soul, and darned if he hadn't become some kind of expert at reading her thoughts simply by looking at her.

"Oh, all right." Disgusted with herself, Josie looked straight at Ben. "I could never fool you for a minute."

"That's right, so don't even try. What's going on?"

"I'm embarrassed, that's what."

"You have no reason to be embarrassed, Josie. It's me. Ben. Your best friend. Remember?"

"I've gone and complicated things so much that I guess I'm having a hard time remembering. Besides, it's been a long time since our study buddy days."

"You haven't changed that much. Have I changed so much?"

"No. It's not that, Ben. It's just…me. I keep wondering when I'm going to grow up. You know? I keep thinking I ought to be doing things differently."

He leaned over and cupped her face. "Don't change, Josie. I like you just the way you are."

She covered her hands with his. "Ben, I think you're the sweetest man I've ever known. You don't know how much your kindness means to me."

He did know, and that was part of Ben's trouble. He kept viewing Josie not as his old pal from college, but as a vulnerable woman who was growing more appealing to him by the minute.

Go slow. He kept forgetting caution. Maybe buying the wine hadn't been such a good idea, after all. He'd wanted to make things festive for her, and instead he'd only made them more complicated. Josie had enough to deal with. She didn't need more problems piled on her plate.

Still…her cheeks were so soft, her eyes so shiny. He held her face a moment longer.

She had another smear of butter on her lips. Did he dare wipe it off? Kiss it off?

He didn't dare. If he started kissing her again, fueled as he was by wine and imagination, he might not be able to stop.

Ben cast around for something to say, something to do besides yearn to hold Josie.

"I called my brother. You remember him?" He leaned back to the relatively safe distance of the sofa.

"Of course. How's Jim?"

"Happy as a lark. Married to a wonderful woman named Sarah. I invited them to the wedding. I hope you don't mind."

"Mind? Of course not. It'll be good to have somebody there who's in our corner."

"You don't think there'll be trouble, do you?"

"Not really. I went to see Ashley today. She was going to be my maid of honor, but I asked her to stay with Jerry Bob and make sure he doesn't come to the church on Saturday."

"You told her the plan, then?"

"I had to. She was aghast at first, then she got quite a kick out of it. She said it was about time I gave Aunt Tess her comeuppance. I'm just sorry I have to do it at your expense, Ben."

"Stop apologizing before I get really mad at you, Josie. You have no reason to feel sorry. I told you I'm doing this because I want to." What would it take to convince Josie that he didn't feel used? Suddenly he thought of the wedding gift. "Wait here. I'll be right back."

"Where are you going?"

"I have a surprise." She'd always loved surprises, and the way she beamed told him she still did.

"Do I get to close my eyes?"

"Absolutely. Close your eyes and don't open them till I tell you."

When he came back he placed the small box in her outstretched hands. She closed her fists around it.

"What is it, Ben?"

"Open your eyes and see for yourself."

He could see the excitement in her, in the way her eyes widened, in the way her body tensed, in the way her mouth parted ever so slightly. When she saw the blue velvet box, she simply sat there, overcome.

For the first time since he'd known her, Ben couldn't read Josie's thoughts.

"Go ahead, Josie. Open it."

The gold locket gleamed against dark blue velvet, and Josie's hand trembled as she lifted the intertwined hearts. She hadn't yet seen the inscription. What would she think?

Ben couldn't wait any longer to find out. "It's inscribed on the back."

She turned the locket over and read aloud, "Ben and Josie, Forever." She questioned him with her eyes.

"I wanted them to put Ben and Josie, Friends Forever, but there wasn't enough room."

"Oh."

What did that mean? That she was disappointed? Relieved? Pleased? And why did her opinion matter to Ben so much?

She traced the locket with her finger as if she were committing it to memory. When she finally undid the clasp and put the locket around her neck, Ben breathed a sigh of relief. He hadn't done too badly, or else why was she wearing it?

"Will you fasten it for me, Ben?"

She held her hair out of the way and turned her back to him. Her neck was long and slender and graceful. Ben wished he were a poet instead of a doctor. Or perhaps a songwriter. It was that kind of neck, the kind that inspired men to write love ballads.

He wanted to bend down and kiss her there, on that soft and tender spot where a damp red curl nestled like a question mark. Then he thought better of it.

It was getting late, and he'd had enough wine to make such an intimacy dangerous.

There was only so much temptation a man could stand. He bent close to fasten the locket. Josie's skin smelled like summer flowers, and Ben had a hard time finishing the task.

"There you are, Josie. All set." He patted her arm in much the same way he'd done so many years ago.

"Thank you, Ben. For everything." Impulsively she pressed the locket close against her skin. "You've not only made a difficult situation more bearable, you've made it fun. How can I ever repay you?"

"Just be happy, Josie."

Chapter Five

Josie had decided the safest way to pull off a wedding with a surprise groom was to remove herself from her mother's house, so she and Ashley had hatched up a bachelor girls' bash the night before the wedding.

Aunt Tess, as usual, protested. "I don't see why you have to do this at the eleventh hour, Josie. And I certainly don't see why you have to spend the night."

"It'll be easier," Josie said.

"Betty Anne's a nervous wreck as it is. How am I ever going to get her to the church on time all by myself?"

"You'll have Uncle Carl to help you." Josie adored her mother's brother. Jovial and kind-hearted, he was the exact opposite of Aunt Tess. Uncle Carl used to tell her the gypsies had left him on her grandparents' doorstep.

"Besides, I have confidence in you, Aunt Tess. You've always *managed*."

"Well, I do like to think so." Aunt Tess patted her beehive. "After all, I did manage to salvage a wedding from that disastrous party."

"You certainly did, Aunt Tess."

Sitting crosslegged on Ashley's bed, Josie recounted her conversation with her aunt, and her friend howled with laughter.

"I guess I should be feeling guilty," Josie said. "But I don't."

"Good. You don't have a thing in the world to be guilty about, except maybe caving in to that old bat about the wedding. Are you sure about marrying Ben tomorrow, Josie?"

"Yes. I'm absolutely positive."

All of a sudden it struck Josie at how quickly she'd said yes to Ashley's question, when only a week earlier she'd been having second thoughts about marrying a man she'd dated for months and known all her life.

Not only that, but she was actually *excited* about the prospect of marrying Ben. She felt giddy and happy and a little bit scared and thrilled all the way down to her toes. Just like a *real* bride. Just as if Ben were the one she'd dated for months, as if he were the man she loved.

Whoa. Wait a minute.

As usual Josie was rushing full speed ahead into territory where even angels feared to tread. Besides that, Ashley was giving her funny looks.

"If I didn't know better I'd say you were smitten with Ben Standing Bear. Not that that would be so hard. He's absolutely gorgeous. Those eyes! And from the way he moved on the dance floor, I'd say the rest of him is not bad, either. Lordy, how come you didn't take a shine to him in college?"

For once Josie was thankful for Ashley's habit of running so far ahead in a conversation that she could forget the first question she'd asked in her rush to get to the next one.

"Ben's a brain, and you know me. When God passed out brains I thought He said *rain,* and I ran for cover." Anxious to get off the subject of Ben, Josie rambled among the dozen or so fingernail polish bottles on Ashley's dressing table. Picking up a magenta one, she read the label. "Persian Paradise?"

"Yeah. I kinda liked the way it sounded."

"I do, too. I think I'll wear it to the wedding."

"Don't you think it's kind of...*purple?*"

"Yes. And not at all what Jerry Bob would approve of. But now, Ben...that's a different story." Josie kicked off her shoes, sat down on the carpet and began to do her nails.

"I think Jerry Bob's sort of sweet. He was extremely grateful when I asked him to spend tomorrow with me."

"Where are you taking him? Somewhere far away from Pontotoc, I hope."

"We're going to picnic on the Tennessee-Tombigbee Waterway. There's a great park just off the Natchez Trace up near the Alabama line. I thought I'd make fried chicken and some of those delicious macadamia nut-chocolate chip cookies."

"Poor old Jerry Bob will think he's died and gone to heaven. I tried to cook for him once and even Bruiser wouldn't eat it." Josie lifted her toes for inspection. "There, what do you think?"

"It's shocking."

"Good. I'm going to do my fingernails the same color. I just wish I didn't have to wear the wedding gown I picked out for Jerry Bob."

Ashley inspected the gown hanging on a hook on the back of her closet door. "If we take off the sleeves and do away with that peplum and get rid of those rosettes on the skirt it would be a simple, classic strapless satin gown. What do you think?"

"I think it would be a miracle. I never did like all that froufrou anyhow."

"One miracle coming up." Ashley opened louvered doors to reveal her sewing machine.

"I keep forgetting you're Betty Crocker and Liz Claiborne rolled into one dynamite package. My only regret is that you won't be standing beside me tomorrow when I get married."

"Don't worry, Josie. I'll be right by your side when the real thing comes along."

"I'm so confused right now I'm afraid I wouldn't know the real thing even if I tripped on it."

"Oh, you'll know, all right, Josie. You'll know."

Ashley had never been married, never been engaged, never even gone with any one person in particular. How could she be so sure?

Josie didn't ask her. Instead she grabbed a seam ripper and plunged wholeheartedly into the remake of the wedding gown.

And when morning came and she stood before Ashley's pier mirror while her friend adjusted her veil, she said, "Wish me luck, Ashley."

"Oh, I do. You know I do." Ashley hugged her tight. "All the luck in the world, Josie."

Josie figured she was going to need it. She waved from the upstairs window as Ashley set out in her red convertible with a basket of Southern fried chicken, and then she drove to the church to face the music.

According to tradition it was bad luck for the groom to see his bride on their wedding day. At least, that's what Josie had told Ben the day they got their license.

"Of course, that's all malarky," she'd added.

"Let's do it the traditional way, Josie." He'd figured they'd need all the luck they could get.

Now, standing in the back room with his brother, Ben almost regretted his decision not to see Josie. What if she'd changed her mind? What if he walked out there in front of a hundred and fifty of Pontotoc's upstanding citizens and Josie didn't show up?

"You look nervous, Ben." Jim handed him a cup of ice water. "It's not too late to change your mind."

"No, I won't change my mind. Today I'm going to marry Josie."

Sarah came through the doors that connected Ben's dressing room with Josie's.

"Of course you are," she said. "And I must say, I wholeheartedly approve your choice." She linked her arm through her husband's. "Darling, are you trying to talk him out of a wedding? If you are, you're in the doghouse."

"Again?" Jim leaned down to kiss his wife, then pulled her close and put his hand on her still-flat belly. "Every time she gets pregnant, I get in the doghouse." Sarah poked her husband playfully in the ribs, and he laughed. "Not that I'm complaining."

"You'd better not."

Looking at the two of them together, seeing their obvious delight in one another, Ben experienced a moment of regret.

That's what weddings should lead to. For a moment he wanted to rush through the connecting door and say, *Josie, let's do this right. Let's have a courtship and see if it leads to a wedding, and if it does, we'll tie a knot that will never be broken.*

He couldn't do that, of course. He'd made a commitment to her already, and if his wedding wasn't the most romantic one in the world, at least it would be one of the most unusual.

"I'd better get back in there with Josie. If I don't, *your* headstrong daughter is going to march out there and order the organist to start the music. She can't wait to scatter rose petals down the aisle.'' Sarah stood on tiptoe and kissed Ben's cheek. ''Thank you for letting her be a part of your wedding.''

''Josie and I wouldn't have it any other way.''

And it was true. Josie had been thrilled when he'd suggested his niece as a substitute for Ashley, and he felt good knowing that he was surrounded by family on his wedding day, especially considering the fact that his reception in this town had been guarded, to say the least.

The first strains of music drifted back to them.

''It's almost time,'' Jim said. ''Are you ready?''

What would happen when Ben walked into the chapel instead of Jerry Bob Crawford? Would there be a scene? And how could he prepare his brother for that possibility without betraying Josie?

''I'm ready…and Jim, no matter what happens, we're going through with this wedding. Okay?''

''You sound as if you're expecting trouble. What is it you're not telling me?''

''As you said, this was all very sudden, and I'm afraid certain members of her family think she's marrying the wrong guy. They were rooting for a hometown fellow named Jerry Bob Crawford.''

''Don't worry. I'll set them straight.''

Ben laughed. ''I knew you would. Just don't take scalps, okay? I'm the one who'll have to live with the consequences.''

''Don't worry. The Bear has become a pussycat since I got married. Just ask Sarah.''

''She'd laugh me out of the room. You're still the Bear and still my hero. Thanks for being here.''

Ben meant every word he said. Memories washed over him—of how Jim hadn't let go of his hand from the time their parents died until Ben could sleep through the night at the orphanage without crying; of how Jim had dedicated his first flight with the naval precision flight team, the Blue Angels, to Ben; of how Jim had struggled back from the paralysis that had cost his career and almost his life; of how his brother had turned tragedy into triumph by opening a flight school to help society's teenage castoffs and misfits.

If Ben could be half the man his brother was, he'd be proud.

"Save the accolades, little brother. They're playing your song." Sounds of the wedding march drifted their way, and the wedding director tapped on the door.

Josie was waiting. As Ben headed toward the chapel he had the sensation that the floor had dropped away and he was floating through a tunnel surrounded by mists. Somewhere far in the distance he could see a tiny beam of light.

When the wedding march started, Josie was standing at the back of the church with her uncle Carl, who would be giving her away. She tried to swallow the lump that had been in her throat since she'd arrived nearly an hour earlier.

"Here goes," she whispered.

Uncle Carl patted her hand. "Everything's going to be all right, Josie."

She'd waited until the eleventh hour to confide in him, and he'd been as supportive as she expected. "Don't you worry about a thing," he'd told her. "When the chips are down, your mama comes through like a champ. The only problem is, nobody ever asks Betty Anne to come through for them. Remember that, Josie. Quit hovering over her the way your daddy did and give your mama a chance to breathe."

"What about Aunt Tess?"

"Pshaw. She's all bluster. You and Betty Anne just need to stand up to her. Or better yet, toss her out of the house."

That was easy for Uncle Carl to say. He'd never had Tess move in with him the way she and her mother had. Tess had moved in to help them after Josie's father died, just for a few weeks, she'd said, and two years later she was still there. She'd leased her own house in Corinth and was talking about selling it.

"Here they come," Uncle Carl said.

Josie lost her breath at the sight of Ben. Maybe it was the tuxedo. She'd never seen him in one, and he was undeniably the most incredible-looking man she'd ever laid eyes on.

That had to be it. It couldn't be the way his dark eyes searched the length of the church until he found her standing in the shadows of the foyer, waiting to walk down the aisle. It couldn't be the way his smile warmed her heart, nor the way her own heart refused to behave.

No, it couldn't be any of those things, for that seemed much too real.

"Pinch me," she whispered. She had to remember that Ben wasn't really the man she loved, and that her wedding was merely a spectacle for the benefit of the Pickens family.

Ben took his place at the front of the church with his distinguished-looking brother at his side. It was a moment before the crowd registered that he was standing in the spot reserved for the groom.

Suddenly there was a collective gasp, and Aunt Tess sprang out of her seat.

Here comes trouble. Josie tensed. If necessary she would march down the aisle and snatch Aunt Tess out of the church. She'd swear she would.

"Where's Jerry Bob?" Aunt Tess said.

Ben's smile never wavered, but his brother turned a fierce look in Tess's direction that would have had most grown men quaking in their boots.

True to form, Aunt Tess was unflappable. "I want to know what's going on."

Suddenly Betty Anne grabbed the back of Tess's dress

and gave a big jerk. Aunt Tess toppled back to her seat like Tinker Toys gone awry.

"Sit down, Tess," Betty Anne hissed. "You're ruining my daughter's wedding."

"Well, I never, Betty Anne..."

"Don't say another word, Tess, or I'll have the ushers take you out." Aunt Tess opened her mouth, and Betty Anne added, "I mean it."

Uncle Carl squeezed Josie's hand. "See. I told you."

It was over. The major trouble Josie had expected had been nothing more than a minor flap. Now she could marry Ben unhindered.

"Can I go now?" Little Miss Elizabeth Standing Bear had been dancing up and down on the toes of her patent leather shoes ever since her uncle Ben had strolled to the front of the church.

Josie bent down and gave her a big hug. "You can go now, sweetheart. And scatter plenty of petals. I want to walk to Ben on roses."

The scent of roses wafted over Ben as Josie came to him through the carpet of pink petals, the gold locket gleaming against her bare skin. For a moment he thought he was in the middle of a pleasant dream, and then she was standing by his side, warm and real, her fingers linked through his.

The music changed, and it took him a moment to realize the organist was playing "Amazed."

"Surprise," Josie said softly, and then she began to sing.

Looking straight into his eyes she poured out the beautiful love ballad she'd sung as a joke at her party. Was this another joke? Another goad for Jerry Bob?

Surely not, for the man wasn't even at the church. What then?

Josie never took her eyes off his, and Ben forgot about questions. Suddenly he realized it was her way of saying thank-you, and he opened his mind and his heart and let Josie sing a love song to him on his wedding day.

"Dearly beloved, we are gathered here today to unite this man and this woman in holy wedlock," the minister said. And so Pontotoc's most controversial wedding began in a beautifully traditional way.

Out in the audience, Ben's sister-in-law had tears in her eyes, and his brother's looked suspiciously shiny. Ben looked at his bride-to-be, intending to give her a conspiratorial wink. Instead he got caught up in the glow on her face.

The vows he said seemed real. The promises Josie made seemed binding. And when the minister finally said, "I now pronounce you man and wife," and Ben kissed his wife, such tenderness welled in him that he wanted to hold her forever.

Jim clapped him on the shoulder as he started back down the aisle with Josie, laughing, at his side.

As they stepped into the sunshine outside the church, just the two of them with the crowd still waiting inside for the rest of the wedding party to leave, they stared at each other, hands and eyes locked.

She was radiant and soft-looking, and he wanted to take advantage of this stolen moment of privacy and kiss her again. *Josie. His friend. His wife.*

Behind them the audience erupted in a buzz of excited conversation. Soon they'd come spilling through the door. The moment was almost lost.

Ben leaned close and suddenly Josie pulled back.

"We did it," she said. "We pulled it off."

Was her determined glee a bit forced, or was he merely grasping at straws?

"Yes, we did, Josie." He reached for her hand, hoping to recapture some of the romance of the ceremony.

Josie gave his hand a smart shake. "Thanks, pal. I don't know what I'd do without you."

He almost said, I don't intend to let you find out, but then the crowd spilled out the door, and he and Josie were borne away to the reception on a tide of well-wishers.

Chapter Six

Ben drove exactly the way Josie remembered, with expert ease. It was the same way he did everything, and that was beginning to scare Josie.

Then how come she was in the car with him heading to the Gulf Coast on a honeymoon? Insanity. That was the answer. And some very determined relatives.

Sighing, she leaned back against the seat and closed her eyes.

"Did you say something?" Out of the corner of her eye she caught Ben's profile. Her husband was so gloriously handsome she couldn't bear to look.

Her husband. She sighed again.

"No, I didn't say anything. Just tired, that's all."

"Lean back and take a nap, then. I'll wake you when we get there."

How? Would he scoop her into his arms and carry her over the threshold? And then what?

Oh, my. The bed. Her mother had said it was king-size, and that explained why she was cruising down the highway at seventy-miles an hour for a honeymoon trip. If she'd thought acting like a blushing bride at the wedding reception was hard, just wait till she had to share a king-size bed with Ben Standing Bear.

It wouldn't take him more than half a minute to find out that the woman he'd married out of pity couldn't keep her hands off him. What in the world was she going to do?

For starters, she was going to quit caving in to her mother's tears and her aunt's strong-arm tactics.

"We can't possibly go on the honeymoon," Josie had told her mother and her aunt Tess while she'd changed out of her wedding gown after the reception, and into the jaunty yellow linen suit Ashley had told her was the perfect going-away outfit. At this rate, the only place Josie was going was the insane asylum.

"That's where your father and I spent our honeymoon."

Betty Anne's lips trembled, and then she began to cry, and that's when Aunt Tess had stepped into the fray.

"Now look at that. You've made your mother cry. I don't know where you got that mean streak, Josie."

From you, Josie wanted to say, but in the interest of peace, she didn't. In fact, she didn't get a chance to say anything, for Aunt Tess was on a roll.

"This honeymoon is my wedding gift to you, and I insist you accept it."

"From the cold shoulder you gave my husband at the reception I'm surprised you want me to spend one single night with him, let alone a full-fledged honeymoon."

Aunt Tess hadn't been the only one, either. Oh, they'd tried to be subtle about it, but Josie had seen the small slights, the unusual reserve. She'd wanted to smack a few faces. Fortunately, Ben and his family hadn't seemed to notice anything amiss. Josie guessed she was more attuned to the nuances of a small town.

Aunt Tess's lips tightened. "The honeymoon was a promotion package, non-refundable."

"Ben and I have made other plans, Aunt Tess." Her protest wouldn't hold water, as the saying goes, and Jose knew it.

"What other plans?"

And though Betty Anne was sitting right there in a straight-backed chair, she didn't say a single thing to help Josie out. Apparently she'd used up every bit of her spunk in her one dramatic moment.

Josie couldn't possibly tell Aunt Tess that she and Ben planned to go their separate ways, and so she asked a question of her own, hoping to turn the tables.

It hadn't worked, of course. Nothing seemed to work with Aunt Tess.

"Why don't you and Mother go? Both of you could use a little vacation. It would do you the world of good to get out of Pontotoc for a while." Not to mention, make things easier for Josie.

Aunt Tess snorted. "I'm not about to sleep with Betty Anne, king-size bed or not. I had enough of her thrashing about and muttering in her sleep when we were kids."

"Well, maybe you can take the honeymoon suite and Mother can get an adjoining room?"

Aunt Tess narrowed her eyes. "I've never seen a bride so anxious to avoid a honeymoon trip. Josie Belle, is there something going on here that you're not telling?"

"Absolutely not." She kissed her mother's cheek. "Thank you for the gift, Aunt Tess. I'm sure Ben and I will enjoy it."

She'd repeated the conversation to him later as they drove away in a shower of confetti.

"There's nothing to keep me from going," he said. "My office won't be open for two weeks. What about you?"

"What do you mean, what about me?"

"Any reason you can't go, Josie?"

"Well, no, actually there isn't. School won't start till the last of August."

"Good, then, it's settled. I'll pack a few things and pick you up in about an hour. Does that give you enough time?"

"Sure."

Josie was becoming an accomplished liar. Six days, six *years* couldn't give her enough time to prepare herself emotionally for sleeping in the same bed with Ben Standing Bear and pretending she didn't like it.

How could she possibly fall asleep with the specter of the bed looming in her mind?

"Wake up, Josie." Ben was bending over her, so close she was only two inches away from his lips. Delicious lips, she might add.

"Are we there?"

"Not quite. I stopped at a food stand and bought crab rolls. I thought we'd have a picnic on the beach, just like old times."

It wasn't like old times, though. She was too aware of the way the moon carved his cheekbones and highlighted his sensual lips. She was much too attuned to the way his legs kept brushing against her thigh as they sat side by side on an enormous beach towel.

Was it accidental? She hoped it was and prayed it wasn't. The simple fact was this: in the space of one day Josie had changed from a woman who knew where she was headed in life to a woman on a roller coaster who had no idea what was around the next curve, let alone what waited for her at the end of the line.

She blamed her condition squarely on Ben. If he kept

looking at her the way he was—as if he couldn't get enough of seeing her, as if he wanted nothing more than to kiss her—she wouldn't be responsible for what she did next.

"Look at that boat, Ben." Anything to get him to quit studying her. "I wonder where it's going."

"Venice."

"You know those people?"

"Absolutely." He picked up her hand and idly began to caress her knuckles. The caress had to be idle, for her old friend Ben would never take advantage of her or of the situation.

"Who are they?"

"A couple of romantics. The man has poetry in his soul and love in his heart, and he's taking his woman to the most romantic city he can imagine."

"Why?"

"Because he never thought he'd fall in love, and now that he has he wants to do everything right."

Josie was enchanted. And fascinated. She'd never seen this side of Ben. Maybe it was because her own problems always forced him into the role of rescuer. Or perhaps it was because the years had given her a different perspective. Whatever the reason, she liked what she saw.

She entered his game with gusto. "What about the woman? What's she like?"

"She's whimsical and bright and funny, somebody who will wear well over the years, somebody he'll find endlessly fascinating."

"What else, Ben?"

"She has red hair, just like you."

Ben caught a strand of her hair and wound it around his fingers. Such a simple gesture, and yet so intimate. Josie held her breath, afraid of breaking the spell.

The moonlight lent him an aura of mystery, and she could almost believe that they were the romantics, waiting to board their boat and sail away to some far-off exotic land where they would live on grapes picked straight from the vine and bread they'd knead together on a large board carved from olive wood.

Suddenly Ben broke contact. It wasn't so much a physical pulling away as a mental one. He lay back on the beach towel with his arms folded behind his head. In the old days, Josie would have flopped down beside him and thought nothing of it.

She didn't dare do that now. In her bid to gain freedom from Aunt Tess had she sacrificed friendship? She hoped not.

She compromised by stretching out and propping herself on her elbow. She'd changed into denim shorts and a white T-shirt for the drive to the coast, but she couldn't bear to take off the gold locket. In the moonlight it gleamed softly against her shirt.

"Ben? I have something to tell you."

"This sounds serious, Josie."

"It is."

"I'm listening."

"You know that I've always liked your brother, and I think Sarah's absolutely top-notch." He watched her, waiting. "I could tell from the way they acted that they thought our marriage was real."

"It was, Josie."

If he'd touched her, if he'd put his hand on her cheek or even in her hair, she would have read all sorts of romantic connotations into what he said. Instead she saw it for what it was—a simple statement of the legal aspects of their union.

"I mean real beyond the legal sense. Sarah opened her heart to me, Ben. She made me feel like a sister."

"She's a good woman."

"I could tell. And I absolutely *hate* what all this has done to your family. I hate it that you had to deceive them, and I hate it that you'll have to disappoint them.''

Ben rolled over and studied her for so long that Josie lost her breath. What was he thinking? Why was he looking at her like that? What was he trying to do? Drive her crazy?

''We're at the beach and the moon is shining. Why don't we just enjoy this…vacation, and let tomorrow take care of itself, Josie?''

If he kept looking at her like that, she knew what tomorrow would bring. Disaster and a handful of regrets.

''Good idea,'' she said, then gathered up the remains of their dinner. ''I'll race you to the garbage can. Last one there's a rotten egg.''

She outran him by a good two lengths. He was winded when he got there, and she punched him playfully in the ribs.

''You're out of shape, Doctor. We're going to have to do something about that. Know any good exercises?''

''They say sex is the best.''

He had to be kidding her. Wasn't he?

''Yeah? Well, maybe you'll find somebody wonderful down here and fall in love.''

He leaned against the can close to her. Too close. She could barely breathe.

''You think so, Josie?''

''Miracles can happen, you know.''

He leaned in, his eyes gleaming. ''They certainly can.'' He was going to kiss her, right here on the beach in the moonlight with a king-size bed waiting for them not two miles down the strip. She braced herself against the can, prepared to weather any assault and still come out with her honor intact.

After all, she'd made a bargain: marry the man, then get the annulment, no strings attached. And that included no kisses that fogged the brain and turned the blood to fire.

He was so close now she could feel his body heat. Josie was burning up, fixing to burst into flames.

"Ben." Her voice was a whisper, a sigh, a plea.

He brushed his lips softly against her cheek. She hoped he didn't notice how disappointed she was.

"Josie. It's been a long day and I'm bushed."

"Me, too. I could use some sleep."

Too late, she remembered that she'd slept most of the trip. Ben's eyes twinkled, but he refrained from comment, which was a darned good thing. Josie was feeling surly and out-of-sorts, and when she got that way she simply wasn't responsible for what she might do.

Chapter Seven

They stood in the doorway of their hotel room staring at the king-size bed as if it had sprouted horns and a tail.

"It's plenty big enough, isn't it?" Ben said.

"Not nearly." Big as he was, there was no way she could keep from touching Ben in that bed.

Too late, Josie realized her mistake. Still surly, she glared at him as if her revealing remark was all his fault.

"Don't you say a thing," she snapped.

"I see you still have a stinger, Josie."

"*I* haven't changed. You're the one who's different."

That ought to hold him. She marched into the room leading with her chin. That's the way she always entered a room when she was mad, and she was good and mad at Ben.

Not about the kiss on the cheek. That had probably been wise considering the circumstances, considering the fact that if he'd kissed her on the mouth she'd probably have stripped him buck-naked and had her wicked way with him on the beach where society not only frowned on such things but threw the culprits in jail.

She didn't want to go to jail on her honeymoon. What she did want was to be carried across the threshold, even if it would be another bald-faced deception. She'd committed a whole string of them today, so what would one more hurt?

She flung her purse toward a chair, not caring that it slid onto the floor and her lipstick went flying off in the direction of the television. Ben was still in the doorway watching her. She could tell by the way the back of her neck prickled. She could tell by the sound of his breathing.

She wished he'd quit. It was getting on her nerves.

Suddenly she was scooped off her feet and hauled unceremoniously against the most delicious-feeling chest this side of heaven.

"Oh. I didn't hear you."

"The Sioux are a stealthy lot."

Josie was having a hard time breathing. Furthermore, she didn't know where to put her hands. Every place she looked was dangerous, from the broad shoulders to the square jaw to the incredible chest.

He stalked toward the door and started marching down the hall.

He was probably going to take her back to the car, dump her inside and take her back to Pontotoc. And who could blame him? She was nothing but a pain in the neck.

"Ben, put me down. What are you doing?"

"Starting all over."

"All over doing what? Where are you going?"

"Here." He stopped at the elevator. "This is where I should have picked you up." He was holding his jaw so tight she could see the definition of the muscles.

"What are you going to do?"

"You ask too many questions, Josie."

His face fierce, he looked every inch a Sioux. Josie could almost hear war drums as he marched back down the hall.

He had taken her captive...and she was loving every minute of it. He didn't stop his resolute march until he got back to the bedroom. The door had shut behind them, just barely missing the latch, and he kicked it open.

Ben Standing Bear not only carried his bride across the threshold, he gave her the most thorough kiss in the entire history of marriage. At least, that's what went through Josie's mind.

And then, quite suddenly she was incapable of thought. He deepened the kiss, and she felt the impact all the way to her toes. They curled under and stayed that way while he cast some sort of Sioux spell over her.

Pressed hard against his chest with his mouth locked on hers working its magic, she felt completely loved and thoroughly ravished.

Good grief. If Ben's kisses could do that to her, what would it be like to share his bed? Not merely lie beside him trying to pretend she wasn't on fire for the man who was supposed to be nothing more than her best friend, but *really* share it.

Was she going to find out?

Ben was still kissing her, and she was kissing him back...body, heart and soul. Although they hadn't moved far beyond the threshold, he had somehow managed to shut the door behind them without her even noticing, and they were in the bridal suite with complete privacy and a full moon shining through the windows and nobody to see if Josie Belle Pickens failed to keep her end of the bargain.

Somebody was moaning, and Josie realized she was the one making those soft urgent sounds—part pleasure, part plea. She should have been mortified, but she wasn't. She was going to do what she'd always done, just be herself.

Damn the torpedoes and full speed ahead. That was her credo.

She settled closer to him. Or did he pull her closer? It didn't matter. What mattered was the way his mouth was still on hers, and the way she felt, as if she'd never been kissed. Not ever. Not once. Not by anybody, anywhere, anytime.

This was the first kiss in the history of romance, and she was the first woman who had ever been kissed.

Good grief, she was lost.

Any minute now Ben would carry her to the bed, lower her to the sheets and make exquisite love to her, and she would die of happiness. It was that simple. It was that wonderful.

And when they returned to Pontotoc she wouldn't have to pretend anymore. She would really be Mrs. Ben Standing Bear, and everybody who had doubted her could just go fly a kite.

Was she falling in love? She had to be. How else could she explain the fireworks that were shooting through her? How else could she account for the stars that were falling from the night sky and landing one by one in her soul?

Every atom in her body was saying yes to him. *Yes, yes, yes.* She wanted to be Ben Standing Bear's wife in every possible way, once and forever.

Ben was playing a dangerous game, and he knew it. Kissing Josie felt too wonderful, too perfect.

When he'd picked her up and carried her over the threshold, he'd told himself he was being noble. He'd told himself he was going to give Josie a honeymoon to remember…in every way except one.

She'd been perfectly clear on that score. And he'd agreed.

At the rate he was going, he would be breaking that

agreement in the length of time it would take to walk across the room to the huge bed that dominated the honeymoon suite.

The kiss he'd meant to be friendly had taken on a life of its own. If he didn't break off soon, it would be too late.

The best way to do that without any misunderstandings was with humor. Josie was his best friend. He just hoped he hadn't ruined their friendship with his impulsive, misguided action.

Abruptly he set her back on her feet. She looked flushed and confused.

"We came through the wedding with flying colors, and now welcome to the honeymoon."

Was he overdoing it? He sounded like a game-show host.

For a moment he thought she was going to punch him, and he didn't blame her. Then the Josie he knew came to the rescue.

"Don't they usually do that by sending a fruit basket wrapped in cellophane?"

"Are you disappointed? I suppose I could wrap myself in cellophane."

"Never mind." Boy, she was really snappish. It must be all that red hair. Redheads were legendary for their tempers, but in all the years he'd known Josie this was his first evidence.

Fascinating. What else was he going to find out about the woman he'd married?

Suddenly she was on all fours crawling around on the floor.

"Josie? What are you doing?"

Hiding a flushed face for one thing. Even from that angle he could see how her cheeks blazed. Call it male pride, but he liked to think he was at least partially the cause.

"I'm finding my lipstick before you trip over it and break your fool neck."

He supposed he deserved that. "Here, let me."

He dropped down beside her and quickly realized his mistake. Side by side with Josie on the floor, he felt how a body can sizzle. He was so hot he was afraid he might burst into flames and set the hotel on fire.

"Got it," she said, and just in the nick of time, for Ben was thinking about kissing her again.

And then what would he say? He's already worn out *welcome*. There was no excuse he could think of to cover what he would have done if Josie hadn't jumped up and left him on the floor feeling like a fool with that damnable king-size bed looming over him.

"I suppose we could erect a Wall of Jericho," he said, when he got off the floor. She was hanging clothes in the closet, and her back was to him.

"What?" She whirled around, hands on her hips. "What are you talking about?"

"The bed. What was the name of that Clark Gable movie? *It Happened One Night*? Remember that sheet they hung down the middle? They called it the Wall of Jericho."

He was prattling on and couldn't seem to stop. Jim would die laughing if he could see his brother now, Ben Standing Bear, the unflappable, totally losing his cool.

"And the walls came tumbling down," she said, and her expression got all soft and glowy. If she kept standing there looking like that he was going to kiss her again, consequences be damned.

They stood staring at each other with the enormous bed between them. He was just getting ready to bridge the distance when Josie saved him—saved them both.

In one of those lightning-quick mood changes he was getting used to, she put her hands on her hips and stuck out her chin.

"Fortunately for us, we don't need a wall." What in the devil did she mean by that? He wasn't long finding out.

''If I recall, that movie was a romance, and there's no romance involved here. Just two good friends, one rescuing the other.''

That said, Josie jerked a frothy lace slip out of her suitcase and flung it across the back of the chair. Next came a pair of panties not big enough to hold a decent sneeze, let alone that beautifully rounded bottom he'd noticed on the beach. Or had it been before?

He lost his train of thought, for the panties went sailing through the air and landed at his feet. Next she sent her bra airborne.

Ben reached up and caught it with his left hand. Reflex, he guessed. From his ball-playing days.

''Drop it,'' she said.

''Where?''

''Anywhere will do. Wait…drop it over by the bed. On your side.''

Humming, she turned her back and dug around in her suitcase until she found what she was looking for—a black lace gown that would make saints take to sinning. Still hanging on to her miniscule bra, he watched while she paced the room, then tossed the gown onto the bedpost.

''Josie, would you mind telling me what you're doing?''

''A little decorating. For the maids.''

''I'm afraid you've lost me.''

''Stage props. Creating an illusion is good theater.''

''An illusion of what?''

He was befuddled. It could be Josie, or it could be the feel of silk in his hand.

''We can't have them thinking nothing went on in that big bed, now can we? After all, this *is* the honeymoon suite.'' That said, Josie smiled sweetly at him then headed toward the bedroom. ''Do you mind if I get the first bath?''

''Not at all. Be my guest.''

She left him standing there with a foolish look on his

face and her bra in his hand. The door shut behind her with a soft click, and Ben sank into the nearest chair. He had the feeling that he'd just made a narrow escape. From what, he didn't know.

She was humming in the bathroom—"Amazed"—and Ben thought he was going to have a heart attack. Here he was, a grown man, reasonable, he'd thought, sensible, not given to flights of fancy. Science. That's what he depended on. Facts. Physical evidence. And yet the simple act of caressing a bit of silk that belonged to Josie felt as if he were touching her. Intimately. In the dead of the night with a full moon turning her skin to silver.

He would sleep on the floor. That was all that would save them.

The bathroom door popped open, and she stuck her head and a good portion of naked shoulder around the door jamb.

"Would you toss me a nightshirt? I forgot to bring it in here."

There was a small mole on her left shoulder he'd never noticed before. He wanted to kiss it. Desperately.

"Ben?"

He stuffed her bra under the seat cushions as if he'd been caught redhanded when the simple fact was, he'd caught her undergarment on the high fly the way he would any object tossed his way.

"What?"

"I said, would you mind handing me a nightshirt? Over there, in my suitcase."

Her suitcase with the red lacy lingerie right on top. He moved the lacy stuff aside in the careful way of a man defusing a time bomb.

"They won't bite." She was giggling.

"What?"

"My panties. They won't bite."

He thought it was best to ignore that remark under the

circumstances. The circumstances being his reddened face and his raging libido.

"What color is your nightshirt?"

"Any of them will do. Just hand me that white one."

It was an oversized T-shirt, and when he pulled it out of her suitcase, he saw the slogan printed on front: Give in to Your Animal Instincts. Save the Dolphins.

It was a long way across the room, and he thought about Josie giving in to the animal side of her nature all the way. If she did, who was going to save Ben?

She'd apparently stepped into the shower when she remembered her gown. Up close he could see moisture clinging to her skin, and he wanted to lick off every drop.

"Here you are." He held out the nightshirt, and her hand closed over it.

"Thank you."

"You're welcome."

Why couldn't he move? And why didn't she? They stood on opposite sides of the door staring at each other. Drowning in each other.

He had to have some fresh air. He had to get a grip. He had to marshal what little shreds of control he had left.

"I think I'll go for a walk while you finish your bath."

"Oh."

Was she disappointed? She looked it. What did that mean?

Ben wasn't going to stick around long enough to find out. He was in enough trouble as it was.

"I won't be gone long," he said.

"Okay. Have fun."

She vanished. The bathroom door clicked shut, and Ben was left standing alone in the honeymoon suite staring at her black gown draped over the bedpost.

It was going to be a long night.

Chapter Eight

Ben was still out there somewhere in the dark, walking off his frustrations or whatever had sent him flying from the honeymoon suite, and Josie was in bed properly covered by her voluminous nightshirt, her half of the king-size sheet and a good portion of the peach-colored comforter. She was hot as hell. And mad, to boot.

It was a darned good thing she'd brought some books or else she'd be out of her mind. Why didn't Ben come back? Suppose he'd been mugged? Or run over? Or shot? Those things happened.

She was torn between racing out into the night to find him or lying down and closing her eyes so she could be sound asleep when he got back or waiting up for him with her book. What the devil was it about, anyhow? She flipped over to re-read the title. Ah, yes. Edgar Lee Masters's *Spoon River Anthology*. It was about dead people and their dead dreams. An altogether appropriate subject, considering her present circumstances.

The last four lines of Herbert Marshall's lament leaped out at her:

> This is life's sorrow:
> That one can be happy only where two are;
> And that our hearts are drawn to stars
> Which want us not.

Josie's star was somewhere on the streets of Biloxi wanting her not, and she had nothing to cuddle up to except a book. She threw it across the room where it whacked the wall and slid to the floor.

Let the maids make what they would of it. She didn't care. She was beyond caring about anything except her own misery.

It was all her own doing, of course. Why, oh why, had she thought being Ben Standing Bear's wife in name only would be easier than facing the town and standing up to Aunt Tess? It was one of the hardest things she'd ever done. In order to get through the next five days she was going to have to use every acting skill she possessed.

The only thing in her favor was that she was a drama teacher. If she lived through it all, the first thing she was going to do when they got back to Pontotoc was file for an annulment.

Josie heard footsteps in the hall, then the key turning in the lock. Ben was back. She snapped off the light, scrunched down under the covers and pretended to be asleep.

Thank God, Josie was asleep. Ben tiptoed across the room and stripped down to his shorts. Running water might wake her. He'd shower in the morning.

He eased into bed, vividly aware of the enticing curve of her hips under the covers and the heady fragrance of her warm skin. Or was it her hair that smelled like some exotic flower?

Probably both. Josie never did anything halfway. Everything about her was double trouble.

She lay perfectly still, but he couldn't hear the sound of her breathing. Was she faking sleep? It wasn't like Josie to fake anything. She led with her chin up and her intentions as clearly defined as if she had red-lettered banners flying over her head.

Ben toyed with the idea of whispering, "Good night, Josie," then thought better of it. The less said the better, considering that it didn't take much to either set them to kissing or set them at odds.

It used not to be that way. Funny, how everything had changed with the wedding.

She rolled in her sleep, sighing, and all of a sudden most of Josie was draped over half of Ben and he felt as if somebody had taken a cattle prod to him. Now what?

He considered making a pallet on the floor, but promptly rejected the idea as cowardly and unnecessary. This was Josie, his pal, not some femme fatale bent on seduction. As she had said earlier there was no romance between them, just a bargain.

Ben lay rigid for a while, *rigid* being the operative word, then carefully peeled Josie off and rolled to his side with his back to her.

That should take care of the problem.

Josie dreamed in Technicolor. She was in the middle of a film where the heroine—that was her part—had just fallen into bed with the hero. They were wrapped together as tight as sausages in a casing and they'd steamed things up so convincingly everybody on the set thought they were in love.

"Josie's in love," they were saying, and the director had

even hired a plane to fly a banner through the sky proclaiming this miracle.

Josie Belle Pickens was a star known for loving 'em and leaving 'em. When she really fell in love, it was bound to be headline news.

She sighed and cuddled closer to her hero. He was incredibly delicious-feeling, and she'd just made up her mind to tell the director she wanted about fifty takes of this scene, when all of a sudden somebody dropped a dinner tray on the set.

Or was it out in the hall?

Josie's eyes flew open. She wasn't on a movie set, at all. She was in the honeymoon suite plastered so close to Ben Standing Bear you'd think they'd spent the night making slow, sweet, glorious love.

They hadn't, of course. For one thing, she'd have known it. For another, Ben didn't feel the least bit romantic toward her. She'd been so hard to get along with she doubted he even liked her anymore.

How was she ever going to unglue herself from him without waking him up? One of her legs was flung over him and her hips were pressed so intimately against his she could feel everything he had. Which was considerable. Mind-boggling. Breath-stealing. And downright delicious.

Her nose was smack dab in the middle of his neck, and her right hand was woven into his chest hairs. What was more, it felt good. *Very* good.

She was wondering how long she could get by with enjoying this new proximity while he slept, when all of a sudden he opened his eyes and stared right at her.

Ben never had been the kind to wake up fast. He blinked then yawned and did a slow stretch, and Josie went along for the ride. She couldn't help it. Her left arm was pinned under him and his was under her nightshirt somewhere in the vicinity of danger.

Not that she was complaining. She wasn't even going to think about the kind of complications she was courting.

"Josie?" Ben was staring at her again, and this time he really saw her. "Omigosh…" He disentangled himself so fast it made her head spin. More than that it made her feel miffed and grumpy.

"I'm so sorry, Josie. I didn't mean to do that." Ben had moved *way* over to the far side of the bed. He might as well have been in Siberia.

"Well, obviously." She threw back the covers and flounced toward the bathroom. She was so mad she didn't even turn on the water to cover the sounds, which is what any normal woman in her right mind always does when she wakes up with a man she's never slept with before, friend or no friend.

Ben was sitting propped on the pillows when she got back. He was sprawled, actually, the way big men with glorious bodies tend to do, with the sheet crumpled artfully around his hips and every last gorgeous bit of his chest exposed for her gratification. She wasn't about to gratify him by looking. Except maybe one small peek. Or perhaps two.

Ben was smiling, darn his handsome hide. What did he have to be so happy about? He was married to a woman he didn't even want.

She scrambled through everything in her suitcase before she remembered she'd hung her shorts in the closet. She stalked over and snatched them off the hanger.

"Josie, are you mad at me?"

She gave him a sweet smile, as fake as any Southern debutante's she'd ever seen. "Not at all. Why should I be mad?"

"I don't know. I just thought you were acting sort of peculiar. That's all."

"That's because you don't know me, Ben. I've grown peculiar in my old age."

"Look, if it's about what happened in bed last night…"

"*Nothing* happened in bed last night."

Ben gave her a funny look, and she knew she'd overdone it. He was on to her. Why had she ever thought she could fool him in the first place? Ben Standing Bear was practically a mind reader.

He climbed out of bed, not the least bit self-conscious about being in his shorts. And why should he be? He looked good enough to eat.

"I thought I would order breakfast served in the room." In passing he slid his hand across the gown she'd hung on the bedpost. The gesture was so sensual Josie nearly passed out from an excess of hormones. "To help preserve the image. Croissants and strawberries. How does that sound?"

Oh, help. Flaky pastries that left enticing crumbs around the mouth, and juicy berries that were best when shared, mouth to mouth, sort of like resuscitation except a thousand times better.

She was a drama teacher, wasn't she? She could play this role.

"Fine." His hand was still on her gown, sort of caressing it, the way she imagined he would her arms if they were draped around the bedpost. Heck, she'd drape her whole body around the bedpost if he'd put his hands on her like that.

"Or would you prefer Southern fare, bacon and eggs and buttermilk biscuits?"

"No. The ripe juicy stuff is best. Especially early in the morning." That ought to hold him for a while.

It didn't. The only reaction she got was the slight lifting of one eyebrow, then he began prowling the room like a big jungle cat on the hunt.

"I'm partial to it in the moonlight," he said, "especially outdoors."

She licked her lips. She couldn't help it. Fortunately, he didn't smile. Unfortunately, he was watching her in a way that made her shiver.

"Sounds primitive to me."

"Primitive but delicious."

They stared at each other, mesmerized. They'd long since stopped talking about picnics, and both of them knew it. Josie clutched her shorts as if she were drowning and they were the only lifeboat in sight, and Ben kept a safe distance on the other side of the bed.

Still, there was so much steam coming off them they might as well have been wrapped around each other so close you couldn't wedge a blade of grass between them

Ben blinked like a man coming out of a dream, then sat on the edge of the bed.

"Afterward..." he said in a far-off, dreamy way.

"After what?" Josie had turned to butter. She sort of melted into the nearest chair.

"After breakfast."

"Oh."

He gave her that *look* again, the kind that made her glad she was already sitting down, since otherwise she'd be pooled at his feet in one glistening glob of adoration.

Oh, darn it, what was she going to do about this? Get out of the honeymoon suite, for one thing. Fast.

"I saw some great boats for rent while I was walking last night. I thought we might rent one and go exploring around the barrier islands. We might even drop a hook and catch a fish or two."

Josie pictured herself in a boat with Ben, the sun turning him into a bronze god while she turned into one big freckle. One big *palpitating* freckle with nowhere to run.

"No, thank you very much."

"You don't like sailing? You used to love it."

"It's not that." Sailing had been fun when Ben was captain of the baseball team and she was Joan of Arc and Carrie Nation rolled into one and couldn't see anything except her causes. Lord, what would she give for a good cause right now. Anything to distract her from her unattainable, unavailable husband.

"We can do something else, if you like. Maybe grab some sandwiches and head across the bay and do the Walter Anderson tour."

She imagined being trapped in the car with him only an arm's length away and her not having the right to reach over and touch him. She'd rather be on a stretching rack in the hot boiling sun.

"I have a lot of things I need to do today, girl things, shopping, the sort of stuff that bores men to tears."

"I don't mind."

What had she expected from a man who was perfect? She cast around trying to think of some other excuse.

"Actually, I was thinking of getting in touch with Francine and the two of us having lunch, catching up on old times, that sort of thing."

"Francine?"

"You remember her, don't you? Blond, blue-eyed, legs about two miles long? The home ec major?"

"I thought you didn't like Francine. Old stick-in-the-mud, you used to call her."

"Oh, well, things change, you know? People get older and more mature, and all of a sudden people you barely spoke to when you were in school become…become compatriots."

"Compatriots?"

"Well, not that, exactly. More like colleagues."

"I see."

If Josie didn't know better she'd say Ben was getting

riled. *Well, good.* She didn't like being the only one who ever lost her cool.

"Maybe strawberries aren't such a good idea," he said.

"Maybe not."

"I'll just take a quick shower and be out of here in a minute. I'll pick up something to eat at Hardee's."

He headed toward the bathroom. *Stalked,* was more like it. Josie got a latent attack of conscience.

"Ben?" He turned and looked at her, and when she smiled, his expression softened. "I really want you to enjoy this vacation."

"Thanks, Josie. I want the same thing for you."

"I hope you catch lots of fish."

"I hope you have lots of fun."

It would be more fun with you. For once she didn't blurt out what she was thinking. She merely smiled and waggled two fingers at him.

When the bathroom door clicked shut, she flung herself across the bed, groaning. How was she ever going to get through the day? Not with Francine, that was for sure. She'd lived in Biloxi for a while, that much was true. But the last Josie had heard, she was somewhere in Wisconsin. Besides that, Josie *still* didn't like her.

Josie had run into her on the beach three years ago when she and her mother had come down for a little trip, and Francine was still the same vicious snob she'd always been.

Why on earth had she made up all that fiction to Ben? Pride, she guessed. She'd stick splinters under her fingernails before admitting to him that she didn't want to spend the day in his company because she was having a hard time keeping her hands off him, and she wasn't about to make a fool of herself over a man who didn't view her that way.

She'd read somewhere that love was friendship on fire. Or had she just thought it up? She couldn't remember, especially in her present state. She and Ben were friends, all right. The only problem was, she was the only one blazing.

What about the way he kissed you?

Pity kisses. That's what. Ben felt sorry for her. That's the reason he'd married her. Ben Standing Bear had always been good at compassion and rescues.

Josie could hear the water running...all over Ben's naked body. She jumped off the bed as if she'd been shot and jerked on her clothes.

It might be rude to leave without saying goodbye, but it was also safe. Josie wrote a note: "Ben, I'm off. Have a good time fishing. I'll see you this evening." She thought about signing it Love, then changed her mind and wrote "Hugs, Josie." Nice and friendly. Affectionate without ripping her heart out and plastering it to the paper.

Josie left while the shower was still running. It was the only way she knew how to stay out of trouble.

Chapter Nine

The thing Ben had always loved about being out on the water was the sense of freedom, the sense of leaving all his troubles on the shore and entering a realm where time stood still, where nothing existed except the sun and the sea and the creatures of the deep waiting beneath the surface to match wits with him. Today, it came as no surprise at all that he hadn't left a thing behind, least of all Josie.

She was beside him, sighing in his ear with every cast of his pole. She was there snuggled close when he sat down to enjoy a cool drink. She surrounded him, all silky skin and sweet scent, when he finally gave up and brought the boat ashore with nothing to show for his day's work except the deeper bronze of his skin.

His heart lifted as he headed back to the hotel. She would be waiting for him, maybe fresh from her bath with droplets of water still on her skin. He would walk through the door and the room would smell like her, like the sweet floral fragrance she'd sprayed on her hair and her skin.

Did she spray it at the base of her throat where he could sometimes see the soft beat of her pulse? On the back of her knees where the skin was so milky white her veins showed blue? On her thighs, where, for one heady moment he'd rested his hand?

What would have happened if he hadn't jerked away from her this morning, gut-punched? He didn't have to search long for an answer. What would have happened would have made annulment impossible. Unthinkable.

Ben already had his face fixed in a smile when he opened the door.

"Josie?"

She didn't answer. He scanned the room, then switched on the lights as if she might surprise him by popping out of the shadows.

Josie wasn't back yet. Ben wasn't going to think about how disappointed he felt. He wasn't going to dwell on the reasons why.

She'd be back soon, and they'd have dinner together and laugh about their day and everything would be back to normal. They'd be Josie and Ben, best friends on a vacation.

Might as well shower while he waited for her. Ben stripped off his clothes and was just headed toward the bathroom when he noticed the red light on the phone blinking.

The message was from Josie.

"Ben, I wonder if you can come and get me. Better bring bail money. I'm in jail."

"Jail!"

Ben panicked. He rushed about jerking on clothes, all the while imagining Josie incarcerated with hookers and cutthroats and Lord only knew what other kind of hardened criminals. He'd heard what they do to women in jail.

When had she left the message? He played it again.

Three o'clock, and it was already six. By now she could be maimed and scarred for life—maybe even dead.

He drove like a madman getting to the jail, weaving in and out of lanes and scooting through almost-red lights, his mind going ninety to nothing the whole time.

Josie, Josie, what have you done now?

Josie could have cried when she saw Ben, partly because she was so relieved, but mostly because he looked so worried.

"I'm here to make bail for my wife," she heard him say, and that made her even more tearful. She was a disgrace to wifehood. It's a miracle Ben even claimed her.

The first words out of her mouth when she was brought to him were, "I'm sorry, Ben. I'm so sorry."

"As long as you're all right. Are you all right, Josie?" Ben went into his doctor's mode, checking her over as if she were a specimen under a microscope.

"I'm fine. Just get me out of here."

He stared straight ahead, just driving. And probably wishing he'd never seen her. Especially wishing he'd never married her.

He hadn't even asked for an explanation, which made her feel even worse. As far as he was concerned, she was apparently just living down to her reputation, Josie the Troublemaker.

"Don't you want to hear what happened?"

"Do you want to tell me?"

"I don't blame you for being mad."

"I'm not mad, Josie, but I *am* puzzled. What I can't understand is how you could have gone to lunch with Francine and ended up in jail."

She was caught in a trap of her own making. She should never have fiddled with the truth in the first place. She'd already lost Ben's respect, and now she was going to lose his trust.

She might think up another story to cover the one she'd already told, a story that would cast her in a better light, but the simple truth was, she was relieved to confess.

"Francine's not in Biloxi anymore."

"I see."

"No, you don't. I knew that this morning." The look he gave her broke her heart. "I didn't want to spend the day with you and I didn't know how to tell you without making a fool of myself, so I made up the first plausible excuse that came to my mind."

"Who can blame you? It was my fault, Josie. I promise you that what happened last night won't happen again."

Here she was, backed into another corner, forced into another lie. She couldn't possibly blurt out the truth.

Oh, but, Ben, I loved what happened last night. I want it to happen again. And more, besides.

She had already complicated Ben's life almost beyond redemption. She wasn't about to compound his problems.

"No, it's not your fault, Ben. It's me. I can't seem to stay out of trouble, that's all."

She hadn't lied, exactly. She had merely skirted the truth.

"Let's get something to eat. Maybe that will make us both feel better."

Over oysters on the half shell she told him how she'd spotted a huge crowd at the beach that turned out to be a peaceful demonstration against the fishermen who were putting their nets in known dolphin waters and carelessly destroying those gentle giants of the sea.

"You were always a sucker for dolphins," he said.

When the fried shrimp arrived she told about the nice old couple from Peoria, Ralph and Sally Beaman, who had come down to the coast for their fiftieth wedding anniversary, and who happened to be strolling along the beach, hand in hand, when they decided to join the cause.

"Did they get put in jail, too?"

"They did. Still holding hands. Every last one of us got tossed into the slammer. We're all such criminal types, you know."

She might as well make a joke of it. Somehow that seemed to ease Ben's anxiety. If she could teach him one thing during their so-called honeymoon, she wished she could teach him to loosen up.

"What happened?"

"I don't really know. I think it was a kid with firecrackers who started it all. The police thought it was a gun, there was a little scuffle and all of a sudden we were all carted off to jail."

He covered her hand. "It's over now, Josie."

"Until the next time," she quipped, and then she saw his face. "I'm sorry Ben. I promise you this. I'll stay out of trouble, at least until after the annulment."

By the time they got back to the hotel the dark mood that had descended on Ben at the restaurant was in full swing. He blamed the long day, too much sun, everything except Josie's mention of ending the marriage.

"I'll bed down on the floor," he said. The sitting area had two chairs and a loveseat, far too small to accommodate his big frame.

"No, let me. You take the bed."

"No. If there's one thing I draw the line at, Josie, it's letting you sleep on the floor."

"But..."

"Josie, don't say another word."

"Okay, Ben."

She disappeared into the bathroom and took the world's longest shower. Probably hoping he'd be sound asleep on the floor by the time she got back. Ben jerked bedding out of the closet and threw it on the floor. Then he stalked around the room checking for irregularities: Martians hiding in the closet, that kind of thing. Why else would he be inspecting the premises?

Disgusted with himself, he picked up the newspaper he hadn't read that morning and tried to concentrate on the world news. Tales of war and mayhem paled compared to Josie's doings.

She emerged fresh from her bath, smiling. And glowing, darn her hide.

"Next?"

He made a sound that was more grunt than anything else, then slid into the bathroom without even looking at her. He couldn't. How could he possibly resist a radiant woman with moisture glistening on her skin?

He turned the water on so hot he could barely stand it, then gritted his teeth while he endured a freezing blast from the cold-water tap. A man in his condition would resort to anything.

She was already in bed when he got out, curled on her side with her back to him. *Good.* Maybe they'd both get a decent night's sleep

He lay down and tangled himself into his covers tossing back and forth for what seemed hours. Then he heard a small sound that ripped a hole in his heart. Josie was crying.

Ben didn't pause to think. He didn't take time to weigh the consequences. He raced to the bed and pulled her into his arms.

"What's wrong?" he whispered.

"Oh, Ben." She curled into him, sobbing, while he soothed her with soft murmurings and tender caresses.

"Shh, don't cry. I'm here, Josie. I'm here."

She cried even harder.

"There, now. Don't cry. Everything's going to be all right."

She wiped her face with her hands and tried to pull out of his grasp.

"How can it? I've made such a mess of things for you."

"That's not true. I make my own choices, Josie. Whatever happens to me is my responsibility."

"Yes, but none of this would be happening to you if it weren't for me."

"I could have said *no,* Josie. I'm not sorry I didn't."

"You're just saying that to make me feel better."

"Do you?"

"No." She hid her face in the sheets, sniffling, and Ben pulled her close. "Why don't you just go back to Pontotoc and leave me down here? I'll catch the bus home or something."

"I'm not going anywhere without you, Josie."

"How can you say that? I've messed up your life."

"You've spiced up my life. I didn't realize how dull I'd become until I found you again."

"You're just saying that."

"I don't say things I don't mean."

She sighed then melted against him, holding on. "You're a sweet man, Ben. I like that so much."

"I'm glad."

She grew quiet for a while, and he was afraid to move for fear of disturbing her.

"Ben?"

"Hmm?"

"Thank you. For everything."

"You're more than welcome. Always."

Silence. Another sigh from Josie.

"Ben?"

"Hmm?"

"You can go back to your pallet now. If you want to."

"I don't want to."

Silence. She snuggled closer. Or was he dreaming with his eyes wide open?

"Josie?"

"Hmm?"

"I'll stay right here. If it's all right with you."

"It's all right with me, Ben."

She wrapped her arms around him, and he could feel the shape of the gold locket against his bare skin. Ben felt branded.

Fearful of repeating his ungallant behavior of the previous night, Ben stayed awake all night. No tangled legs. No stray hands. No improprieties. He was simply holding Josie. The way any good friend would.

She woke up early, propped herself on an elbow and studied him.

"Good morning." Her voice was soft and sleep-filled. He liked it very much. Too much.

"The same to you, Josie."

He lay very still, held in solemn regard of the bluest eyes he'd ever seen. Sky blue. A touch of heaven.

"You didn't sleep a wink last night, did you?"

"Why do you say that?"

"Bloodshot eyes, for one thing. You never have bloodshot eyes."

"How do you know?"

"Because I know you. You always do everything exactly right, and that means getting the proper amount of rest." She patted his cheek, then bounded out of bed, filled with energy. She went straight to her suitcase and started packing.

"What are you doing?"

"Packing for our trip home."

"Aren't you a little premature? We have three more days."

"We're not staying here three more days. We're going back to Pontotoc today. I'll do the driving."

Ben couldn't say he'd be sorry to leave. Restraint can be an exhausting thing. He hadn't counted on needing so much of it. Still, he felt obligated to protest.

"I don't want to ruin your vacation."

"Why not? I've ruined yours."

"No, you haven't."

"Sweet liar."

She dragged the last of her clothes out of the closet and crammed them into the suitcase. Then she started packing his.

"I'll do that, Josie."

"No, you rest. Sleep if you can. I have a few things to take care of before we leave." That was enough to roust him out of the bed. "No need to get alarmed. I'm just going around the corner to the newsstand to pick up a paper, and then I'm going to call Mr. and Mrs. Beaman."

"The organizers of the sit-in?" He hoped his alarm didn't show.

"They didn't organize it, and besides it's not what you're thinking, Ben."

"How do you know what I'm thinking?"

"Sometimes I read minds, too." He could forgive her for anything when she smiled. "The Beamans are staying in a little dumpy place about a mile up the strip. I thought it would be nice if they could move in here and celebrate their anniversary in style. The room's paid up for three more days, anyway."

"Did you know you have a heart of gold?"

"Yes. You gave it to me." She patted the locket around her neck. As far as he knew she hadn't taken it off since he'd given it to her. Ben wasn't going to think about the implications of that right now. If he stayed around Josie much longer he was going to lose his focus. He was going to become one of those people who lived one day at a time with no thought of tomorrow. Like a grasshopper.

He was wondering if grasshoppers had more fun when Josie drifted out the door and he drifted off to sleep.

They were both quiet as they started the long drive back home. Josie felt a sense of defeat, but she couldn't tell what Ben was thinking. He'd insisted on driving, at least until they got out of the city.

She couldn't blame him. The way things had been going for her lately, she'd probably take a magnolia tree home on her front fender.

She tried to lighten the mood with conversation.

"Did you see the Beamans' faces when they stepped into that honeymoon suite?"

"I did. That was a generous thing you did, Josie."

"Ah, shucks, pardner, it was nothing."

Her bad cowboy imitation usually got a laugh out of Ben, but not today. Josie turned her face toward the sea. Soon they'd be leaving it behind.

"Would you stop somewhere on the beach for me, Ben?"

"Sure. Anything wrong, Josie?"

"No. There's something I have to do before we leave, that's all."

Ben pulled over near Beauvoir, the home of Jefferson Davis. "I'll go with you."

"There's no need."

"I insist."

She hated the formality between them. As they walked side by side to the beach, not touching, she imagined how it might have been—kicking off their shoes and walking barefoot through the sand holding hands, occasionally stopping to kiss because the urge was so strong in them they'd die if they didn't.

At the water's edge she pulled a cobalt blue glass bottle out of her purse. Inside she could barely see the outline of the note she'd written.

"What's this, Josie? An S.O.S.?"

"No, S.M.A.S.H., Save My Awful Sinful Hide."

It was the first time he'd laughed since before she got thrown into jail. It was worth the small white lie she'd just told.

Josie knelt down and sent her message out to sea, then stood with her hand shielding her eyes until the blue bottle blended with the waters and was lost to sight.

Maybe a lonely woman across the Mississippi Sound would find it and take hope. Maybe a pair of estranged lovers would find it and renew their vows. Shoot, maybe Kevin Costner would find it and make a movie.

"You're a romantic, aren't you, Josie?"

She couldn't admit to being a romantic, even to herself. If she did she'd cry.

"I'm ready to go now, Ben."

He reached for her hand and held it all the way back to the car. When she started for the passenger side, Ben said, "You can drive now, Josie. If you want to."

She wanted to. Within minutes Ben was asleep, and that's when her foolish tears started. Josie didn't even try to wipe them away. Crying silently, she turned the car north toward home.

Chapter Ten

"We're home," Josie said.

Ben woke up with a start and realized they were parked outside his modest apartment in Pontotoc, and Josie had her hand stuck out as if she expected him to shake it and say, so long, pal, see you later. Boy, was she in for a surprise.

"This is where we say goodbye and go our separate ways," she said.

"Come inside." It wasn't the most diplomatic way of saying *don't go,* but he was barely awake, his brain was foggy and he was upset, besides. It would have to do.

"Good idea. I could use a bathroom break, and I'll use your phone to call a taxi."

He waited till he was inside with both their suitcases stowed in the closet and the door shut behind him before he said anything else. He didn't trust himself. He felt like a frog that had been mashed flat by a log truck in the middle of a hot Texas highway.

She'd vanished into the bathroom, and he smiled when he heard the water tap running the whole time. Latent modesty. Josie was nervous, too.

"There's no need to call a taxi, Josie."

"Why?"

"Because you're staying here."

"I guess I could bunk here a few days till I find my own apartment. I certainly can't go moving back in with Mother and Aunt Tess. They'd have a conniption fit."

"I'm not talking about a few days. I'm talking about a few months."

"That's not what we agreed."

"I agreed to marry you, Josie. I didn't agree to your terms."

A lovely flush crept into her face, and at first he thought it was the blush of a modest woman thinking about going to bed with her husband for the first time. Too late he realized it was Josie on the warpath.

"If you think you're going to take advantage of this situation to...to get into my pants, you're sadly mistaken. I thought you were a man of honor. You've changed, Ben Standing Bear. I don't know you anymore."

"I'm the same stubborn Sioux you knew years ago."

"The man I knew back then would never take advantage of a woman."

Now, he was getting mad, which was totally out of character. Ben had always prided himself on being a calm and reasonable man.

"I'm not planning to 'take advantage' of you, as you so delicately put it. Sneaky tactics aren't my style. When I decide to bed you, Josie Belle, you'll know it."

Too late he saw his slip of the tongue.

"When?"

He wasn't about to back down now. "That's what I said."

"We agreed to an annulment. That means no sex."

"You're the one who suggested an annulment, Josie, not me. And it's not based on sex, it's based on time."

"What are you? A lawyer, all of a sudden?"

"No, I'm a doctor. And a tired one at that."

The steam went out of Josie as quickly as it had come. She put her arms around Ben and leaned her forehead against his chest.

"I'm sorry, Ben. Of course, you're tired, too tired to stand here and argue with me." He hugged her close, and was just going to bend down and kiss her—for old times' sake, of course—when she stepped back, smiling. "I'll stay here tonight, and we'll discuss this in the morning."

"Good. I'll take the couch, and you can take the bedroom."

"No, let me…"

"The issue is not negotiable, Josie."

"Benevolent tyrant."

As it turned out, they didn't wait till morning to settle the issue. Aunt Tess called after they'd had take-out pizza to say everybody was talking about Josie's short honeymoon trip.

"Boy, the grapevine really works fast in Pontotoc, doesn't it?" he said.

"Faster than a speeding bullet."

"If tongues are wagging about our short honeymoon, imagine what they'll say if you move into your own apartment."

"I don't have to imagine. I know. 'What did you expect of Josie Belle Pickens?' they'll say. 'We knew she couldn't keep her man.'"

"They don't have to say that, Josie."

Ben captured her with a frank stare that made her blush. He knew almost to the minute when she changed her mind.

"Can I bring Bruiser over?" she said.

* * *

They fell into a routine: *Strangers When We Meet*, like the title of the old Kirk Douglas/Kim Novak movie, and polite ones at that. Josie had said *excuse me* and *thank you* so much in the last week she was about to explode. Besides, the apartment was barely big enough for two grown people, let alone two grown people and a big hairy dog.

Everywhere she turned, Bruiser was bumping her leg and she was bumping into Ben. In the last week he'd had his hands all over her. Accidentally, of course. If she didn't get some relief she was going to scream.

She thought it would come when school started, but the first rattle out of the trap, one of her students called her Mrs. Standing Bear, which, of course, was the proper way to address her, and all of a sudden she realized she'd have to hear that title day in and day out. And every time she heard it she would know it was a lie.

Josie volunteered for every after-school duty they had, and when that wasn't enough she took up causes.

Ben's practice was growing bigger every day, which was exactly what he'd hoped for when he agreed to become a small-town doctor. One of the top ten in his class, he'd been heavily recruited by some of the finest hospitals in the country, but he'd said no to their offers. He wanted to practice medicine in a small town where he could make a difference.

But more than that he'd wanted to become an integral part of the community. He wanted to live in a small town where your neighbors invited you over for backyard barbecues and your friends asked you to join them for a round of golf and picnics on the lake. He'd missed all that growing up. He'd missed family and home and a sense of belonging. Ben hadn't belonged to anybody except his brother Jim. They'd been two against the world, but now Jim had a family and while Ben was always welcome there, he still felt a huge void in his life.

Plenty of people asked him what to do about their arthritis or their headaches, sometimes even stopping him on the street, but so far nobody had asked him over for dinner or lunch or even for a cool drink of water on a hot day. He was an outsider. He had earned their respect but not their friendship.

From the way things looked, he never would, because he was different and therefore suspect. The townspeople weren't lacking in manners. They were excruciatingly polite to him, even inquiring about his wife, but nobody went beyond the surface formalities. Nobody called him *Ben,* and nobody called him *friend.* Except Josie.

And not even she had done that lately. She was too busy avoiding him.

Maybe Ben wasn't trying hard enough. Maybe being on the outside was his fault.

Glancing at the chart he saw that his last patient for the day was Compton Willis, who had been one of the very first to seek out the clinic. He was a young, enthusiastic farmer with a pregnant wife named Janie, also Ben's patient. A man well worth knowing.

Ben was going to try. And so, after he'd checked Compton's blood sugar and talked to him about ways to keep his diabetes under control, he asked about Janie.

"She's great, except for complaining that she's getting too big to bend over and pick peas. I told her 'Honey, you just stay out of the garden,' and that like to tickled her to death. I told her she didn't even have to cook the durned things, I'd take her out to dinner. Women like that, you know."

Compton's response was more than Ben had hoped for. Flushed with success, he said, "I need to do more socializing with my own wife. Why don't the four of us get

together Friday night and drive over to Tupelo to Va-
nelli's?''

"Well, say, Doc, that's mighty nice of you, but you
know how women are. I'd have to talk to Janie first, and
you know, come to think of it, she said something about
going to her sister's Friday night.'' Compton was sweating
after he finished wiggling out of Ben's invitation. Giving
Ben a lame smile, he added, ''By the way, how's your
wife?''

"Great.'' He made himself smile all the way to the door,
then he retreated to his office and sat down to think things
through.

Perhaps if he battered on the door long enough, in time
he would be accepted. Or it might never happen. Ben might
always be viewed as an outsider in Pontotoc.

And where did that leave Josie? Fortunately for her, their
arrangement was only temporary. He'd promised her six
months, and that's what he would give her. Then he'd get
the annulment and she would be well out of a bad deal.

Meanwhile, he was going to do everything in his power
to make their remaining time together pleasant. He would
start by trying to get them back on a friendly footing. On
the way home from the clinic he stopped to pick up a bottle
of chardonnay and a fat purple candle. Josie loved atmo-
sphere.

As soon as he stepped through the front door Ben knew
she wasn't there. He called her name anyway.

"Josie?'' There was no answer.

He found the note propped on the kitchen table alongside
the stack of letters she'd sat up the last three nights writing
to the city councilmen urging mandatory recycling.

"Ben,'' the note said, ''I'm over at Mother's rehearsing
the music for TKAI with Tammy Reese. Don't wait for me.
Hugs, Josie. P.S. Will you take Bruiser for a walk?''

That was another thing he needed to change. Josie's piano was as important to her as her right arm. Because of him she couldn't even rehearse the music for *The King and I* without going back to school or going home to her mother's.

Ben prowled his apartment looking for a spot to put her piano. Every inch of floor space was taken. He stomped through again, with Bruiser making every step he did.

"I took you in, you big mutt. I'm going to make room for her piano if I have to hold it in my lap."

There was not a single available space…unless he threw out something vital such as the stove or the washing machine or the bed.

He looked at the bed, picturing Josie there. Alone.

"Might as well get rid of that thing for all the good it's doing me, huh, boy?"

Bruiser licked Ben's hand, then trotted to the kitchen and retrieved his leash.

"Okay. I get the message." Ben snapped on the leash. "But get this through your thick skull, Bruiser. Don't try any smart stuff. I'm bigger than Josie, and *I'm* doing the leading."

He opened the front door, and Bruiser shot through like a ball out of a cannon, dragging Ben along behind. They went half a block before Ben could get the upper hand.

It was the first time he'd felt in control of anything since he married Josie. He was so pleased he smiled at the surliest woman in town, old Mrs. Ransom Crumpet, who had last been seen smiling in 1955, the day her husband accidentally did his philandering in a bed of poison ivy.

"Good evening, Mrs. Crumpet," he said.

"Eat prunes," she snapped.

Ben tried to turn right at Court Square, but Bruiser wanted to turn left, and he was tired of arguing, so they went left. That's when Ben saw the house. A perfect two-story Victorian with a wraparound front porch and a For Sale sign in the yard. A house big enough for Josie's piano.

When Josie found the chardonnay and the purple candle still in a bag in the cabinet, she sought advice from her friend Ashley. Advice and relief. It was a woman's way.

Besides, it was the first chance she'd had to see Ashley since she'd returned from her honeymoon. They were in a small café just off Court Square.

"You look stressed out, Josie. What's going on?"

"Nothing. And that's the trouble. Ashley, he bought wine and a purple candle for me. You *know* how I love purple."

"Uh-oh, I already see the handwriting on the wall."

"What handwriting on the wall?"

"I could have told you you'd fall in love with Ben Standing Bear. In fact, I think I did, but you didn't listen."

"I never listen to anybody, Ashley. That's my other problem. I'm like a bull in a china shop, snorting and pawing, breaking things, tearing them up. I'm a mess." She took a soothing drink of her chocolate milkshake. "And for your information, I'm not in love with Ben. We're friends, that's all."

"Who are you trying to kid? This is me. Soul sister. Remember?"

"Oh, Lord, Ashley, I don't know what's happening. First I'm mad that he doesn't kiss me, and then I think I'll sock him in the eye if he does. I don't sleep anymore. Me, the original Rip van Winkle, an insomniac. I lie awake listening to him snore, and I think it's the sweetest sound in the world."

"Good grief. You've got it bad, kid. What I want to know is, what are you going to do about it?"

"I don't have *anything* bad. I'm confused. That's all."

She toyed with her sandwich, suddenly not hungry. "He wants me to go househunting."

"Househunting?"

"Yes, he said he'd planned to buy a house anyway, and he'd like my advice. Besides, he says, it'll be more practical for us to have more space till we've finished this charade."

"He called your marriage a charade?"

"Not exactly. I think he said something like, till we decide what to do."

"Aha."

"Don't give me that *aha* look. What happened with you and old Jerry Bob? I haven't had a chance to ask…. Good Lord, Ashley. You're getting flushed. Was it that bad?"

"No, actually it wasn't bad, at all. He brought a boom box to the picnic. He loved my cooking and I loved his music."

Her own troubles forgotten, Josie propped her elbows on the table and leaned toward her friend. She loved a good drama, and this had all the makings of one.

"And?"

"Nothing. Stop looking at me like that, Josie."

"I will when you tell me the truth. Come, on, Ashley. 'Fess up."

"There's nothing to confess. Really." Ashley pushed her blond hair off her flushed face. "It's just that…well, I think he's a nice guy, that's all."

"He is a nice guy, just sort of dull." At the way Ashley's lips tightened, Josie changed her tune. "For me, that is. I crave excitement, and you know Jerry Bob. He likes everything to be just so so."

"You could be wrong about that, Josie."

"Heck, it wouldn't be the first time."

The waitress came to take their orders for dessert, and in spite of the chocolate milkshake she'd already had, Josie ordered a double chocolate brownie with whipped cream and cherries. Stress always made her crave chocolate. She got that way every time her class put on a play, which was twice a year, late fall and early spring.

Lately, though, she'd been in a constant state of craving. If she stayed with Ben the for agreed-upon six months, she was going to be big as a barrel.

"So, what do you think about the house? Should I go with him to look?"

"Absolutely."

"You don't think it'll look like I'm trying to horn in on his future, or anything like that?"

"Think of it as returning a favor. He did one for you, and now you're doing one for him."

"I never thought about it that way." Josie was so relieved she cancelled her order for the brownie and ordered sherbet, instead. Now she could help Ben find the perfect house. She could walk through the empty rooms and dream to her heart's content, all under the legitimate excuse of *helping* Ben.

"Thanks, Ashley. I feel a hundred times better."

"That's what friends are for. And Josie, one more bit of advice. I think you're trying too hard to make your marriage *not* work. Why don't you just let things take their natural course?"

"I'm scared to, what's why." She might as well have ripped her heart out and laid it on the table bleeding. She tried to laugh it off. "Besides, you know me. Life's a big drama and I'm bound and determined to be the director."

"I guess you'll get your heart's wish soon. What are you doing for your students' first play?"

"I don't think Pontotoc is ready for what I wanted to do. *Cat on a Hot Tin Roof*." Which was exactly the way Josie felt.

"You'd be tarred and feathered, to say the least."

"I promised Ben I'd stay out of trouble, so I'm playing it safe. Mostly. We're doing a musical, instead."

"Well, you look wonderful. Is it the work that agrees with you so much or is it the marriage, Mrs. Standing Bear?"

"Please don't call me that, Ashley."

"You don't like it?"

"I like it too much."

They paid their check, and as they left Ashley put her arm around Josie.

"You're going to get through this, kid." Ashley burst into song. "You've got me and I've got you…"

"…Babe," Josie chimed in, trying to harmonize with Ashley's off-key pitch. Restored by friendship and sunshine, Josie put her sunglasses on and smiled at Ashley in particular and the world in general. "You know what?"

"No, what?"

They laughed at their silliness. Josie was feeling better by the minute.

"When Ben and I get a house I'm going to invite you over for dinner. I've been missing you, you gorgeous creature."

"What will Ben say to that?"

"Lord, Ashley, he never disagrees with anything I say or disputes anything I do. He's so excruciatingly polite and so unlike himself that sometimes I want to scream. Besides, I think he'd welcome a chance to socialize. You know, the whole time he's been here, not a single person has asked us to dinner. Not even Mother."

"That's not like her, Josie."

"Yes, but it's exactly like Aunt Tess. She spreads her poison everywhere."

"They'll come around."

"I hope so."

"And Josie, about Ben… This is a period of adjustment. Give it time."

Josie figured she'd need about a hundred years to adjust to being nothing but polite strangers with Ben.

Chapter Eleven

Josie fell in love with the house the minute she saw it. It was exactly the kind of house she'd always pictured herself living in when she got married, a house big enough to raise a large family and friendly enough to feel warm and cozy and welcoming.

For a moment she forgot the circumstances of her marriage. She raced through the rooms with her arms and her heart wide open.

"Oh, Ben, just look at these floors. Imagine what Oriental rugs will look like against that dark wood. And the windows! Just look at the light. Doesn't it make you want to sing and dance?"

"You like it, then, Josie?"

"Like it? I *love* it. I could marry this house."

Thankful the real estate agent had said, "Take your time, look at your own pace. I'll wait for you back at the office," Josie raced up the stairs and discovered an enormous suite of rooms exactly right for Ben's four-poster bed and some comfortable rocking chairs as well as his antique bookcase. It even had a fireplace.

"Ben, *look.* We can pop corn right over the fire."

"Yes, we can."

The bathroom was a dream. "The tub's big enough for two," she blurted, and when Ben smiled and looked deep into her eyes the way he'd been doing the last few days, Josie felt the roots of her hair burst into flames.

What was it he'd said the day they returned to Pontotoc? *When I decide to bed you, you'll know it?*

Was he getting ready to make good his promise? And what would she do about it if he did?

Josie decided to moderate her enthusiasm. After all, this was *Ben's* house, not hers. She was only a temporary nuisance in his life, like a hangnail that wouldn't go away.

When she saw the rooms across the hall, she lost her resolve. They were full of delightful nooks and crannies, the kind children loved to play in, and they opened to an enormous playroom.

"Paint some murals on the wall, add a couple of skylights and children will *love* these rooms."

He was so quiet she turned around to see if he'd gone back into the hall. Then she wished she hadn't. He was giving her that *look* again, only this time he'd turned up the wattage a hundred percent.

"Do you want children, Josie?"

The way he said it sounded intensely personal, as if he were asking her to sit down with him on a love seat and pick out names for their firstborn. She had to stop thinking that way before she made a hopeless mess of things.

Act, she told herself. After all, she was a darned good actress.

"Well, of course, I do," she said in a nonchalant manner.

"Someday. If I ever fall in love and get married for real. Isn't that every girl's dream?"

Ben looked as if a light had been snuffed out somewhere inside him. The careful stranger she'd been living with for the past few weeks came back.

"I hope all your wishes come true, Josie." The smile he gave her frosted her eyelashes. "I'll be downstairs when you get ready to go. Take your time."

His footsteps echoed like drumbeats in the empty house. *War* drums.

Josie wanted to yell, *Wait! Come back! I didn't mean that.* She wanted to hug him, she wanted to make him laugh, she wanted to see the light in his eyes once more.

She walked to the window and looked out. There were ancient trees in the yard, a huge magnolia with limbs dripping to the ground and a group of oaks with massive branches just right for hanging a swing. Camellias higher than your head would put on a show in early winter after everything else in the garden had gone by, and come spring, the azaleas tucked into all the shady nooks would parade their pink blossoms. Though she couldn't see them, Josie would bet her bottom dollar that in late February and early March, daffodils would pop up by the score, dripping over the sloping lawn like butter.

Her next thought was, I won't be here to see them. She felt the dampness on her cheeks. Mad at herself, she wiped it away, then put on an actress's smile before she went downstairs to meet Ben.

"What's the verdict, Josie?"

There was no warmth in him when he asked the question, no hint of a smile, no light lurking in his eyes. But true to character, Ben had said he wanted her opinion, and now he was asking for it. He always followed through.

Giving him an impersonal answer was one of the hardest things she'd ever had to do. For the last half hour she'd let herself forget the circumstances surrounding their relationship. She'd let herself believe that she would live in the house. That she would sleep in the master suite with Ben. That the two of them would tiptoe across the hall at night to check the crib just to make *sure*.

Before she could answer him, Josie put on her sunglasses so he wouldn't see her eyes.

"It's a wonderful house that will wear well over the years. I don't see how you can go wrong with this house, Ben. Unless, of course, you find a wife who prefers ultramodern architecture to warmth and charm."

"I'll get the car," was all he said.

Jose didn't trust herself to look at his face.

The next morning Ben left for work before Josie got up. She found a note propped on the kitchen table. "I'll be working late tonight. Don't wait up."

When she got to school she immediately signed up to be chairman of the Halloween Festival to raise money for new band uniforms, and then set up a meeting for the following night.

Ben shopped for groceries while Josie was at her fundraising meeting. Two of his patients who saw him turned away and began to whisper behind their hands.

At the meat counter, the butcher hailed him. "Shopping by yourself, Doc?"

"Yes. Josie's at a school function."

The butcher—Max was his name—clucked his tongue and shook his head. "These modern women. Can't live with 'em, can't live without 'em."

Ben always enjoyed loitering over the cuts of prime rib and the thick slabs of bacon and the honey-cured ham. Tonight, though, he hurried on.

Ever since that awful day they'd gone househunting, he

had not referred to Josie as *my wife*. There was nothing like a few shattered dreams to give a man a big dose of reality.

Maybe he ought to thank her. Ben had been in danger of losing his focus. He'd been in dire peril of becoming one of those sentimental people who embraced life with their hearts and arms wide open instead of their ears and eyes.

Somebody like Josie.

"Don't even think about it," he all but growled, and the woman who was pondering which brand of dish detergent to buy gave him a nasty look.

"I *beg* your pardon," she sniffed, then wheeled her cart down the aisle as if a pack of hungry hounds were after her.

Ben blindly dumped frozen dinners into his cart and hurried to the checkout stand. He couldn't get out of there fast enough.

He wasn't accustomed to failure, and yet everything he'd tried to do lately had failed. His attempts at friendship had been rebuffed. His resolution to restore harmony with Josie had bombed. As for the house, who did he think he was kidding? He hadn't needed the house for Josie's piano: he'd needed it as a symbol that he belonged.

When he got home he made notes in his journal. There was nothing as sobering as listing the puny events of your day. Reading them over, Ben decided he was, after all, a mortal, and mortals were made to suffer. It was just his turn. That was all.

Josie's fund-raising committee gathered in her room after school. She'd arranged chairs in a semicircle for a cozier effect.

Clark Reese, the band director, made a beeline for the chair next to hers, then sprawled out in such a way his leg touched Josie's. Trying to be discreet, she moved out of his reach.

"Josie, I'm beginning to think that husband of yours is fiction," Clark said. "When are we going to meet him?"

Josie evaded his question. "He's very busy."

"Is he coming to the faculty party?"

This, from Annette Slocomb who taught math. Her husband, Herbert, came to every school event, and she was suspicious of husbands who didn't. Wives, too. The way she looked at Josie left no doubt of what she thought: the husband was absent, so the wife must be doing something terribly wrong.

Annette leaned toward Josie with an eager I'm-ready-to-give-advice look on her face.

"I don't make social commitments for Ben," Josie said, then smiled to show there was no problem in the marriage, that the problem was in the nosy questions. She was getting ready to ask for a volunteer for the booth all the teachers hated when Annette showed her true colors.

"Is he a full blood or does he have just a tiny bit of Indian blood?"

It wasn't the question so much as the way Annette asked it that got Josie's hackles up. She turned so she could skewer Annette face to face.

"He's a full-blood *Native American*, and proud of it. And I'm proud to be his wife." Josie flipped open her notebook before she did do something she'd regret, such as slapping the superior smirk off Annette's face. "Now, back to business. Annette, I'm assigning you the dunking booth."

When she got home, still shaking inside, there was a note from Ben saying he'd gone to the library, and a voice mail from her mother.

Josie dialed her mother's number. "What's up, Mother?"

"I'm a bit concerned about you, Josie Belle."

"Why? I'm perfectly fine." *Except for narrowly escaping a fist fight defending my husband.*

"What about Ben?"

"What do you mean, what about Ben?"

"Is he fine, too?"

"Yes."

"Where is he?"

"What do you mean, where is he?"

"There's no need to get so testy, Josie Belle. A mother has a right to know these things."

"What things? Would you please tell me what you're talking about, Mother?"

"I hadn't wanted to say anything earlier, but when Tess came home from the library and said she saw Ben there all by himself, well, I just thought it was time to get to the bottom of this."

"I still don't know what you're talking about, Mother."

"People have been talking."

"That's not news. People always talk."

"Yes, but when they're talking about my daughter, that's a horse of a different color."

"No, Mother, it's a horse of the same color. I've always provided fodder for the small-town gossip mills."

"They're not just talking about you. They're talking about Ben, too."

Josie sat down. She didn't want to hear this. She really didn't. Somehow she already knew what was being said without even asking. It didn't bother her so much what was said about her. Unconventional people were always going to be misjudged and labeled. But Ben...

That was a different story. He was as straitlaced as they came. Mr. All America. He'd been the perfect scholar, the perfect athlete, the perfect friend, and now he was the perfect doctor, the perfect man.

He was just getting established in a new town. If Josie had ruined that for him, she was going to die.

Inside, she shrank to the size of a peanut.

"What are they saying, Mother?"

"They're saying the two of you never go anywhere together."

"That's true, but you have to realize that he's very busy with his practice, and I'm very busy at school."

"Still, Josie, he does the *grocery shopping* alone."

"Well, I know how that looks."

"They say you spend all your time at the school with the band director."

"That's an outrageous lie, Mother. We're on a committee together, that's all."

"He's not married."

"A lot of male teachers at the school aren't married. That doesn't mean I'm having affairs with them."

"That word hasn't been used yet, but it's just a matter of time." Her mother fell silent, and Josie tightened her hand on the receiver. "What's going on between you two, Josie?"

Josie was torn between confessing the whole truth, which would put an end to the miserable charade, and protecting her privacy as well as her freedom. When she remembered that Betty Anne Pickens had never really been concerned about what was going on in her daughter's life, the decision was made.

All her mother really wanted to know was how she should respond to the gossip.

"Every newlywed couple has a period of adjustment, Mother. That's what you should tell everybody. Tell Aunt Tess to spread the word. She's good at that."

"She's still talking about selling her house."

"That means she'd move in with you. Permanently. How do you feel about that, Mother?"

"Well, I guess I'm undecided. What do you think your father would say?"

Josie was all set to step into her daddy's shoes one more time when alarm bells went off in her head. She might not always be around for her mother. It was high time Betty Anne started standing on her own two feet.

"Daddy's been dead a long time, Mother. It doesn't matter what he would advise. You're the one who will have to live with the consequences. It's up to you to decide whether you want Aunt Tess as a permanent guest."

"What do *you* think about it, Josie?"

"What I think doesn't matter, Mother. I don't live there anymore."

She gripped the phone and listened to the sound of her mother's breathing.

"Well, I'll think about it, darlin'. 'Bye."

It wasn't until after she'd hung up the phone that Josie realized how tense she was, nor how relieved that Betty Anne hadn't burst into tears. Not over any of it. The gossip or Aunt Tess.

"Maybe there's hope for us all."

She glanced at the clock. The library would be closing in thirty minutes, and Ben would be home.

What if she did something nice to make up for all the ugly gossip? What if she planned a nice surprise to show that she was the same woman she'd always been and that they could still be friends in spite of the marriage? What if she made cookies to show she was sorry? For everything.

One of the things Ben loved about living in a small town was that he could walk almost anywhere he wanted to go. He made his walk home from the library a leisurely one, giving himself enough time to enjoy the sights, giving Josie enough time to be settled at the corner desk in his bedroom grading papers or reading a book or whatever else she did in there all by herself.

Ben passed an elderly couple walking toward the town square holding hands. He'd never felt lonelier.

When he got home he'd take Bruiser for a late-night jog. At least he'd have company.

When he entered his apartment building he smelled something burning. Somebody was going to be ordering take-out food for dinner. He whistled a tuneless song as he went up the stairs. When he got to the top of the landing the smell became stronger. As he approached his door it got even worse.

Ben froze, then he was off and running. He fumbled with the lock and smoke billowed around him as he opened the door.

"Josie!" She didn't answer, and he died a thousand deaths. Suddenly he felt a wet tongue licking his hands, and there was Bruiser, and right behind him Josie.

"Oh, Ben." She threw herself against him, crying.

"Josie, what's happened here?"

With her face buried against his chest, she said, "Warra oooie waa."

He couldn't take the time to decipher. If he did they'd quite likely both die in a flaming inferno. Bruiser, too.

With Josie clinging to him like a potato vine he went through his apartment flinging open windows. When he got to the kitchen he discovered the root of the problem. The garbage can stood in the middle of the floor overflowing with burned food that looked like charcoal briquettes, and another pan full of charred nuggets stood on the stovetop, still smoking.

Holding Josie with one arm, he satisfied himself that the oven was off and there were no smoking pieces of dough inside waiting to burst into flames, then he turned on the exhaust fan and flung open the kitchen windows while Josie hung on like an appendage, crying her eyes out.

Ben melted. He turned inside out. His heart grew two sizes. He developed selective amnesia. Everything she'd said on that fateful day they went househunting was forgotten. Every evening he'd spent alone vanished. Every solitary trip he'd made, every innuendo he'd endured, every ruined night's sleep tossing on the sofa while she lay curled in his bed faded to oblivion.

She was soft and feminine and hurting, and he cared. He cared so deeply it scared him. He cared so very much that he couldn't bear to think about it.

Instead he picked her up and carried her to the living room where the smoke had drifted out the window. Then he sat down with her in the rocking chair. The sofa would have been more comfortable, but here he could hold her like a baby and rock her with a steady soothing rhythm.

"It's all right, Josie. No harm's done except a few black smudges on the wallpaper and I'll clean that off. The main thing is that you and Bruiser are all right." She didn't say anything, but she wasn't crying as hard as she had been.

"You *are* all right, aren't you, Josie?"

"Hmm."

"You didn't burn yourself, did you?"

She didn't move, didn't lift her head off his chest. He could barely make out her muffled "No."

"That's good, then." He rocked a while in silence, then remembering how Josie loved music he tried to sing "Amazed." He botched it so badly that he should have been embarrassed. The funny thing was, he wasn't.

So Ben just kept on singing. Singing and rocking and holding on to his Josie.

Josie had never felt more cherished. She could stay right where she was for the next million years or so. Ben's sing-

ing was so far off tune even Bruiser left the room, but to
Josie it was the most beautiful sound in the world. If it
wasn't the sound of love, it was surely the sound of a deep
and abiding friendship.

Ben knew all the words to the song, which amazed her
but shouldn't have. He excelled at everything he did, even
rocking, especially rocking. She began to swing her foot to
the rhythm of the rocking chair and to hum along and pretty
soon she realized that Ben had stopped singing and was
listening to her.

When the song ended she stayed where she was. Maybe
it was selfish of her, considering the way she'd treated him,
but what the heck, she was only human. She could be selfish sometimes and the world wouldn't come to an end.

"I love it when you sing that song, Josie, or even just
hum it. You have a really great voice."

"Thank you."

"Sometimes when I'm getting ready for bed I hear you
in the bedroom singing snatches of the songs from the musical you're directing, and I just stand outside the door and
listen."

Josie's heart hurt to think of Ben standing outside a
closed door. Any closed door. Especially hers.

*Oh, Ben, what have I done to you? What have I done to
us?*

If she didn't change the subject she was going to start
crying again. Maybe she should get off his lap. Or would
that look like another cold shoulder? She decided to stay,
and it was nice that she could use kindness as her motive.
It kept her from thinking about the hard questions, such as
What is being in love and am I in it?

"I didn't mean to almost burn the apartment down, Ben.
I'm sorry I scared you."

"You had me worried there for a while, Josie."

"I was trying to make cookies."

"That's what those blackened objects were?"

"Yes. I was making them for you." The rocking chair was still going and it never lost its rhythm, but Ben's arms tightened around her ever so slightly. She wanted to see his face, but she didn't want to make a big to-do of it, so she just stayed right where she was, curled comfortably over his heart.

"That was sweet of you. You'll never know how much that means to me."

His voice had dropped an octave the way men's voices do when they've done some wonderfully romantic thing like hugging you and rocking you in a rocking chair, and all of a sudden they're beginning to turn their thoughts toward heavier matters, like desire.

Josie had better set the record straight at once or she was going to end up in that four-poster bed with Ben, without a single protest on her part. How could she protest something she wanted to happen?

That just goes to show the state a woman's mind gets in when she's narrowly escaped some disaster, especially one of her own making.

"I wanted to make up for all the trouble I've caused you," she said.

He didn't say anything, but he did stop rocking. What did that mean? Was he upset? Relieved? Disappointed? She wasn't fixing to find out. Nosirree, Bob, she was going to stay right where she was, curled up to him like a bunny in a burrow.

"And all the gossip," she added. "And all the loneliness."

"Are you lonely, Josie?"

"Well, I'm not talking about me, I'm talking about you."

"How do you know I'm lonely?"

This time she did look at him. There was something in

his voice that was impossible to ignore, something she recognized and understood.

Sitting up in his lap, she cupped his face and pressed her nose against his the way the old Josie would have done with her best friend Ben.

"Because," she whispered, "I know how lonely it is to be living in the house with somebody who barely acknowledges that you exist. I know the terrible isolation of sleeping in a bed all by yourself and feeling as if you're the sole survivor of a spaceship wreck on Mars even when there is another person in the next room. I know how it is to go to bed at night and wrap your own arms around yourself because there's no one to do it for you. I know, Ben, and I understand."

Electric with emotion, they sat in stunned silence while Josie's revelations echoed around the room. What had started out as a friendly chat had turned into an airing-out session. Josie had just ripped her heart out and laid it bleeding at Ben's feet.

Years of feeling like an outsider in her own home; years of feeling as if she were viewing her parents with her face pressed against a windowpane suddenly coalesced, and her repressed emotions tumbled free.

That's how wonderful hugs can be...and how dangerous. They make you feel safe. They make you feel loved. They make you believe you can tell the truth without fear of reprisal.

Josie sat very still in Ben's lap, waiting for the world to come to an end.

Instead he stood up and carried her to the bedroom and lay down beside her.

"Lean on me, Josie," he said.

He held her as tenderly as a baby, held her that way all night long, and in the morning when she woke up, Josie discovered a smooth clean place in her heart where the cracks had been.

Chapter Twelve

Ben was whistling when he walked through the doors of his clinic—ten minutes late according to the clock. Although he usually didn't tolerate tardiness, especially in himself, he decided that this morning had been worth it.

"Feeling better?" he'd asked Josie when she sat up in bed this morning.

"Hmm, yes, thanks to you." Tousled and appealing, she'd bent down and kissed him lightly on the lips.

He bounded out of the covers like he'd been shot. "What do you say to breakfast together, then? We haven't done that in a long time."

"Too long," she said.

Perched on the their balcony like two birds, they'd shared orange juice and small tidbits of their day while Ben had pondered the wistful quality of Josie's voice when she'd said to him, *too long.*

Soon he was going to have to do some serious thinking

about Josie, but not this morning. Right now the order of the day was greeting his receptionist.

"Good morning, Nettie Jean," he said.

She tapped her watch as if she couldn't believe what she was seeking. "Will wonders never cease? You're late, Doc."

"It looks that way, doesn't it?"

"You're gonna tell me the clock is wrong?"

"No, I'm going to tell you I've joined the human race. Maybe."

"Let me bid you welcome." Laughing, Nettie Jean bustled off to the coffee machine and served him a steaming cup.

"What time's my first appointment?"

"Not till nine-thirty. Oscar Levitts."

He checked his desk for the lab report on work he'd ordered on Oscar, then remembered that it wasn't going to be ready until this morning. Ben decided to save his lab technicians a few steps by going across the hall to get it.

He opened the lab door just in time to hear the tail end of gossip about his wife.

"...and they say she's down at the school all hours of the night rehearsing for that musical she's doing. Without the doc."

Ben froze in his tracks. The bearer of those bad tidings was none other than Marilyn Jones, thirty-five, mother of four, pillar of the community and darned good lab technician.

"Well, I hear she's been squiring around all over town without him, and leaving poor Doc, bless his naive soul, to do all the shopping and all the cooking." This from Charlene Rasberry, her assistant, who brought her yarn to work every day in case she had a minute to crochet booties for their pregnant patients.

Ben hated gossip above all things, but he couldn't bring

himself to leave. This was Josie they were maligning. He needed to know what was being said about his wife.

"What did he expect when he married her? That's what I want to know. She's always had a reputation for trouble."

"He didn't expect anything, is my guess. They say he married her out of pity. Clytee Crawford told Aunt Martha she'd never been so relieved over anything in all her life as she was the day Josie Belle walked down the aisle with somebody besides Jerry Bob."

"Well, all I can say is, poor Doc."

For a moment Ben was paralyzed by anger. He thought about going back into his office and quietly shutting the door. Instead he strode into the lab. Both women looked as guilty as if they'd been caught stealing eggs.

"I need the lab reports on Oscar Levitts...unless you're busy with other things."

Marilyn outran her shoes to get the report, and bumped smack into Charlene. If he hadn't been so mad, Ben would have laughed. As it was, he took the report back to his office and shut the door. He still had nearly an hour before his first patient, an hour to think of a solution.

In the end, he knew there was only one: rescue Josie one more time, and then set her free. It was a good plan that would have only one casualty. Him.

Josie was surprised to find Ben at the apartment when she got home from school.

"You're home early."

"Yes. Slow day at the office."

She smiled. "Is that bad or good?"

"Both." Something was up. She could tell by the way he looked at her.

Josie felt as if she were drowning in quicksand. He was going to ask for an immediate annulment. He was going to say, *look, let's just get this over with,* then shake hands and wish her well.

She could postpone the inevitable by diverting his attention with a funny story. Or maybe she could get him laughing about Aunt Tess's impromptu visit to the school.

That's what she would do. After all, nobody would be hurt if she postponed the bad news for a little while.

"Aunt Tess dropped by to see me today."

"Any reason?"

"She said she was just checking to see how I was doing. Then she nosed through everything in my room, including the closets. She even looked behind the window shades."

"She's about as subtle as a Sherman tank."

"When I asked her what she was looking for, she said, 'Nothing,' then she proceeded to ask me when I'd last seen the band director."

Josie started laughing, then realized Ben wasn't even smiling. Her plan had backfired.

"Ben, what's wrong?"

"Gossip. That's what's wrong, Josie."

"Sticks and stones may break my bones, but words can never hurt me." The rhyme had been Josie's mainstay when she was growing up. Somehow it didn't do much to soothe her now.

"Yes, they can, Josie. Sometimes words are more dangerous than blows because their cruelty is insidious."

"People will always talk. There's no way to stop them. The best thing to do is just settle in till it blows over."

"I won't have people talking about my wife."

"Thank you for the thought, but there's nothing you can do."

"Yes, there is."

There was fire in his eyes and the sound of drumbeats in his voice. Delicious shivers ran through Josie, and unconsciously she shifted away. Ben Standing Bear on the warpath was far too dangerous for comfort…and far too sexy.

"Do I want to know what?" she asked.

"I think you should since you're central to the success of the plan." The way he smiled made her think of a panther that had cornered his prey. "We're going to fight fire with fire, Josie."

He was *telling*, not asking. Josie had always liked that about Ben: he knew exactly when to be kind and gentle and exactly when to be a warrior.

The warrior in her kitchen was turning her into a maiden longing to be captive. It was a role she'd never played. Not once in her life. Even with Jerry Bob. What *he'd* turned her into was a woman who didn't dare let somebody else take charge, a woman who protected her independence with a fierceness bordering on the paranoid.

"It sounds intriguing." *Exciting, mind-boggling, breath-stealing. Oh, help. If he keeps looking at me like that, I'm lost.* "Tell me more."

"Are you all right, Josie?"

He put his hand on her forehead. She started to tell him that wasn't the part of her anatomy on fire, but she didn't. It was taking all the willpower she had just to keep breathing.

"I'm fine," she said. "Just a touch of a headache."

"Here, sit down." He pulled out a chair and eased her into it. "Let me make it better."

If anybody could make what ailed her better, it was Ben Standing Bear. The pill he handed her wasn't exactly what she had in mind, but she swallowed it anyway and chased it down with the water he brought.

"So, what's your game plan, Doctor?"

"You will become my wife in every way."

She nearly choked on her water. Ben patted her on the back, then knelt beside her and checked her pulse, which was probably racing like an aging greyhound trying to make the finish line. Darn his gorgeous hide, did he have to hover? Did he have to keep touching her? Everywhere he'd put his hands, she felt branded.

He smiled at her. "I think you'll live."

"I like your bedside manner."

"You haven't even seen it yet."

She'd never seen eyes so deep. She was going to drown in him and be content the rest of her life.

"Tell me…" She licked her lips since his were off limits. "I…what do you have in mind?"

"We'll be seen together in public, go out more, and when we do, we'll act like a loving couple."

"You mean hold hands?"

"Among other things."

"I see." And what she saw had her heart in overdrive. "And when do we start…being happily married?"

"Tonight. Unless you have rehearsals?"

"No. Nothing my assistant can't handle."

"Good. Get your glad rags on, Josie. We're going out to dinner and the movies."

"My glad rags? Are you becoming Southern, Ben Standing Bear?"

"Not a chance. I'm just trying to blend."

She didn't know what got into her—joy, she guessed—but she raked him boldly from head to toe.

"Take it from me, Ben. You'll never blend. Thank God."

Ben had never expected his first audience to be Jerry Bob Crawford. His concern was not for himself, but for Josie.

As they entered the restaurant he took her elbow, then leaned down to whisper, "Trial by fire."

She followed his subtle nod to the table opposite theirs,

then immediately dragged Ben in that direction, smiling and waving.

"Well, look who's here," she said. "Jerry Bob and Ashley." Josie leaned down to kiss them both on the cheeks, then moved so close to Ben she might as well have been sitting in his lap.

Ben steeled himself against the thrill of having Josie in his arms. He was playing with fire, and already he could feel the heat of the flames. He tried to focus his attention on the task at hand.

Jerry Bob looked as disturbed as Ben felt, but Ashley covered for him.

"We're keeping each other company on an otherwise boring Friday night," Ashley said. "Won't you and Ben join us?"

The last thing Ben wanted to do was have dinner with Josie's ex-almost-husband, but he waited to take his cue from Josie. What she did thrilled him in more ways than one.

"No, thank you. I want this man all to myself tonight." She dropped her voice into the range of sultry, then stood on tiptoe and kissed Ben full on the mouth. "Is that all right with you, darlin'?"

"Sounds good to me."

Josie turned back to her friend. "Ashley, we haven't visited in a blue moon. Let's have lunch soon."

"Let's do."

"How about tomorrow?"

"I can't tomorrow, Josie. I have other plans. But soon, I promise."

Ben played the loving husband as they followed the waitress to their table, which wasn't hard to do. The hard thing was letting Josie go, even long enough to pull out her chair. He made a big production of hovering over her. The scent of flowers wafted from her hair and skin, and he saw no reason not to bend down and kiss the side of her neck.

And not just for appearance's sake. For the first time since their wedding, he could openly do what he'd wanted to do all along.

"Do you think Ashley looked a little pale?" Josie said after the waitress left with their order.

"I didn't notice."

How could he? As far as Ben was concerned, when Josie was in the room she might as well be the only woman there.

"Well, she does. And what in the devil is she doing with Jerry Bob?"

"Maybe she likes him. Would it bother you if she did?"

"Absolutely not. Ben, this is not what you're thinking."

"And what would that be?"

"That I have feelings for him."

"Do you?"

He felt a stillness inside himself, almost a paralysis, as if his next breath depended on her answer. Just when this shift had taken place he didn't know, but all of a sudden he realized how important Josie was to him. How much that had to do with friendship and how much it had to do with emotions far more complex was something Ben didn't want to think about.

He needed to focus on the issue at hand, which was rescuing Josie's reputation. By George, when he finished with this town, *nobody* would view Josie as a woman he'd married out of pity. They would all be calling him the luckiest man alive because Josie Belle Pickens was his wife.

After that...

No, he wouldn't let his thinking roam beyond tonight. Tonight he and Josie would be the perfect lovers, at least in the eyes of the townspeople.

"Ben..." Josie reached for his hand across the table, and he felt how small-boned she was, how fragile.

She needed someone to take care of her, to rub her feet at night when she came home from rehearsals tired, to hug her close in the rocking chair when she was blue, to sing to her and make her laugh. Josie needed someone to love her, someone to make her believe she was the most wonderful woman in the world.

For one heady moment he thought he might be that man, and then he remembered all the reasons he couldn't be.

"I *do* have feelings for Jerry Bob," she said.

He felt as if a knife had laid open his heart, and then he saw the devilish twinkle in her eye. Ben decided to play along.

"Before tonight is over, I hope to persuade you to change your mind."

"And how would you do that?"

"Do you want me to tell you or to show you?"

"Show me."

"Here? In public?"

"Why not? My reputation's in tatters anyhow."

He should have known better than to challenge Josie. Now what was he going to do? Ben Standing Bear, the new doctor in town, decided there was only one thing to do.

He went around the table, pulled his wife into his arms and gave her a kiss so thorough it should have been outlawed in public. Probably it would be tomorrow. He could picture the headlines in the *Pontotoc Progress*: City Bans Kissing.

In that case, he decided to make use of what little time he had left, and so he let her catch her breath, then kissed her again.

This time when she pulled away she was as flushed as if she'd been running in hundred-degree heat.

"Ben, I think there's something I should tell you."

"You want to leave without dinner and go straight home to bed? Is that it, my sweet?"

"Shh. Mertie Fae and Leon Jenkins are about to fall out of their chairs eavesdropping."

Ben smiled. That was exactly what he wanted—to give the town something different to say about his marriage.

"Well, my love, shall we leave now or would you like something else sweet before we go?"

"Aren't you overacting a bit?" she whispered.

"Maybe you should give me a few private lessons?"

He loved the way her eyes sparkled and the way she felt leaning back in his arms. He was even beginning to enjoy making a spectacle of himself. The world would be a better place if more people displayed affection instead of anger in public.

"Maybe I could," she whispered, and he reached for her hand across the table.

The gesture had nothing whatsoever to do with putting on a show for the public. What it had to do with was companionship and warmth and a tenderness almost too much to bear.

Sitting across the table from Ben holding hands, Josie could almost believe it was love. He caressed her knuckles as Lucille put their plates on the table. And while she poured their iced tea Ben made erotic circles in Josie's palm.

"Anything else I can get for you?" Lucille asked.

Ben smiled at her and said, "We're fine, thank you," and that's when Josie knew she loved him.

Wasn't that just like her to come to the biggest realization of her life in a restaurant while a waitress poured iced tea instead of in a beautiful garden while the moon was shining or even in their little apartment while Ben was brushing his teeth, for goodness sakes? And now every time Josie thought about being in love with Ben she would remember Lucille, whom she'd known all her life but had never had any dealings with except to say hello in passing. Lucille with the big dark mole on her cheek and too much blue shadow on her eyes.

Josie didn't believe in coincidence: she believed in fate and divine cosmic order. Somehow Lucille had been picked as the catalyst, and Josie wanted to jump up and hug her neck.

Instead she said, "Thank you, Lucille," with such fervor the poor woman spilled tea. And Ben, Josie's hero, her warrior, her love, helped swab it up and even had Lucille laughing about what she'd only recently considered a major disaster.

Josie could hardly sit still. She wanted to shout her love from the rooftops. She wanted to broadcast it to the town. But most of all, she wanted to tell Ben. She *had* to tell Ben.

Every word he said during dinner was surely a pearl, because Ben was so brilliant, but Josie couldn't hear what he was saying for the clamour of her heart. So she nodded and smiled and gazed into his eyes with such longing she wondered that he didn't read her thoughts.

"Is anything wrong, Josie?"

"Wrong? No, everything's perfect, Ben. Just perfect."

"You've been so quiet, I was worried. What would you like to see this evening?"

"You," she whispered.

He leaned across the table and kissed her. Josie knew it was all part of the game, but the glow in his eyes gave her hope. She clung to it like a drunken sailor to a lamppost.

"That sounds good," he murmured.

"Ben?"

"What?"

"Can we skip the movie?"

"Yes. What would you like to do?"

"Take me home and I'll show you."

Chapter Thirteen

It was a heady experience, this being in love. On their walk home, Josie's feet hardly touched the ground. She wanted to grab Ben around the waist and shout her love up to him. She wanted to run all the way home so she could shut out the world and be with Ben. Only Ben.

How could she have been so blind all those weeks, all those years? How could she not have known that what she felt for him was too rare, too strong, too precious to be anything except love?

Even though it was dark and very few people were about, he held her hand all the way home. Could it be that he cared for her? Could it be that he loved her and didn't even know it?

Or what if he didn't love her at all? What if he was merely pretending for the sake of the town?

Josie couldn't think about all that right now. The main thing was to get home, get out the wine and create a mood, set the stage. Then…

"We're home, Josie."

The apartment loomed ahead, as overwhelming as the king-size bed in Biloxi, and Josie was on stage without a script. She'd just have to ad-lib.

Lacing her arms around Ben's neck, she stood on tiptoe and kissed him. And suddenly she didn't have to ad-lib, for he was kissing her back, kissing her with such fervor she melted and might have fallen onto the sidewalk if he hadn't held her up.

She made soft humming sounds of pleasure, and so did he. It was extremely gratifying and extraordinarily hopeful.

"Shall we go inside?" she whispered when they came up for air.

Smiling, Ben picked her up and carried her all the way up the stairs and through the door. Inside, he didn't put her down: he allowed her to slide slowly till her feet were on the floor and every inch of the rest of her was touching him. Intimately. Chest to chest, hip to hip, toe to toe.

She rubbed her face against his throat and felt the way his pulse raced. Emboldened, she leaned back, licked her lips and said, "Ben Standing Bear, you're the most delicious man I've ever known, and I'm going to eat you up."

"Is that a warning, Josie?"

"No, Ben. It's a promise."

He bent close and almost kissed her again. She could tell he wanted to. She could see it in his eyes, feel it in the tenseness of his body.

With his lips only inches from hers, he said, "I just happen to have a bottle of very good chardonnay in the kitchen. Do you want some, Josie?"

"I want some of everything you have, Ben."

"Then wait right here."

He hurried into the kitchen as if he were on fire. Wouldn't it be nice if he were? Wouldn't it be wonderful if he came back and suddenly confessed that he loved her and had loved her from the time they'd said their vows, and their marriage was real, after all, and she would never have to be lonely again?

Josie began to hum. Ben stood in the doorway holding the wine and two winestems in one hand and a glowing candle in the other.

"That's our song," he said.

"Yes, it's our song." She smiled at him, and when he put the candle on the table she said, "Purple, my favorite."

"I know."

He pulled her down onto the floor beside him, then handed her a glass of wine and wrapped one arm around her. She leaned her head into the crook of his arm, right where she belonged.

"Heaven," she said, and he kissed her softly on the lips.

She almost told him she loved him, but she wanted to pick the perfect time. Besides, what if he didn't want to hear it? What if, the minute she told him, he ran as fast and as far as he could go? Josie couldn't bear to lose him. Not yet.

And so she sipped her wine, and gazed into his eyes and was happy she had candlelight.

"More, Josie?"

"Oh, yes. I want more of everything."

Josie was throwing herself at his feet, and all he did was pour her another glass of wine. *To tell or not to tell, that was the big question.* The way things were going—cooling down instead of heating up—if she told him, she'd probably put an end to the evening right then and there. Josie sighed.

"Anything wrong?" Ben asked.

"No. It's just me, I guess."

Putting some distance between them, he scooted back and studied her. She hoped he couldn't see her well enough by candlelight to read what was on her mind. Her love was new and therefore scary. She was walking on shaky ground. The urgency she'd felt at the restaurant to *tell* Ben had evaporated in a haze of uncertainty.

Why didn't he say something?

"Do you want to tell me about it, Josie?"

"About what?"

"About whatever is bothering you."

She'd always done that with Ben, and he'd always let her talk uninterrupted, then given her such wise advice that she used to laugh and call him Solomon.

Where was that ease when she needed it? Did love have to destroy their friendship? Did it have to change everything?

What she did tonight would change her life. That much she knew. Love burned through her like a comet, but for the first time in her life Josie chose caution. For once in her life she didn't leap without looking, she didn't race pell-mell into the fray.

Oh, she was going to follow her heart, make no mistake about that. But the thing she'd never realized was that the heart had its own wisdom. The trick was to listen.

"I don't want to talk about it, Ben. Not yet." She had one more good sip wine left in her glass, so she lifted it high. "Let's toast, Ben."

"That's a good idea. What shall we drink to?"

He poured himself another glass of wine. She'd never seen him drink more than two. Maybe he wasn't as unflappable as he let on. Or maybe he was scared, too. Men got that way sometimes, though few ever admitted it.

"To us, Ben." *Careful,* she warned herself. *Not yet.*

"To us," he added. "Forever."

Funny. He'd left off the *friends* part, just as he had in the locket. She put her left hand over the locket and pressed it against her heart.

''We make quite a team,'' he said. ''I think we succeeded in our mission, don't you?''

''Absolutely.''

''More wine, Josie?''

''No. I'm a little bit tired. I think I'll turn in.'' She kissed him lightly on the lips before she could change her mind. '''Night, Ben.''

''Sweet dreams, Josie.''

She walked straight to the bedroom without looking back. If she looked back she was lost.

The door closed behind her with a decisive click. Ben lifted his glass.

''To us, Josie.'' He drained the glass, then poured himself another. ''Forever.''

He was beginning to get a buzz. ''Better stop while you're ahead, old boy,'' he muttered.

There were no sounds from the direction of the bedroom. Was Josie undressing? Already in bed? Ben stared at the door as if his thoughts would make it magically fly open, as if the power of his own longing would propel Josie into his arms.

And then what? What about their agreement?

In a few short weeks their marriage would be over. That's what they'd decided, hadn't they? When had everything changed? When had he come to the conclusion that the last thing in the world he wanted was for his marriage to Josie to end?

His brain felt muddled, his thinking fuzzy.

''But not fuzzy enough.'' He sloshed the last of the wine into his glass. He was courting a hangover, but what the heck. A hangover looked good compared to that closed door.

Josie stared at the ceiling trying to figure out what to do about her newly born love, but all she could think of was

Ben sitting on the other side of that closed door. Shut out. Lonely.

She couldn't bear it. With her nightshirt flying out behind her like the wings of some skinny-legged white bird, she flung open the door.

He was slumped on the floor right where she'd left him, staring into the candle flame. He'd put on a CD, and the deep rich voice of Etta James crooned "The Man I Love." Josie took it as a good sign.

"Ben?"

His eyes burned when he looked at her, burned right through her gown and seared her heart. Josie padded across the floor barefoot. It was the longest walk of her life. She was one of the children of Israel, walking across Egypt, following hope the way you'd follow a star.

Stretching out her hands, she whispered, "Come with me."

He didn't ask where, he didn't question why, he didn't hesitate. When his hand closed over hers she pulled him upright, then steadied him as she led him into the bedroom.

"Lie beside me, Ben. Just hold me. Let me hold on to you."

He lay down fully clothed, and she slid across the bed straight into his arms. He folded her close, and she felt safe and whole. All her life she'd been searching for a man like him, a warm and witty man who combined the lively curiosity of a child with the strong intellect of a well-educated adult. And underneath it all flowed a deep river of passion. It roared through him, a wild thing, barely harnessed.

"I love you, Ben," she whispered.

Ben took her lips, and the river left its bank and carried her off where the only thing that mattered was two people, joined, two best friends who had finally found their way home.

* * *

"I love you," she said once more, and Ben fought his way through the fog to strip off his clothes. Then he climbed back into bed and rolled Josie on top of him while Etta James sang "Embraceable You."

Her hair made a curtain around his face while he kissed her, and he was surrounded by the smell of flowers.

"You smell good," he said.

"You *feel* good."

He couldn't bear not to kiss her, and so he covered her mouth once more. She was sweet and savage, light as a feather, soft as a dream. When he rolled over, he took her with him, and she was there waiting for him, warm and inviting. Ben Standing Bear slid to the place where he belonged, where he'd always belonged and it felt like coming home.

Such sensations rocked him that he didn't move, didn't want to move, and he was filled with wonder.

"Who would ever want to leave this?" he said.

"Don't leave," she whispered. "Not ever." And she began to move beneath him in a rhythm as old as time.

In the next room the incomparable Miss James sang about love being as deep as the ocean, and Ben felt the truth of the music in his bones. Somewhere deep inside him caution struggled to be heard, but he was beyond hearing. There was only the night and Josie in his arms. Nothing else existed. Nothing else mattered.

The love they made was slow and sweet and of such tenderness the senses were almost overwhelmed, while in the background the haunting love songs of Billie Holiday as sung by Etta James gave way to the sounds of Marcus Roberts playing Gershwin for lovers.

They were the songs he'd heard Josie singing and humming at random moments—taking a late-night shower, pouring orange juice into a tall glass while the early-morning sun shone in her hair, bent over a set of her students' papers, walking down the street with Bruiser acting like a snobbish music critic.

The music took on a new dimension. The lyrics belonged to the two of them together on the double bed where Ben lay flat on his back with his hands around Josie's narrow waist and she poised above him offering her breasts like cups to the gods.

Marcus Roberts's piano asked the musical question, "How Long Has This Been Going On?"

"Forever," Ben whispered, and Josie leaned down to steal his heart with a kiss. "Just stay, Josie, stay there forever."

Through his fog of wine and passion he saw her sweet, bewitching smile.

"May I taste you?" she asked, ever so softly.

The prim question was delightfully at odds with her lush wanton side and Ben was so filled with wonder at his good fortune he could only nod. Then she took him in her mouth and he was transported.

The music flowed around him, over him, through him. Josie was the music, and he immersed himself in her siren song.

Finally they both found release, and as he rolled to his side, keeping her firmly in his embrace he was vaguely aware of the last song Marcus Roberts played—"But Not for Me."

And then the music stopped.

"Stay by my side, Josie," he said. "Don't let go."

"I won't. I promise," she whispered, then she pulled the cover over them and Ben fell softly into sleep.

Josie cuddled as close to him as she could get. "I love you," she said, although she knew he couldn't hear. Wonder-filled and wide-eyed she listened to the soft rise and fall of his breathing.

The moon laid a path across their bed and Josie lifted

herself on her elbow to watch him sleep. He slept soundly, peacefully, one hand folded on his chest and the other holding on to her.

Questions began to race through her mind. What would happen tomorrow? Would he be glad? Sorry? Would he leave? Would he stay? What would he say?

Hush, she told herself. *Be still.*

Nobody could predict tomorrow. Least of all Josie. Ben was in her bed and she was in his arms, and for the moment that was all that mattered.

Chapter Fourteen

Something woke Ben before daylight, some internal alarm signaling danger. Suddenly he remembered what it was: he'd crossed the invisible barrier with Josie. Even now she was cuddled close, one arm thrown around his waist, her cheek pressed against his chest.

What have I done?

With war drums beating in his head, he disentangled himself and eased out of the covers, then he stood beside the bed studying her. Her camellia skin flushed a deep rose and her hair a bright halo, she looked like a fallen flower.

He was filled with such regret he had to leave the room, or else the sight of her would be his complete undoing. He tiptoed out, his head pounding with each jarring step.

In the kitchen he drank two glasses of water quickly, then leaned against the cabinet with a third. His hangover was a monster, but he couldn't blame his actions on the wine. He'd known exactly what he was doing when he climbed into Josie's bed. He'd known exactly what he wanted.

Memories washed over him of the night spent in her arms, and he smiled in spite of himself. She was all his fantasies rolled into one, and then some. Together, they'd been wonderful.

What had he expected? A friendship such as theirs was a rare and beautiful thing, and over the last few months it had transformed into a deep and abiding regard that went beyond trust, beyond respect, and even beyond love. What he felt for Josie was a miracle.

He wished it could be different. He wished he could wake her up with a kiss and they could sit on the balcony drinking orange juice and laughing, just two good friends who'd shared a night of passion. If that were so, he could stay and they could even share the same bed, and when the time came to say goodbye they could go their separate ways without regret.

Unfortunately, that wasn't the case. While he hadn't been on guard Josie had crept into his heart, and now she was burrowed so deeply that when they parted Ben would be only half a man.

His heart hurt at the thought of leaving, but there was no other way. He and Josie had always been honest with each other, so staying and living a lie was out of the question. Staying and pretending everything was a lark would be betrayal of the worst kind, both to himself and to her.

Ben had to go. Not because he didn't love her, but because he loved her too much.

He was a virtual outcast in Pontotoc. He'd die before he'd subject Josie to ostracism in her hometown.

He drained his glass, then turned toward the window to watch the sun rise. Nature generally had a buoying effect on him, but today he was unmoved, earthbound, his feet so leaden they might as well have been nailed to the ground.

Soon he would go and wake Josie and tell her his plans, but for now he would try to wrest some energy from the sun.

When Josie woke up in an empty bed she knew something was wrong.

"Stop being silly," she whispered, then she hugged Ben's pillow to herself and tried to recapture the glorious sense of well-being she'd felt the night before. Every detail of their lovemaking was etched so clearly in her mind she might as well have been sitting in a plush seat at the theater watching a movie, complete with sound track.

Though she hadn't paid particular attention at the time, she recalled every song that had played while she was in Ben's arms, wonderful love songs of Gershwin and Billie Holiday, each word a jewel, each musical phrase imbued with special meaning because of Ben.

Remembering was sheer bliss, and Josie allowed herself that happiness before she climbed out of bed, shrugged into her nightshirt and went in search of Ben.

She found him in the kitchen looking out the window. She read tension in every line of his body, from stiff posture to the taut muscles that corded his back.

Standing in the kitchen that suddenly seemed as foreign and parched to her as the Sahara, she wanted to run away as fast as she could go. The foreboding she'd felt in the bedroom became a full-fledged case of fear, and she had to wrap her arms around herself, she felt so cold.

When Ben turned and saw her he didn't smile. He didn't come to her, either, which was even worse.

"Josie? Are you all right?"

Yesterday Ben would have put his arms around her and held her close while he asked the question. He would have picked her up and carried her to the rocking chair where he would have sung soft songs to her, off-key.

"I was, until I discovered you weren't in bed with me."

"I'm sorry about that, Josie. I didn't mean to wake you."

"It's not lack of sleep that's bothering me. I'm scared, Ben."

"There's no need to be. I'm going to make sure you come out of this all right."

He'd confirmed her worst fears. She must have quit breathing for the room began to spin and when she tried to find Ben's face she could see nothing but shadows. She gripped the back of a chair and made herself focus. She was not a weakling, and she refused to act like one.

"I don't think I want to hear this, Ben. How about eggs?"

"Eggs?"

"Do you want eggs for breakfast? I think I can scramble some without burning them."

"I don't want anything to eat, Josie."

"Juice, then? How about orange juice?"

"Orange juice will be fine."

She took her time pouring the juice. Every minute she stalled was one more minute she had with Ben.

"Why don't we take this out to the balcony?" she said, trying for perky and failing miserably.

"That's fine."

Ben followed her out, careful not to touch her, she noticed. They sat in chairs facing each other, with Ben looking at her as if he were trying to commit her to memory. She knew that's what she was doing with him. Memorizing him. Storing up every detail of him for the long, lonely days ahead.

They sipped their juice in silence for a while, not even speaking when a cardinal flew in and landed on the branch of an oak that spread a canopy over their table.

Ordinarily one of them would have pointed it out, and they'd have entered into some lively discussion about its color and its mating habits. Once Ben had told her that cardinals mate for life, and that he'd seen a male sitting in the middle of the road mourning his fallen mate, that the bird had fluttered anxiously on the side of the road while Ben's car passed by and had then taken up his vigil once more.

She wondered what the cardinal would have done if his mate had merely left him.

What was she going to do?

"Josie, I didn't mean for last night to happen."

"Ben Standing Bear, if you say you're sorry I'll never speak to you again as long as I live."

That made him smile, and Josie grabbed hope by the throat and hung on so hard she figured she was choking it to death.

"I'm sorry I caved in to temptation. I can't say I'm sorry for the rest of it, Josie."

"Good, because I'm not." She came within an inch of telling him she loved him again, but for once she listened to the voice of reason. A man in the mood to leave was not a man in the mood for confessions of the heart. "I'm *glad* it happened, Ben."

"You are?"

"It was the best thing that ever happened to me. It was absolutely wonderful."

He gave her a look that would stop a breaking heart, and for an instant she dared hope.

"I wish things could be different, Josie."

"You're leaving, aren't you?"

"Yes. I'm leaving."

"I can't say that I blame you. I mean, look what I did. I hog-tied you and roped you into a marriage you didn't even want…"

"Josie…"

"...and the first rattle out of the trap I got thrown in jail..."

"Josie..."

"...and then I nearly burned your apartment down, and besides all that you've had to sleep on the couch."

Big fat tears were rolling down her cheeks, but it didn't matter anymore. She could turn into a pitiful wreck of woman and it wouldn't even matter. Nothing mattered except Ben, and he was leaving.

Suddenly he was out of his seat and kneeling beside her chair. He cupped her face and wiped her tears with his fingers, and smiled a smile that broke her heart all over again.

"Listen to me, Josie. Are you listening?"

She nodded, and he brushed his fingertips lightly over her lips. Her breath got caught in her throat. Could it be that he would change his mind?

"My leaving has nothing to do with you. I don't have a single regret about marrying you or about anything that happened afterward."

"Not even the jail episode?"

"Not even that."

"You're just saying that to be kind. I know you, Ben. You're the sweetest man alive."

"Don't pin any medals on me, Josie. I don't deserve them."

He traced her lips one last time, then returned to his seat on the other side of the world. At least, that's what it felt like.

She would die if he left her. It was that simple, that powerful, that true. Would he stay if she begged?

Even she wouldn't stoop that low. But she would ask why. She had to know, otherwise she would drive herself crazy with self-blame.

"Why are you leaving, Ben?"

"Trust me, Josie. I have my reasons."

"I want to know what they are."

"Does it matter?"

"Yes, it matters. It matters so much that I won't sleep a wink if I don't know."

She probably wouldn't sleep a wink, anyway. She'd gotten used to having Ben in the house with her. But it was more than that, ever so much more. He wasn't merely somebody in the house, he was the other half of herself, the half that made the difference between a humdrum daily existence and a heart-stealing roller-coaster ride through Wonderland.

"Josie, I came to this small town because I wanted to make a difference. I not only wanted to provide quality health care, but I wanted to be a part of the community. I wanted to make friends. I wanted to be a real part of small-town life, not just the doctor, not just somebody people come to see when they are sick."

Josie knew exactly where he was leading. He'd come up against the wall that people like Clytee Crawford and her own Aunt Tess built. While the South had a well-deserved reputation for hospitality, the reality was that powerful cliques existed, cliques that dictated who got in and who stayed on the outside. Nowhere were these groups more noticeable than in small Southern towns.

"Give it time, Ben. Sometimes we're slow to accept strangers."

"There's a difference between being a stranger and being an outsider."

"That will change, Ben. You'll see."

Was the pleading for herself or for him? Was she telling the truth or was it all wishful thinking?

"I don't know whether the town's attitude will change, but I do know this. As long as you are legally my wife you're going to be tarred with the same brush. I can survive it. I've been a loner all my life. But I won't subject you to it.''

Josie could have countered with all kinds of arguments. She could have told him she loved him and nothing else mattered. She could have told him she was made of sterner stuff, that she was not the kind of woman who ran from every little confrontation, that she was not the kind of clinging vine who collapsed at every disappointment.

But she knew Ben: once he'd made up his mind there would be no changing it. Besides, she wasn't about to cast herself in the role of beggar. She had her pride.

The fact was, she'd told him she loved him and he hadn't said it back. There was nothing more heart-wrenching than unrequited love.

Furthermore, she had her temper, and she could feel it rising. Maybe that was all that could save her.

''You won't change your mind.'' It was not a question: it was a statement.

''No, Josie. I won't change my mind.''

''And so you're going to renege on our agreement.''

''I wouldn't put it that way.''

''How would you put it, Ben? You've figured all the angles. By yourself, I might add.''

''Now, Josie…''

''Don't you *now Josie* me! I'm not the same starry-eyed little coed you bossed around on the college campus.''

''If anybody had called you starry-eyed you'd have boxed their ears, and you didn't listen to a word of advice I gave you.''

''If I had I might have stayed out of trouble, is that what you're saying?''

''I don't want to fight with you, Josie.''

She was getting madder by the minute, and fighting was exactly what she wanted to do. She wanted to hit something, and hit it hard.

"I never figured you for a coward, Ben."

The astonished look he gave her was genuine, and she almost pulled in her horns. But she didn't. Horns weren't going to win the war, but they'd get her through this battle. She'd worry about the next one when it came along.

"Remember the Alamo," she said.

"I do. Everybody died."

"Not without a fight."

"Josie, I don't know why you have to make this so difficult. I thought we were friends. I wanted us to part that way."

"I'll just bet you did. Well, I'll have you know that I don't want to be friends with a man who sleeps in my bed then turns tail and runs."

She'd finally made him mad. *Good.* Anything was better than that cool facade.

"Are you saying I'm a coward, Josie?"

"If the shoe fits, wear it."

"I've never been a coward."

"Oh, yeah? Well, what do you call a man who turns a woman into a one-night stand?"

"Is that what you think of last night, Josie?"

"No, but apparently *you* do. Josie Belle Pickens with the swinging door. Hello, goodbye, see you around...if I see you at all."

She'd never seen Ben as mad. Unlike her father, who used to turn red in the face and explode, Ben turned to ice. The kind that would freeze you with a glance, the kind that would slice your heart if you got close enough.

Unconsciously, Josie took a step backward, but it wasn't enough to save her. Ben stalked her with the fierce intensity of a mountain lion going in for a kill.

"Now, Ben..."

She held out one arm like a traffic cop, but he kept on coming and didn't stop until he was so close she could see the fire in the center of his eyes. It burned Josie all the way to the roots of her hair.

If she took one more step backward, he would realize what he was doing and stop. If she said the magic word, if she said *please,* he would say *I'm sorry* then stop his determined march.

But Josie didn't do any of those things. Her chin came up and she took her stand.

Ben snaked out his arm and reeled her in with such force her body made a soft *whump* against his. Her blood roared so loudly she couldn't think. Her heart thumped so hard she couldn't breathe.

He tipped her face upward and slammed his mouth down on hers. She meant to resist, but how could a rose stand before a warrior? The only way she knew was to pull in her thorns and try to overpower him with sweetness.

She parted her lips and challenged his tongue in a sensual duel that steamed up the kitchen windows. *This is war* her mind said, while her heart said, *this is love.*

Cupping her hips he drew her close then began an intimate dance that sent reason flying out the window. Josie wanted him with every atom in her being. Love flowed through her like a river, and she was lost.

With their mouths and bodies locked in erotic combat, he walked her backward toward the bedroom. Josie was going to win the battle: Ben was headed straight to her bed.

But in winning the battle she would lose the war. She knew that as surely as she knew her name. With each step they took, victory slipped through her grasp.

She had to let him go. She had to send him on his way. But not yet, not until she'd tasted him a little while longer, not until she'd felt how his skin burned against hers.

With pleasure-sounds humming in her throat, she became Ben's willing captive. When they were halfway across the living room, he swept her up, stalked into the bedroom and kicked the door shut. Eyes blazing, he lowered her to the bed.

"You are *not* a one-night stand, Josie."

Too full to speak, she reached for him, and he took her mouth once more in a fierce and tender kiss. His hands roamed freely under her nightshirt, setting off fires that were achingly familiar.

Josie almost lost her resolve. *Just a while longer,* she told herself, *and I'll let him go.*

The stakes were high. She didn't want Ben to come to her out of guilt or a misplaced sense of loyalty. She wanted him to come to her freely. And forever.

With his hand pressed flat over her belly he made soft, erotic circles that moved ever lower, and when his fingers slid inside her, Josie erupted with such force she had to bite her lower lip to keep from screaming.

Levered over her, his face so close she could see fire in the center of his eyes, he took her mouth in a fierce kiss that stole her breath.

"Tell me you don't want this, Josie." His face was a study in torture, his voice a sound that broke her heart.

Every fiber in her being screamed at her to give in. She was burning, *burning,* and only he could quench the flame. But to give in would be to lose him.

Even as his body pressed ever closer, even as his fingers played their magic, even with his lips only inches away, Josie told him no. She told him goodbye.

"I don't want this, Ben."

Shock froze him. For a moment he was poised over her like a storm, and then inch by torturous inch he pulled away.

She held back her tears, bit back her anguished cry.

He towered over the bed, but she didn't move. She couldn't. Misery paralyzed her.

"I'll find another place to stay." His voice chilled her

to the bone; his face froze her soul. "I'll tell people you kicked me out. I want you to do the same."

Without another word he left, closing the door softly behind him.

Chapter Fifteen

Ben came to get his clothes while she was at school. When she got home she found a note propped on the kitchen table.

Josie,
    I've found a place to stay. Here's the number in case you need me. I'll sign the annulment papers whenever you're ready.

Take care, Ben.

She slumped against the kitchen table and cried until she was limp as a corn silk, and then she washed her face, ate tuna straight from the can, graded papers and cried again.

After she'd wiped her eyes on a paper towel, she checked her telephone messages. There were two: one from her mother and one from Ashley.

"Josie," her mother said, "Aunt Tess heard about the breakup at Simpson's Drug Store. She's fit to be tied. Everybody's talking. Give me a call."

"I'll just bet they are," Josie snarled, then she played the second.

"I'm concerned about you, Josie," Ashley said. "I heard what happened with Ben. Come over here or I'll come over there and you can talk, rant, cry, whatever. Call me."

Josie couldn't bear to talk to her mother or Ashley. It was enough that she had to talk to her students at school. She couldn't bear to face anybody who would offer her sympathy or advice. She couldn't bear to sit quietly while somebody told her she'd *get over Ben*. She didn't want to hear platitudes such as "It's all for the best," or "Things have a way of working themselves out."

She was like an old cat: she had to curl up in a dark corner and lick her wounds. Alone. She'd come out of isolation when she felt stronger. If she ever did.

For now she would weep.

Ben made sure word got around that Josie had kicked him out. It was the first time in his life he'd ever been responsible for circulating a rumor. In addition to telling everybody from the butcher to the postman to his secretaries and office nurses about his marital woes, he had to play the role of broken-hearted husband.

Not surprisingly, it was easy to play. Ben didn't have to fake a haggard look. He hadn't slept since he'd moved out on Josie. He didn't have to pretend he was shaken to the core. Any fool looking in the mirror would see what a toll losing her was taking.

How had it all happened? How had these feelings crept up on him? How did they get past the guard he kept? How had they circumvented his well-known focus?

Ben was filled with remorse. He could blame his first loss of control on the wine, but there was no excuse for the second. He had turned into somebody he didn't know.

At random times during the day he found himself thinking about Josie, wondering how she was. Twice in the first week after he was gone he picked up the phone, started dialing her number, then replaced the receiver. He didn't want to intrude. He had to let go.

Josie needed to completely disassociate herself from him. She needed to get on with her life, to find somebody *acceptable* to Pontotoc society, somebody whose standing was so high in the community she would feel girded and protected by the townspeople, but above all loved.

Was she doing that? Moving forward? Getting on? Bouncing back?

What if she wasn't? What if she was lonely and feeling rejected, unprotected, unloved?

By the end of the second week he couldn't stand the suspense anymore. As soon as he saw his last patient on Friday he called her number. The answering machine clicked on: "Hi, this is Josie and Ben. Leave a message."

Josie and Ben. The two of them. Together. A team. Best friends. Forever.

She hadn't changed the message. Did that mean she still thought of them that way? She was too busy to bother? Too sad?

Ben couldn't stand not knowing. What if Josie was depressed, which was totally out of character for her? But still, it could happen.

He drove by the apartment and didn't see a sign of her. Then he cruised by her mother's house. Like a teenager. Like a grown man who is suddenly floundering around in unfamiliar territory, uncertain of every decision he's made lately, particularly the ones connected to Josie.

Disheartened, Ben started back to his own furnished apartment, two rooms and a bath, no balcony and barely enough space for his books, let alone a piano.

He wouldn't let himself think about a piano because that brought to mind images of Josie standing at the front of the church singing "Amazed" or bending over her students' papers humming "The Man I Love" or standing barefoot in the kitchen pouring cereal into a bowl, humming "Someone to Watch Over Me."

Or Josie spread across the bed, silk and flame, while Etta James crooned love songs.

He was going home and pack up all his CDs. He decided that he was going to rid himself of every reminder of her.

And that's when he saw her walking Bruiser toward the town square. If he turned right she'd never see him. If he turned left there was no way she could avoid seeing him.

Ben turned left.

Josie looked into the mirror at the weepy, blotchy-faced person she had become and said, "Okay. Enough of this nonsense. No man alive is worth all these histrionics."

She washed her face and combed her hair and even put on some makeup, then she called Ashley.

"Good grief, Josie. I was beginning to think somebody had kidnapped you. Why haven't you returned any of my calls?"

"That's what I'm doing now."

"Well, it's high time."

"Do you have plans for this evening, Ashley?"

"Nothing I can't cancel. Come on over and I'll cook peanut butter and jelly sandwiches."

"Whatever happened to fried chicken and macadamia nut cookies?"

"Uh. Just the mention of all that rich food makes me sick."

"You! The Betty Crocker of Pontotoc! Are you dieting?"

"You could say that. Gosh, Josie, I can't wait to see you. It feels like a hundred years. Hurry."

It was the first time she'd laughed since Ben left, and it felt good.

"Is it all right if I bring Bruiser? We'll walk over so he can get his constitutional."

"Sure. I'll be happy to see the big lug."

Josie hooked Bruiser to his leash. "We're going to Ashley's by way of the whole town, and I want you on your best behavior. Do you hear me?"

He swung his tail in a wild arc that bruised her shins, then gave her his goofy, tongue-lolling grin as if to say, "Who? Me?"

"Yeah, you, you big ox. No monkey business, now."

She opened the door, bracing herself to be dragged down the street at the speed of a flying bullet, but to her surprise and delight, Bruiser acted as sedate as a little old lady going to afternoon tea.

When Mrs. Crumpton Wages stopped them on the street in front of Simpson's Drug Store, he didn't try to pull her arm out of the socket, but flopped down at her feet and waited.

"Josie. Looks like your dog has finally learned his manners."

"Yes ma'am. It looks that way. How are you, Mrs. Wages?"

"Can't complain. Except with my knees. I had to go to the doctor last week, Dr. Ben." She gave Josie a sly look. "He's such a good doctor, and seems like such a nice man."

"Yes, he is both."

"Then how come you kicked him out?"

"Is that what people are saying?"

"I got this straight from the horse's mouth. Dr. Ben, himself."

Ben, Ben, why are you doing this?

"Well, sometimes things don't work out in a marriage,"

she explained, "no matter how good the two people are or how hard they try."

Mrs. Wages clucked her tongue, then patted Josie's hand.

"Everybody's on your side, you know, you being home-town folks, and Dr. Ben being…well, you know."

Josie's hackles came up. One of the things she hated most was prejudice, and she was going to fight it, no matter what the cost.

"No, Mrs. Wages, I'm afraid I don't know what you're talking about."

"Well, dear, after all he is an Indian…"

"He's a Native American. Full-blood Sioux and very proud of his heritage. As proud as you are of yours."

Glennella May Wages was founder of the Pontotoc chapter of the Daughters of the American Revolution, and took every opportunity to parade her family tree.

Glennella May fluffed herself out like a mad hen, and gave Josie a gimlet-eyed look.

"I'll have you know *my* relatives fought for their home-land."

"So did Ben's. And they were here first."

"Well, I never."

Glennella May almost outran her shoes getting away from Josie.

"Well, Bruiser, I guess I blew that." She clicked her tongue, but he didn't budge. Apparently he found the cool sidewalk more to his liking than trudging along at a sedate pace behind Josie.

While she tugged his leash, Josie continued recounting her sins.

"It's not as if I don't already have enough enemies in this town. She was probably the only person in Pontotoc on my side besides Ashley and Mother, and maybe not even Mother, and what do I do? I alienate her."

Bruiser gave her a doleful look as if he sympathized with

her completely, but not to the point of cooperation. His haunches were glued to the sidewalk.

"Bruiser, if you don't come on here, I'm going to go off and leave you."

She tugged once more, but he called her bluff. There was no way she was going to force his cooperation because she was no match for him. Josie was thinking of the ultimate bribe, ice cream, when all of a sudden Bruiser shot off the sidewalk, jerked the leash out of her hand and bounded straight for the town square.

She went in hot pursuit. Fortunately there were no cars coming except that of Buford Langston who never drove over twenty-five anyway because he said high speeds wore out his car. It was Second-World-War vintage and likely to last the rest of his life if his own prediction came true. He'd said he wasn't planning to live past ninety-two, and he had turned ninety-one last Christmas.

Josie dodged around his front fender, and he didn't even have to hit his brake.

Waving and smiling his toothless smile he called out through his open window, "How de doo, Miss Pickens. Nice day for a drive, ain't it?"

"Yes sir, it is."

He waved, then tootled on. Obviously he wasn't taking sides about anything, let alone her marriage. Of course, even if somebody tried to enlist him to one side or the other, he wouldn't hear a word they said. The last thing he'd heard was the cannon shot off in the town square to celebrate the end of the Korean Conflict.

"Bruiser, come back here," Josie yelled, then she saw the cause of his excitement.

Bruiser took a flying leap at the object of his affection, and if Ben hadn't been such a big man he'd have toppled, along with the bench he was sitting on.

"Hello, boy. Did you miss me?" Ben leaned down to pat the dog's head, and Bruiser licked his face all over.

Josie froze. She was torn between running in the other direction or running toward him and doing exactly what her dog was doing. Quite simply, she wanted to lick Ben all over also.

At war with herself, she stood apart from them, hoping she might fade into the shadow of the nearby oak tree. Ben looked up and smiled, and Josie was drawn to him the way a moth is drawn to flame.

"Hello, Josie."

"Ben."

"I'm sorry I caused all the commotion." He didn't know the half of it. "With your dog, I mean." Or perhaps he did.

She stopped two feet short of him, unable to go any closer. She didn't want him to see how her hands shook or the way a nervous bead of sweat rolled down the side of her cheek.

"You didn't cause a commotion, Ben. Bruiser is being his usual disobedient self."

"I'm glad to see him. I've missed the big guy."

What about me? she wanted to ask, but of course she didn't. She had her pride, and she was clinging to her self-control by a thread. If she didn't get off the town square soon, she was going to explode, and it wouldn't be a pretty sight.

"Come on, Bruiser. Here, boy."

Bruiser looked at her as if he'd never seen her before, then turned his tongue-lapping attention back to Ben.

"Don't go like this, Josie."

"Like what?"

"As if we were perfect strangers."

Josie's thin control snapped. "How do you want me to act, Ben? Like one of those gushing belles who pretends everything's all right, even if the house is burning down around their ears?''

"Can't we just be friends?"

"How typically male. You come on like gangbusters, then you get scared and run away, and then you want me to act like your best buddy so you can salve your conscience. Sorry, Ben. My friends don't walk out on me. They stick around, no matter what."

"I thought I explained my reasons, Josie."

"Did it ever occur to you that when two people have been intimate, that implies a commitment? One of them shouldn't just decide on his own to end it without even giving the other one a chance to express an opinion."

"I'm sorry you feel that way."

He was not sorry he'd walked out, not sorry he'd ended the relationship, not sorry they would never lie in bed in the moonlight together or sit on the patio feeding each other strawberries.

Josie was so mad she could bite tenpenny nails in two. She was so mad she could have stomped her foot and made a hole all the way to China.

"Bruiser, come here this minute, or I'm going to give you to the dog pound."

He knew she meant business, for he skulked over with his tail between his legs and his soulful eyes begging her forgiveness. She stooped to pick up his leash.

"Josie... Don't go like this. Don't leave mad."

If she didn't leave mad, she was going to leave crying, for the tears were pushing against her throat, ready to burst forth.

"It's the only way I can leave, Ben."

She whirled around and marched off with as much dignity as she could muster, which was considerable. Hell hath no fury like a woman scorned. She was thinking in Shakespearean again. Maybe there was hope for her, after all.

Chapter Sixteen

True to her word, Ashley had made peanut butter and jelly sandwiches.

"Low-fat bread, sugarless peanut butter and spreadable fruit instead of jelly," Ashley said, waving her arms toward the table.

"You look pale, Ashley. The firm's working you too hard."

Ashley was a legal secretary and her hours were often as horrendous as those of the lawyers she worked for. After Ashley'd inherited her aunt Hettie's estate last year, Josie'd asked her why she didn't quit her job, but Ashley said she'd go crazy being a lady of leisure.

"I'll tell them you said so." Ashley swept toward the table trailing Jungle Gardenia perfume and a tie-dyed caftan. "Let's eat. I'm starving." She poured two glasses of skim milk and set out pottery plates with hand-painted roses and linen napkins with lace edging.

Josie grinned. "At my place you'd be lucky to get paper plates. Heck, you'd be lucky to get a peanut butter sandwich."

All of a sudden she started crying. Ashley came around the table and put her arms around Josie.

"I don't even have a place," Josie sobbed. "It's Ben's apartment. He even paid the rent. And I can't go home. Mother and Aunt Tess would drive me crazy. It's such a mess, Ashley. What am I going to do?"

Her best friend smoothed her hair and squeezed her hard, then went to get a box of tissues.

"Here. Wipe your face and blow your nose and you can tell me about it."

Josie swabbed her eyes and honked her nose, then reached for another tissue to mop up the fresh set of tears that rained down her face.

"The whole town's talking about it. What is it you don't know, Ashley?"

"The most important thing of all. Do you love him?"

"I *hate* him. He made love to me then walked out. I saw him in the park, and he's not the least bit sorry. He's just…big and gorgeous and wonderful and…oh, Ashley, I love him so much I can't *breathe* without him."

"Then we've got to figure a way to get him back."

"He won't come back. He's the most stubborn man alive."

"Why did he leave? Did he say? And what did you say? I don't know what happened at all. Gossip is never the same as the truth."

"He didn't give me a chance to say anything." Josie's emotions swung wildly between despair and anger. Right now, anger had the upper hand. She tore viciously into a sandwich. "It was that quick." She snapped her fingers. "First, he's in my bed making me feel like I own the world, and then he's out of the door."

"See. I *knew* you loved him."

"Yeah, well, he doesn't love me back."

"I'll bet you a million dollars he does. Men get scared, that's all."

"How do you know?" Ashley gave her a funny look, then lowered her head over her food. Josie was immediately contrite. "I'm sorry, Ashley. I didn't mean that. No wonder Ben walked out. I'm a nasty-tempered witch."

"You are no such thing. You're a good woman with a broken heart. Now, tell me why he left."

"He said he's an outsider in this town, and he won't subject me to that."

An image of Glennella Mae Wages came to her mind, and Josie's volatile emotions swung toward rage. She banged her fist on the table, and Bruiser leaped up from his snooze by the window.

"Can you believe it, Ashley? The gall of this town. The nerve! They flock to him to take care of their aches and pains, but when it comes to socializing with him, he's an *Indian*. It makes me so mad I could bullwhip the whole town."

"I have a better idea."

"You do?"

"Yes. We'll change the town's attitude."

"I don't see how we can do that. I've never even been able to change their attitude about me, let alone somebody else."

"We start by spreading a little of Ben's money around."

"Maybe I'm losing my touch for intrigue, Ashley. I'm afraid I don't get it."

"Dear old Aunt Hettie is going to help us, God rest her soul. Since I came into her estate I'm probably the town's biggest philanthropist, though nobody knows that."

"What does that have to do with Ben?"

"I was just thinking about writing a very large check to

the town's parks and recreation department to help fund the new little league baseball stadium. Anonymously, of course. Except this time, I'll drop a few broad hints that will lead them to believe it came from the new doctor in town. That, plus the rumors we spread should do the trick.''

''Good grief, that's brilliant, Ashley. Money talks, to coin a dazzling new phrase. I didn't realize I had such a devious friend.''

''You don't know the half of it.'' Ashley padded barefoot into the kitchen and came back with heaping bowls of ice cream topped with whipped cream and cherries.

''I thought this was an Ethiopian supper.''

''Supper was. Dessert's a different matter.'' Ashley set the confections on their plates, then ate earnestly before she went back to the matter at hand. ''I thought we'd follow up the donation with a letter from Ben expressing his interest in the sport of baseball…he used to play, didn't he?''

''He was the best. He could have gone pro.''

''Perfect. In his letter he'll tell his background of college ball and volunteer his services as a little league coach.''

''I suppose you're going to write the letter.''

''Absolutely. And you're going to steal his letterhead.''

''Great. I knew I liked this plan.''

''And while you're at his office stealing his supplies, you're going to flirt like mad.''

''I will not.''

''Do you want him?''

''More than I can say.''

''Then you'll be witty and vivacious and charming and flirty. And just when he's charmed out of his pants and thinking you must be crazy about him, you drop a little hint that your newfound vivacity is due to another man.''

''I've never been less than straightforward with Ben, Ashley. He'll catch on to me in a minute.''

''I knew you'd do it!''

"I didn't say I would."

"Yes, you did. A woman will do anything to have the man she loves. Meanwhile, do you want some more ice cream?"

"More! Good grief, Ashley, if I eat any more I'll look like the Goodyear blimp."

"I take that as a yes."

Josie laughed as her friend padded back into the kitchen to scoop up seconds on ice cream.

"I feel better than I've felt since Ben left, Ashley."

"Good. That's what friends are for. To pick you up when you fall. Let's take our ice cream to the sofa. This hard chair is killing my back."

After they'd settled on Ashley's chintz-covered sofa, they discussed what Josie would wear for the seduction.

"It's not a seduction, Ashley."

"How can it not be? If you love someone, all encounters are a seduction." Ashley licked the whipped cream off her bottom lip. "I think you should wear that red dress you wore to the prenuptial wingding with Jerry Bob."

"That's an evening dress."

"So what's to keep you from dropping by late, on your way to a big shindig?"

Josie laughed. "I think the wrong one of us went into drama. I never knew you had it in you, girlfriend."

"There's a lot more to me than meets the eye."

"I'll say. Some man is going to be very lucky to get you. Speaking of which…you haven't said a word about yourself. What's happening with you?"

"Got a week or two?"

"You bet. Fire away."

"Some other time, Josie. For now, let's concentrate on you. Let's talk more about our plan. You can spread the rumor of Ben's philanthropy at school, and I'll take care of the law community."

"And Aunt Tess can tell the rest of the town."

Ashley's face lit up. "That's brilliant, Josie. I wish I'd thought of that myself. Can you imagine the old biddy's face when she finds out the man she's dished the dirt on is suddenly the man everybody with a pet project wants to suck up to?"

They laughed until they had to hold their sides. Then Ashley finished off Josie's second bowl of ice cream, put on some shoes and took Josie and Bruiser home in her car.

When Josie walked into his office in her eyepopping red dress, Ben nearly fell out of his chair. He glanced at his intercom as if it had suddenly grown horns and a tail. It wasn't like Nettie Jean to let somebody come into his office unannounced. It wasn't even like her to let anybody come into his office without an appointment, period. She guarded his privacy with the determination of a bulldog and the zeal of a Baptist preacher in a room full of sinners.

Josie propped one hand on the doorframe, and flashed him a brilliant smile.

"I'm afraid I conned your secretary into letting me see you. I hope you don't mind."

She didn't speak so much as she purred. And, by George, Josie was *posing*. She had something up her sleeve, and as soon as Ben's heart slowed to normal he was going to figure out what it was.

"Of course not, Josie. You know you're always welcome. Won't you sit down?"

He hurried around his desk to pull out a chair for her, but he was too late. She'd already perched herself on the edge of his desk and crossed her legs. Her long, *gorgeous* legs clad in silk stockings that had some sort of sparkly stuff that winked at him every time she swung her foot.

Ben watched her swinging leg, mesmerized.

"You're sure?" Josie asked, then pouted her full red lips at him.

Ben wasn't sure of his name. He wasn't even sure he was breathing. If she kept swinging her leg like that and pouting those kissable lips at him he was going to need a transfusion.

"Sure about what?"

"That you don't mind my being here?"

"Absolutely not. Make yourself comfortable."

"I already did."

"So I see."

Ben didn't know which was more dangerous, standing close to Josie in her killer red dress or sitting behind the desk with her on it. He chose the latter, not because it seemed safe, but because he needed something to support his legs. They felt rubbery, as if he'd breathed too much oxygen and his face was about to kiss the floor.

Actually, what he wanted to kiss was Josie, starting with her red lips and moving straight down to her cleavage. No sooner had he sat down than she leaned *wa-a-ay* over and put that part of her anatomy on display.

"Ben?" He'd never heard her voice so sweet and sexy. Or had he? He was having trouble remembering.

"Yes?" He would have said yes to anything she wanted.

"I hope you don't misinterpret my visit."

He didn't know how to respond to that without stepping into a hornets' nest, so he kept quiet and waited for Josie to reveal herself.

Strike that. She was already revealing more of herself than Ben could bear. He waited for her to reveal her *purpose.* That was it. Ben tried to focus on Josie's purpose, but he kept getting distracted by the parts of her that kept popping out of that scarlet seduction she called a dress.

"I came by to give you something," she said.

She'd already given him a racing pulse and labored

breathing and temporary insanity. What more could she give?

"I don't think it's fair that I'm living in an apartment where you've already paid the rent, so I came to reimburse you."

"Forget it, Josie. It's the least I can do."

"No. I insist, and if you refuse I'm going to be extremely upset."

Would she leave if he took her money? If she stayed on his desk much longer he wouldn't be responsible for the consequences. The thing that was uppermost in his mind was spreading her across his desk and seeing how much of her beautifully revealed bare flesh he could kiss.

"All right, Josie. You can pay the rent on the apartment."

"Great! Is a check all right?"

"Certainly. If it bounces, I know where to find you."

Funny he should mention bouncing. She leaned over once more and began digging around in her purse while her breasts moved in wonderfully enticing ways.

"Aha. I knew it was in here somewhere."

When she handed him the check she was practically prone on his desktop. Ben longed for a bucket of ice water to dump over his head. Anything to cool him off.

His hand closed over hers, and for a moment he was looking directly into her eyes. Her pupils were unnaturally large and bright. She was playing a game. But what? If he weren't so distracted by the scenery she provided he might figure it out.

"Ben? I'm suddenly so hot...and thirsty. Would you mind giving me something *bi-i-ig* and cool?"

Whatever she was playing, he was beginning to enjoy the heck out of it. This was a side of Josie he'd never seen, this coquettish vamp with the face of a saint and the body of a siren.

Now that the shock was wearing off, maybe he could throw in a bon mot or two himself.

"How big, Josie?"

"About like this." Without missing a beat she extended her index fingers and showed him a measurement. Horizontal, he noticed.

"I see you still have an appetite for king-size things."

The little hoyden actually ran her tongue over her lips.

"Yes. I'm very greedy."

"Then let me see if I can't whet your appetite."

He stood up and towered over her, pleased to see her squirming. What would she do if he kissed her? Gazing down at her he was sorely tempted, but the thing was, he didn't know what *he* would do.

He'd learned the hard way that Josie was a dangerous woman. It was so easy to lose control around her. And then he'd be right back where he started, entangled, with no easy way out.

There was no way he would subject Josie to the isolation of being paired with a man the town refused to accept.

"I'll get your drink."

He left abruptly, and when he got to the kitchen he leaned over the sink and splashed cool water on his face. The brief respite gave him a chance to regroup. He'd never known Josie to resort to games, and he'd certainly never seen her play the coquette. Why now?

Every detail of their last evening together came to his mind, but the thing that stood out most was what she'd said. "I love you, Ben."

Was that why she had come today? Because she loved him? He'd heard that women would go to any lengths to save the man they loved, but he'd always thought it was one of the many fallacies about relationships. He also knew that it was not smart to generalize, that individual behavior varied.

Where was his big brother when Ben needed him? He was tempted to give Jim a quick call. That's how desperate he was. That's how desperate Josie had made him.

Still…no matter what she felt for him or he felt for her, nothing had changed. And short of a miracle, it wasn't going to.

The smart thing to do was take her a glass of water and tell her goodbye. Again. Painful as that would be.

Ben got the tallest glass he had and filled it to the brim. When he returned to his office he was relieved to find Josie sitting in a chair, though there was not a single thing sedate about her. Even sitting she exuded more sex appeal than most women would if they were doing an impromptu strip on top of the dining-room table.

"There you are," she said.

When she left the chair and came toward him it was no ordinary walk: it was an unfolding, like one of those accordion-pleated fans painted with exotic scenes and brilliant colors. With every step she took, she dazzled him.

"I was beginning to think you were lost." She wasn't speaking so much as purring, and though he knew it was an act he could feel the sensual pull of her voice all the way to his toes. "I was beginning to feel abandoned."

Just when he'd steeled himself against her pretty pout, she moved in on him—red skirts whispering against his leg, warm white hand on his arm, heady fragrance intoxicating him, big blue eyes sucking him in.

"I have what you want, Josie."

"You *certainly* do, Ben."

He offered the water, then held on just to feel the tips of her fingers. A crumb in a banquet hall. A single drop of water in a parched desert. Ben Standing Bear had turned into a desperate man.

Later he would wonder how Josie had done that, but at

the moment all he could do was try to hold firm against her sensual assault.

Josie held the cool glass to her cheek, then with her eyes locked on his she slid it slowly into her cleavage.

"Hmm," she murmured. "That feels good."

Finally she drank her water, but he couldn't seem to look away from the moisture beaded on her skin, shimmering along the tops of her breasts where she'd held the cool glass.

Ben knew what he was going to do, what he *had* to do. He was going to kiss her there, on the soft exposed flesh, still damp and shining. It was inevitable.

Like a man sleepwalking, he reached for her, and suddenly Josie whirled away and grabbed her purse, all business.

"Thank you for the water, Ben, and for being so nice about taking the rent and everything."

"Don't go, Josie."

"Oh, but I have to. I can't keep Jerry Bob waiting." Gut-punched, Ben stared at her. "We're driving over to Tupelo for dinner and a concert. That's why I'm wearing all these glad rags."

Still reeling from the news that she was back with her old flame, Ben moved to the relatively safe distance of the chair behind his desk. Josie hadn't dressed for him. She hadn't flirted for him. She hadn't put on that outrageous display with the glass for him.

She was merely in high spirits because she was back with the man she loved. Ben felt like a fool.

"You and Jerry Bob are back together again, then?"

Flushed and smiling, Josie popped her hands on the desk and leaned toward him, exposing more of her still-moist cleavage than was good for his blood pressure.

"No, but you understand how these things go. Once

you're intimate with a person, there's a bond that's hard to break."

Josie and Jerry Bob... Ben was going to be sick. And there was no way in hell he was going to tell her to have a good evening.

She waited for his response, still posing over his desk, her eyes riveted on his. Silent, he held her stare. At least, here was a game he could play. If she thought she could best a Sioux at stillness, she was sadly mistaken.

The sound of their breathing was loud in the deathly quiet of the room. It shifted from the ordinary intake of oxygen to the uneven gasping of denied desire.

She leaned closer, bearing her full weight on her hands. His daily planner where she rested her palms skidded forward, and Josie with it. The top half of her hit the top of his desk with a soft thump.

Ben kicked out his chair and scooped her up from behind. She leaned back against him, trembling.

"Are you hurt, Josie?"

"Only my dignity."

Wounded dignity had never felt so wonderful. That's what Josie thought as she lolled in Ben's arms. She wanted to wallow there for the rest of the evening, and if he gave her the least encouragement, she would.

His arms tightened around her, and Josie's heartbeat sped up. He was going to turn her around and kiss her and she would unzip her dress, then they would lie on the scarlet pool of silk together where they belonged.

Ashley would be thrilled at the success of their plan. Josie was already composing her triumphant message when Ben released her.

"I'm glad you could drop by, Josie."

If she cried now she would undo everything she'd struggled for. She made herself flash him a dazzling smile.

"Careful. I'm liable to take that as an invitation to come again." She didn't have to make herself put her hand on his cheek. She didn't have to give herself a pep talk in order to trail her fingers across his lips. "You take good care of yourself, Doc. You hear?"

"You, too, Josie."

She turned at the door and looked back, then she wished she hadn't. Ben looked so forlorn she wanted to cry. In fact, she did, but she waited until she was in her car.

Chapter Seventeen

Josie waited until after Ashley had mailed the contribution on Ben's letterhead to visit her aunt Tess. She went unannounced, counting on the element of surprise to advance her cause.

Tess was in the kitchen arguing with Betty Anne over the chicken they were baking.

"Hello, everybody," Josie said.

"Hi, dear." Josie's mother looked relieved to see her. "You're just in time to help me with dinner. Come on over here and help me get this chicken in the oven."

"You don't have enough paprika, Betty Anne. Here, let me fix that."

Tess grabbed the paprika, and her mother surprised Josie by jerking it out of her sister's hand and slamming it back into the cabinet.

"I'll thank you to remember this is *my* house, Tess."

"Well, that's a fine howdy-do. After all I've done for you."

Instead of crumbling, Betty Anne stared her sister down. Her face flushed, Tess turned her venom toward Josie.

"I suppose you dropped by to unload your troubles. Everybody knows what a disaster you made of your marriage. If you'd listened to me in the first place, none of this would have happened."

When Betty Anne slammed the oven door and turned around, she had her hands twisted nervously in her apron, but there was nothing timid about her expression.

"That's enough, Tess. You've been on Josie's case ever since you moved into my house, and I'm sick and tired of it."

Grinning, Josie clapped her hands. "I see you've found your spunk, Mother."

"What she's found is her spleen, and if she thinks I'm fixing to put up with it she's got another think coming. Josie, kindly tell your mother I'm moving out."

"I heard it with my own ears, Tess, and all I have to say is it's about damned time. All you've done since you've moved in here is boss me around and say harmful things about my daughter and her husband. It's no wonder the poor man left. By the time you got through spreading your poison around town, folks thought he was little better than a horse thief."

"I'm not fixing to stand here and listen to that, Betty Anne. I'm leaving."

Hoorah, Josie wanted to say. In fact she wanted to race up the stairs and help her aunt pack her bags, then stick around till the taxi came to take her back home. But that wouldn't do a thing to help Ben. Josie had to do some quick thinking to come up with a plan that would help Ben and her mother, both.

"Don't go like this, Aunt Tess."

"For Pete's sake, Josie, let the old battle-ax go before she changes her mind."

"Now, Mother, before she gets halfway to Corinth both of you will be wishing you hadn't quarreled."

Betty Anne untwisted her hands from her apron and rammed them into her pockets. "I don't take back a single thing I said."

"Well, if you think I do, you're just plain mistaken, Betty Anne Pickens."

Josie slid around the warring sisters and started making orange-spiced tea, Aunt Tess's favorite.

"Is that cinnamon I smell?" Tess craned her neck and sniffed like a bluetick hound hot on the trail of a rabbit.

"Yes, it is. Sit down, Aunt Tess. I'll pour you a cup." Tess sat stiffly at the far end of the table. "You too, Mother. I want to talk to both of you."

"If it's about your marriage, dear, all I can tell you is that your father and I never quarreled a day in our lives. I'm afraid I'm not very good at giving advice in that department."

"If you ask me, you're well rid of him, Josie Belle. And if you're lucky, Jerry Bob will forgive and forget."

Josie reigned in her rising temper. The worst thing she could do right now was argue with her aunt Tess. She had to practice the art of war in its purest form: best the enemy with superior tactics, not brute force.

Accordingly, Josie affected a meek attitude and a mournful look.

"You're probably right, Aunt Tess." Betty Anne raised her eyebrows, then opened her mouth to protest, but Josie gave her mother's shins a nudge under the table. "It just seems such a shame, though. All that potential."

Aunt Tess perked up. "All what potential? What on earth are you talking about, Josie Belle?"

"I'm talking about Ben. I mean, if I'd known all this was going to happen, I might have thought twice before I split up with him."

Josie was plying to her aunt's weakness: she couldn't stand not to be the first to know—and spread—the latest gossip. In order to make her story believable, though, Josie had to pretend reluctance to tell it.

"All of what what was going to happen? I can't make heads nor tails of a thing you're saying. Get to the point, Josie Belle."

"You mean you haven't heard?"

It was the perfect touch. Aunt Tess stiffened as if she'd been shot through the heart.

"Well, I wouldn't go that far. But I'd like to hear it straight from the horse's mouth."

"My daughter's not a horse."

"Oh, for pity's sake, Betty Anne. Don't start. You know what I mean." She turned to her niece. "Well, Josie?"

"Ben wouldn't want me to say anything. He's a very private man, especially when it comes to his philanthropy."

"Good lord, you mean he's the one that sent that hundred-thousand-dollar check last week to the parks and recreation department?"

"I didn't say that, Aunt Tess."

"How did you know that, Tess? The paper said it was anonymous."

"I have my sources." Tess gave her sister a smug look, then turned her beady-eyed scrutiny on Josie once more. "I'll bet you a pretty penny he's the one gave that quarter of a million to the library. He's in there all the time."

"I really can't comment on that, Aunt Tess. All I know is that Ben Standing Bear is the most generous man I've ever known, and it wouldn't surprise me a bit to see him named Citizen of the Year at Clytee Crawford's masquerade."

"I always knew he had potential." Aunt Tess nodded to herself. "Yessir, it took marrying into the right family to bring it all out."

Aunt Tess fairly fidgeted with excitement. Here was big news that she would spread with great relish, not only spread but embellish.

Josie curbed her exultation and made herself give a dramatic sigh. She had to get Aunt Tess to stay a few more days, just long enough to spread the word that Ben was Pontotoc's most generous citizen.

"I don't think I can face going to that ball without family support. Aunt Tess, if you'll consider staying here until after Clytee's big event, I'll drive you up to Corinth then stay the weekend and help you get your house back in shape."

"Well..." Tess cut her eyes toward her sister. "I'd like to help you out, Josie Belle, you being my niece and all, but I don't want to stay where I'm not welcome."

Josie nudged her mother once more under the table.

"I'm willing to let bygones be bygones, Tess," Betty Anne said, "provided you'll kindly keep your mouth shut about my cooking."

"I've always liked your chicken, Betty Anne. I just like to stir up a little trouble every now and then. It keeps me sharp and it keeps you on your toes."

Her mother and Aunt Tess were laughing when Josie left to visit Ashley. She came to the door in a baggy sweatsuit and bare feet.

"I hope you don't mind if I stretch out. My feet are killing me." Ashley promptly lay down on the sofa and put her feet on a stack of throw pillows.

"I brought dinner." Josie held the bag of take-out fried chicken aloft.

"Yum. I'm starving. You know where the china is."

"China, my hind foot. We're going to eat out of the box. I'll just set up the TV trays."

While Josie was laying out their dinner, she regaled Ashley with the story of how she'd hoodwinked Aunt Tess into becoming Ben's greatest champion. Ashley laughed until tears rolled down her cheeks.

"By the way, I think having him named Citizen of the Year is a great idea, Josie. I'll get the ball rolling on that."

Josie snorted. "Are you kidding? Clytee would as soon name a rattlesnake as name Ben. We might have turned into pros at scheming, but even we aren't that good."

"She'll change her mind."

If Josie hadn't been so busy thinking about Ben she might have noticed the smugness of Ashley's smile. As it was, she merely reached for another fried chicken leg. Intrigue made her hungry.

It must have made Ashley hungry, too, for she was already on her third piece.

"What makes you say Clytee will change her mind? Do you know something I don't know?"

"Yes, but we'll get to that later. First, I want to hear about your visit with Ben. We never did get a chance to talk. How did it go?"

"Great...I guess."

He looked at her as if he wanted to eat her up. As if she were special. As if she were the woman he would call *wonderful* the rest of his life. But just when she thought she had him, Ben had pulled away.

Josie ran her hands through her hair. Even though Ben hadn't kissed her, it had all seemed intimate, somehow, and she couldn't bring herself to tell Ashley the details. It would be wrong. An invasion of Ben's privacy...and hers.

"I don't know what to think about our relationship anymore, Ashley. In fact, we *have* no relationship."

"Did you do everything I suggested?"

"Yes, red dress, bogus dinner date and all. You'll never guess who I named as my date." Ashley's fork stopped midway to her mouth.

Josie knew the value of a dramatic moment, and she

dragged out the suspense before she announced triumphantly. "Jerry Bob!"

Ashley's fork clanked against the TV tray and her chicken rolled onto the carpet. Josie was stunned by her friend's reaction, but not nearly as stunned as she was when Ashley stooped to the floor to clean up the greasy mess. As she leaned over, her engorged breasts and burgeoning abdomen strained against the sweatshirt.

Josie stood up so fast her chair fell over backward. Ashley stood up slowly, her hands stretched over her growing belly.

"Now you know," she said.

"Why didn't you tell me, Ashley?"

"I've been wanting to, but there never seemed to be a good time."

"I've been a selfish brat, all wrapped up in my own problems while you've been going through a pregnancy all by yourself."

Or had she?

Ashley hadn't been dating anyone or Josie would have known about it. They'd always told each other who they were seeing. Except in the last few months. Since Josie had married Ben. Since she'd been so busy falling into unrequited love she couldn't see her nose in front of her face.

Suddenly the truth began to dawn.

"Who's the father, Ashley?"

"I think you know."

I think he's sort of sweet, Ashley had said. *I'm making fried chicken and macadamia nut cookies.*

And then there'd been that fleeting look of guilt on their faces when Josie and Ben had seen them at the restaurant.

"Not Jerry Bob. Tell me it's not Jerry Bob."

"It's Jerry Bob." Ashley blushed. "I love him, Josie. And have for a very long time. Even before the two of you started going together."

Josie took all of this in silently. Some friend she'd turned out to be, so self-absorbed she'd paid only cursory attention to what was happening in her friend's life. Ashley had always seemed steady and perfectly capable, a woman at ease in her own skin. It was easy to lean on people like that, and difficult to imagine how they would ever do anything so rash as getting pregnant out of wedlock or falling in love with their friend's fiancé.

"So, where is he?" Josie asked. "And why aren't you married?"

"He asks me to marry him approximately six times a day."

"I don't understand. You said you loved him. Don't you?"

Ashley sank onto the sofa and patted the cushion beside her. Josie sat down and they linked their arms around each other, then leaned their heads together.

"It's all about the baby, Josie. He wants his baby but I don't think he ever got over you."

Ashley began to cry, and Josie held on to her, blinking back her own tears.

"That's just plain not true, Ashley. I don't think he ever loved me, not really. He just loved the idea of me, somebody so different from his mother." She hoped what she was saying was true. It sounded like it *could* be, and if it made Ashley feel better, that was good enough for Josie.

"Jerry Bob takes sex *very* seriously." Now that was a truth Josie knew for a fact. She warmed to her subject. "He would never engage in a casual affair. I'll guarantee he loves you. Some men need a little nudging in order to say the words, that's all."

Ashley straightened up and dried her eyes on the tail of her sweatshirt. "Fortunately I don't have to work. I'm perfectly capable of raising this baby all by myself."

"Is that what you want to do?" Ashley shook her head. "I thought not. So, what are you going to do about it?"

Ashley had never been able to resist a challenge, even from the time they were kids. She stood up, reached into the box and began to parade around the room, gesturing with a fried chicken wing.

"First I'm going to march into Clytee Crawford's office down at Crawford Tractors and tell her the good news."

"She doesn't know?"

"I asked Jerry Bob not to tell her."

"My Lord, that *proves* he loves you. He tells his mama *everything*."

"Not with me, he doesn't." Ashley looked fierce and fragile at the same time. Josie applauded her. "So I'm going to tell Clytee that if she wants to see her grandchild she'll name Ben Standing Bear as Citizen of the Year."

Josie felt the thrill of victory all the way to her toes. Being tapped for that honor would ensure Ben's place in the community. And then nothing would stand in their way.

Nothing except love. She and Ashley were in the same boat: both wanted men who apparently didn't want them back.

"Where does that leave you and Jerry Bob?"

"The same place it leaves you and Ben. In the hands of fickle fate."

They reached for the comfort of Southern fried chicken at the same time, then looked at each other and laughed.

"So," Josie said, "what are you wearing to the masked ball?"

Ashley licked the grease off her fingers. "I'm planning to go as an elephant. What about you?"

"Given all this dastardly plotting I've engaged in, I probably should go as Machiavelli."

Chapter Eighteen

Ben heard about the baby at the library. He was browsing through the classics looking for a copy of Melville's *Moby Dick* to get him through another long evening alone when he heard two women gossiping on the other side of the stacks.

"Are you sure it's true? She's been separated awhile, you know."

Ben tried to tune them out. He even thought of whistling a song to let them know they had an audience, but suddenly he was riveted.

"It's true all right. Clytee said she saw Josie buying baby clothes right and left, big as you please."

Josie. Pregnant.

Ben tore out of the library so fast he forgot to put the book he was holding back on the shelf. The security strip on its spine beeped when he tried to pass through the doors, and he felt like a criminal.

He hurried to the desk and checked it out, then raced out the doors as if his pants had caught fire. When he got outside he couldn't remember where he'd parked his car.

Fortunately the parking lot was small, and in a matter of minutes he'd located it and was tearing through town toward Josie's apartment.

She didn't answer the door, and Ben stood on the street with his neck craned upward so he could see if her lights were burning. There was a small one on in the kitchen.

"Josie." He called softly, hoping he wouldn't attract attention, but when old Mr. Lancaster in apartment 2A stuck his head out the window, Ben felt like Stanley Kowalski in *A Streetcar Named Desire,* standing in the street yelling "Stel-laaa!"

"She's ain't here, Doc."

He and Josie used to laugh and call Cleveland Lancaster the house police, for he knew every move the tenants of the apartment building made.

"Do you know where she is?"

"Down yonder at the school, rehearsing that play of hers."

"Thanks, Mr. Lancaster."

"Don't mention it." Cleveland was tucking his head back in the window like a turtle, then changed his mind and poked it out again. "Hey, Doc. Heard you was gonna be a daddy. Congratulations!"

Was Ben the last to know?

By the time he got to the school he'd manufactured a whole scenario in which Josie was already giving birth and nobody had bothered to tell him until he heard it, incidentally, at the hospital.

"By the way Doc," a nurse said, "your wife's in there having your baby."

Following instinct and the lights burning in the window, he strode into the auditorium intent on calling Josie out as if they were characters in an old Western, only this time the duel would be verbal. Then he saw her. Ben's heart stopped and his feet were nailed to the floor.

She was in the center of the stage dancing with an imaginary partner while a CD played "Shall We Dance?" Ben hadn't seen her since that day she'd taken him by storm in his office, all dressed up in red. Hadn't wanted to see her.

And now he knew why. There was no way he could look at her and not know he loved her, not know he'd loved her all along, from the moment he'd said his wedding vows. Even before that. From the moment she'd climbed up on that stage at her engagement party and crooned a love song to him.

The warring within him suddenly ceased. Ben knew what he hadn't known the day he walked out of their apartment, the day he left her for a cold lonely bed and a life without laughter and sunshine. His high-flying ideals weren't worth a hill of beans in the face of a love so strong it pulled his heart out by the roots. His noble notions of protecting her from the censure of the town were a heap of ash compared to the river of need that ripped through him and tore him apart.

She'd said she loved him, and he loved her. Nothing else mattered. They would face whatever the future dealt together. And if this town kept thumbing its nose at them, then they'd find one that wouldn't.

Just Ben and Josie. Plus one. The baby.

His heart started pumping again, and he moved down the aisle listening to the sweet sound of her voice as Josie explained the scene to her students.

"The dance is a pivotal scene in the play because this is when the king realizes he loves Anna. They've sparred throughout the play, and now they are dancing and gazing into each other's eyes and falling in love. You have to make the audience *feel* that."

Even as far back as the sixth row, Ben could feel Josie's passion. How had he ever been able to let her go? How had he ever walked away from that?

"I'm not sure I can do that, Mrs. Standing Bear. I don't have much experience with that mushy stuff."

The speaker was a strapping young man with dark hair and black eyes, shoulders the size of a fullback's, strong powerful-looking legs and big bare feet the size of Virginia hams. Josie had chosen wisely. He would make an impressive King of Siam.

"What do you love best in the world, Jason?"

"My motorcycle."

"That's it, then. When you look at Belinda, imagine she's your motorcycle."

Everybody laughed, the boy she'd called Jason and a beautiful ethereal-looking blonde who stood in hoop-skirted splendor waiting her turn to play falling in love. Obviously Belinda had the role of Anna.

"Let's try that again. Shall we?"

"Could you show us one more time, Mrs. Standing Bear?"

Seventeen years old was too young for a boy like Jason to understand that someday a certain girl would come along and his motorcycle would turn into a pile of nuts and bolts with a noisy motor, and he wouldn't even remember the night so long ago when he'd thought he would love his machine forever.

"All right. One more time." Shading her eyes against the glare of stage lights, Josie called toward her tech crew. "Larry, let's take 'Shall We Dance' from the top."

Music filled the theater and Josie embraced the air and gazed up at her imaginary partner.

"It's always better with two, Josie." Loving the look of surprise and wonder that came into her face, Ben stepped onto the stage and swept Josie into his arms.

"Always." Her voice was so soft he had to lean down to hear.

"Is this the scene where Anna and the king fall in love?"

"Yes."

"Then let's show your students how it's done. Shall we dance?"

She nodded, but that was all he needed, because the way she was gazing up at him was a classic example of a woman deeply in love. Ben prayed she meant it. He prayed their time apart hadn't destroyed her feelings for him.

As he swung her into the dance, he fervently hoped she wasn't merely acting.

Her heart was in her eyes. Josie couldn't help herself. Here was Ben, and she was hopelessly in love and there was no way she could pretend otherwise.

One of the things she'd always loved about him was the way he danced, the way he held her, not so close that she didn't have freedom of movement and not so far away that she couldn't follow him, but exactly right, guiding her with his hands and his body so that the two of them moved as one.

His eyes gleaming, he leaned close and whispered for her ears only, "How am I doing, Teach?"

Any better and her hair would catch on fire.

"Great."

That wouldn't do, that sexy murmur that was a sure signal to Ben that she was over-the-moon crazy for him and all he had to do was snap his fingers and she'd fall into his bed like a ripe plum. Where was her pride? Where was her spunk? Where was the woman who had sworn to herself that she would learn to play the game, that she would play hard-to-get, that she would hold out for declarations of love and nothing else would do?

"You're a very good actor, Ben."

He spun her to the far corner of the stage out of earshot
of her students.

"I'm not acting."

"Oh."

Boy, when she set out to play hard-to-get she broke all
track records. The women who knew the value of a cold
shoulder every now and then were the ones men wanted
the most. Ashley had told her that. At the time Josie had
thought it sounded cruel and calculating, but now she
wasn't so sure.

She'd bared her heart and soul to Ben once, and look
where that had landed her. All alone.

Still, shouldn't a man and woman be able to tell the truth
and have everything work out all right in the end?
Shouldn't a man and a woman who had been friends for
years be able to sit down together and be frank about their
feelings without fear that one of them would walk out the
door and leave the other one sitting home alone waiting for
the telephone to ring?

Making a feeble attempt to get the upper hand, Josie
looked at her students. Jason and Belinda watched with rapt
attention, not because they were taking notes on acting, she
was sure, but because they'd never seen her husband. Ben
Standing Bear in the flesh was a glorious sight to behold,
especially when he was in his Sioux warrior mode, out to
take captives, in this case, Josie.

Didn't he know he'd taken her captive the minute he'd
walked back into her life? No, even before that. Long ago
while she was still in school she'd given her heart to him.

"Belinda, do you get the general idea now?"

"Oh, yes ma'am. The way you're looking at Dr. Standing Bear is pure magic." And so it was, so it was. "If I
could play the role that way I'd have the audience en-
thralled."

Belinda was not only a straight-A student, but an astute

and enormously talented young woman. She was going to have the audience in her thrall anyway, but Josie was thrilled that she wanted to do her role and the play justice.

"How about you, Jason?"

"I'll try to do it that way but I don't think I have Dr. Standing Bear's charisma. He'd make a great King."

As far as Josie was concerned, he was already king, and she couldn't wait to be alone with him. She was dying to know why he had come after all these weeks of silence. Could it be to tell her that he loved her?

"Why don't we call it a night? It's been a long rehearsal and we still have a few weeks to go."

"Don't you want us to try the dance, Mrs. Standing Bear?" This from Belinda who always wanted to go the extra mile.

"We'll try it first thing tomorrow. Meanwhile, why don't you practice in front of the mirror, use your facial expression to convey feeling, see how it looks? Okay, guys?"

They nodded, sliding their eyes toward Ben. And who wouldn't? She wanted to slide her whole self in his direction, straight into his arms.

"Okay," they said.

"Good rehearsal. See you tomorrow."

They were so slow getting their costumes off and getting their props back into place, Josie wanted to scream. She could feel Ben watching her, waiting.

At long last her crew filed out, trailing book bags and letter jackets and goodnights. Finally she was alone with Ben. And she didn't know what to do. She didn't know what to say.

The woman who taught acting didn't have any idea how to act with her own husband.

Suddenly Josie had a sinking feeling. She'd never filed the annulment. Maybe that's why Ben had come.

"Aren't you going to look at me, Josie?"

She faced him reluctantly, like a woman on a game show who had picked door number three and is afraid a tiger will jump through. He was leaning against one of the columns on the set, looking every bit as delicious as she remembered, and then some.

He was waiting for her to say something, but before she could speak, Josie had to teach her heart to behave. She swallowed the lump in her throat, then took a deep breath.

"It's good to see you," she said. "How have you been?"

"Lonely."

"Me, too."

Whole worlds can be wrapped up in a man's stare. The one Josie saw was marvelous, full of soft summer nights under white cotton sheets and evenings of wine and music on the front porch swing and standing side by side in the kitchen exchanging kisses while Ben stirred up something wonderful to eat and Josie tried to keep from burning the toast.

"I think we should do something about that." His voice was deep and full of magic, and Josie wanted to wrap herself in him and stay forever.

"What do you suggest, Ben?"

"For starters, I suggest we hold each other. You're too far away."

His eyes were electric, and Josie was jolted all the way down to her toes. They started toward each other and she was so caught up in the nearness of Ben, she didn't see the stage prop in her path, a velvet-covered ottoman.

It caught her at the knees and she toppled. Ben reached for her, but he wasn't quick enough. She landed in an undignified sprawl, her belly pressed into the ottoman, her torso and legs dangling over either side.

She stared morosely at the floor. So much for romance. With a sound more akin to a wounded bear than anything she'd heard, Ben scooped her up and squeezed her so close she could barely breathe. It was wonderful. She could stay right where she was for the next century or two.

"I'll never forgive myself if anything's happened to the baby," he said.

The baby? What baby?

She almost blurted it out, but an instinct for self-preservation, long buried, rose to the surface. Her father used to tell her she would be better off it she'd just listen every now and then instead of roaring full steam ahead.

So Josie listened. And what she heard shot her hopes right out of the sky.

"Are you all right, Josie?" Holding her by the shoulders, Ben inspected her face. "Is there any pain? Any bleeding?"

Ben thought she was pregnant. He thought she was the one having the baby. But why?

Suddenly Josie remembered the shopping spree she'd gone on on Saturday afternoon. In an attempt to boost Ashley's spirits, she'd bought every cute baby thing the town of Pontotoc had to offer.

Snippets of conversation came to her, Lenola Jones down at the Storks R Us commenting as she sacked the receiving blankets and booties and sleepers in every color the store had, "You must be excited about the baby, Josie."

"I'm thrilled," Josie had said, adding a white teddy bear to the stack.

"What about the Doc? I guess he's on cloud nine."

"Oh, yes."

What else could she say? Not a soul knew about Ashley's baby except Josie and Jerry Bob, and she wasn't about to betray her friend. So naturally Lenola thought it was hers, given the fact that nobody in his right mind practically buys out the store for a baby shower, and Josie had confirmed with her own lips that Ben was the proud father-to-be.

And naturally Lenola had told her best friend, who happened to be Clytee Crawford, and now the whole town was talking. Again.

Obviously Ben had heard.

That's why he had come. To claim his baby.

Her dreams of love in tatters, Josie jerked herself out of his reach and smoothed her shirt back into her jeans.

"Leave me alone." It was as close to a snarl as she could get. Nothing makes a woman madder than to be wanted for all the wrong reasons.

"I'm going to take you down to the clinic and examine you, just to make sure."

Oh, help. Her stretched out on a table wearing nothing but a paper sheet and Ben with his hands all over her. Rediscovering her body. Discovering the truth.

He reached for her, but she danced out of his way.

"Don't touch me."

That stopped him in his tracks, and Ben Standing Bear was not an easy man to dissuade. Josie probably had her *condition* to thank.

"I know you're worried about the baby, and believe me, Josie, I do understand why you wouldn't want to come to me after the way I walked out on you. But I'm going to make up for all that. I'm going to take care of you."

All because of the baby. Every word he said was a stake driven into Josie's heart.

"Just go, Ben. I don't want to talk to you, I don't want to see you."

She saw the fire that came into his eyes, and if she hadn't known him so well she'd have trembled. Ben Standing Bear had the look of a man who would crush anything that got between him and the thing he wanted most.

"If you think I'm going to walk away and leave my

child, you're mistaken. I thought you knew me better than that.''

She *did* know Ben, and what he said was the gospel truth. As long as he thought she carried his child, he would pursue her. And it wouldn't be casual, either. He would pursue her with the relentlessness of a Sioux warrior.

The simple thing to do would be to tell him the truth. But there was the matter of keeping Ashley's secret. Then there was the matter of pride. Josie's.

Ben had already made his motives plain, and if she backed down now, he might persist anyway, just in case she wasn't telling the truth. And then, what if she did get pregnant right off the bat? It had happened to Ashley. It could happen to her.

She'd never know if Ben wanted her because of herself.

There was only one thing to do: best by superior tactics. In this case, evasion.

''The baby's not yours.''

''Whose baby is it, then?'' He sounded like a calm, reasonable man, but his face gave him away. It was thunderous. ''Josie, I'm waiting for your answer.''

She couldn't say *none of your business,* because as long as he thought he might be the father, it was definitely his business. There was only one thing left to do. Tell the truth.

At least the part of it that would serve her immediate purpose.

''It's Jerry Bob's.''

Oh, help. She was weaving another tangled web that would surely end in somebody getting hurt. When was she going to learn?

Ben wasn't the kind of man to spread gossip. She could tell him the whole truth with complete assurance that he would never betray Ashley. *Then* she would send him on his way. And maybe, just maybe, if she got very lucky and if the moon turned blue she'd get another chance to love him and find out if he loved her back.

"Ben…"

She paused and put her hand over the gold locket he'd given her, for courage. But Ben had already stalked off the stage and was lost in the darkness of the vast auditorium. Josie shaded her eyes, trying to see him beyond the bright stage lights, but all she saw were shadows.

"I love you," she whispered, and her voice echoed all the way up to the balcony.

Josie Belle Pickens was standing center stage playing the most tragic role of her career, the woman who had lost the only man she would ever love.

Chapter Nineteen

By the time he arrived at work the next morning, Ben had managed to tamp his fiery rage down to a glowing ember. His anger wasn't directed at Josie, but at himself. He'd quit the battle too soon. He'd gone to win back the love of his life and had ended up alienating her even further.

"'Morning," he all but growled.

His secretary looked up at him, startled.

"Somebody die in your family, Doc?"

"Sorry. It's nothing personal," he said, then shut himself in his office and brooded.

His mail was neatly stacked on the front of his desk, and as he methodically went through it, he tried to figure out what he could do to rectify his mistakes with Josie.

All of them.

The signature on the letter he was holding caught his attention. Clytee Crawford. What business could she possibly have with him?

He quickly scanned the text, then sat back astonished. She wanted him to be guest of honor at her masked ball. *Guest of honor.*

Ben glanced out the window to see if the sky was falling and he hadn't even noticed. Clytee Crawford despised him.

She was bound to have ulterior motives. Still, wasn't this exactly what he'd wanted? Admission to the town's closely knit society?

He would go, out of curiosity if nothing else. Besides, Josie might be there. It would give Ben the perfect opportunity to court her.

That's exactly what she needed, and that's exactly what he intended to do, Jerry Bob or no Jerry Bob. Josie wasn't married to Crawford; she was married to Ben. What belonged to her, belonged to him, and he would love that child, no matter who his biological father was.

Besides, if she were in love with Jerry Bob, wouldn't she have run to the nearest lawyer to get annulment papers drawn?

Relief flooded him, and along with it a clear course of action.

Ben opened his next letter. It was from Opie Claude Jernigan at the parks and recreation department. He wanted Ben to coach a little league baseball team and ended by saying he'd call sometime next week to find out when it would be convenient for Ben to have dinner and discuss the matter.

"It must be raining," Ben said. "Manna from heaven."

His elation was tempered by regret. There had been no reason to leave Josie, after all. If only Ben had waited. Apparently all this had been in the works all along, and he had been too impatient to give the people time to accept him.

Ben leaned back in his swivel chair with his hands

clasped, dreaming and scheming. He was going to storm Josie's fort as it had never been stormed.

Victory wouldn't come easy. Anybody who knew Josie knew that. But Ben wasn't in for a short skirmish; he was in for the whole war.

And eventually, he would win. Anybody who knew *him*, knew that.

Satisfied, he picked up the phone and set the first part of his battle plan into action.

Josie and Ashley were sitting on the floor in front of Josie's TV sharing a bowl of popcorn with Bruiser and planning more devilment.

"I think we're becoming devious women, Ashley." Josie was only half joking. She'd always despised deviousness in anybody, and policed herself rigorously for any signs of it, so she could stamp it out before it got a toehold.

"I haven't told anybody any lies. Have you?"

"Not outright."

Ashley reached into the bowl for a handful of popcorn. She was growing bigger by the minute, it seemed. Soon she'd be in maternity tops, and her secret would be out.

"The end justifies the means," she said. "Keep thinking about the end."

Josie tried, but she couldn't picture it.

"How did it go with Clytee?"

"Cool at first, and then when the fact of the baby sank in, I thought she was going to get down and kiss my feet in gratitude. She *adores* her son and would do anything for him. I have to admire that." Ashley tossed Bruiser a few kernels of corn then helped herself to another big portion.

"How about you, Josie? Anything from Ben?"

Josie told about Ben's visit to the rehearsals.

"You mean he thought it was *your* baby?"

"That's right."

"And he thought you and Jerry Bob…" Ashley smacked her forehead. "Oh, Lord."

"You know me. I leave a trail of confusion wherever I go. I was just getting ready to tell him the whole truth when he walked out. You're not mad, are you, Ashley?"

"Mad? *Mad!*" Ashley wrapped her arms around herself and held on. "I think it's the funniest damned thing I've ever heard." Giggles bubbled up and spilled over. "Trail of confusion won't begin to describe it. Together we've managed to leave a trail of mass hysteria."

They gave each other the universal look of women who are partners in crime, the one where humor is evident in the sparkle of eyes and laughter is caught in the throat, getting ready to explode.

Josie and Ashley let it explode. They laughed so hard they had to hold on to each other to keep from toppling to the floor.

Seeing opportunity, Bruiser sank his head into the bowl and began happily gobbling all the popcorn.

Finally Josie and Ashley wiped their eyes on the dish towel they'd been using for a napkin. "My fine linen," Josie had called it.

"Just look at us," she said. "You as big as a barrel without a husband to your name, and me with a husband who thinks I'm having another man's baby."

"Yeah. Just look at us."

Ashley caught her lower lip between her teeth to hold back her laughter, but it didn't help. They both cracked up.

As women do everywhere. Laughing to keep from crying.

The best way to get the phone to ring was step into the shower. Josie started to let it ring, then changed her mind, grabbed a towel to wrap around her wet hair, and dripped water all the way across the floor.

"Hi, Josie." She'd know that voice anywhere. "It's Ben."

She didn't want to get the chair cushion wet, so she sat down in the middle of the floor.

"I know," she said.

"How are you?"

"You mean, how's the baby?"

"No, I mean how are *you?*"

"You ask because of the baby."

Silence. Josie twirled the phone cord around her middle finger, then untwirled it. Now was the perfect time to tell him the truth. And yet, there was still the question of love. Did he or didn't he?

And anyway, when she told him she'd lied—not lied, exactly, but withheld vital information—she needed to be able to look into his eyes.

"That's not why I called."

"Then why did you call?"

"To tell you I'm taking you to Clytee Crawford's masked ball."

"You mean, to ask me."

"No, to tell you. You're my wife, and I'm taking you. I'll pick you up at seven."

"Of all the gall," she said, but she was talking to a dead receiver. Ben had already hung up.

Ben stared at the phone. He'd done it. He wasn't necessarily proud of the way he'd handled things, but he'd made it perfectly clear that Josie was to be his escort, then he'd hung up before she had a chance to change his mind with argument or charm. With Josie, he never knew what was coming next.

The thing to do, of course, was leave before Ben got there. That would show him she wasn't easy. That would show him she wasn't going to be bossed around.

It would also be rude, not to mention ungrateful. After all Ben had done for her. After all their years of friendship.

Josie paced the floor with Bruiser taking every step she did, sometimes whining and licking her hand. She patted his head.

"Don't worry, boy, everything's going to be all right. I'm just nervous, that's all."

She would sit down if she could, but she was afraid she'd split her dress. It was as tight as hide, lowslung and outrageous, the dress Rhett Butler had made Scarlett O'Hara wear to Melanie's party, a scarlet dress for a scarlet woman.

Of course, that wasn't the reason Josie had chosen the costume. Lately she'd been such a scheming woman she decided to dress the part.

And now she was getting her choice. Any minute now Ben would walk through the door and think she'd dressed to entice him

Bruiser whined again, sat back on his haunches and thumped his tail hard on the floor.

"You're absolutely right, boy. I should change."

She wondered if she had time. If she had her old Halloween costumes she knew she would, but they were still in her closet at her mother's house. The best she could hope for was time to slip into jeans and a shirt, tie a bandana around her neck and tell everybody she was a cow hand.

Miss Scarlett's dress wasn't made for hurrying. Josie had managed to make it halfway across the room when she heard the key turn in the lock.

And then Ben was in her apartment, and Josie forgot everything. His chest was bare, his feet were encased in beaded moccasins, and the rest of him was stuffed into deerskin pants so tight they defied reason. Genuine, from the looks of them. There was no way he could have gotten into them unless they'd been stitched right onto his body.

"I used my own key," he said.

"Good Lord," she said.

They stared at each other, electrified, hypnotized.

"You look sensational, Josie."

"So do you."

The truth just rushed out. Josie couldn't have stopped it if she'd tried. Ben's eyes glinted with humor.

"I thought I'd fulfill Clytee Crawford's fantasy."

Lord, the way he looked, he was going to fulfill every woman's fantasy. Josie kept that tidbit to herself.

What he was doing was not only bold but brilliant. He was going to turn Clytee's vicious *Indian* label into something so spectacular it could only be called proud and noble.

Josie applauded him, and Ben grinned. For a moment they were best friends again, and it occurred to Josie that she was going to lose something precious if she didn't end her charade with him soon. Very soon.

Ben whipped out his mask and put it on. "How's this for a disguise?"

"I don't think you're going to fool anybody."

There was no way they could miss that naked chest, all that gorgeous bronzed skin, the sharp definition of muscle he'd kept toned with years of rigorous attention to health and body.

"I don't think you will either, Josie. Not even with a mask."

He moved in fast, like a lightning bolt that struck without warning, searing and stripping away all her outside layers until there was nothing left of Josie but her beating heart. In one swift motion, he pulled her into his embrace then bent over her as if they were engaged in the last steps of the tango.

"Ben..."

What had she meant to say? *Don't. Do.* She had time for no more, because his lips were on hers and nothing existed except that time, that place, that kiss. Everything that had gone before was no more than a forgotten memory, swept away in the tide of passion that stormed her.

Bent low over her, he devoured her lips. That was the best word she could think of, the stuff of movies and novels and late-night television that left you panting in your chair at midnight wishing for more.

She was panting, all right, melting, dissolving into a palpitating mass of willing flesh. Mercy, Ben had her so hot she was going completely out of her mind.

Out of the corner of her eye she saw the door a few feet away and the room beyond, the bed with its white spread waiting to be mussed by two lovers who couldn't keep their hands off each other.

With every fiber in her body she wanted Ben to take her there. She wanted to lose herself in him and be reborn.

First, though, she had to clear the air, tell the truth. When he paused for breath she whispered, "Ben..." and then his lips were on hers once more.

And his hands. Wonderful, expressive hands, sending shivers all over her. He supported her with his right while his left traced an erotic line from her breasts to the indention of her small waist to the flare of her hips.

"Nice," he murmured, and then he did it all over again. Suddenly he lifted his head, his eyes filled with suspicion. "You're awfully trim for somebody who's pregnant."

His eyes pierced through her as he ran both hands down her sides, following her curves, passing over the flat planes of her belly, then back up to the soft mounds of her breasts.

"Amazing. Not an outward sign. Not even the breasts."

She jerked back, enraged. "I'm not your patient."

"No, you're my wife."

"I can take care of that tomorrow."

Stalking off was difficult in her tight dress. The best she could manage was a dignified mincing step. Still stung, Josie grabbed her wrap, if you could call it that, a frivolous feathered concoction she flung around her neck where it lay like a cat curled on a windowsill. Not the look she'd hoped for.

"Josie, I don't want you to take care of that. I want you to be my wife in very sense of the word."

"Because of the baby?"

"Yes," he said. "Naturally..."

Josie didn't even wait to hear the rest of it. She slammed out the front door and was on the sidewalk before Ben caught up.

"Josie, come back inside. I think we need to talk."

"We'll be late, and it won't do to keep Clytee Crawford waiting."

Ben had never seen Josie like this. He helped her into the car still puzzling over her behavior, but not so much that he didn't notice the way her dress molded her hips. He experienced such a wave of desire he had to stand on the sidewalk and compose himself before he could get into the car.

They rode in silence through the darkening streets. Where were the good old days? Where was his best friend who talked to him about everything?

Ben blamed it on her pregnancy. Hormones gone wild. Everything out of whack.

"Which way?" he asked.

Josie gave directions, and as he pulled into the driveway she thawed a little.

"The perfect touch would be a stallion."

"A stallion?"

"Yes, except this dress is so tight I don't know that I could ride."

Memories washed over him as he parked the car—Josie with her hair lifted off her neck, her breasts swaying above him, a look of pure cat-like satisfaction on her lips.

"I don't think a woman in your condition should," he said.

Josie gave him this *look*. He couldn't describe it, couldn't decipher it.

"I'm not pregnant," she snapped, and then she bailed out of the car and stalked into the house.

Ben stood in the dark like a man shell-shocked. *Not pregnant.* What in the world was going on here?

He followed after her, calling her name, but she had already disappeared into the crowd of masked revelers.

Gone to find Jerry Bob, no doubt. But why? To tell him she'd miscarried? Been mistaken?

Ben had to find her. He pushed his way through pirates and cowboys and showgirls and prim school marms, as well as several wild animals and an enormous cow whose back half kept splitting off toward the bar.

"Herman, you come back here," the front end of the cow bellowed, but the tail kept on going.

It would have all been comical if Ben hadn't been so desperate to find out what was going on. He craned his neck over the crowd and spotted a pink elephant underneath a potted palm, deep in conversation with a matador who looked vaguely familiar.

Suddenly the elephant and the matador were joined by a fiery redhead who was turning heads right and left. Josie.

Ben had started toward her when a bejeweled matron dressed like Elizabethan royalty caught his arm. She pulled off her mask and there was Clytee Crawford.

"I'm so glad you could come, Dr. Standing Bear." Her smile looked genuine.

There was nothing to do but speak to his hostess. With a last glance toward Josie, he turned to Clytee.

"It's my pleasure. And thank you for that gracious letter."

He meant what he said. Not only had Clytee asked him to be the guest of honor, but she'd offered profuse apologies for her earlier rudeness. "It appears I've let myself become fossilized," she'd written. "My world view has become so narrow that I can do nothing more than parrot dead ancestors whose prejudices should have been buried a long time ago."

"I hope your being at my masquerade means you've forgiven me, Dr. Standing Bear," she said.

"It does, and I have."

Clytee crossed her hands over her heart. "You don't know how relieved I am. I'd hate to think I was headed into grandmotherhood with that on my conscience."

"Congratulations." He tried to sound normal, casual. "I suppose Jerry Bob is happy?"

"Yes, I never thought I'd live to see the day, after that wedding fiasco and all." Clytee blushed. "No offense meant, Dr. Standing Bear."

"Please, call me Ben."

I'm not pregnant, Josie had said.

Filled with confusion and despair, Ben tried to think how he could diplomatically get to the bottom of all this. How was a man supposed to ask if his wife was carrying another man's baby?

There was no diplomatic way. He would just have to blurt it out.

Clytee saved him the trouble. "They'll have a quiet wedding, of course, under the circumstances, but I couldn't be happier. Ashley is a lovely young woman."

"Ashley?"

"Yes. I think she'll make a wonderful Crawford. I believe you know her. She and your wife are good friends."

Josie was still by the potted palm, and now Ben knew why the matador looked so familiar. It was Jerry Bob. Obviously the elephant was Ashley.

He couldn't wait to get to his wife.

"Will you excuse me, Mrs. Crawford. There's something I need to take care of."

"Oh, can it wait?" The lights dimmed then brightened once more, and the orchestra struck up "For He's A Jolly Good Fellow."

Clytee tugged Ben's arm. "This is the highlight of the evening," she said. "And you're due on center stage."

Ben followed Clytee Crawford to the front of the ballroom, with one last glance at the woman in red.

Chapter Twenty

Josie had her arm around the elephant. "Here it comes, Ashley. The moment we've been waiting for."

"I've already found what I've been waiting for." Ashley gazed up at Jerry Bob with what Josie suspected was an adoring look. Behind the elephant suit she couldn't tell.

Josie experienced a moment of envy. To have the man you love tell you he loved you right back had to be the best feeling in the world. She wouldn't know. And now she never would.

When she'd confessed her little white lie to Ben, she'd blown every chance she'd had of happiness. She would never have what she wanted, what everybody wanted if they'd only admit it—a place to call home and somebody waiting there who loves you.

Up front, Clytee was introducing the Citizen of the Year, but Ben was nowhere to be seen.

"Our Citizen of the Year is a man who has quietly gone

about doing good works in our town," she said. "A man who came to us a perfect stranger and ended up opening his heart and his clinic to the people of this town. While the rest of us were playing golf and bridge on Saturdays, he was in his clinic providing free treatment for those who could not afford medical care."

Josie was surprised, not that Ben had done it, but that she hadn't known. "Did you know that, Ashley?"

"No," Ashley whispered. "But it has to be so. Clytee always does her homework."

"This is not a new venture for him," Clytee continued, "but a project dear to his heart. While he was in medical school he organized his fellow interns into a team that treated thousands of patients free. He gave up weekends and holidays for the poor while still maintaining his status at the top of his class.

"I present to you Dr. Ben Standing Bear, a man we are proud to call our own."

Changed into a tuxedo, Ben walked onto the stage to thunderous applause. Josie's was the loudest of all. Ben was being honored, not because of their scheming, but because he deserved it. Tears streaked down her face and ran from underneath her mask. She didn't even bother to wipe them away, but hugged Ashley and whispered her goodbye.

"You're leaving? You'll miss the dance."

"I know."

Ashley squeezed her hand. "He'll come back to you, Josie. I know he will."

Josie didn't plan to stick around to find out. She couldn't bear another disappointment, another lonely evening sitting in her empty apartment with a telephone that didn't ring.

She hugged Ashley. "Have fun," she whispered, then she went in search of her mother.

Aunt Tess was the one she found. "I'm ready to go home now," Josie said.

"It can't be soon enough for me. I feel ridiculous in this gorilla suit." Aunt Tess walked toward the exit so fast Josie had to step double-time to keep up with her.

"Where's Mother? Didn't she come?"

"She came all right. But she's not going home with us." Tess burst through the French doors, jerked off her gorilla head and took a deep breath of fresh air.

"What do you mean, she's not going home with us? Did the two of you quarrel again?"

"No. Now that I'm leaving we get along better than we ever have. Betty Anne's staying here."

"How's she going to get home?"

Josie looked over her shoulder, trying to spot her mother, the beruffled Little Bo Peep through the open doors. She finally saw her with the Big Bad Wolf.

"Him." Tess nodded toward the wild animal who was at that very moment stealing a kiss from the blushing woman wearing the ruffled hat. "That's Leon West under all that ridiculous fur."

"The postman?"

"He's had a thing for Betty Anne for years, and she's finally decided to live a little."

Josie was glad somebody could. All she wanted to do was crawl in a hole and hide.

"Let's go to Corinth," she said, then she followed her aunt to the car.

Josie wasn't at her apartment. That much was clear. Ben stood in the middle of her bedroom listening to the echoing silence.

After he'd received the Citizen of the Year award he'd searched all over the ballroom for her. Finally Ashley, sans her pink elephant head, told Ben that Josie had left right after the presentation.

And then she'd said, "Don't be too hard on her. Sometimes her zeal to take care of other people puts her in a bad light, but she's the finest, most caring woman I've ever known. I hope you know how lucky you are to have her in your life. I know I do."

Chastising Josie wasn't what Ben had on his mind.

On Sunday, after the ball, Josie called her mother from Corinth. "Has Ben called?"

"No."

"Come by?"

"I haven't seen him, dear. Were you expecting him?"

"No. I wasn't expecting him."

"How are things up there?"

"We got the house cleaned and all Aunt Tess's things unpacked."

"That's good. I'm glad you were there to help her. When will you be home?"

"Sometime this afternoon. Around four."

"I'll see you then. Oh, I almost forgot. There's a package here for you. It had to be signed for, so Leon brought it here."

"Who is it from?"

"There's no return address."

"Is it bigger than breadbox?"

Betty Anne laughed. "You never could stand the suspense. Do you want me to open it?"

"Go ahead. I'm dying to know."

She heard her mother's footsteps tapping across the floor, going to get scissors, no doubt. She pictured Betty Anne's slight frown of concentration as she tore into the box. Then she heard a soft exclamation.

"Good grief." After a brief fumbling, Betty Anne came back on the phone. "You're not going to believe this."

"What? Tell me, Mother."

"It's a blue glass bottle."

What seemed a lifetime ago, Josie had stood on the shore and tossed a blue glass bottle into the Mississippi Sound, then watched until it vanished from sight. Had someone found it, then? But how did they know where to send it? She hadn't even signed her name.

"Oh, and Josie, there's a message inside. Do you want me to get it out and read it?"

"No. I'm coming right home."

The message was simple: Love is all that counts. Nothing more. No salutation. No signature.

It wasn't the message Josie had sent sailing into the sea, but it was so close she got goosebumps. Nor was it the same bottle.

That night she set the mysterious bottle on the bedside table where the tiny glow of her nightlight reflected off the glass and shot a path to the door like a blue beacon lighting the way home.

On Monday, Josie was relieved when she looked at her daily planner and discovered she'd scheduled a brief rehearsal after school, which didn't leave her any time to go and see a lawyer. The annulment would have to wait.

She couldn't keep postponing it forever, of course. If the six-month period expired, Ben would be stuck with her. Or stuck with divorce.

"I won't think about all this today," she said, and then she thought of nothing else.

Obviously he wanted her to get it over with or he would have called. But what if he was sick or hurt? What if he was waiting for her to apologize for everything?

The list of her sins was so long she didn't want to think about that, either.

By the time she got into her car and headed home she had a splitting headache.

Seeing a buffalo on her sidewalk didn't help. It was blocking the path to her door. There was no way she could avoid the crowd that had gathered around to gawk. She'd just have to hold her head up and march on. The way she'd always did.

"There she is," somebody shouted, and a splinter group surged her way.

Had she won the lottery? Josie was stopped in her path by people, some she knew, some she didn't. Mr. Lancaster was front and center, of course. Nothing ever happened in the apartment building that escaped his notice.

"I told 'em you'd be here in a minute. If they'd just hold their horses you'd get home in time to claim that buffalo."

Josie wondered if she were still in her bed asleep, and all this was a strange nightmare.

"Are you Josie Standing Bear?" A man wearing brown overalls with Classic Instruments stitched onto the pocket pushed his way to her. She managed a nod. "Sign here."

The clipboard he thrust at her was real. The pen, too. If she didn't come to her senses she was going to claim ownership of that ghastly buffalo sitting on the sidewalk.

"What is this?" she asked. "I didn't order anything."

"All I do is deliver, lady. Sign, please."

"But I don't want it. Can't you just take it back?"

"I can't do that. My job is to deliver." He pushed his cap to the back of his head. "Look lady, all I need is your signature then you can call the store and work out whatever you want to with them."

Josie signed.

"She's all yours, lady."

"I was afraid you'd say that."

Josie approached the thing on her sidewalk with caution. As she got closer she saw that it wasn't a buffalo at all, but a big fake fur throw with wooden legs, a twisted rope tail and a papier-mâché head that looked suspiciously like the one in her prop room back at school.

"I can't wait to see what's under there." Mr. Lancaster was right at her elbow, grinning from ear to ear.

"Neither can I." As Josie grabbed the tail and pulled she made two great discoveries: curiosity is a great cure for a headache, and a grand piano looks right at home no matter where you put it.

All her life she'd wanted a grand piano, dreamed of it, schemed for it, hinted about it. And now, finally, it was hers.

"I never dreamed I'd find what I wanted under a buffalo," she said, and she was laughing and crying at the same time.

"There's a note." Mr. Lancaster, acting as self-appointed director of the drama being played out on the sidewalk, snatched the note off the piano and handed it to Josie.

"What's it say?" he asked, peering over her shoulder.

Josie read in silent wonder, then afterward she was crying so hard she couldn't see the note, let alone speak.

"A Sioux always claims his bride with gifts," a voice from the back of the crowd said, quoting the note. A familiar voice. A voice that stopped Josie's heart.

And then Ben emerged from the crowd, his eyes gleaming.

Taking her hand, he finished, "I love you, Josie. Forever."

"I can't believe you did this," she said. She couldn't quit smiling. She might never stop.

"We started this courtship with an audience. I thought it appropriate we end it the same way."

"How do you want it to end?" she whispered.

"Like this." He swept her into his arms and kissed her to thunderous applause. Kissed her thoroughly. Kissed her so long and hard she lost all her breath and most of her senses.

"Encore," Mr. Lancaster yelled, and Ben smiled down at Josie and said, "Shall we?"

"Yes." She puckered up for another kiss, but Ben surprised her by opening the piano and playing the first notes of "Amazed."

She'd never missed a cue in her life, and she wasn't about to miss this one. Sitting on the piano bench she played their song while Ben stood beside her and sang.

Nobody seemed to mind that he sang off-key. Least of all Josie.

Chapter Twenty-One

As soon as they'd finished their love song, Mr. Lancaster shooed the audience away. "Show's over," he said, then tipping his hat and grinning, he walked back into the apartment building and shut the door.

Josie was having a hard time believing that she, of all people, was front and center in a drama with a fairy-tale ending.

"You're not mad at me? After all..."

Ben put his hands over her lips. "I love you, Josie," he said, and to prove he did he kissed her till she believed him.

"But where will I put the piano?"

"I'll show you."

Never one to wait for surprises, she asked, "Where are we going?"

"Home."

"Where...?"

Laughing, Ben put his finger over her lips. "Not another word till we get there. Promise?"

She nodded. He gave the address to the movers, then drove her through streets as familiar to her as her own name, streets where she'd learned to ride her tricycle, then her bicycle, streets where she'd walked Bruiser and greeted friends and dreamed her dreams.

And suddenly there was another of her dreams staring her right in the face and all she could say was, "Oh, Ben."

"We're home, Josie."

It was the house they'd looked at in the summertime when the roses bloomed beside the front porch and a mocking bird sang to them from the ancient oaks. The roses were fading now, giving way to the fall camellias that bloomed behind the new porch swing. The mocking-bird still sang in the yellow-leafed oak while a rabbit chased his brother through the cones that had fallen beneath the giant magnolias.

Ben carried her over the threshold, then kissed her again and didn't stop until he had to tell the movers where to put the piano.

"Want us to throw this old thing away?" One of the movers held up the fake buffalo.

Josie and Ben looked at each other and grinned.

"No," they said.

The movers spread the fake fur on the polished wooden floor as if it were the finest Oriental rug.

"There's no accounting for some folks' taste," they muttered as they went out the door.

As soon as it clicked shut behind them, Ben picked Josie up and lowered her to the rug.

"There's a rumor circulating in town that Dr. and Mrs. Ben Standing Bear are going to have a baby."

Josie looked up into the smiling face of the man she'd

loved for so long she could barely remember anything that had gone before.

"I know a way to make it come true," she whispered.

She reached for him, and Ben unveiled his bride, then rescued her.

Forever.

* * * * *

Coming in July 2004
from Silhouette Books

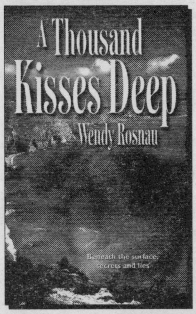

Sly McEwen's final assignment for top-secret government
agency Onyxx had gone awry, leaving only questions behind.
But Sly had a feeling Eva Creon had answers. Locked inside
Eva's suppressed memory was the key to finding the killer
on the loose. But her secrets may have the power to destroy
the one thing that could mean more than the truth…
their growing love for each other….

Available at your favorite retail outlet.

Forrester Square

LEGACIES . LIES . LOVE .

A story not to be missed…

In July, Forrester Square comes to a gripping conclusion!

ESCAPE THE NIGHT

by top Harlequin Intrigue® author

JOANNA WAYNE

Returning to Seattle after many years, Alexandra Webber meets Ben Jessup, who now lives in her childhood home. When recurring nightmares and memories of a long-ago night begin to haunt and endanger Alex, Ben vows to protect her.

HARLEQUIN®
Live the emotion™

If you enjoyed what you just read, then we've got an offer you can't resist!

Take 2 bestselling novels FREE! Plus get a FREE surprise gift!